TAG

STEPHEN MAY

Cinnamon Press

Indepe   tional

Published by Cinnamon Press
Meirion House
Glan yr afon
Tanygrisiau
Blaenau Ffestiniog
Gwynedd
LL41 3SU
www.cinnamonpress.com

The right of Stephen May to be identified as the author of this work has been asserted by him in accordance with the Copyright, Designs and Patent Act, 1988. © Stephen May 2008. ISBN 978-1-905614-37-0
British Library Cataloguing in Publication Data. A CIP record for this book can be obtained from the British Library

All the characters in this book are fictitious and any resemblance to actual persons, living or dead, is purely coincidental.

Designed and typeset in Garamond by Cinnamon Press
Cover design by Mike Fortune-Wood from original artwork 'young woman face abstract' by 'madartists'; agency: dreamstime.com. Printed and bound in Great Britain by Biddles Ltd, King's Lynn, Norfolk.

The publisher acknowledges the financial support of the Welsh Books Council.

To Carole, Caron and Hannah

Gifted women all of them

For their help with this book many thanks are due to:

David Armstrong
Adrian Barnes
Heather Beck
Suzanne Berne
Jan Fortune-Wood
Ilona Jones
Camilla Hornby
Paul Magrs
Duncan May
Anthony Roberts
Nicholas Royle
Marjorie Sandor
Christopher Wakling
MMU online MA class of 08
The Arvon Foundation

TAG

ONE

There is a baby crying. Yelling its little heart out. Really screaming. A group of kids, fourteen or fifteen year olds are gathered around a buggy. That screaming. It just twists your insides. A girl reaches into the buggy. The screaming doesn't increase in intensity but neither does it diminish. The girl brings out a swaddled bundle. She's calm despite the noise. The girl holds the baby up by the throat with her left hand. She pulls back her right fist and smashes it into the baby's face.

The other kids laugh.

The baby stops crying.

The kids laugh some more.

Someone sniffs.

'That wasn't very kind, Mistyann.'

There's an adult in this group. A woman. Nervous. About fifty. Badly dressed.

'Worked though Miss, didn't it?'

This isn't a real baby. This is the School Baby. This is a baby whose job it is to go home with pupils and irritate them so intensely, that no-one will want to go out and get a real one. This is a baby whose mood swings and tantrums are programmed by Miss Midgley, the Health and Social Care Technician. This is a baby that begs to be given a slap.

'And what will you do if she cries at home tonight Mistyann, hmm? What if your, er, unusual, er, child-care methods don't work? What if Baby carries on screaming through the night hmm? What will you do then?' Snort. Sniff.

'I'll kill her miss. I'll rip her head off.'

'Miss?' Another kid now. A boy. Small. Spots. 'How do you know it's a she miss?' The kids laugh again.

'It's got no cock you div!' Someone shouts but Spots persists.

'Yeah but it's got no it's got no it's got no other bits neither.'

'It's a eunuch,' says Mistyann. Clear. Firm. She's got authority. 'It's a little baby eunuch.'

Mistyann's good with words. Mistyann's Talented And Gifted. We did a test. 198. Highest score in the year. So she's coming with me on the special course in Wales. Eight specially selected fifteen year olds from across the country are going. And I'm going because apparently I'm Talented and Gifted too. I'm an Advanced Skills Teacher. It says so, on the certificate I've got in the downstairs toilet at home.

'Mr Diamond, look.' They've seen me now. 'Mistyann's murdered the School Baby'.

'Ring the police, Sir. She's a killer, Sir. She's a psycho.'

Just then the baby cries. It's heart-breaking how real it sounds. The baby sobs and chokes. Sounds like she's waking from terrible dreams into somewhere worse.

'It's a miracle!' I cry, all theatrical. Everyone laughs. Except Mistyann.

'Fucking eunuch,' she says her voice stretched and tight, 'I thought I'd killed it.'

'Babies are tough, Mistyann,' I say.

'Not that tough,' she says, her eyes on mine unblinking. Her hands white around the buggy. There's a pause. A bell rings and tugs the kids towards the buildings.

'Don't forget the course, Mistyann,' I say. 'We need your yellow slip.'

Mistyann nods, turns and walks away. The School Baby cries and cries. Mistyann turns back, the clouds lifted from her eyes. She's bright, smiling.

'You have to punch it, Sir! Like I did. It'll shurrup then!' She skips away, fizzing with energy. A mongrel terrier darting between all those zombie sheep. There's a heavy sigh next to me.

'You're going to Wales with Mistyann Rutherford?'

'That's the plan, Mrs English. She's officially part of the TAG crew. Talented and Gifted. 198 on the Cognitive Reading Score. A genius in waiting.' There's a pause. A sniff, I think. Or a snort. Or a dismissive remark.

Mrs English sniffs. I award myself five points. Then she snorts. I award myself another five.

'Oh she's clever alright,' Mrs English does not make this sound in any way good. I award myself another five points. The maximum mark. Mrs English heads after the kids.

'Time to go in,' she says.

'I've got a free,' I reply and Mrs English sniffs again, as I should have guessed she would. She snorts.

'Alright for some.'

As she turns away, I punch the baby.

The crying stops.

TWO

I'm a fucking genius. That's what Mr Negus says back in Nursery. He uses that funny voice old people use to kids that they think are sweet.

'Do you see the car, Mistyann?'

And I say, 'Which car do you mean, Mr Negus? The green Subaru? The blue Saab 9000? Or the iron-car with the ugly dent in the side?' I'm nearly three. Iron cars are what I call Robin Reliants. They look like irons you see. And that's when he says it. He doesn't say it to me. He says it to my mum.

'Claire,' he says, 'your kid is a fucking genius.' Mr Negus is the care-taker at Edith Cavell Lower School but he knows my mum from when they were both at Pilgrim Upper. He's got a dog, Sally. An Alsatian, beautiful and big. Looks like a wolf. I see them both sometimes, out walking. Sally, that's the dog, looks sad now. Course she's got to be like proper ancient and old age makes you pure sad if you're a dog or a person.

'Old age definitely ain't for cissies.' Nan says that, and she should know. She's proper old. Sixty at least. She lives in Manchester and that's not for cissies either. They are always stabbing and shooting each other up there. Nan says that she doesn't mind that so much, it's the bleeding rain she can't stand. When she wins the lottery she's going to buy a caravan and live in Spain with her toyboy. That's what she says.

When we're little and see Mr Negus and Sally we scream and hide behind our mums' legs

Mr Negus says, 'She's alright. She wouldn't hurt a fly.'

And I say, 'But I'm not a fly, Mr Negus, I'm a girl.'

And Mr Negus says, 'Oh yeah, that's right. Yeah she does likes to eat girls I must admit. Flies are safe. Girls are not.' And we all scream some more. It's like a stupid little joke that we have between us.

Anyway. Mr Negus is the first person to call me a genius. 'What's a jeenus?' I say.

Mum says, 'A genius, Mistyann, is a fucking pain in the arse.' She says it nice though, with a smile in her voice.

And I say, 'Don't swear, Mummy. It is very rude.'

And Mum looks at Mr Negus and laughs.

'See what I've got to look forward to? Years of being bollocked by my own kid.'

That's a long time ago now. Before Ty, and before William and Harry were born. Before all the trouble.

Not many people call me a genius now. They call me GIFTED instead and it always sounds like it's being said in capital letters. They also make it sound a bit like a disease. They kind of whisper it. But whisper it noisy, if you know what I mean. Today I've mostly been writing my name over and over on my new bag. I haven't done that since I was eleven. I've even been putting little smiley faces in all the 'O's'. I can't even remember when I last did that. My new bag is cream and it says 'Books and Things' in big black fuck off letters. It's not the sort of thing I normally buy.

Things you should know about me. I'm Mistyann Rutherford. I'm fifteen. I live – used to live - in Manton Heights which is an estate of shoebox houses in Bedford but, IN NO WAY IS IT A COUNCIL ESTATE. That needs to be said big, cos they all have heart attacks round here if anyone says that they can't afford their own houses. Seems weird to me. If you rent you can live where you want for as long as you want. You can move on or out whenever you want. But if you buy you're stuck in some poxy little house somewhere you don't really want to live.

I live with my mum, Claire, who is a bit of an alkie plus she's depressed about Ty going off with that slag. And I live with my little brothers William and Harry. They are eight and five and not my real brothers. They're half-brothers. William was Mum's scheme to keep Ty living with us and Harry was Mum's revenge on Ty when it didn't work and he was off shagging the tart who lives in Clapham Road. We're not sure who his dad is. Mum won't say. I bet he's an embarrassment. Pure married or minging or gay.

My dad's still alive but he lives in Scotland and he's a loser anyway so I don't see him much. I used to email him telling him how well I'm doing at school and asking for cash. That was when I was at St Teresa's Catholic High School, which sounds floss but isn't. It's just the school all the Irish and Italian and Polish kids go to. And the only other things you need to know are:

I still like cars

I like football, even though I don't watch it much anymore and

No-one ever needs to feel sorry for me.

THREE

You should have been in court today. It would have made you laugh. My solicitor was an acned kid called Wayne King. Yes, really... A typical set one boff. Food, you'd have called him. Someone asking to be eaten.

You told me to go to a decent firm and I did—Porter and Sons, established in 1956—but the old hands clearly knew that I was a lost cause. They wouldn't touch me. Why would they? Poor old Wayne got lumbered.

I felt almost sorry for him. Wayne looked like some awkward wading bird; all knees and elbows protruding from impossibly scrawny limbs. You definitely look older than him. His Top Man suit was a size too big and he reeked of Lynx and morning masturbation. Sorry, but there it is. You're not going to read this and I'm not going to censor myself. Call it a pact. Poor old Wayne looked so thoroughly, geekily adolescent that I kept expecting him to get out his Game Boy whenever proceedings adjourned.

It won't surprise you to learn that he was rubbish. Not that it mattered. He could have been Perry Mason and it wouldn't have mattered. Maybe it mattered to Wayne. Maybe he really felt that he could pull off some kind of miracle and make his name. It was never going to happen.

Think what he had to work with. A self-confessed alcoholic. A teacher caught abusing a position of trust. And worse, a man convicted by the tabloids of the most appalling of modern crimes—that of being a 'sad loner'.

It didn't help that Wayne completely misread the magistrate. You know about magistrates, Mistyann? I know that you have come across them. Part-time volunteers who spend their free time judging their fellow citizens as an alternative to working in the local thrift shop. Most of them are ladies of a certain age. Tories of course. The one I got even looked like Maggie Thatcher in her peak years. And everything about poor old Wayne was calculated to annoy her. The cheap suit, the acne, the ridiculous teenage haircut —asymmetrical mullet, not the hair of a serious advocate— the spineless blushing and, most of all, his PC habit of calling her 'Madam Chair'. All of it was bound to get on her tits.

Magistrates sit in threes but it is only the chairman that you have to worry about. They are the most experienced and Maggie was clearly not the type to brook any serious debate. You could tell at a glance that her word was going to be Law in this case.

As poor old Wayne stumbled through the mitigation he grew more and more skittish at the disapproval radiating down from Maggie's stare. Eventually he called her 'Madam Chair' once too often and she could bear no more.

'Mr King,' she snapped, forcing him to break off from his laboured spiel. Making him jump. Poor old Wayne panicked and dropped his notes. He was using a lever-arch file containing notes as densely scribbled as some ancient Anglo-Saxon manuscript. Improv, like so much else, was clearly not his forte. After a pause for him to scramble around the front benches picking up his scattered manuscript, Maggie got to the point.

'Mr King, I am not an item of furniture. Please desist from referring to me as though I were.'

Poor old Wayne looked like his arse had been spanked. He stammered, swallowed and gasped. Eventually he choked out a kind of damp apology and we all moved on, the rest of his oration being delivered in a pathetic schoolboy whisper.

I felt for him when, as he staggered to a close, Maggie rose imperious as a battleship.

'The bench will retire.'

And it was at that point that I laughed out loud. She didn't want to be a chair, but she didn't mind being a bench. Maybe the old battleaxe knew exactly what she was doing, but I'm not sure. Old prejudices die hard and I still don't like to credit Tories with a sense of humour.

Whether she was making a deliberate gag or not, I don't suppose laughing in court did me any favours. In any case, Mistyann, I don't think anyone's really interested in my version of the whole Welsh debacle.

Do you want to know what I'm up to these days? I don't teach any more. Had you heard that? I do shifts with the Undead and I watch telly and I surf the net. And, yes, I'm thinking of putting that band together with my mate Cog. After all, it's only been what, twenty years?

It's my mate Cog that really wants to re-form. He's the driving force.

'Come on,' He says more or less nightly on the phone, 'It'll be a laugh. And it's not as though you've got anything else on. No marking or anything.'

No marking, no five a side, no running, no snooker, no nothing it is true. I don't go out much. It's all a bit too dangerous these days.

I've known Cog since 1977. 1977 imagine that. Good Queen Lizzie's Silver Jubilee year. It's September. I've been at my new school for less than three weeks. We're doing PE.

'What do you mean you've forgotten your kit? I don't know what your last school was like, Diamond, but this is a serious place. You can get undressed anyway. You'll do in PE in your pants. Come on, we're all boys here. And at least it's not swimming today.'

The new school is big on swimming. It has a huge pool, bigger than the public one, and if you forget your swimming kit, you swim naked. I'd heard stories about this place before I arrived, but I'd never believed them.

1977. Silver Jubilee year and I'm wearing my last clean pair of pants. My silver Jubilee briefs. Tiny, covered in a union jack and with the smiling official portrait of Her

Majesty and the Duke of Edinburgh stuck fast on the crotch.

I'm the new kid. I'm four feet nothing tall. I'm eleven years old. I wear glasses. I'm shit at rugby. I've already learned that Mr Cheshunt's mantra, 'Come on lad, the bigger they are the harder they fall' is a big fat lie. Stopping some of these kids is like stopping a charging rhino. Dive at their feet? I don't think so.

I have no friends at this school. I've been plucked from the comp to go to the Modern school. Well, it was modern in 1802 or whatever. A scholarship kid with his fees paid by the council, detested equally by staff and students as an oik getting above his station. No allies. And now I'm nearly naked. I'm wearing comedy pants. I'm blushing pinkly with my whole body and the teacher, a sniggering sadist called Mr Gamble is saying.

'Get into pairs.'

No one comes to join me. I can see that there is one group of three but Mr Gamble doesn't make any of them become my partner. He says, 'You'll just have to do these exercises on your own, Diamond. Do the best you can.'

It's then that Cog comes over.

'Hi,' he chirrups, 'I'll be your partner. If you want.' If you want. How impossibly gallant is that?

Cog. Charles Oscar Greenwood. My oldest friend and now half of my entire corps of friends. Times like these you find out who you're friends are. And mine are Cog and Army Dave. That's it. And compared to being stripped nearly naked in your first week at an all-boys school, and in this way exposed as someone who wears a picture of the Queen next to his cock, the humiliation of courts and magistrates is nothing, believe me.

FOUR

I sign the stupid yellow form myself. Mum's never going to get round to it.

'In a minute,' she says, and everyone knows that 'in a minute' means fucking never. Anyway, she doesn't want me to go on the trip. I'm too useful. Who gets William and Harry to school? Me. Who feeds them home? Me. Who clears the place up? Me.

Mum used to be proper house-proud, now she just screams about living in a tip and does sweet FA about it. She'll start sometimes. Some mornings we're woken up by the hoover going at 7 o'clock. She loves old disco and it'll be on mega-loud with mum in her thong singing about dancing in New York City, while going mental with the hoover. She never finishes. We get up, get breakfast and go to school and when we come back the hoover will be parked in the kitchen and mum will be yelling that she doesn't get a minute's peace. Or sometimes she'll be in bed. Whatever, the house will be in a state. In fact it might be worse than usual 'cos she'll have got all William and Harry's toys out to 'sort through' and left them all over the floor.

Harry's got this one toy, a horrible plastic doll with an evil face that he calls Tim. Don't ask me why. Ty gave Tim to Harry and he was battered then. I think he comes from a car boot sale and he's got pen all over his face from where Harry drew on him. And he's got one arm 'cos William gets jealous and operates on him with a pair of scissors.

'He's got cancer Harry. I had to cut his arm off to save his life.' So then Harry goes and destroys all William's Lego models. It's pure total war for a while and they are only four and six then. Anyway I come home once and mum is sitting in the middle of the lounge, toys and bits of crap all round her, and she's howling. Proper howling like she's in agony and she's holding this Tim doll real tight. Freaks me out this does. Scares the shit out of me. Much more than when she goes berserk and starts calling us names.

She tries to be a good mum but she's just a bit pants at it. And I think that's okay because you can't be good at everything for ever. It's like footballers. I like Roy Keane. I like him because he was proper small at home in Cork in Ireland and everyone told him that he would never make it. But he refused to listen and he made himself stronger, fitter, harder than everyone else and he became the best and got signed by Manchester United. Then, in that World Cup, when all the other Irish players are just happy to be in Japan and wanting to party, Roy goes crazy because he can't see the point in playing if you're not trying to win. Roy's retired now. Had a hip that was a bit dodgy, knew he wasn't good enough anymore and quit just like that. He's a manager. A star one. He doesn't take any shit.

Other footballers who aren't as sorted as Roy don't choose to give up. Football gives them up. Some of them get into drink and drugs and have to have liver transplants. Mum's like that in a way. She's a talented mum but she let herself get tired. Couldn't keep up. It happens in football, TV, music, everything. Like I used to think Ant and Dec were well funny, now they get on my tits. Okay, I might have grown up a bit but I also think they're just not as good as they used to be. A bit tired, a bit smecked. Course you don't actually stop if you're on telly—you just get sad. And my mum's like that too. She should stop being a mum. She should get her liver transplant or whatever she needs and just do something else, but you can't if you're a mum.

Anyway. I sign the stupid form myself. I can do mum's signature perfect and no-one ever looks at the signature. But before I do that I have to check some things.

'Mr Diamond?'
'Yes, Mistyann?'

'Mr Diamond, is it true that where we're going there's no TV?'

'No TV. No radio. No internet. No CDs. No mobile phones. I told you, Mistyann. It's paradise.'

'Sounds boring. What about newspapers and stuff?'

'None of those either.'

'And how far is the nearest town?'

'Six or seven miles I think, Mistyann. Though there is a village nearer than that.'

'What about you, Sir? Will you take a radio and that?'

'I might try and smuggle in a small wireless, Mistyann. For the cricket.'

'You can't do that!'

'Very passionate, Mistyann. Why not?'

'Cos it would be cheating. You can't have one rule for the kids and another for the adults. Wouldn't be right.'

'Mistyann, it happens all the time. I can vote, drink, smoke, drive, get married, do the lottery, buy a kitchen knife. All things that you can't do. Not legally anyway. I don't have to wear a school uniform either. It's a cruel world, Mistyann, where double standards operate all the time. You should be used to that by now.'

It's a weird thing to say about a teacher but Mr Diamond is the most like a film star of all the blokes I know. He's only about 40. That's not that ancient. He doesn't really look like a teacher. He sort of looks a bit like Tom Cruise, only taller cos Tom Cruise is a bit of a midget. He's got all his hair and he's thin. He hasn't gone lardy and grey and smelly like most teachers. He goes running and plays football and all that, so he doesn't look old. He just likes to use an old fashioned way of talking. But he's got a good voice. It's deep and he speaks slowly like he's tasting all the words. Mainly he sounds a bit like there's a well good joke going on somewhere. Love that.

I've always loved having him talk to me like that. Just me and him. Even in Year 7. Sometimes, when we get a bit of a groove going, it's like we're in a play. Not one where all the words are written down, but the kind where you make up the words as you go along but somehow the words don't turn out to be ordinary words. Even if they are, me and him can make ordinary words sound better. Just like words in a play. And he always looks right at you, which most teachers, most grown-ups, hardly ever do. Anyway it's important that I get the answer I want.

'Sir, I don't think you should cheat. If you take a radio I ain't going, Sir'

'You aren't going. You aren't going.'

My heart sinks. I've heard that stupid expression before but this time I proper feel it. I feel my whole heart sink towards my stomach. I'm thinking that Mrs English, or someone like her, has fucked it up for me. She hates me. She really does.

'Why not? Is the trip cancelled?'

'No, Mistyann, it's just that you don't say 'ain't'. You say 'I'm not'.'

'Jesus, Sir. You can be so boring. I'm NOT going if you cheat.'

'Mistyann, I'm just trying to give you some free grammar advice here. You'll thank me one day'

Yeah, right. As if.

'Forget it, Mistyann. Okay I promise. I will not take any modern receiving equipment to Cefn Coch even though the second test against the Windies begins that week, so help me God. Is that okay? And since when did you get so keen on people following rules, Mistyann, eh?'

That's the other thing I like. The way he says my name a lot. Love that. Not enough people do that.

'And it's true that the course is during half-term, Sir?'

'Yes, Mistyann. Rather unbelievably I'm giving up my precious rest and recuperation offered by the February half-term to escort a group of the county's most precocious brats to a strange and distant land, one peopled by painted savages who persist in speaking their own tongue despite a much better alternative now being freely available.'

'What are you on about, Sir?'

'I'm on about the Welsh, Mistyann.'

'They speak English, Sir.'

'Mostly that is true, Mistyann, but not where we're going. Where we're going it's the full on Cumree, dai-boyo-bach-bungalow-burning-experience. Cumree is spelt C-Y-M-R-U by the way and it's what the Welsh call Wales.'

'Why do they burn bungalows?'

'Because English people buy bungalows and only live in them at weekends and the Welsh say that the English have put the prices up so that they, the Welsh, can't afford bungalows of their own. So they burn them.'

'Isn't that fair enough then, Sir?'

'I suppose you could argue that, though personally the mystery is why the English would want to live there.'

'Don't you like the Welsh then, Sir?'

'Listen, Mistyann. Racism is a terrible thing. I think that we're all agreed on that aren't we?'

'Course. My brother's black.'

'Yes. Well. Racism is a terrible thing. But it's also a powerful human impulse. So God invented the Welsh. The only people it's okay to be racist about.'

He has these little jokes does Diamond. I bet they get him in trouble loads when he's out and about. I bet he gets in some right rucks. Anyway I get all the information I need. So the next day I hand in the form.

I know that Diamond thinks I'm asking all these questions about TV and that because I'm a stupid little kid who can't imagine going a day without watching cartoons. Which just shows you how people, even people like him, can't see beyond the obvious. Really pisses me off sometimes. And I can't believe we're going to a place called Kevin Cock.

FIVE

Poor old Wayne tried to use the fact that I was 'subjected to an all male environment at a formative stage' as part of his explanation for what he called 'my disastrous, but momentary, loss of control'. Crap. Even I don't buy that. And Maggie was having none of it.

And in any case at the Modern we weren't without feminine influence. Ms Marsden was the music teacher and she ran a little lunch-time club for kids who preferred records to rugby. It was important that we called her Ms rather than Miss; it felt significant, even if we didn't know why. We did know that it annoyed other members of staff.

'Oh you're in Mizz Marsden's class. Lucky you.' They would sneer.

We were allowed to bring records to the music club. We could play them in turn and talk about why we liked them. You were allowed to discuss the record for the same length of time as it lasted. This meant that my Ramones singles didn't get much discussion at first but that Roland Marshall's Barclay James Harvest tracks got a lot of undeserved focus. But we loved it in her room. It was warm and safe and we felt like a little gang.

Ms Marsden was cool. Twenty-five-ish, she wore men's clothes, three piece suits, slightly—and only slightly—accessorized and feminised. A pair of strange, vaguely ethnic, earrings one day, a vivid pink scarf the next. She had an intense, severe expression. Her face, which was pale and devoid of make-up, was like the surface of the moon; pitted with craters and oddly shaped scars. She was no beauty, but she had a sharp angular look and a smile that could be quite annihilating. She looked like no-one we had ever seen and the rest of staff hated her. I think we were all in love.

I remember you saying that you don't like music, but it's hard for someone my age to understand that. For us it became the main thing. Music meant more to everyone then. It was harder to find for one thing. You didn't hear punk classics played in Asda the way you do now.

It was in Ms Marsden's lunchtime class that I heard Joy Division for the first time and Echo and The Bunnymen and The Doors and The Velvet Underground and The Kinks and Roxy Music and Patti Smith. And Bowie, of course. Ms Marsden had a major crush on Bowie and she looked so great, her hands moving like strange hawks in the air, as she described seeing Bowie's farewell Ziggy concert that we were fans before we'd heard a note. About a year after the music club had formed, Ms Marsden started setting homework.

'Go home and listen to Peel tonight,' she'd say, 'There's a Slits session on.' Or she might say, 'Old Grey Whistle Test tonight, gang, Comsat Angels and Dr John.' And the following day we'd argue and shout and talk and play records. It was a proper education and after a while the Barclay James Harvest stopped coming in and instead we'd compare The Only Ones with Lou Reed or The Clash against vintage Stones.

She had a whole syllabus worked out. One half-term we listened to early rock 'n' roll. Elvis, Little Richard, Wanda Jackson, Carl Perkins, Charlie Rich and Gene Vincent.

'This is the stuff that turned the Beatles on.' she said. 'We ought to know about it.'

Another term it was vintage soul. James Carr, Curtis Mayfield, Marvin, Aretha, Otis, Smokey. I don't remember when we started bringing in fewer records to allow more time for hers, but I also don't remember caring.

Outside in the cold and the rain, County House would prepare to do glorious battle on the rugger field against Churchill House—who were boarders and the sons of army and air force officers—in the first round of the Cock House Trophy. And from our eyrie in the music block we would literally look down on them and laugh. From where we sat they looked like so many misshapen crabs conducting some bizarre mating ritual. And there was no doubt that Ms Marsden encouraged our laughter. We were insurgents against the established order.

It really was called the Cock House trophy too. Teams of boys competing to be called Cock House. Those Victorians had a real sense of humour. I'd love to hear what you'd make of that: The Cock House.

I'm thinking of buying a ticket to London. Spending some time there, just walking the streets. Is it a good idea do you think? Of course I'll have to fill in a form, ask permission, promise to be good. It's like being back at school this, Mistyann.

SIX

I nearly don't make it out the house.

'Mistyann! Mistyann! Harry's fucking puking every fucking where!' This is typical of Harry. Little brat can tell when I want to do something and does everything he can to wreck it. See, if he's sick then I'll have to baby-sit him while mum goes to work. Even if she wasn't working I'd have to stay at home and look after him cos mum pure hates the littleuns when they're ill. Sometimes she doesn't like them much when they're well either. And then sometimes she hugs them all day long and calls them her 'little chickens' and calls Harry 'bun-bun' and 'noo-noo' and all crap like that. But that doesn't happen often, and I'm not sure they like it. I think it scares them cos it's not normal and it's not what they're used to.

Anyway today Harry is puking into the washing up bowl and William is creating because he can't find his mobile. Little fucker's only eight. Shouldn't have a phone. Ty got it for him of course. It's got wi-fi, TV, MP5, about a million games, all the bollocks. I moaned about it for ages. I've only got a crappy little phone that doesn't even do polyphonic or the web. I mean I don't really care but it's not right that my little brother should have the dogs of a phone when I've got a shitty old thing, but Ty says he doesn't want William to be called a ragga at school.

I say, 'What about me then?'

He says, 'But Mistyann, you are a ragga.'

And William laughs his nasty little laugh and I go upstairs and wipe his toothbrush under the rim of the bog and put it back. Stupid little rat is sick for two days.

Ty turns up at our house about twice a year. William's birthday and sometime around Christmas and every time he has loads of presents. He's like William's own personal Santa. If Santa could be black. Ty's fat with the kind of stupid little beard lardy blokes have because they think it hides their chins. It doesn't. Ty's always laughing this big old fake ho-ho-ho laugh. And he drinks sherry. Likes to think he's got a bit of class does Ty. That's why he gets wankered on martini and sherry and stuff. Can't get lushed up on lager like normal people. He's a twat.

Anyway, his precious William is pure whinging big time about his mobile and Harry's coughing and crying with sick all down his jumper and I'm worried that mum is going to notice that my PE bag is about 15 times its normal size in a minute.

'He's fine,' I say 'He's faking. He's trying to bunk off. He's probably got SATs or something.'

I feel a bit bad about this cos Harry looks at me and his eyes are huge and full of tears. He looks well sweet my brother. He's got all this mad curly red hair and a cute little round face and eyes like chocolate buttons. Red hair and brown eyes. It's proper unusual and everyone says he's adorable. And he can be. As long as he gets everything he wants. So he's looking up at me all outraged.

'I'm ill, Mistyann! I'm really really really sick.'

'Really thick you mean.' That's William being really bloody helpful. And so Harry starts crying.

And Mum goes, 'Oh God, I can't stand it, Mistyann. You deal with this. I've got to be at work.'

I know that there's no point complaining but I do anyway.

'Mum, it's an important day at school today. We've got a test.'

'You don't learn anything while you're taking a test do you?' she says. 'People worry too much about exams if you ask me.'

'I didn't ask you. Who would ask you anything? You don't know fuck all about anything.' I say and she tries to slap me but I'm too quick and move away.

'Mistyann, just look after the boy, okay? Just start your half-term a day early. Jesus, it's just a day.' And suddenly she looks proper smecked. I hate her when she does that 'I'm all exhausted' thing.

'He's your fucking kid!' I yell, but she's already in the hall putting on her coat.

William's still whining on. 'Mum, what about my mobie?'

'It'll be where you left it.'

'It isn't. It isn't. I always put it in a special place and it's gone. Someone's nicked it.' And obviously he has to blame me now. 'I bet it's you, Mistyann.'

'Why would I want your stupid phone?' I say.

'Because yours is pathetic and rubbish and old and doesn't do anything.'

'It makes calls,' I say, 'It receives calls. What else do you need a phone for?'

William looks at me like I'm mad. And of course calling people is the one thing that William never does on his phone. He listens to music and wastes aliens and vids his mates twatting each other and all that, but he doesn't call people. Who would he call? He used to phone his dad but Ty changed his number after a couple of weeks and wouldn't tell him the new one. Said he didn't want to be bothered by kids ringing up and stopping important calls getting through. Which means calls from his fuckbuds I guess.

Mum says, 'Fuck this, I'm off.' And she's out the door and gone.

I get down after her and yell down the street, which I know she hates. 'You're the worst mother in the whole fucking world, you know that? Worse than Rosemary West!'

She turns around. 'Get back inside you little bitch!' she hisses.

And off she goes to spend the day filing nails and asking people about their holidays and telling people they look lovely and being nice. She works in a beautician's, my mum. Mad isn't it? Talks about setting up her own business. As if.

Rosemary West is this woman who killed loads of people, or helped her husband kill them. They even killed their own daughter. My Dad is obsessed with crime. Murders especially. Only things I ever see him reading are quiz books and books about famous killers. He let me read the one about Rosemary West when I was nine. Gave me nightmares.

Just then I hear this choking sound and turn around just in time to see Harry vomming over himself. He's missed the bowl by like at least a kilometre. William is staring at him proper fascinated.

'You. Fuck off to school,' I say.

'But it's only ten past eight,' he whines back, 'and I haven't got my phone.'

'If you mention your phone again I'll batter you,' I say, 'School. Now.'

And he looks at my face and decides to go which is a miracle. So at least he's out the way. I look at Harry, who seems a bit better. I take William's mobie out of my bag and check his credit. He's got £20 on it. God knows how, probably Ty playing Santa again. I phone 999 and tell them my little brother's vomiting everywhere and we wait for five minutes till the ambulance arrives. Harry's well excited as I tell the paramedics that he seems a tiny bit better but that I've been proper worried and that my mum is out because she's run to the neighbours for help. No, I don't know which neighbour, she's in a bit of a panic and so they say that they'll take Harry to A&E to have him checked over. And they give me the number of the hospital and tell me that I'd better wait for my mum so I can tell her what's happened and they promise Harry that they'll put the siren on. Then they go and I can finally get out of the house and get to school.

Before I do that though, I get changed. I was going to do it at school in the bogs but now that Mum's not here I don't have to worry about her getting all sus, so I can put on my travelling-to-Wales gear at home.

When I leave the house I've got five minutes to make it to school so I use William's bike with all my gear over my shoulders. Halfway there I realize that I've forgotten the lock, which means it will definitely be nicked while I'm away, but I think—fuck him. Fuck him. And I wonder what Mum will do when I don't come home from school. And I decide she'll probably do fuck all. Which is good. Which is what I want.

SEVEN

The night before the trip to Wales I went to play pool with Cog in the Three Horseshoes in Bletsoe. They had a doubles tournament on. It was a quiet night, the winter rain keeping a lot of the younger punters indoors, so we won. An outrageous flukey double gave us the title, which Cog accepted graciously by chanting football style at the locals.

'Who are yer! Who are yer!'

He followed up with a chorus of 'You're not singing any more...' before we were given our prize—a bottle of Liebfraumilch, presumably one that had been mouldering away since the heyday of sweet German wines back in the 1970s—and asked to leave.

A night of extraordinary success couldn't be allowed to end with me dropping Cog off at his door before returning home to complete the marking that was waiting for me like a sullen, neglected wife. No, it was a special night, so Cog came back to drink the Liebfraumilch; the first time, incidentally, that booze had ever crossed the threshold of my little house. But I was confident in my abilities to withstand the temptations of this particular vintage. If I was going to fall off the wagon it wouldn't be into the sickly stickiness of cheap Kraut plonk.

There was a moment of crisis when my lack of a cork-screw was discovered. We could only settle down when the old gent next door had been roused to furnish us with the necessary. I had no wine glasses obviously, so Cog sipped at his drink from my old 'Coal Not Dole' mug. It seemed to put him a nostalgic mood.

'Hey, Jonny do you remember the night we supported The Fall?'

Of course I did. It was the night I got to finger a Danish teacher-training student called Sabine. Our band really did its job. We were all virgins before the advent of Be Nice, but within three gigs we had all managed to make significant sexual headway.

It's always been a source of wonder to me. It's girls who do music when you're young. It's girls who are ferried from piano to gym to ballet to horse-riding. It's girls who fill the ranks of the school orchestras. A boy will get an imitation Strat for his fifteenth birthday and four weeks later he's on stage, stumbling through a sausage-fingered version of Seven Nation Army. Meanwhile the beautiful all rounder whose tits he gets to grope at the post gig party has grade eight bassoon and can play the entire works of Shostakovich. I've never really managed to get my head around that. Why would you want to be the girlfriend and not the star?

'You know, Mark E Smith said that he loved us and that we could go on tour with them. We should have taken him up on that.'

'Bollocks. You're suffering from False Memory System my friend. His tour manager said we were okay and that we could support them again in London if we paid them two hundred and fifty quid.'

'We should still have done it. Things could have been different.'

'Cog, you're a chartered surveyor. A successful professional. I'm bringing great literature within the grasp of the proles. We do important, worthwhile jobs.'

We had a good laugh at that.

'Do you remember Ms Marsden's band?'

'Tower of Strength in the Horse and Groom? How could I forget?'

It's hard to imagine there being a modern equivalent of the Gloom, as we called it. You'd know it as the Bedford branch of Pret a Manger. Back then it was where all the local bands played. A venue so scummy that the last landlord died in 1989, not of cirrhosis of the liver but from a necrotising super-bug infection of the kind normally only found in Rwandan refugee camps. And amid this small-town temple of the squalid there was Ms Marsden on the Gloom's tiny stage shouting, 'Christ was a liar. A fucking liar!' over and over to a squall of feed-back. She was wearing a wedding dress, an ivory vintage gown that pushed up her breasts, always hidden at school under a black polo neck; a voluptuous impersonation of a restoration beauty. In my first glance I could see acres of snow-white cleavage on display, all set off with a delicate tattoo of a strawberry. The dress was slashed raggedly and diagonally from her right hip to just above her left knee. She also sported black fish-nets and, on her right thigh, we could clearly see the garter belt and suspenders.

I know. How crude. How lacking in guile this seems now. But remember this was before Madonna, before Britney, Kylie or Beyonce or any of the modern parade of under-dressed, overly pneumatic disco vamps.

After the breasts/dress/legs, I noticed the hair. The bristly crop was now platinum. Her head glittered where it caught the light. Her face, normally pale and yoghurt fresh, was as immaculately made up as any long haul air hostess. She was stunning. Her cheek bones were sculpted and her eyes a suitably luminous cat-green. She was sparkling, cosmetically enhanced by secret processes that boys of my generation never got to know of.

It's different for lads your age. I think twenty years of *FHM* and *Men's Health* have given boys an insight into the running of the modern face. In 1983 this information was distributed on a strictly need to know basis and only women needed to know.

'She was crap wasn't she?' Cog was laughing at the memory. 'Passing out was the best response, mate.'

I nearly died at that gig. A near fatal combination of two bottles of red Martini, the boots of the Churchill house rugby team who we'd played in our Cock House semi, and the heat and humidity of the unventilated pub conspired to induce major organ failure.

Everyone always got a right kicking playing the boarders. They only ever got outside by volunteering for extra sport practice. They were, to all intents and purposes, professionals. Not only that, but they carried deep grudges against their opponents who were able to watch Top of the Pops or Starsky and Hutch; privileges which were denied those who lived at school.

It took ages for anyone to call an ambulance because:

a) Everyone thought that I was just a lightweight who couldn't handle his booze

b) Cog had dragged me to the bogs because he didn't want to be thrown out once the bar staff had spotted me comatose and

c) Ms Marsden came and told Cog that calling a fucking ambulance would ruin her special night and she wasn't going to lose her chance of being signed because of some prick of a kid getting wasted. She let him know that she had heard for a fact that there were A&R men coming specially from London in time to catch her second set.

Apparently she came right into the gents, opened my eye with one exquisite thumb and sighed, 'He'll be okay. Prop him against a wall or something. He's just wankered. This is a big night for me.'

Betrayal. The hard edge of this is something we have to keep bumping into again and again if we are going to learn the lesson of it. But I think Ms Marsden's betrayal of Cog was worse. Me she just left to die in my own piss. He had to suffer the fact that her band was shit. Really, really shit. In my front room Cog closed his eyes to picture it all.

'They were like King Crimson. They were like Jazz. They were like a jazz band trying to do punk. Four bald guys and Ms Marsden doing all that stupid poetry over the top. I tried to like it, I really did, but by song three I thought, I have to check on Diamond. It was just such a relief to be away from that fucking racket man'

And I was thinking that if Ms Marsden and her group had been any good at all, he'd have been moshing at the front and I'd have been dying in the stinking bogs of the Horse and Groom.

'I mean, after all she said about music. After all she taught us…'

'I know, mate. I know.'

And once again we told each other the whole story of that night. The sirens, the irritable ambulance man who paused in his fixing of tubes and wires to lecture someone who had referred to him as a paramedic.

'You've been watching too many American movies, sonny. We don't have paramedics here. I drive ambulances. I'm an ambulance driver. We don't need poncy titles.'

And there was the beautiful girl who had wept when she saw my face as they carried me outside and, of course, Cog told the story of how Ms Marsden, face shiny with sweat and fury, had tunnelled through the crowd to spit, 'You fucking, fucking kids. That's it. No more music club. I'm not wasting any more time on you, you TONE DEAF TWATS!' And she really did say it like that. As though it was in capitals.'

'That was the name of our band wasn't it? Tone Deaf Twats.'

'For about ten minutes.'

'That's right. Then Sid and Jacko joined and it was Be Nice.'

Cog was silent for a while sipping at from the mug which, I noticed now, was chipped. When had that happened? I loved that mug.

'And you're off to Wales tomorrow with this genius feral child.'

'Yeah. For my sins. Seven days with Ariel La Rock, Educational Psychologist to the stars, guru of the academic talent spotters.'

'It's funny isn't?' Cog was thoughtful now. 'I mean you were a genius yourself. I mean the scholarship and everything. And we were all so impressed with you at school. I mean the way you seemed to sleep through the lessons and then come to life whenever you were asked a question and always seemed to have the right answer. It was awe-inspiring. We were all a bit scared of you. And you were so quick at everything. I mean you picked up guitar in what, a week?'

'Bit longer I think and I was always pretty average. And I got a C and a D at A level. Hardly genius scores. I went to Essex for God's sake—the University of Clearing.'

'Yeah. But you were also pissed most days, so actually it was a real achievement. Me, if I have one glass of wine I can't even do the *Sun* cross-word. You're the cleverest man I know, Mr Diamond.'

'You're also bladdered.'

'True. True.'

We called a cab and, after he'd gone, I sat thinking about the day I'd got the offer of a scholarship to the Modern. I hadn't wanted to go. I wanted to go to Pilgrim Upper with my mates, but there were my mum and dad bursting out of their clothes with pride.

'Why didn't you tell us you were a genius, son?'

'I'm really proud of you, Jonathan...'

'The Modern. Imagine...'

'Means school on Saturday mornings mind...'

'That'll be alright he only watches rubbish on TV then anyway. What's it called? The Multi-coloured Swapping Shop?'

'They finish at twelve. Still be home in time for Football Focus.'

'I think it's rugger at the Modern, Nick.'

'Good. Toughen him up. Football's a girl's game now. All long hair and kissing. What's that about?'

'So. What do you think, Jon?'

'The council will pay the fees.'

'It's a real honour…'

'I always knew you had brains. Somewhere…'

'Your decision. What do you say?'

'What about my friends?'

'You ungrateful little get…'

'You'll still see them, Jonny. We're not moving. They all live round here. Come on Jonathan, it's such an opportunity…'

It hadn't turned out quite the way it was meant to. I think I was meant to get straight A's and head off to Cambridge to lose the mockney accent and dedicate myself to advancing our understanding of the world or some such bollocks. Instead it was the dogged pursuit of a drinking career that started at school, worked on with real fervour at the University of Clearing and developed with admirable single-mindedness through the jobs held for a couple of years, then the jobs held for a few weeks. Before long I was working the night shift as what is euphemistically known as 'a carer' for the ancient and the mad. The people I called the Undead.

Sluicing the commodes of the very old and very ill is a good job for the alcoholic. You're permanently anesthetised to the stench and, almost uniquely among modern western businesses, there are no deadlines. You and your charges can drift together towards death.

For three years I tended the scabs and bowels of the Undead. You don't get fired from working with the demented. It would be like sacking someone from carrying out the dead from the plague houses of seventeenth century London. It's a dirty job but someone has to do it. Someone else. Someone who can't do anything else.

For a long time I thought I would never leave them. That I would be there mopping and stroking and soothing and breathing sweet vodka-coke over the restless gurglings of the Undead forever. I thought that I would stay there until the cruel thief that stole their identities came to add mine to his collection. That happens. It's far from unknown for attendants in homes for the geriatric mad to move quietly from warder to patient.

Cog had left half a mug of the Liebfraumilch. I took a deep sniff and recoiled from its cloying bouquet. Christ, how do people drink that stuff? It's like some sort of chemical weapon. It should be banned by UN convention. I opened the door and threw it outside into the garden. It struck me that it was an odd thing to do. Maybe I was worried that it would corrode my sink or something. But after I'd tossed out the wine I stood for a moment looking out into the drizzling night. I'd known this road all my life. There were no surprises waiting for me in Gladstone Street.

If I was to look outside my front now, Mistyann, I'd see your mum. I know I would. She'd be sitting as she does every night in that silver 4x4. Sitting, drinking, smoking and staring at my front door. The phone calls have stopped. The abusive ones and the silent ones. The haranguing in the street has mostly stopped too. She's opted for this unnerving passive stalking. I can't say it's worse, but it's not good. Really not good.

EIGHT

I get to the car park yeah, and the only person around is Carboot. He's crying. Carboot is always crying. He's like pure total food. Everything about him says kick the shit out of me. Carboot's name is Dale. Car Boot Dale. Funny huh? You know who makes that name up? Our teacher. Mrs Duck in Year Three. Pretty fucking cruel cos Carboot is in and out of fucking foster homes and when he's with his mum she forgets to look after him. So when he's back living at home he pure reeks or he doesn't have a coat. I don't think she's evil, Dale's mum, she just doesn't know how to deal with her kids. This is how bad she is: she's so bad *my* mum takes the piss out of her. My mum slags her all the time.

'She's an effin disgrace,' Mum says, 'She wants putting away. She wants her kids taken off her full time.'

And this is my mum talking. Mad. And if his mum wasn't bad enough Carboot is like proper scrawny with this proper bad acne. He looks like he got chicken pox and then it never left. And he stammers. Kid's got no chance. Food.

But he lives down my road and I kind of look out for him when I can. But he's pure hard work. He doesn't do himself any favours. I mean here he is fucking crying again. He's asking to be twatted.

'Alright, Dale?' I say, He looks at me blank. 'What's up?' I say. 'Come on mate—ain't telepathic, you're gonna have to give me a clue at least.'

Carboot looks at me. He can't talk. His mouth is full of tongue and his nose full of snot and his eyes full of tears. He looks like he needs squeezing out. He looks like a dish-cloth left in dirty washing up water. He looks a state. He unzips his coat, shows me what he's got on underneath.

What has he got on underneath? Fuck all. Diddly-squat. There's just his white skin stretched over his ribs like a manky sheet over a cheap bed.

'Jesus, Dale. You let them take your fucking shirt. What is wrong with you?'

He swallows, dirty tears leak down his face, like fucking slugs crawling along a garden path. Slow and disgusting.

'I cccccccouldn't help it.' He sniffs. 'They made me.'

'No one makes you give them your shirt, man.'

'They did!' He looks desperate

Here's the thing about bullies. They are not cowards like teachers say they are. Stand up to them and you will get battered. Grass them up to a teacher and you will get battered. Whatever you do, you will get battered. It's what you do after you get battered that is crucial. You have to keep at them. Whenever you see them, no matter how many there are you've got to pile in and when they put you on the deck you've got to keep getting up and you've got to hit first and hit fast and you mustn't avoid them, you've got to seek them out. You've got to make the bullies sick of you. See them in town? Then you've got to be over the road and in their face. See them out with their mum and dad? Get over there and give them a mouthful. Or a face full of spit. The more public the place the better.

Yeah, you'll get battered. You'll get battered again and again and again, but in the end they're gonna give up. In the end they'll be avoiding you and the places you go. In the end they'll be hiding from you or wanting to be your friend. Carboot? He's a three stone streak of piss. But if he kept coming back. If he kept after the cunts who took his shirt then eventually, eventually—they'd leave him alone.

You've got to make the bullies bored of you. It's like the postman. If some annoying little yappy dog keeps going after his ankles every time he tries to deliver somewhere then he'll kick it a few times but in the end he's just not going to go there. He'll miss that house out. You've got to make the bullies change their route. Carboot though, he hasn't got what it takes to be an irritating little mongrel. He can't jar people off enough.

'Who took your shirt, Dale?'

'Them lot. Carter and that.'

Angel Carter. Tits like Katie Price. She's only sixteen, but they can't be natural. Someone must have paid for them. Looks like a Page Three model but I swear she's another one who is like Rose West inside. Thinks she's it.

'Why?'

'Said it was for a fashion project. Said she just wanted to take a picture of it. A Polaroid. Said she'd give it straight back.'

'Why did it have to be your shirt?'

'Said that it needed to be small and and and and and and…' His voice drops to a whisper, 'stink'

'For her pro ject.' I say it like it's two words like the Americans do cos I like the sound of it that way. Pro. Ject. 'And then what?'

'I didn't want to take it off but there were loads of other kids around and and and and I…'

'You felt you had to…'

'Yeah.' Even Carboot knows how lame all this is sounding.

'And then they fucked off with it. Classic.' I look at William's phone. I'm meant to meet Diamond in five minutes. I know where Carter and her fan club will be. There's a corner by the performing arts block where the CCTV can't clock you and where the teachers never go. They never go there cos that's where the lushing and the smoking and shagging goes on and they don't want to know about it. If they do go past it's by accident and they pretend they don't notice. Nikki Long gave five year eleven boys a blow job there last term, one after another, for a dare. The new RE lady, Miss Hopkins, walked right past. Didn't do nothing, didn't tell no-one.

Five minutes.

'Come with me, Dale.'

I drop the bike—someone will nick it this week anyway, might as well be now—I grab him by the hood of his coat and pull him into school and head for the performing arts block. There's a little staff bog there and I go and find what I'm looking for.

'Keep look out. Let me know if there's any teachers coming.'

But there aren't. The drama and dance teachers are always late. JD says to me once. 'The thing is, Mistyann, they don't have any marking.' That doesn't make sense to me. That should mean that they're on time in the mornings. He gets sort of stressy, like I'm missing something really obvious. 'Don't you see? It means that unlike say your diligent, dedicated and, some would say, foolish English teachers, who spend every night huddled at the foot of a veritable Everest of Year 9 practice SATs, your average performing arts teacher can be out honing his or her dance skills at Esquires or The Pink Toothbrush till the early hours.'

'You mean they can go clubbing, Sir?'

'Yes, they can go out drinking and clubbing safe in the knowledge that they will not be falling behind in the assessment of Key Stage 3 attainment targets.'

Makes sense when he says all that. And sure enough there aren't any staff in the PA block. Anyway I get what I want and head out of the bog and along the dance corridor. At the end is the fire door and the other side of that is where Angel Carter and her mates will be standing, smoking and laughing about what a feeble piece of food Carboot is.

Carboot is puffing along behind like Thomas the fucking Tank Engine. Jesus. I want to bully him myself. I stop outside the fire door and check the phone again. Three minutes. For some strange reason it feels important that I'm not late.

I kick open the door. Carter and her mates are all looking the other way. As they turn around I count her, her munter friend Carly Storey, Ricky Bedwetter (Richard Leadbetter—he acts the tough guy now, but he was a right gumbo in primary and I don't ever let him forget it), Danny Kazantis and Jezza Doyle. Only five. The thing that makes me laugh is that they all try and hide their fags. Cos of course their first thought is that I'm a teacher. Ricky actually drops his and stubs it out under his Reeboks. And they're all meant to be so hard. Pathetic. I don't have time to mess.

'Carboot's shirt,' I say. 'Give.'

'Or what?' This is Angel, but she's pure faking it. She's shitting herself really. You can always tell. But I don't have time for the usual chat so I produce my secret weapon—the bottle of bleach I won from the staff bog. They don't leave this stuff in the kids' toilets. Most of the time there isn't even bog roll in there.

'Oh, I'm scared,' she says and sort of rolls her eyes. And the thing is—she is, but she's doing okay for a bimbo. You got to give her that.

'You fucking should be,' I say and I unscrew the cap. 'I don't have time to piss about. Give him his fucking shirt.'

She gives me some serious face. I don't care—she's going to give me what I want in the end. She's not going to risk those whore looks. Thinks she can be the next Abi fucking Titmuss. The seconds tick by. I count them. One elephant—two elephant—three elephant. I learnt that in Year 6 science. If you count normally then you go too quickly. You put an elephant in and it gives you exactly a second. So you can time experiments and stuff properly. Six elephants go past and Angel cracks.

'God,' she says, 'No need to go off on one. Was just a fucking joke.' And she pulls out Carboot's shirt from her bag. She chucks it to him without looking his way.

'There. Wouldn't want your BOYFRIEND catching cold now, would we?'

And off they go, all of them trying to give me the hairy eyeball as they do. Like I give a shit. I look at William's phone. One minute. Carboot is already undoing his coat. He's so thin. He's like one of those Africans you see on the news.

'Listen, Dale mate. You know you're going to get battered don't you?' He nods. 'Maybe not today. Maybe not even next week with the half term and that. But you are going to get it.' He nods again. 'That's life. But at least you aren't going to look like a sad twat at the start of every lesson.' He nods, miserable. 'Hey, Dale,' I say 'It's okay. I'm actually proud of you. The way you take it. The way you suck it up. It's impressive. Really. It is.'

And then I do something that surprises me. Surprises me, fucking shocks him. I hug him and I can feel his bones through my jumper. 'It's gonna be okay in the end.' And just at that minute I mean it.

And I head back to the car park. And the bike's lying where I left it, which is a fucking miracle. I look towards the main entrance and there's Jonno Diamond just coming into the car-park in his stupid fake James Bond car. It's one of those cars without a roof and he gives me a wave. I'm on time and it's going to be okay.

NINE

The Undead. Funny isn't it, that in the rich West, those who can't look after themselves are cared for by an army made up of illegal and semi-legal immigrants, junkies, recently released prisoners and people who, for whatever reason, can't get any other work at all. The mad, the bad, the brutal and the Bulgarian. And the desperate. Don't forget them. And, yes, there are one or two saints as well. A couple of despicable Mother Theresas with a morbid addiction to doing good—but for the most part it's just us. The dregs.

Of course if the demented old were not quite such leaky bags of liquid waste then the job would have its entertaining moments. Just today Walter Pullinger told me in patient detail how he invented Interpol, but the Queen stole his idea. Walter is a former captain of industry and is now a fully nappied-up six foot, six stone baby. A baby that you occasionally catch snogging Miss Ewart, an eighty-three year old ex-headmistress of some posh Ladies College. Tongues and everything. These lighter moments are few and far between, however. Most of the time in The Elms you are just wiping up shit. Real or verbal.

Dementia itself is not too bad: it's the moments of clarity that are so upsetting. This is one of several areas where we alcoholics can sympathise with the Alzheimer's victim. The haziness about time, the holes in the memory, the waking up bruised and not knowing why, forgetting the faces of loved ones. All of these are points of kinship. But of all the places where our experience corresponds, the most terrifying is in knowing the horror of the truly lucid minute. That time when, through no fault of your own, you are confronted with the enormity of how fucked up things are. At least the alcoholic can medicate reality away with a swig from one of the emergency stashes he keeps for just such an occasion. The senility sufferer has to wait for the next neural failure and that might take days. That's the thing with these temperamental synapses—sometimes they hold up much better than you think.

It's in the cogent moments that the demented rant and rave and rage. It's then that they perceive the agony of their situation. If you want to earn the grateful smile of a dementia sufferer, leave them alone with a large bottle of vodka when they are in a sane phase. The paracetamol they can usually find for themselves.

Here's another frightening fact about the Undead. They're always telling you to have sex. Men with arms like frosted twigs lunge and grip you as you pass bearing a steaming bedpan or lukewarm plate of lunchtime slop.

'Get it while you can, son. Get it while you can,' they croak before dropping back exhausted but happy—knowing they've passed on something vital, something that you need to know. And the women are always taking their clothes off. Hardly a day goes past without some former pillar of the community, some ex Lady Mayoress or WI chairwoman shrieking and stripping and attempting to flee towards the park to expose the slack balloons of her dugs to whoever might be walking a dog or playing Frisbee with their kids

You were early on the day of the trip to Cefn Coch. Early and dressed pretty much appropriately. I had feared you might be a bit chavvy. Sorry, but there you are. But you were just wearing jeans and a fluffy pink jumper. You looked almost demure.

I parked the car—it's gone now—next to you and wound down my window. Now that I was closer I could see that you were made up of course. Your mouth a red slash across your freckles. I hadn't expected that. Where was the snot-nosed urchin of the playground? Most kids your age put on make-up and look younger. They look like infants dressing up. You really looked the part. You looked twenty. You looked brazenly, adultly gorgeous and it made me edgy.

'Mistyann,' I said, 'We're going to Wales.'

'So?'

'So you don't need the slap. It'll be wasted on them.' I offered you my hankie. You laughed, hard and spiteful.

'Yeah right. As if. Took me ages to do this.'

What was the point in fighting? I took in the rest of you. You had trainers on obviously, but not the great white container ships most of the Year 10 kids seemed to float on. These were regular sized and even a bit battered. They looked almost like you could run in them. You only had a small bag too. The kind of rucksack you might put your PE kit into. And you were holding on to a rather flash mountain bike.

'It's okay, Mistyann,' I said as I lifted my own suitcase from the back seat of the old MGB. It was the love of my life, though I was losing the suppleness you need for climbing in and out of sports cars. Pretty soon I'd be doing Pilates and yoga just so I could get in and out of my car. I loved it though—the way she bounced and rocked over every minor bump, the way her engine gurgled and crooned like a happy child. I loved the smell. Back in the day I used to take that beauty out just so I could drive at 60 through some dormitory hamlet with its po-faced 'please drive carefully through our village' sign, its smug red phone box and its faux rustic pub serving lukewarm 'families welcome' roast dinners to lukewarm families.

Sometimes I imagined that this is what all the young battle of Britain heroes felt like as they rolled and twisted their Spitfires across the sky while the country was shitting itself down below. Sometimes I wished I could still drive pissed. I tell you, there's nothing like throwing an MGB around a country lane with a couple of pints of Bombardier sloshing around your stomach to bring on the Biggles fantasies. But it's pretty good even without the ale.

You looked at me steadily as I heaved myself out of the bucket seats and reached into the back for my brief-case,

lap-top and faithful carpet bag; a gap year relic from Peru.
Not a memento of my gap year, I should add. I got it last
year from some Latin American Studies student on eBay.
Lovely piece of kit. That's gone too now.

'Trying a bit hard there, Sir.'

'What do you mean, Mistyann?' You gestured at the car.
'I'll put that down to envy, Mistyann.'

And you laughed again, but pleasantly this time.

'Are we going to Wales in that, Sir?'

'No, Mistyann. I wish we were. The old girl could use a
decent long distance run. That's when she's at her best. But
no, it's taxi to the station, train to London, tube to Euston
and then to Betws-y-Coed via Chester, Llandudno Junction
and Dollgoddengodden or somewhere, Al Qaeda and
Richard Branson permitting—then we'll probably do the
last ten miles by a combination of chariot and pit pony. But
I can assure you that we're not going by bike.'

You looked at the bike and coloured.

'It's my brother's. Can I put it in your office?'

'Have you seen my office, Mistyann? There's barely
room for all my junk. There's barely room for a chair.'

'You can take the front wheel off. Go on, Sir. It'll be
nicked otherwise. Or trashed. You know it will.'

This was true. I had arranged for Cog to pick up and
look after the MG for a week because of just such a well
founded fear of youth crime. I probably sighed.

'Come on then, Mistyann. Best be quick, the taxi will be
here in five minutes.'

I swear you almost skipped to the office. On the way we
passed a couple of Year 11s, both over six feet and with
small goatees. Jermaine Feaver and Kirk Long. Their school
uniform made them look like they were on their way to a
fancy dress party, or as if they were in a play.

'Like your new girlfriend, Sir.' Jermaine grinned as we
passed.

'You want to be careful, Sir,' chimed in Kirk.

They're decent lads. Thick as shit of course. They were both on this scheme where they spent half the week at college learning something worthwhile, but Friday was one of the days when they had to hang around school, when they could have been at a lathe or laying bricks and generally making themselves useful. They took it quite well, considering. As long as you didn't try to get them to do anything educational they were okay. Do anything for you. A smoke, a beer, a condom, they'd give you anything they had and they always had these essentials.

We were at the office now and I did some of the usual fumbling with keys. Being a head of department is uncomfortably like being a jailor. St Theresa's was a nice school, full of nice kids, but still we locked every door behind us, and the whole teaching staff jangled as they walk. I sensed your agitation.

'Mistyann,' I said, trying to disguise the sudden irritation I felt, 'Are you always this jumpy?'

'Course,' you said.

'It must be a very hard way to live.'

'Keeps you thin though.'

'Thin isn't everything.'

'No,' you said, 'Thin isn't everything.' You paused. 'Thin with big tits. That's everything.'

I resolved not to spar with you for the rest of the trip. I opened the door and, by twisting the front wheel, somehow got the wretched bike in, bundled on top of my desk like it was some kind of installation.

By sucking in my stomach and squeezing round I could get to the blinds which dangled uselessly like the sails of some wrecked yacht. They neither let the light in, nor kept the room shaded, but this time a sharp tug brought the whole blind down reasonably smoothly. I was surprised. A major feature of the British education system is that no part of it, from the Local Authority all the way down to the Venetian blinds, ever works properly.

'That'll stop your brother's bike exciting the kleptomaniac instincts of Year 7,' I said and turned with difficulty to find you just inches behind me. 'Come on, Mistyann,' I said. 'It's claustrophobic enough in here.'

And of course at that moment there was a knock on the door.

'Mr Diamond, your taxi's here.'

The door opened and it had to be Mrs English. The downward curve of her mouth revealed distaste for the state of the room, disgust that it contained Mistyann and myself, and real pain at the sight of a bike on top of the various official school documents. She sniffed.

'You hear that, Mistyann? Our carriage awaits.'

And I found myself telling Mrs English about you having no lock for her brother's bike and the need to put it in a place of safety. I got another sniff and, as we passed the office where the receptionists were beginning the first tea and ginger nut ceremony of the day, she pulled me inside.

'Wait here a moment, Mistyann,' she said. You rolled your eyes. I gave you a wink.

'A word to the wise, Mr Diamond,' Mrs English began, 'You really mustn't allow yourself to be in a closed room with a Year 10 girl. Particularly not that Year 10 girl.'

'Why not Mrs English?'

'Oh come on, Jon, in the current climate… male teachers are so vulnerable…'

I became aware that the biscuit ritual had paused. Mrs English continued, her audience secured. 'I mean to be in a small room with the door closed and the blinds drawn. It looks bad.' She paused for dramatic effect, to allow the office ladies to savour the full significance of her words. 'I mean… in this day and age… where it is so easy for parents or children to make wild allegations…'

'Don't worry, Mrs English, you can rest assured that if I decide to shag any of Year 10 I'll make sure that I've done a proper risk assessment and filled in the appropriate forms.'

Mrs English sniffed. She really had to get that sorted.

'I'm just trying to tell you what it could look like to anyone with a malicious agenda.'

'I know what you're saying, Jean, and I'm grateful.' I was gratified to see her wince at this casual use of her first name by an inferior. 'But the taxi...' I gestured through the window to where a burly man was bulging out of his XXL England soccer shirt and pacing up and down by a silver Merc.

'Enjoy yourself in Wales,' chirped Janet, the head's PA. Fifty-five and easily the sexiest woman on the staff. Of the entire school staff, there were probably only three you'd tolerate being stuck in a lift with and Janet would be in everyone's top three I reckon. I had the suspicion that I'd be in her top three too. The competition wasn't overwhelming of course.

Most of the other blokes on the staff were burnt out cases. Cynical, weary, grey. Sitting in the staff room waiting for the end. Even if the end was sixty, seventy or eighty terms away. There were people on the staff who were counting the days away like lifers.

I bet I'm not in Janet's top three now.

It occurred to me that I had been standing silent far too long.

'You okay?' said Janet.

'I'm fine, Jan, fine. It's just the thought of Wales.' And I gave her my How The Welsh Became material, about them being the only ethnic group it's okay to be racist about. And it went down a storm. Janet hated anything PC. Mainly because it was her who had to compile and process all the equal ops forms and, seeing as you can't get on a bus or buy a stamp or—more crucially for school life—give a kid a detention without filling in an ethnic monitoring form, it took up a large part of her working day. Through the window I saw the taxi guy look at his watch. I hurried out, answering Jan's cheery, 'Don't do anything I wouldn't do.'

50

with the response, 'Gives me quite a lot of scope that, Janet' and had the satisfaction of hearing her dirty laugh.

'Miss Thornton's a bit of an old slapper isn't she?' This was you trampling on my fantasy before I'd properly shaded in the details.

'Mistyann, we need to get this straight—we are still in a school situation. You are still meant to show respect to your elders. In other words you can't go around slagging my colleagues in my hearing.'

You sighed in a way that Mrs English would applaud and then we reached the taxi and fuck me if he wasn't a sigher and a sniffer as well. He was letting me know what he thought of our lateness. In fact he was letting us both know, you and me, what he thought of the whole modern education system with its laxness and slackness and general bad manners. I decided to take my revenge by being ridiculously chatty all the way to the station.

'Very friendly, Sir. To that old taxi guy I mean.'

You seemed to unwind a bit when we found our seats on the train to St Pancras. You'd got yourself some kind of nuked cow pat from the buffet car and you were watching it carefully as it sizzled and smouldered on the table next to you. You'd got a wire running from a metal credit card up to one ear. I made the mistake of asking about it.

'VXL 90 MP4 player, HD-DVD player, everything player. It's the total dog's. Not just a phone. No-one has just a phone now, Sir. Where have you been? My dad got it for me.'

You had a book open in front of you—something called *Dark Sister*. I'd never heard of the author but clearly it was a proper book, not the dreaded Teen Novel.

'You've really got this multi-tasking thing down haven't you, Mistyann?'

'What?'

'I mean eating, listening, reading, talking… it's very impressive.'

'Yeah well I'm gifted aren't I?' And you smiled. You really have an amazing smile, Mistyann. You should use it more. All the defences drop and you shine. Really shine.

Where do you go, all you underclass beauties? The checkout girl with the porcelain skin. The wasp waisted barmaid with the generous mouth and the easy laugh. The occasional pre-Raphaelite muse you see in the park or hanging around the bus station. Where do you go? Twisted out of shape by boys mostly. Saddled with kids and houses and organizing the lives of the helpless and hopeless. Doesn't take long for the skin to go, the hair to dull, the eyes and the spirit to harden to a survivor's toughness.

You were watching me.

'You're a right day-dreamer, Sir. Sometimes you just disappear. Like just then. One second you were here and the next you were gone. Disappeared like Bilbo.'

'Bilbo?'

'Don't be thick, Sir. Bilbo in that book *The Hobbit.* God you read it to us in Year 8. It's only two years ago. Get with the programme, Sir. You know. He puts on the ring and vanishes.'

'Mistyann?'

'Sir?'

'You don't have to call me 'Sir' all the time. I mean you don't normally. At school I mean, so I'm wondering why you're doing it so much now. It feels like you might be being a bit ironic.'

You looked blank.

'But you told me to, Sir. You told me to treat you proper. Like we were at school.'

'Yeah, but it sounds like what the army might call dumb insolence. Like you're taking the Michael, extracting the proverbial. Oh for God's sake, Mistyann. I feel like you're taking the piss.'

'Me, Sir? Never.'

I rolled my eyes, fished around in my bag for my Walkman and my book.

'Mistyann, I'm not as recklessly modern as you. I can only do two things at once. So if you don't mind I'm just going to listen to The Clash and read some Martin Amis.'

You know it wasn't me that was meant to be taking you to Wales? It's only because the woman who was meant to be in *loco parentis* had a sick child that I was drafted in. Otherwise you might be doing your GCSE's and I might be —oh I don't know—applying for deputy headships somewhere.

TEN

Travelling with Diamond's okay. He doesn't talk. Just listens to his old man music with his face turned down like his dog died. He doesn't have an MP3 player, not even an Ipod like the other men teachers. He has a thing that plays cassettes. Fucking cassettes. How sad is that? He makes me think about my dad up there in Scotland acting the big man cos he wears a suit to work.

'I'm the first person in my family to wear a suit to work, Mistyann. First person who needs more than one tie.'

Big fucking deal. He works for the Social. When he moved he said, 'Gotta go where the work is, hon. They'll always need Benefit Officers in Bonnie Scotland.' It's a joke. I don't get it. My dad thinks he's funny. He memorises jokes. So I used to memorize them. Used to make me piss myself, my dad. He doesn't now.

The other thing my dad likes is pub quizzes. He's always been in a quiz team. And this is how serious they take it— they rehearse. Quiz league is on Thursdays so they practice on Tuesdays. Sundays too sometimes. How mad is that? They sit there, him and his friends, and ask each other questions. Name the horse that came second in the 1961 Grand National. What was the name of the dog that found the World Cup when it was stolen in 1966? Who was Prime Minister when Queen Victoria died? What is the chemical symbol for Aluminium? All that. Mental. If it isn't a quiz day or practice day he sits at the end of my bed and gets me to read random questions from these quiz books he has. Paperbacks so big they hurt my wrists to hold them.

Mum is shouting up the stairs. She's going, 'For fuck's sake, Len. It's eight o' clock!'

And he goes, 'Just a couple more minutes, my love.' And then twenty minutes go past and I'm hardly able to keep my eyes open and Mum really starts to do her nut.

'Len, give her a break, she's fucking five years old.'

And Dad smiles at me. 'What's the point in having a gifted child if she can't help you win the quiz league?'

And then he goes downstairs and it all kicks off between him and Mum. Yelling and screaming and things breaking and all that. And I put the covers over my head and they smell of Dad. They smell of Marlboro Lights and Real Ale. Smoky and sweet. I used to love that smell. I can't remember any of the jokes. I can remember the capital of fucking Azerbaijan—it's Baku—but I can't remember a single joke, which tells you how crap they must have been.

I look at Diamond sitting opposite and wonder if he and my dad would get on. I think he'd think my dad was a twat, but maybe Dad would be different around Diamond, not so much of a gumbo. My dad thinks that knowing facts means you're brainy, means you're clever. Actually it just means that you've got too much time. Anyone can learn stuff, like anyone can eat. So you know the names of all the Doctor Whos—so fucking what? What good does it do?

Diamond gets in a bit of flap when the ticket collector comes. He's a real indie kid and pure reckons himself. Tries to do some old chat. I can't be bothered with him.

I watch the countryside go by for a while but it's flat and boring. Everything is so teeny—the houses, cars, fields, everything. Then I remember something.

'Sir… Mr Diamond… Jon…'

He doesn't look up. Stupid fucking tape machine thing and his stupid fucking book. I pull his sleeve. He looks up and carefully takes out the earphones.

'What is it, Mistyann?'

'Want to hear a joke?'

'Go on then.'

I say it all in a rush, 'Stevie Wonder is being interviewed and the interviewer asks what it's like to be blind and Stevie Wonder says…'

'It could be worse. I could be black.' Diamond finishes the joke for me. He looks at me for a few seconds and I know what he's thinking.

I say, 'I know what you're thinking.'

'What am I thinking, Mistyann?'

'You're thinking, I wish I wasn't taking her away for a week, aren't you?'

He doesn't answer straight away. 'No,' he says at last. 'I was thinking that I wish that they still let people smoke on trains. I've given up but I find I remain a very keen passive smoker.' He pauses. 'Who is Stevie Wonder, Mistyann?'

'I don't fucking know,' I say. 'Some black geezer.'

'He was a singer. He is a singer. A good singer.' He pauses again 'It's a racist joke, Mistyann, you do know that don't you?'

'Bollocks,' I say.

Afterwards I think: No Mr Jonny Clever-arse English teacher Diamond, it isn't racist. It's a joke about how thick racists are. In the joke Stevie Wonder hates blacks, even though he is one, and it shows how crazy it is to think that a person's skin colour even matters. And then I remember who Stevie Wonder is. I remember that song 'I Just Called to Say I Love You'. He's not good. He's shit. But I don't get time to say this because then there's an announcement and all this scrambling around with bags and all that.

And then we're in London. I've been before. Came with my dad when I was six. We went to the motor show. I remember it was the first time I saw a Smart car.

Dad said, 'Not bad for a toy, is it, Mistyann?'

It's different now of course. Now I could get well lost in London. No one would find me. I could get a job. I'd get an apartment in a sky-scraper so I could look out over the whole city. It must be amazing at night. Like living between two universes. All the stars above and all the street lights and shit below. It'd be like being a fucking angel or something. London's pure total the sickest.

ELEVEN

'Have you got some ID?'

'What do I need ID for? It's a fucking train not a nightclub.' Ticket Boy coloured in confusion. 'Well it's just that you look a bit older than fifteen. I have to check if you can really claim a cheap fare.'

'She's in Year 10,' I said. 'I'm her teacher.'

His eyes bulged a little. 'Crikey, I thought you were her dad. I thought you were his daughter.'

'Jesus, no,' you said forcibly.

'That's a bit too forceful, Mistyann. A bit hurtful.'

'I wouldn't want you as my dad,' you said, fumbling in your bag for a library card or some other ID.

'It's okay,' said Ticket Boy, 'I trust you. You just look older that's all.'

You flashed him a smile, which is what I guess he was after all along. He didn't give a shit about you travelling under age. He was just finding excuses to give the girl a compliment.

'Teacher eh?' Ticket Boy said, eyeing me coolly. 'Working for the Clampdown.' And he grinned.

And I saw myself through Ticket Boy's eyes: forty-ish bloke, suit jacket combined with jeans and T-shirt, camper shoes; beginning to go to seed. My whole look screaming: teacher on a day off. Or worse, my manner, look, speech, all shouting fucking social worker. It didn't help that Ticket Boy was about twenty-two and managed to wear that Virgin Rail panto outfit like it was something he picked up in a vintage clothes store and was wearing because he liked it.

'I heard you say you were listening to The Clash,' he said, 'My dad likes them. They're okay. Which album is it?

'London Calling,' I said and immediately regretted it. I should never have allowed myself to get suckered into conversation.

'Yeah, that's the one everyone goes for. Personally I think the first album has the edge. It's more in your face. More direct, more political. Ticket?'

I scrabbled around for my ticket. It's always in the last pocket you go for. This gave Ticket Boy time to follow up his critique of my musical taste with, 'Course my favourite from that era are the Gang of Four. Were you into them at all? I mean you hear their influence everywhere now. Franz Ferdinand, bands like that, they wouldn't exist without *Entertainment* and I'll tell you who else is due for a critical re-assessment, The Au Pairs. Bedford to St Pancras, that's great, sir, thank you.'

I bet he's in a band. Every young bloke who can't play sports is in a band. The good looking ones sing. The rest aspire to be bass players. Britain is, as Army Dave once observed, a nation of bass players. In other words a nation of megalomaniacs with low self-esteem. Ticket Boy looked like your archetypal bass player to me.

An old guy piped up from across the aisle. 'It's going to take you a long time to check all the tickets at this rate, sonny.'

'Yeah, best get on.' Ticket Boy winked at you before shuffling down the corridor.

'What was that all about?' you said, a few minutes later after Ticket Boy had finally crossed into coach E.

'Oh, what conversations between men are always about, Mistyann. It was about putting me in place, about showing me that there's a new kid in town and that old geezers like myself have out-lived our usefulness and should do the decent thing and crawl off and die.'

'I thought he was trying to impress you…'

'Sadly no, Mistyann. I would love to believe that, but no. I think he found me ridiculous and you intriguing.'

The rest of the Bedford to London stretch of the journey was happily uneventful. Flitwick and Harpenden passed in a blur. Luton squatted briefly at the side of the track like a tramp taking a dump and we were suddenly in the grimy modernist bus shelter that is the new St Pancras. You were awed.

Bedford is fifty one miles from London and yet you'd hardly ever been. Some kids from Manton Heights hardly go into town. You were like a two year old pointing out everything.

'Look, a busker, a real busker!'

Everything got the same delighted squeal—red buses, black cabs, beggars, everything.

'We have beggars in Bedford, Mistyann.'

'But not like this. Not with attitude.'

Yeah, nor are the Bedford *Big Issue* squad quite as dead-eyed and smack-jawed, but it was a laugh travelling through London with someone genuinely entranced at the wonder of it all. I could see you sucking it all in, fuel for the future.

'This,' you said, opening up your arms to embrace the whole stinking vortex of the city, 'This is well ace.' I knew that there was no higher praise. I was touched.

'We've got an hour or so, Mistyann. Do you fancy a wander around Soho?'

You were quiet as we moved around that strange cluster of streets and I wondered if I'd done the right thing bringing you here. Dean Street; Wardour Street; Carnaby Street; The French House; the Coach and Horses; the gay men who cluster surprisingly threatening outside the coffee shops in Old Compton Street; the Chinese; the porn shops; the old guys with the red and ruined faces. All of this was like a definition of glamour to me when I was in my teens. Now I found myself trying to see it through your eyes, and everything became dirtier and sleazier than I remembered.

'Which one do you think is a terrorist then, Sir?'

I hadn't broken you of the Sir habit yet. And my personal jury was still out on whether or not you were taking the Mick.

'What?'

'Who is the terrorist? There must be one. All these people. All these foreign people, one of them has got to be a terrorist.'

I looked around. 'Plenty of tourists, Mistyann. No terrorists.'

'You don't know.' And I realized that the danger of the city was a big part of its thrill for you. We passed some so-called sex cellar where a girl with a dead face was standing on the door half-heartedly trying to tempt punters. I was reminded of a trip twenty years ago to Amsterdam, of an eager Dutch lad doing the same job but with feeling.

'Live sex show. The girls like on the counter yeah? You can actually touch the girls yeah?' And his final selling point, 'You have your student card, yeah? Students get 15% discount on all sex, drinks everything.' We declined, Cog and I, and later we were confronted by a huge North African near our hotel who, upon having his generous offers to provide us with dope, smack, crack, speed, acid, women or boys all turned down, had fixed us with a withering glare. He ended up, snarling, 'So why the fuck did you come to Amsterdam?' It was a good question, and one that we didn't really have an answer for. So we legged it. He was six foot five for fuck's sake and had all the frustration of the commission only salesman after a bad day. We were right to run.

Now you were laughing.

'What's the matter?' I said, puzzled.

'That girl. The one trying to get people into to watch the sex show.'

'What about her?'

'She pure looks like the girls that work in Boots. She has the same make-up, the same expression, everything.'

And you made your face go dead calm and emptied your eyes while smiling at the same time. You had the exact same rigor mortis look of the sex show girl. My stomach turned over.

'See. Boots make-up girls and sex show girls. They're the same, aren't they?'

'Come on, Mistyann. Time to go. Wales is calling. Can't you hear those sheep?'

'Baaa.' You said, too loudly. 'Baaa. Baaa.'

TWELVE

Turns out Llandudno Junction is a real place. Sounds like it should be in *Postman Pat* or *Fireman Sam* or something. And there's snow everywhere. There wasn't any till we pulled into this station but here it's everywhere. And makes everything look even more like a toy railway station. I love snow. Love it. Always kills me. Makes me feel like Christmas. Not like Christmas Day cos that's always shit. But like the first bit of Christmas in November, when the lights and the decorations go up in the town and you start hearing carols in the shops. That makes everyone happy. It's the feeling that something good might happen soon. By the time the actual day comes round and everyone's skint and fighting and puking and rowing and that, then you know you've just been tricked again. That first bit's good though—hearing 'Hark the Herald Angels Sing' in Accessorise or somewhere. I always love that.

We go to the café that is pure nasty and proper packed with old fogeys and munters and everyone is wet and all their clothes are steaming and it's too hot and we have to share a table with this old lady dressed like she's going to climb Everest, big walking boots and a woolly hat and all that. She must be baking. And the other person at our table is a girl who just sits and cries. She doesn't make any noise but tears sort of leak down her face. She's about twenty maybe, a bit fat. Pure ordinary looking. Quite a pretty chubby face. Blonde hair a bit messy. Looks like a student, only not a trendy one. No one takes any notice of her but I see JD just looking at her. He doesn't say anything till they announce our train. Then he gets up, gathers all our stuff together and leans towards the crying girl.

'It'll be alright. Whatever it is, however bad you feel now, it will get better. Even this will pass.' She looks at him proper shocked and JD goes a bit pink, and then he turns to me and jerks his head. I smile proper hard at the crying girl. As we leave the café and hurry along the platform to where this *Mickey Mouse* train is pulling in I look back. I see that she is pure sobbing now and that the old lady has got her arms around her. The old lady meets my eyes. She looks well worried. I give her a little wave and then the train stops and we get on. When we're sat down I say, 'Well done, Sir.'

'I don't know,' he says. 'I think I might have made things worse.'

'Duh,' I say, 'You think?'

'But you've got to do what you can. Make people feel they're not alone.'

I want to say, 'But people are alone,' but I'm also thinking about Carboot Dale and the kicking he's going to get from Angel Carter and her mates, so I don't say anything else.

There's another announcement and I decide that actually I like Welsh. All the sentences sound like waterfalls or something. I tell Diamond this.

'Sounds like the kind of language witches would have. It's the sickest.' I say. I'm not even sure that he hears me. He's just looking out of the window. Looking at the snow. He's done his Bilbo trick again.

THIRTEEN

What did I learn about you on the trip to Wales that I didn't know already? Not much really. That you were foul-mouthed and foul-tempered? I knew that already. That you were an instinctive comedian? I knew that too. You were telling me about the time the head of your primary school suggested that you go to Anger Management.

'What did you say to that, Mistyann?'

'I said,' and you leaned across the table right into my face so that your nose was just about touching mine. 'I said, "I'm not doing anger fucking management" and I punched the wall like this!' And you brought your hand hard down on the table with a bang and everyone in the carriage jumped and it was especially bad because I had deliberately booked us tickets in coach B—the quiet coach—but you just laughed and wriggled back in your seat. 'Anger fucking management. What's that when it's at home?'

We had sat in silence most of the way out from London. No cocky bass-playing Ticket Boy this time. Instead we had a sullen Slav who came past twice pushing a trolley.

'Any drinks? Sandwiches? Snacks?' All mumbled in a choked monotone that broadcast quite clearly his views on the vagaries of a globalised labour market that had made him a trolley dolly between London and Wales. Maybe he was a doctor back in Krakow or wherever. But he didn't attempt to de-construct my taste in music and you ignored the looks he flicked at you as he passed. You just sat quiet and read *Dark Sister* like any Set 1 boff and I read *Time's Arrow*, listened to *London Calling* and periodically sneaked a peep at your perfect frown. And I felt weighed down somehow, like I was living on a denser, more difficult planet than this one.

We used to do a couple of Clash songs in Be Nice. We didn't do 'Clampdown' but we did 'London's Burning' and

'White Riot'. We changed the lyrics to, 'All along the A6…' and got in as many Bedford references as we could building up to a chorus of, 'Bedford's Burning with Boredom now!' Always went down a storm. Better than our own stuff anyway.

There's a demo tape somewhere of three of our own songs. We were going to put out a single. Hostile Youth, another local band, were going to have one side and we'd have the other. Cabbage's mum—Cabbage was a behemoth in a frayed leather jacket, 20 stone of wobbling lard and their lead singer—was going to pay half and we'd pay the other half. But Cabbage was pictured in *Searchlight* moshing at a Skrewdriver gig and that kind of killed the idea. Skrewdriver being the original Nazi punks and cheer leaders for the National Front. Cabbage—Paul Stanley—he's a Probation Officer now. Of course he is. I wonder where our tape went.

'What music do you like, Mistyann?'

'I don't like music.' You didn't look up from your book.

'Come on, Mistyann, everyone likes music.'

You looked up now. 'I don't.'

And for the first time I noticed that your eyes sometimes have the oddest glitter. I should have left you alone, let you get on with your book. But I didn't. The full stop in your voice irritated me.

'What about TV? What do you like to watch?'

'TV is crap.'

'Yeah, most of it, but everyone likes something. Come on. There must be something. People your age watch TV all day every day. Don't you all watch a million hours a year or something?'

You put your book down and stared at me like I was a moron. You sighed and for a second I was reminded of Mrs English. I almost laughed.

'People. Kids. Have the TV on, but that doesn't mean they are watching it. Middle aged people watch telly. Kids just have it on in the background. We don't watch it. We're too busy.'

And that felt right actually. It felt plausible. It's true. It is the forty-somethings who lapse into a nightly lassitude with a drink and a bag of fancy crisps while the kids get on with stuff. You see it at parents' evenings. Parents, who are fat and cushiony versions of their children, sit there trying to work up an interest in homework policies, while making it clear how much they resent being dragged away from *Emmerdale*. Meanwhile the offspring fidget and twitch beside them, clearly straining to run outside and do stuff.

'Well,' I said, 'What do you do? Don't watch telly, don't listen to music, what else is there? I can't imagine you at Guides...' You shrugged. I carried on. 'Come on. There must be something even if it's only swigging cider outside Maccy D or a little light joy-riding...' I stopped, suddenly shocked at how sneering and bitter I sounded.

'Yeah, Sir, then we all go dogging...' You sounded tired.

'No need for the Sir.' I intoned automatically.

'Can I read my book now then?'

I shrugged and then thought that to leave it there would mean that I'd been drawn into communicating on your level and clearly I was nowhere near as fluent in the language of shrugs and sighs and eye rolling. So I injected as much brio into my voice as I could. 'Yeah, sure. What is it about anyway?'

'Dunno. Magic, herbs, witches, ghosts.' You showed no enthusiasm.

'But it's good, yeah? You'd recommend it?'

''Salright.'

I wondered what you would say if my young self walked into the carriage with his array of blond and blue spiked hair and his nine and a half stones of tightly controlled outrage, his habitual swagger and slur, his broken-spined copy of *Metamorphosis and Other Stories* in one hand and his can of Red Stripe in the other. What would you do if he were to sway in here with his translucent skin, his army surplus jacket and those black drainpipes that stopped dramatically three inches above his monkey boots? Would you be intrigued? Impressed? Amused? Bored? Scornful? Indifferent?

And then he did get on.

Fifteen minutes later as we pulled out from changing trains at Llandudno Junction, my younger self got on and made his way down the aisle of our coach. Okay, the hair was a bit different, a black-brown bird's nest rather than the peacock spikes I was sporting in 1986, and the coat was a ragged Oxfam crombie rather than the Bundeswehr jacket I favoured then, but everything else was pretty much the same. The sparrow legs, the black drain pipes, the monkey boots, the pinched white skin, the cheek bones like Nazi razor blades, the black hollows around eyes reddened by provincial amphetamine, student union lager and bad sex; the bony fingers clenched around the Red Stripe, the book—I couldn't quite read the title—everything that mattered was the same. It was the look I recognized; the same stare that came right back at me from a thousand pieces of ID. The same anxious belligerence I had seen in my bus pass, rail card, University registration card, passport. The ghost of myself coming down the aisle. I was spooked for a long moment.

My ghost was being tugged along by a girl maybe four or five years old dressed like a little punk rocker herself. She had a miniature hoodie on with 'Mayhem' spelt out in zigzag capitals and she was dressed in torn chocolate and strawberry striped leggings above tiny DMs that had been customized in a deliberately primitive style: daisies, cows and dogs tippexed on. The imp's hair was shaved at the sides but left to hang over her face in a fringe that resembled a donkey's tail. She had a nose stud.

She tugged my ghost to the table across the aisle from us. Behind him huffed a large middle aged woman carrying two carrier bags. She was tented in a shapeless black dress, her eyes heavily outlined in kohl, her hair crimped and the colour of midnight. She was sporting a wicked looking spike beneath lips that were painted a rich purple. She was about six foot tall and the top of her witchy coxcomb seemed to brush the top of the carriage. She looked like you imagine Boudicca might if Boudicca was fixated by late eighties High Goth couture.

I looked over at you. 'The Goth Family Robinson,' I murmured just too loud and got a dead look back. 'Never mind,' I said.

I glanced back over to my ghost and his companions. Boudicca was clearly twice his age and I wondered if she was mother to him and grandmother to the baby crustie, who now sat solemn, motionless and day-dreaming across the table from her in the window seat, or whether she was mother to them both.

Boudicca caught me looking and held my gaze while at the same time taking the Red Stripe from my ghost's fingers. My eye flickered to the book unopened in front of him and my heart lurched. Kafka. Shit. Unbelievable. Meanwhile Boudicca tipped back her head and swallowed deliberately, her long neck working with surprising grace. I noticed that my ghost was gazing seriously at that same Arctic expanse. Boudicca finished the can, placed it back down on the table, looked at him and smiled. She and my ghost began to kiss. They began to snog in a way that would get them banned from any swimming pool. They started slow but the heat quickly turned up and hair and cheeks and necks and shoulders were soon being covered by moving hands. The girl moved her gaze to the window. I couldn't take my eyes off the mismatched carnal wrestling of my skinny doppelganger and the matronly Goth-queen. I felt your eyes on me. I turned my head. You were smirking as I knew you would be.

'Bit pervy, Sir,' you whispered, but not that quietly. I put my fingers to my lips.

'What?' I mouthed.

'Staring at them like that.' You made a goggle-eyed, slack jawed face of such comic accuracy that I found myself smiling.

'What do you think of the boy?' I hissed. You shrugged. 'Good looking? Ugly? What?' You shrugged again.

'Didn't really look at him.'

'I used to look like that.'

You laughed. 'Yeah, right.'

'I did. Dyed hair. Skinny jeans, everything.'

'I bet you looked a mess.'

'Yes. Yes, I probably did.'

You sat back in your chair and apprised me coolly. You looked suddenly and completely adult.

'You look better now. You look better than he does anyway. You'd look alright with some decent clothes.' You leant forward, suddenly grinning. 'You need a wife, Sir. Someone to look after you.'

The couple across the aisle added sound to their previously silent piece of amateur eroticism. Unpleasantly wet sounds. Moist whispers, damp moans. You twisted around in your seat. 'God, they're still at it. Here... Here!' You raised your voice 'It is the bleeding quiet coach, you know!'

The couple disengaged. My ghost slumped back in his seat staring ahead while Boudicca shot us a look both baleful and ferocious. I stared back. I saw Boudicca contemplating the pros and cons of a confrontation and you could see her work out that, while I might be a pushover, a middle class straight in sensible corduroys, the kid with me had an obvious sociopathic streak that might prove more tricky. You weren't bothered. You'd made your point.

'How far have we got to go now anyway?'

'We'll be coming into Betws-y-Coed pretty soon,' I said.

'Betsy Co-ed and Kevin Cock. Why do all these places have the names of cartoon people?' you said.

'It's a cartoon kind of country,' I said, too loudly, without thinking. I felt heads turn in my direction. Across the aisle the little crustie kid piped up. In Welsh. It's still a shock when you hear little kids use minority languages like this. It's easy to think of Welsh, Gaelic and the rest as being thoroughly grown up affectations. But she got no response and tried again, in English.

'Can you read me a book?' My ghost and Boudicca automatically and simultaneously batted her away.

'Not right now.'

'Ohhh.' The girl looked so crushed.

'I'll read you a story, darling.'

And you were up and across the aisle with one easy swing like a baboon. The kid's parents, if that's what they were, were too astounded to react.

'What have you got there?' You were cooing now. 'Ah, *The Enormous Crocodile*. That's the sickest story, man. You don't mind, do yer?' you said to Boudicca, combining a grin with exaggerated boot-girl estuary vowels. Boudicca, uncertain how to respond, looked across to me. I smiled and shrugged. My ghost gazed directly at you and smiled. I noticed his crooked teeth and ran my tongue across the equivalent tumbledown graveyard in my own mouth.

'No, sweetheart, you go right ahead.' And then he grinned over at me while squeezing Boudicca's hand. He looked back to you and the kid.

'But not too loud, eh. It is The Quiet Coach after all. Got any more lager, love?' And Boudicca fished in her carrier bag and passed him a can. And then she dived in again and came up with another can which she pushed

70

across to you. All of them Red Stripe, my poison of choice till I found myself climbing my own home-made twelve steps. I felt a little pang. Not a craving for alcohol, more a faint nostalgic tremor. Red Stripe is not, you see, despite popular belief, a Jamaican drink. Red Stripe is brewed and bottled on the site of the old football ground in Bedford. I started drinking it in the sixth form and carried on at college, every swig giving me a little hometown warmth.

'Cheers.' You smiled and snapped back the ring pull. Great, I thought. Day One of the Gifted and Talented experiment and our star pupil is swilling strong lager with the counter culture. I closed my eyes, put the headphones back in. Guitars, bass, drums. And Strummer was suddenly alive again, alive and snarling in my head.

I tried not to imagine the headlines should anything kick off this week. What could it be? TEEN IN SCHOOL TRIP DRINKS SCANDAL or PARENTS RAGE AT UNDER-AGE DRINKING. Headlines which now seem ridiculously mild and which I'd clearly take in preference to the ones I eventually got.

I tried not to imagine Mrs English's sour smile of triumph and instead to relax and do the journey maths. Thirty minutes to Betws-y-Coed, twenty-five minutes cab ride. Less than an hour. Not that far. I'd get some Clorets at the station and explain the ground rules to you. Again.

FOURTEEN

After a while I get jarred with Diamond being all quiet and mardy and I realize I kind of know fuck all about where we're going so I get Diamond to explain it to me.

'Didn't you read the information pack, Mistyann?'

'Of course not, Sir. Looked proper boring and well long.' He didn't expect me to read it I can tell.

'To be absolutely honest, Mistyann I didn't give it that much attention myself. But thanks to a partnership between the Department for Children, Schools and Families and the Onelife Foundation, Britain's leading creativity development enterprise, you are going to be given a chance to develop your innate creativity with a Top Mind-Mapping Life-Coach and Cognitive Behaviour Creativity Specialist. Whatever that means.' When I don't say anything he carries on. 'It's some American psychologist who is going to unleash your potential, Mistyann. God help us all.' And I can hear the smile is back in his voice.

'Let's have a look, Sir.' He passes over the pack and I flick through. 'Ariel La Rock?'

'Yes. Just possibly not the name she was born with. She's a celebrity child guidance guru. Transformed education for the gifted in the States apparently and we have a governing class obsessed with what America does.'

I've heard this before. In lessons Diamond is always banging on about America and Iraq and Vietnam and the Sudan and oil and gas and how America wants to rule the world and that. And I think: Of course they do. Everyone wants to rule the world. Who wouldn't? Man U don't say, 'Oooh let Accrington Stanley win the premiership now, we've had our turn'. If America is the most powerful country then they are going to make the rules. End of.

'But what are we actually going to do?'

JD twitches. 'I'm as much in the dark as you. I imagine it might involve some drama games, writing, some team building, problem solving exercises, getting in touch with your inner Führer. Usual nonsense. The point is, Mistyann, that you have been selected as one of the future leaders of our nation. This is the fast track to a seat in the House of Lords or something important like being Controller of Reality TV for *Channel 4*.'

'I fucking hate reality TV.'

'Yes, but Mistyann, you hate nearly everything.'

Which is so not true. I like football. I like cars. I like boys. Some of them.

'Are you saying you like it? *Big Brother*? And all that?'

'Of course I don't like it. But you're meant to.'

I've tried to get into reality sometimes just so I won't be left out when people are talking about it at school but it fucks me off, everyone's all like me me me and I know too many people like that already. Mum likes it though. She talks to the telly when *Big Brother*'s on. Shouts advice and that. Like the people on it are her mates. She gives William and Harry a chubba chub each so they won't talk or fight through it even though the little fuckers should be in bed anyway. Then she pours herself a pure fuck off glass of wine and spends an hour swearing at the telly. It's mad.

'Come on, Mistyann,' She says once. 'At least try and get interested. It's nice to do things as a family every now and then.' She's making an effort so I try to be nice back.

'It's just not my thing, Mum.'

She goes pure heavy mental. 'Just fuck off then!' she yells. 'Always trying to ruin things you are. Spoilt bitch.'

So then I go upstairs and think about phoning Childline but I don't. And do you know why I don't? Cos I suddenly imagine how embarrassing it would be if it turned out that they knew you. I mean imagine if it was Mrs English or someone who was a volunteer at the end of the line.

Imagine her sniffing and saying 'Mistyann? Mistyann Rutherford, is that you?' Fucking do me in that would.

The train pulls into this station that makes Llandudno Junction look like King's Cross. It's pure miniature. There's snow everywhere and a glittery frost on top of the snow. It looks all fairytale-ish. Like Narnia or somewhere. It's well ace. Love it.

And we find there's a taxi waiting for us and Diamond talks to the taxi driver about the stuff people talk to taxi drivers about—football, the weather, all that time wasting bollocks. Diamond is pretty good at the questioning thing cos we find out loads. The taxi driver isn't Welsh, he's from Essex and his wife is from Essex, but they've been here seventeen years and their kids were born here, so their kids speak Welsh and do it at home sometimes to piss off their parents. And I think it must be ace to have a secret language, this code your parents can't understand. Most adults don't understand kids anyway, but to have a proper language which only the kids can speak. How killing is that?

We go down this twisting lane that's like the down bit of a roller coaster, and we do that for miles and miles only it's even scarier cos it's in the dark and then suddenly this castle appears. It's like Dracula's house or something, made of black stone with weird turret things and I can see this mardarse bloke standing in the headlights with his face all scrunched up. I can already see he's food. Diamond pays the taxi and the loser comes towards us with his hand out.

'You must be Mistyann,' he says and I take his hand. It feels like a dead fish, all limp and damp. 'Well,' he says and he opens his arms. 'Here you are!' Like he's showing us something proper decent like a Ferrari or something. I look at Diamond and he's frowning. And I think what the fuck are you so worried about?

FIFTEEN

The warden, Ray, was making a speech. We were in a room furnished in the style of the bohemian class of some distant era; sitting on worn but high quality sofas, decorated with throws with swirls of aboriginal art.

There were nine kids in the room including you. And even though you were chewing your lip and fixing your face into its habitual scowl, you were the most prepossessing. But it was a close call. In teaching you learn to notice the trouble first and the good-looking ones next. Good-looking trouble is the nightmare combination and you had that of course, but you weren't the only one. You sat next to this coffee-coloured beauty and there was something in that girl's poise that suggested danger. She sat perfectly still, her back as straight as any Royal Ballet principal dancer. She looked like the result of a lab experiment that had managed to merge the DNA of Zadie Smith and Kate Moss.

It took me a second to take in the odd thing about this line up of Gifted and Talented. I should have guessed; a government project had to be 'inclusive' and 'embrace diversity'. These kids looked like they were lined up to star in some advertising campaign for Benetton or Coke.

Nine kids: Three white girls (you and the two who looked like plump young dinner ladies.), Black boy, Black girl (this was Zadie Moss) Chinese boy, Indian boy, White boy. The final kid was a white boy whose selection was doubtless in no way hindered by his being sat in a wheel chair. All genuinely gifted no doubt.

Ray's speech was twenty minutes of propaganda about the life-transforming power of the Onelife Foundation. He told us that we were all 'special' because we had been selected for this opportunity and that however creative we felt we were now, we would be even freer in our thinking in a week's time. All of this was delivered in an anxious monotone that suggested that he felt creativity was a nasty little bug that might cause stomach cramps and diarrhoea.

He looked around and I noticed how years of compulsory niceness had smoothed and thinned his features so that everything had become milky. He had a milky covering of almost blond hair curling around his crown, a milky caterpillar of hair along his top lip, milky eyebrows, milky voice and a milky look in his sad grey eyes. He had had, I felt sure, a milky life.

As Ray reminded us in his tentative, milky way of the rules of the house—no TV, no internet, no mobile phones —I took another look around his audience. Wheelchair Boy was very deliberately making notes in one of those trendy little moleskin notebooks, Chinese Boy was frowning and your eyes were darting around the room like a cat that has been reliably informed of the presence of mice in the place somewhere, your body hunched and taut. Zadie was looking at her legs, presumably as surprised as the rest of us at their inordinate length, while the Asian kid stared fixedly at Ray as though fearing that if he looked away he might suddenly do or say something interesting just to spite him. Black Boy was looking at me. As I caught his eye he smiled, a sudden flash of beautiful, radiant ivories that instantly made my mouth feel furred and rancid. I nodded back, careful not to show my own piss-coloured gravestones.

I, and from the rabbitty look of him, Ray, anticipated some mutiny at this point, but the kids accepted the loss of their mobiles without protest. It was the first real indication that we were not dealing with normal children. It was only Amber, the other teacher, who looked aghast. Poor thing, I expect that she had never in her life used a payphone. She rallied quickly though.

'Ray, I'll need to keep my mobile for emergencies and for keeping in contact with my head of department.'

That's the benefit of an Oxbridge education for you. Speed of thought. Milky Ray capitulated without a struggle.

'Er, yes, I suppose staff should have mobiles.' I had the school mobile. A bog-standard Nokia. The Morris Minor of phones. I still didn't have one of my own, something that was a source of amusement to my peers as well as the kids I taught. It was like I'd confessed to not having a chair or a bed. I didn't care. As far as I was concerned I was the freest guy I knew. No-one could ever get hold of me on a whim. No-one could ever phone demanding to know where I was.

Amber was in her early twenties, but looked about sixteen. When you and I had walked into the big self-consciously rustic farmhouse kitchen, she was texting someone. She continued to text while nodding lethargically in my direction by way of greeting. I nodded back and Ray fussed with cups and milk and sugar.

'She's terribly bright. First from Cambridge. God knows what she's doing teaching,' he whispered.

I watched her toss that hen party hair—black on top, platinum underneath—the look you generally see accessorized with too much flushed flesh and a bottle of Vodka Ice—and I knew that I was going to have a keep a tight check on myself not to get too irritated. This was a teacher? This was a Cambridge graduate?

With the ground-rules established Ray cheered up and trundled through another few minutes of basic house-keeping. All the food was 'totally organic and fair trade of course'. Of course. I stole a glance at you to see the impact of this phrase. You were impressively impassive.

Everyone was to help themselves to breakfast and lunch. And Ray stressed that it was all very much Jamie Oliver rules. Everything we consumed was going to be good for us. He paused again. Here was another bomb to be stepped over as lightly as possible. Amber wriggled, someone might have sighed, but that was about it. I was beginning to think that these kids weren't so much gifted as lobotomized.

Ray explained the procedures for the evening meal. 'After tonight you lot will be doing the cooking. Er, nothing to be afraid of. You do it in groups, so you'll cook every other night and wash up on the nights that you don't cook.' He took a deep breath, a signal to himself that there was a jokey passage coming up. 'I know that some of you can cook already—some of you can cook but just don't realise it yet. And in any case our experience is that in any group someone rises to the top to take on the chef role. Someone always turns into er Gordon Ramsey and the only time we get problems is when er two people rise to the top. And then we have to hide all the sharp implements. You can't have two Gordon Ramseys. Not in our kitchen. It's just not big enough. But no really, you'll be okay. We provide detailed recipes and all the ingredients. It's all idiot-proof. I should know, I've tested all the menus myself.' And he smiled in that milky way that you'll remember.

The Chinese Boy guffawed. The sudden bark of his laughter startled us all before calling forth puny smiles that glimmered briefly before expiring at Ray's feet. You yawned. Ray sighed and rallied to finish the talk. The gist of is it was that this was a commune. 'You've seen your rooms. You know that Cefn Coch is emphatically not a hotel', that he and his wife, Susie, were always around to help, to please be careful if we left the site and to be sure to let someone know. 'The villagers are alright but don't think you'll charm them with your English ways.' He bustled off to make squash for the kids and I headed outside for a fag.

I found a sheltered spot well away from the glowering, head-masterly presence of the house and stood gazing at the view. It was bleakly impressive. The snow had turned the farmland into a bright foaming sea. It was a clear night. One of those nights when you feel exhilarated by nature and oddly thrilled by evidence of the futility of human endeavour. One of those nights when you think 'it's all bollocks anyway'.

There was a sudden movement at my feet and I found myself staring into the eyes of a black cat.

'What are you staring at?' I said and the cat legged it. From behind I heard movement.

'Talking to yourself, Sir. You're losing it.'

'Mistyann. Bloody Hell. You nearly gave me heart attack.'

You sniggered.

'That Ray. He's a twat isn't he?'

I didn't answer but tried to savour my second long drag. I coughed. Violently. You laughed.

'You want me to show how to do that, Sir?' And then we agreed that Ray was, indeed, a twat. I felt bad when you added that he was, like, so obviously a teacher as well.

And of course it was obvious that Ray was a failed teacher. Everything about him suggested it. I had a sudden mental picture of kids running over desks and fighting and throwing stuff while Ray pretended not to notice the anarchy around him. I felt sympathy for Ray then. And of course you caught on in that supernatural way you have.

'Never mind, Sir. He's out of it now. He's got it easy.'

'What's your room like, Mistyann? Made yourself free with the mini bar yet?'

Even in the icy dark I could feel you tense.

'Room's alright—but I'm sharing with a right stuck up bitch. "Yah, look, I hope you don't mind but I like to get up to practice yoga at 6.30am. I absolutely can't function if I miss it".'

I laughed. You'd got that cut-glass RP thing down perfectly. 'Mistyann, you're priceless do you know that?'

'She's meant to be black as well. She don't talk like a proper black girl.' So I knew that you were in with Zadie.

At dinner—baked potatoes, quiche, salad, served to us by inscrutable moon-faced and silent Welsh teenagers—Ray told us that Ariel had arrived but that she was very jet-lagged and that we would meet her at the Saturday morning session scheduled to take place in the LRC at nine sharp.

Somebody—the Chinese boy—asked, 'Please... what is the LRC?' and you muttered, 'It's what they call libraries now. Learning Resource Centre, innit.'

Ray coloured and stammered, 'Er yes. It is the room we used to call the library but we're planning to put a computer in there... and anyway our research has found that students find the term library off-putting...' and then he faded out in front of his audience's clear disdain, before fading in again to tell us that tonight's ice-breaking session would be held in the more informal setting of the sitting room.

After dinner a queue formed by the payphone which was housed by the front door in a genuine GPO red callbox. Three kids weren't in the queue Zadie, whose real name was Charlotte, non-wheelchair White Boy and you. I guessed that this was because you were the kids who'd disobeyed orders and kept your mobiles. Ray put the phones he had collected in a little safe on the wall. And then spun the numbers on the combination lock with unnecessary force.

I found you in the kitchen washing up with two of our waitresses. All three of you were laughing.

'They're teaching me Welsh, Sir. It's well hard.'

'Nothing rude, I hope.' I said with what I hoped would be a winning smile. Neither of the Welsh lasses responded and both looked at the floor. I asked if you'd called home.

'No point,' you snapped. 'They know where I am.'

'Mistyann,' I tried to keep my voice even, 'I'm only asking.'

One of the waitresses said something quiet and quick to her mate who looked right at me and laughed nastily. After a second, you joined in, your laughter forced, making you sound like a fox barking and I heard myself sigh. 'I'll leave you to your er lesson.'

I headed for a few quiet moments in my room. You get used to that sort of thing in teaching. Random laughter is part of the weaponry of the students in their ongoing insurgency against authority and it's best to ignore it. The worst thing for any authority figure is to be drawn into a confrontation that he daren't lose but can't win. My years in teaching taught me to choose my battles with care.

Amber and I had been allotted rooms in a special staff suite, separated by a bathroom that we shared. My room was identical to the room I had at Uni. Clean, comfortable, tiny. It just needed a poster to transport me back to the eighties.

I spent most of my time at the Uni of Clearing drinking, taking drugs, getting off with people and playing in shit bands. And so did everyone else I knew. After a while I spent more time being chucked out of bands than I did rehearsing with them. You know how it goes: the would-be guitar hero tells you the band is splitting up and then you hear that the rest of them are rehearsing with a new singer under a new name. The band didn't split up; they just chucked me out. In a nice way.

And I spent quite a lot of time getting dumped by a succession of Emmas and Sophies and Lucys who spent the first couple of weeks of our romances thinking I was a riot and the next couple of weeks getting pissed off with the caustic remarks and disgracefully intermittent erections. After a couple of weeks I was usually history, filed under 'learning experiences' and replaced by Toby who was studying Social Policy.

I also spent time in one-to-one therapy sessions with tutors who told me that I could really achieve great things if I'd just get my act together and with bank managers who wanted me to do penance before granting me a new overdraft.

Going to a bank then was like going to church for confession. You would list all the sins you had committed with their money and they would grant you absolution by way of more funds. As long as you looked suitably remorseful you usually got the cash. It helped if you got to know your confessor personally. I reckon I saw Mr Gooding twenty-five times in three years. By the end of my course he was practically my closest friend.

I was lucky, I guess. These days all these transactions are done by remote control and Mr Gooding has been replaced by a random Indian grad student reading from a script.

I left university with a desmond—a 2:2, oh how witty we were—a stubborn genital wart, an overdraft that would have bought me quite a nice little house and an hour's worth of demos of the longest lasting of my uni bands—the Electric Full Stops.

It felt like a thousand years in the past. And so I already loved this little room at Cefn Coch. Nothing in it. No junk, no clutter. It was heartening to sit on the bed, pick up a book and realize how little you really need. A book, a bed and a shower down the hall. All the rest is bollocks, isn't it?

I padded out and along to the bathroom next door. Perfect. Along with the complimentary soap and shampoo there was a shower cap. I came back into my room, took the chair from under the desk by the window and, by standing on it, found that I could place the shower cap over the smoke alarm. Hurrah. This is why humans and not apes or cockroaches rule the earth, because we have the ingenuity to neutralize attempts by state-sponsored nannies to subdue us. It was a simple shower cap but it was also a weapon in the war against the health and safety Nazis. I smoked my second cigarette in ten years and listened to my faithful Walkman. A fuzzy C90 that Cog had put together a few years before. Every track a modern classic. And I fell asleep. Smiling.

SIXTEEN

I'm with the kid in the wheelchair. We're playing this game that's meant to break the ice and get us all to be friends. What we've got to do is to find out all we can about our partner in one minute and then we swap over. When it's our turn to talk about ourselves we can only answer the exact questions they ask, we can't just give our life stories.

I find out that his name is Pete, that he has muscular dystrophy, that he's expected to be dead before he's 21, that he supports Spurs, that his dad tried to kill him two years ago cos he couldn't cope with having a disabled son but that he got a suspended sentence, that he has a brother and sister both older than him and that he used to have a pet rabbit called Guinness because it had a white head and a black body and that he reckons that he's been chosen for this course not because he's gifted or talented but because his teachers feel sorry for him. He tells me that his big ambition is to see Spurs play in the champion's league before he dies. I tell him that he's got no fucking chance.

When we swap over he doesn't find out much about me. I tell him some stuff, but his questions are pants and anyway we get talking about Keano and don't have time for much else.

Then we have to feed back what we've learned to the group and I'm not sure that Pete wants everyone to know about the whole dying thing so I stick to the stuff about Spurs and the rabbit and I can see everyone looking at me, thinking that I've really missed the point and that makes me fucking angry.

I already know a bit about the fucking snob, Charlotte, that I'm sharing a room with cos she told me. Didn't ask about me of course, but managed to let me know that she was a veggie 'Practically a vegan actually', lives in Primrose Hill, wherever the fuck that is, and that her dad owns practically half of Nigeria and he's a chief and she's a princess or something. She's going to be a lawyer and then go into politics.

'Intellectually, I think I'm a social democrat so that would normally mean Labour, but in terms of career advancement I've got to think about the Conservatives. I mean an articulate, high achieving black lawyer—they'll be desperate to find me a major job, won't they?' Those are her actual words.

And later she says all this to Dalwinder, the Asian kid, so it's so obvious that it's a routine. Not even a good routine.

We're all roughly the same age and going round the room we find out that Dalwinder is from Hounselow and that his dad works at Heathrow. He speaks about four languages. The Chinese kid is called Stephen and he's a poet. The other white kid is a boy with proper long hair called Zak. He says that he doesn't go to school, that his mum educates him at home.

At first I think that it must mean that he's been chucked out but it turns out that his mum never let him go in the first place.

'She's like this mad hippie, yeah?' he says, and then he says that he can't read very well. 'But I can play anything on the guitar and I'm really into conceptual art, like Tracey Emin and Sam Taylor Wood and Damien Hirst and that, yeah?'

The other boy is this black kid called Julius and I decide that he's the one that I'm going to shag. He's the best looking but it isn't just that. He seems sort of shy and finds it hard to look anyone in the eye, but he smiles at everyone. And just looks decent, you know? I mean you can always tell who are the phonies and the fakers and the jerks and this kid, Julius, just looks like he won't fuck you around. Also he doesn't say that he's a poet or an artist or nothing. He's paired up with Zak and Zak says, 'This is Julius Bedeau and he wants to live a beautiful life.' And Jon asks Julius what he understands by that and he just spreads his arms out and smiles. And he's got this most amazing smile. I mean black kids often have dutzi smiles, but Julius's really is the dog's. I'm definitely going to shag him.

We do some other games after that. We have to tell the whole group something that is true but that we think will surprise them. I think about telling them that I slept with a bloke for money once, but then I think what if I can tell from their faces that this doesn't surprise them? So I tell them I can make myself faint whenever I want to, which I used to do all the time at primary school when I was bored. I think about doing it just to show people I can but in the end I decide I'm not in the mood. The other kids say some stuff but none of it is surprising, not really. Ray tells us that he once had a mental breakdown and thought he was Jesus. He says he started to get better when they took him to the mental home and there were already three other Jesuses on his ward. And that's sort of interesting but not the sort of stuff you should tell a group of kids you're meant to be looking after.

JD tells us that he was in a band once, but no one looks very impressed. Then we play this game where Ray shouts out a number and we have to get into groups of that number and then he shouts an object and as a group we have to become that thing like an aeroplane say, or a duck. It's a dumb game but at least it gets us moving around. And then Ray says that we'll start the serious stuff tomorrow when Ariel is here.

My room is big and decorated in white with two beds in it, like William and Harry's room but about 50 times as big and we've got our own bathroom. But Charlotte is going to be in there most of the time. I can tell. She spends about an hour in there just taking her make-up off and cleansing and that and comes out looking just the same. I get so bored waiting for her to come out that I just get into bed. She's proper shocked.

'Mistyann, that's like really gross. You've got to take your make-up off, that's like the Law, okay?'

But I tell her I can't be arsed and she looks at me like I'm scum and I think about getting out of bed and wiping her toothbrush around the rim of the bog, but suddenly I'm totally smecked and anyway what if she's sick in our room? That would be like so shit.

When we're in bed she says, 'Mistyann?' and I go, 'Yeah?' and then she says, 'Have you ever thought about being a lesbian?' And I tell her no. And she says that everyone in her school is a lesbian right now.

'It's like the fashion,' she says. And she says that the other fashion is to be anorexic. And I ask her how much it costs her dad to send her to the school and she says 'It's like 15K a term or something.'

And I think that she's just a lying bitch and tell her that I'm going to sleep and just before I go to sleep I think that it's funny that I never have thought about being a lesbian. Not once. So I think about it now. And I think that doing it —the sex and that—that might be alright but all the talking and being supportive and having to tell girls that yeah they look great and no they're not fat. Drive you mad that would. Do you in.

SEVENTEEN

The first thing I heard on waking from the usual anxious dreams was the clatter and clang of multiple breakfasts being rustled up somewhere deep inside the castle. And surely that was bacon I could smell? I was already salivating as I pulled random clothes from that old carpet bag, so it was only later that I found I'd twinned a salmon pink Van Heusen shirt with a brown V-neck M&S jumper with ancient Levis with a hole in the knee. Fine for a student with literary pretensions but less than serious for a forty year old senior teacher and stand-in parent. And I never got the breakfast.

I was following the cheerful clash of crockery and being led by the nose towards that wonderful bacon scent right up to the kitchen door. Beyond it I could hear the chatter and hum of strange voices and suddenly it sounded like hundreds of people in there. I couldn't face it so I did a sudden swerve through a fire exit and found myself in a little wooded arbour, the crunch of snow keeping time like a funeral snare under my feet.

I moved away from the bushes and came upon a view that was almost Antarctic in its expanse. A blinding, brilliant white stretching as far as you could see. It was easy to see how people could panic and hallucinate in snow that unforgiving. But at that moment it was thrilling.

I lit a cigarette and turned back to look at the house which, in the early morning, rose as black as the surroundings were white. With its insane turrets and narrow mullions it looked more than ever like a film set. Something Terry Gilliam might imagine. Clearly it was a Victorian fake. The dream of some industrialist with a fortune built on sending kids and women down the mines, which he then spent on creating a new Camelot.

I was lost imagining a time where a ruddy mine-owner would have gathered his family about him—how many kids would he have had? Eight? Nine?—and read them *The Rime of the Ancient Mariner* while a fat, apple-cheeked housekeeper bustled around with mulled wine and pastries. Then I was startled by a voice at my elbow.

'Hello, Jon. No breakfast? Or have you had it?' Ray's wife, Susie, stood smiling and with her was a tall woman with a mane of mad blonde hair who'd sat in on the ice-breaking session. She hadn't joined in but had taken notes in a furious scribble. Now that she was close up I saw that she also had an intense, slightly pop-eyed stare. I gestured with the hand holding my fag.

'This is breakfast I'm afraid. It's a new high nicotine diet. It really works. I'm thinking of patenting it.'

Susie laughed and introduced me to her companion. 'This is Kendra, she's here as a care-worker for Pete, you know, the boy in the wheel-chair?'

I asked her what that was like and her mouth thinned which I took to mean that it was not quite the life that a younger Kendra might have had planned for herself.

We made small talk which is, I find, the time when you find out most about people. When people are confessing or, to use the language of the AA group, 'sharing' then they are story-telling and as such they are editing, shaping, nipping and tucking their lives for public consumption. It can be entertaining, but it's rarely anything like the truth. In genuinely trivial conversations people give themselves away. One five minute chat about sweet Fanny Adam will generally tell you all you need to know.

Over the next five minutes I learned that Kendra couldn't decide whether she hated Pete or loved him, but also that that she very definitely hated nearly everything else about her life. She managed to communicate this very clearly through a series of twitches and monosyllabic whispers, while all the time keeping her eyes fixed on me in a way that was unsettling. I also learned that Susie was a wit and clearly wore the trousers in her relationship with Ray. I asked her what it was like to be an Asian women in this part of Wales and she laughed.

'I usually introduce myself like this: "Hi, I'm Susie, I'm the mail order bride" and I watch them get all flustered. But it's what they all think.' She anticipated my next question by saying, 'I'm not by the way. Ray was travelling around the world after his breakdown, trying to "find himself". Lucky for him, he found me instead.' And she laughed again.

I told her that she lived in a beautiful spot and she said that I should see where she comes from.

'It's alright here in the snow, but mostly it's grey in this country. Cold and grey. Cold grey rain, cold grey houses, cold grey people. We're going back to Malaysia when we can.'

I learned something else from Kendra. She told me that she thought Pete was really pissed off with you, Mistyann.

'I don't know for sure. He hasn't said much, but I think he told her lots of personal things—about his illness I mean —and she didn't share it with the group. It would annoy him, I think.'

After they'd gone in I spent a few more minutes smoking another cigarette, staring into that hypnotic blankness and thinking that if I was in a wheel-chair and had to spend my days with a little team of Kendras to wipe my arse, then everything would annoy me.

EIGHTEEN

Sure enough Charlotte is up pure fucking early. I never realised meditation and relaxation and all that could be so bloody noisy. She's groaning and moaning and ooohing and aahing and sighing. It sounds like she's being tortured. I try to shut it out the way I do when William and Harry and Mum are all going off on one, which happens most mornings. But Charlotte Snob doing yoga makes way more noise than Harry and William fighting. It's mad.

Anyway, in the end I can't fucking stand it so I get up, have a piss, chuck a jumper on and go exploring. I hear Charlotte go, 'Where are you going?' as I leave, and she sounds just like Harry. I don't answer. Just keep on going and I'm thinking about Harry and how he is. Perhaps he really is sick. Most kids get rid of bugs in twenty-four hours —we learnt that in Health and Social Care—but what if it was something serious? For a second I miss him. I proper miss all of them. God knows why. They probably haven't even noticed I've gone yet. When they do notice, Mum'll just think I've run away again. I've done it twice before.

Second time I went to Scotland to see my dad. Thumbing it all the way there. Takes two and a half days and ten lifts to get from Bedford to Burntisland in Scotland. Eight blokes and two women pick me up. I'm only thirteen but no-one tells the police, no-one tries to take me home. I tell them all that my mum's mad, which is kind of true anyway, and that my dad's expecting me. Tell them that Dad was meant to come and get me but that his car's broken down. And I have these pretend phone calls with my dad while I'm in the cars. I make this big deal about memorizing the numbers when I get in. I get my phone out.

'Hi, Dad, it's me,' I say. 'Yeah I've got another lift. Number plate is R71 KDW. Says he's taking me forty miles up the A1. I'll ring again when I get out.'

Course I can't really call cos I don't have any credit. I shit myself thinking that someone will call me while I'm pretending to be on the phone and then I'd be pure busted, but no-one does.

I tell them that my dad's a police inspector and that because his car was knackered I'd started hitching without his permission, but he's letting me carry on seeing as how I'd started, and seeing as how the only alternative would be staying with my mum who was about to be put in the mental home. It's a bollocks story but I think no-one feels like testing it out in case it turns out to be true and they look like an idiot. Even so, one bloke shows me his dick.

I know it's going to happen. He's been right chatty and then he starts to get quieter and quieter till he's hardly saying anything at all. Then he pulls off the road down this proper dead country lane. And he stops and turns off the engine. I'm shitting myself, but I have my fingers around this little vegetable knife I've taken from home and I'm thinking when he goes for me I'll go for his throat. I'll go super-nova. Mental. That's what Ty always says.

'In a fight you've got to go super-nova right from the off. No fucking around. You got to mental them. You might only get one chance. Mental them. It's the only way.'

One of the few sensible things he's ever said.

Anyway, this driver is sat there and I'm sat there and then he gets his dick out and it's flopping across his lap. It's not even proper hard, just a bit sort of swollen. And he's not looking at me, just sort of looking down at his cock and suddenly I just know I'll be alright so I tell him to put it away. I don't have to shout or nothing.

I just go, 'Can we get going now?'

And he looks kind of relieved and we drive back onto the motorway and he drops me off at a service station and gives me a tenner. I tell you people are well strange sometimes. But he's the only proper weird pervy one. The other blokes are okay. I like the drivers who just turn the radio up when you get in like they're saying "I'll give you a lift but I don't want to have to make conversation". Suits me just fine.

The women pick-ups are more annoying.

Both of them are really different from each other, but they both jar me right off. I mean one is proper young and has punk hair all different colours and she's pure totally pierced and all that and she has one of them Herbie cars painted bright yellow. And the other's this old lady in a car that's so boring I don't even notice the make or the colour. But both of them turn out to be nearly the same. They both keep on and on asking questions. In the end I have to start to cry just to get them to shut up. That totally works. Shuts them right up.

My dad goes mad when he sees me. I get a train the last bit. The punky woman drops me right in the centre of Edinburgh and I get a train with the tenner the perv gives me. I go right across a mad old iron bridge to Burntisland. Do you know it's not really an island? It is a shithole though. People used to go on holiday there once. Fuck knows why. It's the shittiest place I've ever been. It's a good place for Dad cos there are lots of people there who don't work. I stay there two days and then he drives me back. He drives all the way through the night and just drops me at the end of Manton Lane. And then my mum goes fucking mental and we have the police round and everything. I bet the neighbours hate us. They'd get the council to evict us if they could but they can't because it's our house. Well my mum's house. She's got a mortgage and everything. She's proper proud of that.

The first time I run away is the year before. I'm going to go to London with my first proper boyfriend, Warren Parkes, the one who bought me the sovereign ring with the word "bitch" engraved on it. Loved that ring for a while. Thought it was the sickest. The total dog's.

We only make it as far as the bus station. We are going to do the whole Romeo and Juliet thing. We are going to go to London and we think buses run all night, but they stop at eight o' clock or something so we hang around for a bit and then have to go home. It is well embarrassing. I think Warren could nick a car or something but he doesn't know how, which is pathetic. I reckon every boy should be able to get into a car. Okay, maybe not one of the new ones with immobilizers and all that, but an old crap car like a Sierra or something. I could do it, but I don't know, maybe I don't want to show him up. Boys hate that. When you can do something better than them.

So I'm thinking about Harry and William and home and everything and I find myself in the big old dining room where we had dinner. It's a dutzi room. It's got this table that all of us sat round and there would have been room for a few more people too. It's like a table you normally only see in paintings with Lords and that getting pissed around it and eating huge turkey legs with their fingers. And the room has these massive windows which look over the hills and I'm looking out the windows and I see like this weird thing. There's this person all done up like a warrior from one of those Kung Fu films that Ty likes to watch with William. It's got a hood that hides its face and these like baggy pyjamas that you see Arabs and that wearing and it's doing this kind of slow motion dance. And the maddest thing of all is that it's waving this huge fuck off sword in front of it. It's a proper sword. Big and curving and it looks wicked in the moonlight or starlight or security lights or whatever. It looks proper sharp that blade and this thing is making all sorts of strange shapes with it.

So I'm just stood there at the window watching when the figure turns towards me and pushes the hood back. Of course it's not a weird creature really, it's a lady. And she smiles and waves for me to come towards her. And I don't really want to but I do. She's got a pure nice smile and a beautiful face. A pop idol face. She looks like a celebrity or something, like she's someone I should recognize.

The dining room has one of those French door things and I think it's going to be locked but it isn't and so I go outside.

Close up, the lady looks more ordinary, though still beautiful. She has blonde hair scraped back from her face and pure pale skin and these amazing green eyes, almost like alien eyes or cat's eyes or something and she is leaning on the sword like it is a walking stick and she's smiling and her teeth are perfect. All even and white and the only other person who has teeth that perfect is my Nan, my dad's mum, and her's were false. You just know that this lady doesn't have false teeth. And she's smiling like she has been waiting in the garden just to meet me. She holds out her hand.

'Hey,' she says. 'Kinda early to be up isn't?' And I realize that she's American. I nod and then think that I should say something.

'Charlotte is doing stupid frigging yoga in our room.'

It's all I can think of. And this lady raises an eyebrow and I realize that she has been doing some sort of yogary thing too. That's what all the slow motion dancing was about. God.

'Are your teeth real?' I say. 'Only my Nan had teeth a bit like yours but hers were false. They were plastic.' And I can't believe that I've said it. Talk about fucking rude. But this lady just laughs.

'Well, it depends what you mean by real I guess. They are not plastic. They're porcelain veneers over real foundations.

I guess that you wouldn't call them false but you could call them renovated.'

And then I realize who she must be.

'You're Ariel,' I say. 'You're our guru.'

And she laughs again. 'Who told you that? Who said I was the guru?'

'Oh, it's just something that Mr Diamond said. He's my teacher.'

'Ah. So you must be Mistyann, right?'

I nod.

'You see I've done my homework. Yes, Mistyann, I'm Ariel La Rock and I'm not a guru. I'm an educational psychologist who specializes in helping people fulfil their potential, that's all.'

'Is it your name real?' I ask this because I remember what Diamond said about it when we were on the train. This makes her laugh again and I feel good about that and I think that I always feel good when I make people laugh.

'You could say that my name is renovated too. Ariel is my real first name but La Rock was my second husband's name. I kept it when we got divorced because I liked it better than my first husband's name which was—' She stops here and looks all around like she's looking out for people who might hear and then whispers, 'Hamburger.'

I laugh now. 'You are joking.'

'No,' she says, 'Actually Hamburger is quite a common name in the States. My original name is Smith. 'There's a pause and then she says, 'I bet I looked pretty strange out there, huh?'

I nod and then explain how I thought she looked like a ghost, dancing.

'A ghost dancer? I kinda like that.' And then she says 'Hey Mistyann do you want to see something really cool?'

So we walk around the house a bit, crunching over the snow which is all sparkling and we head for this high wall covered in white where the snow has fallen on the ivy that covers it and there's a little wooden door, like a fairy tale door. We have to duck to get through it. And on the other side is like a secret garden. It's big with a high wall all around. The snow is really piled up in the corners and in the middle there are all these snowmen things. Only they're not like the normal snowmen you see, you know just big round balls for bodies and smaller balls for the heads. These are more like the masks African tribes wear. But made of snow. Statues of snow masks. And they're proper big. As tall as me most of them. There's about eight of them and they have dutzi eyes. The eyes are these perfectly round black stones. Not pieces of coal, these eyes look completely round and shiny.

'Easter Island statues,' says Ariel.

'What?' I say and she says how these snow head things are like these strange stone statues that they have in a place called Easter Island. They're amazing. Pure freaky.

'Did you do them?' I say even though I know she didn't. And Ariel laughs.

'No, I was just looking for somewhere private to do my tai chi and came here. It was just too spooky to do it with these fellows watching so I went back to where you saw me. But it's kinda awesome, isn't it?'

And we stand there looking at the snow heads which pure do look like they could speak or put a spell on us at any second. I don't know how long we stand there because it gets light around us. The sky gets pink behind the snow heads and I suddenly notice that all my bones feel like ice and I have to clamp my teeth together to stop the clicking up and down like those stupid wind-up toy teeth you see in joke shops. Ariel notices and smiles and says, 'Brrr' and rubs her arms and we go back towards the house. We meet the cat on the way and Ariel stops to make a fuss of it and tickle its whiskers and when we get in the dining room she says that she's got to go and get changed so she goes one way and I go towards the kitchen.

In one of the cupboards there are four variety packs of cereals. I open all of them and take out all the little boxes of the coco pops. That might seem mean but coco pops are the only ones I like and breakfast is the most important meal of the day. Everyone is always saying that, aren't they? I eat one bowl of coco pops and by the time I finish I can hear people starting to get up—there are showers whooshing and stuff—so I put all the other boxes of coco-pops into this cotton bag that I find hanging on the kitchen door knob and head back to my room.

As I get to towards the main stairs I can hear voices arguing. I stand and listen for a little while until I recognize a voice. It's Pete having a right go at someone, calling them a stupid cow and a twat and an imbecile. If I'd wanted to hear that kind of shit I could have stayed at home.

When I get back to the room I get straight back into bed and try and get warm again. It takes ages and as the blood goes back into my wet feet it really hurts and I realize that I've hardly ever been proper cold before.

Charlotte is all made up like she's going to spend a day working in Boots, except that she's got this mean look which would put anyone off buying anything. Her mouth's all tight and thin, she's frowning and she's got lines across her forehead that make her look about fifty.

'Where have you been?' she says, making a special effort not to look at me.

'Nowhere,' I say. And that's it. We don't speak again till dinner.

NINETEEN

All the adults met before the morning session. We met in the LRC as Ray persisted in calling it. I wondered idly about rebranding books themselves. Perhaps we could call them HLDs—Handheld Learning Devices—and perhaps the nations' kids would be transformed into readers overnight? The most ridiculous thing about changing the name of that particular library was that it was such a classic example. There were shelves floor to ceiling bowed and groaning under the weight of leather-bound tomes. And these really were tomes: majestic slabs of compacted knowledge.

Aside from books there was a solid oak table and a number of chairs backed in worn red leather of the kind you might expect to find in the board room of a superior private bank. Sitting around it with me were Ray, Amber, and Susie. We did more chit chat for a while. I asked Ray why he gave up teaching and he gave me a sharp look and I remembered that he hadn't actually told me that he ever was a teacher. It was your observation. But in the end he just muttered the usual excuses. Behaviour, paperwork, marking etc. All perfectly valid but just looking at him you can guess that disorganization, inability to keep order and all round milkiness had something to do with it.

Amber made a call to her boyfriend—a litany of DIY instructions—and then a call to her mother that ended with the request that her mum popped round to her house to check that the boyfriend was doing what he was supposed to. I felt like phoning him myself to tell him to run for the hills or just kill himself.

I still wanted to ask Susie more about being a Malaysian immigrant in this most tribal and clannish area of Wales but, with Amber's calls home defiling the library quiet, I didn't get the chance and then Kendra stumbled in. She was all breathless apologies and it transpired that she was late because her charge, Pete, was being a real turd.

'I don't know what's got into him. He's just being so vile and unreasonable today.'

And I thought—he's a teenager, they can all be vile and unreasonable. It's one of the symptoms of adolescence. Even the crippled ones are going to be prone to it. More prone to it probably.

Ray reassured her. 'We're still waiting for Ariel,' he said, and explained that she was really jet-lagged and we should give her a few more minutes. Of course just as he finished saying this, in she came looking like she could run a marathon.

She was wearing jeans and a vintage AC/DC T-shirt and, I'm not an expert, but she didn't seem to be wearing make-up. She was naturally flawless and grinning. A real grin, not a professional smile but a sunburst of genuine warmth. I imagine that she was used to people falling very quickly for the Ariel La Rock phenomenon.

She worked us over pretty effectively. In just under fifteen minutes she had set out her general philosophy, her aims and objectives for the week, and her methodology. And she did it lucidly, crisply and concisely. I can't recall an actual word that she said but I do know that she was witty, charming and businesslike. By the end of that quarter of an hour we were all signed up as part of Team La Rock.

Up to then I'd seen the project almost as an anthropological exercise. I thought that the week might do you some good and that I might learn something from watching how people behaved under these sorts of conditions. I hadn't expected to feel enthused about it. Ariel was good at projecting passion for her work and it was contagious. I mean Amber even put her phone down and, when it pinged the arrival of a text, she actually switched it off.

Isn't it interesting that I can't now think why her ideas seemed so impressive, just that they made perfect sense at the time? She was a fantastic saleswoman.

You know that she's up for election to the Iowa state senate now? I've been following her blog. I don't think she writes it herself—I picture a breathless intern pleased to be part of the Ariel La Rock phenomenon. You won't know this but she met our Education Minister this week. Proof that she's becoming a major political player. And there's a photo of her playing the clarinet at a school for kids with moderate learning disorders. No, she's definitely getting on. The people of Council Bluffs and Sioux City are going to have to be very strong-willed to resist her.

The last thing she did on that first day was to tell us something about a truly amazing snow installation in what she described as the 'Secret Garden'.

Ray looked worried. 'Do you mean the vegetable garden? I hope the kids haven't been playing about in there. Old Owen the Gardener gets really upset with people mucking about amongst his root crop. Sees it as his private domain. We'll have to tell the children it's off limits, I'm afraid.'

Susie gave him an odd look.

Ariel smiled sweetly at him.

'You should see this, Ray. It really is something special. I'm sure even Owen the Gardener would be impressed.'

After the talk she kept me back to thank me for coming. Said that she knew it was short notice and that she appreciated it and so on. I'm a big boy now but I found myself growing shy and flustered in the presence of so much flaunted radiance. Anyway, I think I muttered that it was no big deal. And she smiled and put her hand on my arm.

'Jon,' she said, 'Don't give me that English modesty. You gave up your vacation to supervise these kids. That says something to me about your character. I'm so impressed. And I've met Mistyann. She's a bright spark, isn't she? I can see why you recommended her. I really think she's going to grow here. So good job, Jon.'

And she gave me the full film star mega voltage smile and executed a parade ground turn and I watched her perfectly aerobicised arse stride off to take the first proper session. That arse—ass, whatever—will come in handy when it comes to shaking up the state senate. Even Republicans are human.

I was thinking it was no big deal for me to be in Cefn Coch. I didn't do much with the holidays generally. For a start there was generally a hundredweight or two of marking to be done. And the rest of the days saw me catching up. Catching up with mates, catching up with DVDs and films, catching up with music, even catching up with the odd book. The invitation to come on this trip at least told me how far back into the normal world I'd come. To be an Advanced Skills Teacher, trusted to take kids away; it was a vindication of my recovery.

So later I shivered out across the strange lunar beauty of the snow and found this walled garden and, as I stood there staring at that bizarre installation, I was thinking about the long route to Llangow and Cefn Coch. I was thinking what a magical thing I'd managed to do. I'd kicked the booze. I had a proper job. More than that I had the respect of my peers and now I was working with the best mind in my profession to change the lives of some of the brightest kids.

I stared into that implacable, hypnotic view feeling free of cynicism. The air was so cold that every breath hurt and yet I felt good; so alive that it was hard to keep from shouting out.

Today, Mistyann, was a bit different. Today I was posting pap into the face of a guy with Huntingdon's Chorea. That's the disease that did for Woody Guthrie. Google him.

Technically Mr Sykes isn't one of the Undead because he's still got most of his marbles. You can see them shining behind his eyes. But he can't walk, talk or move at all. Not so much as an eye-lid. Nevertheless you can feel his rage. A boiling keg of hate under pressure. Makes Pete the Wheelchair Boy seem serenely accepting by comparison. I tell you, it's a strange, almost moving thing to be up so close and so personal with that volume of corked and silent evil.

And yes, I'd say I feel a bit resentful about being back here with my people, the Undead. And yes, sometimes I'd like to wreak vengeance on those I consider responsible. And yes, sometimes I do feel that you, Mistyann, are one of those people.

TWENTY

We're sitting on cushions in a circle in this sort of barn thing. It's a big empty space with giant tea chests full of god knows what pushed against the back wall. It's got a springy floor like the one in the dance studio back in the performance art block at school and a proper high ceiling with these giant black beams going across. It's got these tiny windows. It's a humungous space and feels weird with just a few of us in it.

Pete and Charlotte are both proper moaning. Pete lists all the stuff on TV he'd normally be watching and Charlotte tells the group about the shops she'd be going to. None of the rest of us is listening but they don't notice or care. I sit opposite Julius so that I can watch him and decide that I have done the right thing in picking him to fancy.

He really is beautiful and I'm trying to think of words to describe his skin, when he looks up and catches my eye and smiles and it's a dutzi big happy smile. The only thing that freaks me a bit is that he's got this look in his eyes like he knows I fancy him. But then I decide not to care about that because we're only here for a week and if he knows I'm after him it will make things easier. Also, probably everyone fancies him all the time anyway. He's probably used to it. And at least he looks happy about me fancying him which is the main thing.

Then I notice that he has snow around his trackie bottoms and it comes to me that he maybe he made the wild snow heads that I saw with Ariel and I'm suddenly a bit sort of—hold on, I mean getting up early to make something so crazy, that's wild but it's kind of mad as well. A bit freaky. It puts me off him in a way.

The thing is—I don't actually reckon I am a genius. Or GIFTED or whatever. I just don't take any shit from anyone. Also, I don't care about fitting in with everyone else. There are kids I know that are way cleverer than me but they pretend not to be. Leanne Redgrove for example. She was the biggest brainbox in primary school but she spends every lesson now trying to wind up the teachers.

JD likes to suck on pens. It's like a habit he has. So one day Leanne gets in a bit early and sticks a bic up her fanny. Then she puts it on his desk and hides all the other pens. Course after about ten minutes he sticks the pen in his mouth. Everyone is pissing themselves. And it's funny. Course it is. But kids like her think you should be fighting teachers all the time and I just think: why bother? Most of the teachers just seem sad and tired. And that's no reason to bully them. I fucking hate bullies.

Leanne Redgrove should be a good girl too. Her mum is a health visitor. She lives up Kimbolton Road where all the big houses are.

All the teachers are part of the lesson. Kendra, Amber and JD. Ariel calls it a workshop. But it's a lesson really. Ariel gets us going with some warm up exercises. We do some stretching stuff for ages and then she makes us get into pairs—I go straight for Julius and Ariel produces these special blindfolds and we have to blindfold our partners.

Before I put the blindfold on Julius I look around at everyone else because I want to know who has gone with who. JD is with Amber. Kendra's with Pete of course, and Dalwinder is with Zak. Anna and Julie are with each other and Charlotte has to go with Stephen. I can see that she's not happy with that.

It's funny having adults doing it with us. And I think about what it would be like if schools were open to grown-ups too. My mum is always banging on about how A star she could have been at school if she hadn't got into boys and that and how she wishes she could go back and do history and French and everything. No-one would give the teacher any shit with Mum in the room. If she wanted to get on with her coursework or something and thought Leanne Redgrove or Angel Carter was stopping her, she'd twat them. Teachers can't touch kids these days but if there were other adults in the class being students, well, *they* could, couldn't they?

A teacher could come up to Mum after a lesson and go 'You know, Claire, that girl Redgrove is holding the whole class back.' And the next day Leanne would be off school or she'd be in but she'd have this massive black eye and she would be well quiet in lessons.

Ariel says that she doesn't want the adults sticking with each other. She says that we are all a team and that she doesn't want clicks forming. And I smile at JD because I know that the real word is cliques, but he doesn't see me looking. He's frowning, looking well serious.

We name each other person A and person B and the As blindfold the Bs. I blindfold Julius and then the people without blindfolds get all the tea chests and scatter them across the floor to make an obstacle course. Then we have to guide our partners through it using just a hand on the shoulder. Then we guide them using just one finger. And last of all we guide them using the faintest touch we can.

'Now As, see if you can swap partners without the Bs even noticing,' Ariel says.

Charlotte is right beside me in a second and I move my finger off Julius's shoulder at the same second that she puts her's on.

'Good, now try to do this several times. Try to swap partners as many times as you can.' I get to guide everyone round the room at least twice without bashing into any chests. It's a laugh. Charlotte doesn't even try to swap partners any more. She stays with Julius.

The weirdest bit is when I get to guide JD around. It feels funny knowing that I could get him to crash into a table or something. He has to trust me to keep him safe and he doesn't even know it's me that is in charge of him. Guiding Pete is different. That's a bit of a joke. Course you don't have to put even a finger tip on his shoulder you just swap places behind the wheelchair. Later he tells us that he could tell exactly who was pushing him. I think he's lying.

Then we swap over, so if you were guiding before, now you are being guided. I'm standing with JD when Ariel tells us to stop so now JD is my partner and it's proper strange having Diamond put the mask over my eyes. I feel my face getting hot and it's like there's a big lump right inside of me and I can feel my shoulders go tight.

I stand there listening as they move all the chests around to make a new obstacle course. JD has a strong hand on my shoulder. Even when he's just got his finger on my back he feels sort of tough. I've never thought of him as hard before. He's always been just a teacher. I feel this electric crackle down my arm and I'm quite pleased when I can feel someone else taking over.

It's weird to have random fingers come and take over and move you about. And it's strange how they all have different styles. Some sort of prod you and push you, and others just kind of leave their fingers resting on you while you feel your own way forward. I guess that the forceful people are Julius and Zak, and that the softer guides are Stephen, Julie and Anna. The last time I feel people swap it pure feels like no-one has even a fingernail on my back. I stop because I think that no-one is guiding me. But when Ariel tells us to take the blindfolds off I see that Stephen is behind me with his little finger just on the top of my jumper. I look at his finger. He whips it away and shoves his hand deep in his pocket.

'I thought that we were coming here to work,' he says, under his breath, but I can see Ariel over his shoulder and she looks our way so I can tell that she's heard.

Basically, this class is like a drama class. It's the sort of thing we do in performing arts with Ms McFarlane who is like this young teacher that does wacky stuff.

We spend the whole morning playing games. We play Grandmother's Foot-steps and What's the Time, Mr Wolf and Cat-and-mouse and Bull-dog and loads of stuff that I haven't done since Year 1. It's like a kid's party and we all get into it in the end. Everyone gets proper hot and sweaty. Even the snobby kids like Charlotte and Stephen start to run about. Even Amber. Even JD. Pete's funny because if it's a running around game then he acts like Kendra is a horse, saying 'giddy up' and 'Whoa, there!' cos she has to push him all the time. And if it's a dancing game like musical statues then he does all these twizzles and wheelies and stuff.

We're all pure smecked by the end and we just sit on the floor and I can hear my heart going bang bang bang. It must be well exhausting being a little kid. I don't know how they manage it. I don't think William manages it now. He's like a little robot always plugged into something. I think that you never see William without some kind of cable going into him. There's always a PSP or MP3 lead or a head-set lead. Harry might still manage the being a kid thing for a little while and I say to myself that I'll try and make sure both my brothers have some proper kid-fun when I'm back whether they want to or not.

JD comes over and his face is all shiny and I see two little rivers of sweat running over his cheek-bones. They sort of come together under his chin and swell into one big drip that goes plop onto the floor in front of me. It makes me laugh.

'God,' he says, 'I haven't done anything so energetic since... well, ever.'

And I tell him about my idea for having adults being taught in schools at the same time as kids and how it would improve behaviour and everything and he just laughs, which pisses me off a bit but I don't say anything because Ariel calls us over and we all sit around her on the floor like five year olds do at story time.

She tells us that she's going to use play as a way of bringing out our creativity. She says that our imaginations are most powerful muscles.

'I want to remove all the blocks that you put in your own way.'

She says that when we can triumph over the obstacles that we create for ourselves then the barriers other people use to stop us will seem puny and easily dealt with.

'The point of life is to find out who you are and then to become that person,' she says.

And she says that we'll be doing a range of activities that will reveal our true natures. She says loads more but those are the main things that I remember.

When she stops speaking Charlotte says, 'I think I already know who I am. Ariel.' And I swear I can feel the whole room go, 'Yes, you're a stuck up bitch'. No one actually says it, but you can feel the words appear like a giant thought bubble above everyone's heads. Stephen asks, 'Will we be doing any work? I mean any actual written work?' And some others join in. There's like this little chorus. Julie and Anna go all boffy and say that yes, they would also like do some real work. Some writing. I can't remember all of Ariel's answer but I do know that she says, 'All I'm going to ask you to do is to produce something or do something extraordinary. Something that is worthy of your own personal unique gifts and worthy of the faith your teachers have placed in you.' And she goes on to talk about the amazing snow statue in the secret garden.

'One of you has got the right idea. Get out and use what's around you to make your mark.' Julius is sitting on the end of the row and he just looks at the ground all modest. A lad who doesn't think he's it. You know how bloody rare that is.

'We'll be doing a mixture of tasks and some might involve writing but others will be practical and by the end of the week you've got to do something that celebrates the uniqueness that is you. Something only you could have done.'

To be honest it's hard to concentrate on all of Ariel's little lecture cos Dalwinder's leg is touching mine. I don't notice at first because the pressure is proper light. It could be accidental I guess. But I test things out by moving my leg away a bit and yeah, sure enough, Dalwinder's leg follows mine like it's being pulled. I look at him out of the corner of my eye. He looks like he isn't noticing the whole leg game thing. He's just staring straight ahead. Dalwinder fancies me so I've got that to deal with now cos my plan is still to shag Julius. The more I see him, the more I like him. He just moves so well. You just know that he'll know what to do.

I've never even snogged a Pakistani lad before, even though there are loads of them in Bedford. Not in Manton Heights mind, they're normally in Queens Park where the Mosques and the temples and that are. There aren't many in school either what with it being for Catholics and everything. It's funny cos black kids, proper black kids, Afro-Caribbean kids are it and everyone fancies them. I reckon you could be the geekiest, weediest black lad going and you'd still get girls trying to get off with you, but Pakistani boys aren't it. Doesn't mean you can shout at them though like some people do. At our school the Stanies get called Bin Laden so much that they don't even complain about it; maybe they don't even notice it.

We have a fancy dress disco in Year 6 at primary and this one kid—Nazim Ankarath—comes dressed as a suicide bomber with a big belt with bombs made from black painted bog roll middles stuck to this heavy belt like the kind Ty uses for his weight-lifting. He also has on this padded body-warmer and a heavy rucksack. He doesn't look like a real suicide bomber but the teachers go mad. They call his parents and then there's a tribunal thing and he's suspended till the end of the year and it's written about in the *Bedford on Sunday* and all that. Then one morning there is Nazim's face on the front of the *Sun* or the *Mirror* or something with the headline BABY BIN LADEN'S SICK BOMB STUNT.

And there are two weird things about the whole thing. The first one is that Nazim Ankarath is like this proper quiet hard-working kid; a real egghead who goes to one of the floss schools after Edith Cavell. And the other thing is that he's not even a Muslim. He's a proper strict Christian. Every Christmas Nan comes down and makes us go to church and there he is praying and singing and everything.

One of the big troubles with people is that they can't take a joke. I've always thought that. No-one's ever funny anymore. Not on telly, not anywhere. Maybe they passed a law and I was too young to be told about it. And things—movies, books, magazines, whatever—that are meant to be funny are just dumb. Comedians. They are just so not funny. But if you laugh at things that really *are* funny—then people just give you shit. You should be allowed to laugh at everything, shouldn't you?

I wonder a bit about shagging Dalwinder and I realize that I don't even know if Stani boys are allowed to touch white girls or anything. I think we're off-limits for Muslims like bacon sandwiches and sausage rolls and eating with your left hand, and it means I kind of miss some of Ariel's chat but there's more stuff about finding the hero inside yourself even if she doesn't use those exact words and I'm thinking that I'm glad that I can't see JD cos he'd roll his eyes or produce this funny face and I'd be laughing. He hates all this sort of talk. And all the time Dalwinder's leg lies against mine like a little radiator producing heat from my thigh to my knee.

After a bit Ariel tells us that we've got a break and then we are going to tour the grounds and find a special spot that will be our own personal creative zone.

'A place where you will have complete artistic freedom,' she says. 'Freedom to experiment including, of course, freedom to fail. Remember what Beckett said, "Fail. Fail Again. Fail better." No-one achieved anything who didn't fail first.'

As I'm going out of the barn, Ariel stops me.

'I love your plan to let adults into schools, Mistyann. It's such a good idea. It's the kind of visionary thinking I'm hoping that this course will inspire in everyone.' And she asks me if I'll write an article about it for this online education magazine she runs and I tell her that I'll think about it but I'm chuffed that she's asked me.

We go across from the barn back to the main house to have a drink and a biscuit. It's been snowing again while we've been in the lesson and all our earlier tracks have been covered up and everything looks new again. Kendra is really struggling to push Pete's wheel-chair.

'You need a snow plough on the front of that thing, Pete mate,' says Zak, but then Julius and Dalwinder go over and pick Pete up in his the wheelchair and carry him across the snow to the main house.

Kendra is screeching, 'Be careful! Be careful!' Like she's proper panicking and Pete does kind of look like he could fall out of the wheelchair and onto the snow at any moment. The wheelchair with him in it is obviously heavier than the boys expected. Pete seems okay though. He's got this look on his face like he's a king and Dalwinder and Julius are his servants.

He says, 'Jesus, don't fuss, Kendra. It's nice to be a normal height for once.'

So she says, 'Don't blame me if you fall.'

And then he says, 'I won't blame you, Kendra. I'll sack you.'

He is kind of a wanker that kid, even if he is in a wheelchair, even if he is going to die. If I'd been carrying him I'd have fucking dropped him there and then. I expect JD to be in the kitchen but he's not so I can't tell him about Ariel asking me to write for her magazine. Instead I have to listen to Stephen go on about how he expected to be doing some proper work during this week.

Stephen's a tall kid with heavy black glasses and a bowl hair cut that makes him look much older than fifteen. He looks about forty-five and he talks like an old man too—like some mad old professor. He should be wearing a bright white coat like scientists wear. His voice is too loud and he puts his words down in steady rows like he's laying bricks.

'No wonder this bloody country is going down the pan. They take their brightest students and make them play kids' games. In China children are probably designing new cars that don't use fossil fuels and we're playing blinking blind man's buff.'

He's proper cross. I don't know why he's chosen me to say all this to but the good thing is he doesn't expect me to say anything back. When he stops I can't think of anything to say but Zak's there.

'Don't sweat it, man,' Zak says. 'Take a chill pill. Go with the flow. Now who's for a cup of the hot and steaming?'

I decide to go outside and see what the statues look like now that there's been more snow.

TWENTY-ONE

Just walking around the house in the snow made me feel like Scott of the Antarctic. Or like Bono in one of those early U2 videos. The whole scene generally had the look of an eighties pop promo—the gothic house rising blackly from the stark quilt of snow. The misty hills crowding around the edge of the horizon. The mint-fresh blue of the sky blemished only by the toothpaste stripes of a passing plane. Easy to imagine Bono striding across this landscape singing hymns of non-specific melancholy. And as fake as an eighties pop video too. The gothic house was a kind of school. The stripes didn't tell a story of a romantic flight to freedom. They were mile high skid-marks charting the progress of some Easyjet cattle transport towards a wintersun hell.

Only the cold felt properly authentic. We're not used to the physical constriction of cold anymore; the way it compresses the chest so that every breath has to be fought for. I spent a few minutes in silent study of the clouds my breath formed in the over-oxygenated air, before I was reminded to have a cigarette. I breathed in deeply, revelling in the tearing sensation this caused behind my ribs.

I explored the grounds of the house, taking childish pleasure in leaving abominable snowman prints through the virgin white of the gardens. It was built on a south facing shelf with one jagged black molar of a hill rising behind it, too sheer for the snow to settle on except around the lower slopes. I struck out from the medieval front door and headed under a stone arch flanked with thorny bushes. This brought me into a garden enclosed by dry stone walls. A further archway beckoned maybe fifty feet away and I headed for that and rested there, marvelling at just how breathless even travelling that short distance made me.

Lighting a new fag, I moved into another garden which had a small wooden door set into the wall that ran along the back. I struggled up the slope, suspecting that this dwarf-sized entrance would lead into the 'Secret Garden' where Ariel saw the snow statues she was so lyrical about.

They really were something. Even half-buried amid the morning's snow-fall, the heads looked unearthly or like offerings from some much older civilization. It was too cold to stand for long in one spot so I moved back out of this garden and towards another exit which led into the surrounding woods. Nestled among the trees was a little cottage made of blackened stone. The front steps had had snow scrupulously shovelled away and a thin carpet of grit to prevent accidents. Someone had been reading the health and safety manual I thought—someone's done a risk assessment.

What a strange black house it was. The sort of hidden home you could imagine jeering mobs dragging old women from to lynch. The home of witches and outcasts. Just beyond the main house walls and surrounded by mud, rock and black branches. In summer it must be like having a home in a hedge with all that dense foliage around. I guessed that this was where Ray and Susie lived and wondered briefly about the interior. I wondered about how much of Asia Susie had been allowed to bring with her. Ray looked like a hoarder to me, a collector.

I pictured him with his vast vinyl collection and his books and comedy tapes. He looked the sort. The sort who would have kept all his old *Beanos*. How much order would Susie have imposed on this bachelor landscape? Or had she just added her own vivid Eastern clutter to the beige wash of Ray's life? I wonder now if I actually envied Ray a bit. Envied him his escape from teaching to this Celtic idyll. Envied him his vivacious wife. Envied him his ability to have one glass of wine and then stop.

On that first night there was, for the adults, wine with the meal. No doubt it too was 'totally organic and fair trade of course'. I declined, of course. Amber asked me neutrally, conversationally, did I not ever drink? And I had answered neutrally, conversationally, that no, I didn't.

'I'm an alcoholic,' I said cheerfully.

You should try it. It's the sort of thing you'd enjoy. It's a conversational suicide bomb. If ever you want to blast a hole into the hum of inconsequential chat try confessing to a drink problem. It's like dropping a glass on a stone floor. The effort is minimal and the crash and confusion quite satisfying.

After a pause I said that it was no big thing and that I hadn't had a drink for twelve years but that I found it best to say that I was an alkie straight out to save people the effort of continually asking me if I was sure I didn't want just a small one.

They say that you can't stop drinking without help but I did. I tried AA a few times but never got my head around admitting that there was a power higher than myself into whose hands I could entrust myself. Neither did I like the general standard of dramatic monologue when it came to the part where people had to share their experiences. Sometimes you got a share that was just electrifying, a piece of real theatre but, for the most part, the stories and the rambling delivery of them was depressingly similar. I never needed a drink more urgently than when I had just left an AA meeting.

Fortunately for my liver I didn't have to go to many. I don't think I would have had the stamina for it. Instead Dad died. Face down in his muesli. No warning.

Dad had a full English every day of his adult life until he was fifty. Then he switched to Alpen. A year and a half later he was dead. And he still out-lived his own father who was 49 when he suffered a stroke watching England play

Argentina in the quarter finals of the 1966 world cup. The only decision Thatcher ever made which had Dad's full support was the sinking of the Belgrano.

'Who gives a shit that it was steaming home? Those dirty spick cowards killed your grandfather. They deserved whatever they got.'

He was convinced that it was watching the way the Argentineans fouled Hurst and Moore and the boys that drove Grand-da's blood pressure so dangerously high.

I had my ultimate drink just before I went in to see Dad's body at the General Hospital. A double, maybe a treble voddy from the little flask I bought in Camden Market back in the days when drinking was just a hobby, not a full-time job. I had, because I was crass, Joy Division's 'Dead Souls' on the Walkman. Moments later, faced with the genuine catastrophe and horror of a finished life, the thick medicine dancing in my belly seemed unforgivably sacrilegious. And the music just ridiculous. Vainglorious and hollow next to the real drama of an ordinary working man lying dead on an NHS bed.

I left the hospital, put the tape and the hip-flask in the nearest bin, spent my last fiver on a short back and sides and, in my imagination at least, filled out the application form for teacher training there and then. It can't have been as movie dramatic as that, but within a few days I had left the Undead and was twitching and sweating on a plastic chair waiting for an interview at the Higher Education College in Polhill Avenue; Bedfordshire University now. A teacher. I was going to give education a human face. I was going to be an antidote to the bullies and cynics that allowed me to fuck up my own school days.

I got back to the big house exhausted. A morning playing party games, followed by a tramp around the grounds in the snow contemplating my past had left me wiped out. I needed a nap. These days my naps sometimes start before I actually get up. These days I'm like an elderly dog, dozing my way through my final years. They say that forty is the new thirty. In my case they are wrong. Forty feels more like the new eighty-two.

But back then I was a napping novice, so I slept poorly until pulling myself out of some dangerous dream to wake to a thirst and a headache, finding you staring down at me, Mistyann. Apprising me with your most solemn look.

'Everyone's going sledging, Sir,' you said at last, 'I was wondering if you wanted to come too? I did knock, Sir. Honest.'

When we got to the slope in front of the house a scene of Victorian Christmas card jollity confronted us. Happy children scarved and gloved in all the colours of the rainbow were shrieking with delight. It was a scene straight from one of the end of Dickens' novels; when the inheritance has come through for the good, kind, deserving children while the wicked have been punished by death or penury. This impression was heightened by seeing Pete whizzing down the slope in a race with the cocky indie kid, Zak, like a regular Tiny Tim Cratchit.

'Now, God bless us, everyone,' I muttered.

'You've got to stop that, Sir,' you said.

I affected puzzlement, 'What?'

'The pure random quoting from old books.'

And then you grinned and were off, kicking your way through clouds of powdery snow to join the merry gang of your peers.

Milky Ray was supervising the sledging—there were probably hundreds of directives from the Health and Safety Executive prohibiting this kind of reckless pastime on residential trips and Ray had the anxious look of a man who had inwardly digested every one. He looked like he was going to be sick. I couldn't resist it.

'Charge!' I yelled, as dramatically as I could, and, pausing only to scoop snow into rough balls I lurched ponderously forward in your footsteps. Every few steps I launched feeble snowballs towards the lads, who whooped and rose to the challenge. As I ran down the slope towards them, straight into the ragged volley of surprisingly accurate and forceful snowballs from Dalwinder and Zak, I suppose that I was trying to achieve two things. I wanted to be seen as a good sport and I wanted to give Ray a heart attack. But within seconds I was just a kid playing in the snow. It's exhilarating giving in to all that Lord of Misrule stuff; to just let go of authority and the pomposity that goes with it.

And the real delight of the snow ball fight and the sledging and the rest of it was to see these kids get into it as a gang. It occurred to me that most of these children were freaks and weirdoes in their own schools. Hurting, most of them.

Your arrival amid the mob had been greeted with muffled claps and kisses from the girls and a volley of snowballs from the boys. The highest possible expressions of delight. And I was struck again by the thought that one of the things about truly gifted kids is that they are gifted at everything. Not just the dreary roll call of GCSEs and attainment targets and cognitive reading scores, but also making and keeping friends, building social networks. Lots of kids can pass exams but the real all-rounders—the truly exceptional—will also have legions of protective admirers. I'd noticed at school how no-one seemed to mind you getting top grades with so little effort. Most of all, no-one seemed to mind your uniqueness. Kids are normally pretty unforgiving about difference but chavs and indie rockers, geeks and gangstas, emo-kids and glue-sniffers were equally happy to be around you. Bullies just stayed out of your way and it was really only the occasional teacher, ones with their own exceptional talent for bitterness—like Mrs English— who tried to get you to know your place.

See, Mistyann, you were better than the best of them and when I think of you now I see you winning friends wherever you are. Not just getting by. Getting on.

We went down the improvised toboggan run together, do you remember? You insisted on going in front while I sat behind as the brakeman, ready to dig my heels into the snow if need be. It was faster and more frightening than I had expected. The lads had worked hard to make that slide as dangerous as possible and we seemed to get up a lethal momentum in seconds. You were yelling, but not with fear, and I was thrown forward and gripped you tight around your thin waist. There seemed almost nothing to you. Your body was a thin steel cord inside that nylon jacket. And when we spun around at the bottom of the slope the sledge tipped up and we rolled together briefly before sliding apart. And I lay there winded, every attempted breath making me cough, listening to you laughing. And then you were up, racing back up the slope with the sled bouncing behind you. You were at the top by the time I had recovered sufficiently to rise onto my elbow. Then there was a little knot of smiling women pulling me up. Ariel, Kendra, Susie.

'Not so much like Tom Cruise now, is he girls?' This was Susie laughing as I got gingerly to my feet. Hard to believe these days but I used to get that a lot. 'Oi, Tom' kids would shout if they saw me in the Harpur Centre or 'How's the baby?' Or, even, and most creatively, 'What's that scientology all about then, mate?' Seems incredible now. You should see me, Mistyann. I've put on two stone, most of it around my face. I never really bought into the Tom Cruise comparisons, but now when I look in the mirror I see Mr Potato Head. A face of lumpy roundness with chins that jostle for room like so many cheap, fatty sausages.

'At least I do my own stunts,' I said, and winced and staggered. And the three of them made a good-natured pantomime of helping me to the top of the slope.

TWENTY-TWO

I'm checking my messages in the bog. In what Charlotte calls 'the en-suite'. There are three. Two numbers I don't know and one from home. I call the message number. It's William and he's in tears. Jesus.

'I know you took my phone and I've told Dad.' He hangs up. No 'How are you?' or even 'where are you?' God, he is such a whining brat. The next is from Ty of course.

'Girl, you have gone too bloody far this time. You come back home, you give the phone back to your brother or you are going to get your ass whipped. I'm telling you, girl. I'm not fooling with you. Come back right now, you hear.'

I play his message again to guess his mood and decide that he just sounds tired. Obviously William and Mum have been twisting his melons. I don't think he cares. I listen again. He definitely sounds more smecked than anything.

Mum's message is scary even for her. She's yelling so much I have to hold the phone away from my ear. I'm convinced Charlotte can hear it in the bedroom. I cut Mum off, open the bog door and look at Charlotte lying on her bed flicking through some hair magazine. She looks up.

'What? What?' She obviously hasn't heard jack. I go back inside and lock the door again. I can hear her whining

'What are you doing in there?'

Petulant. That's the word for her. I say it out loud in front of the mirror, splitting it up into different parts. I like the way it makes my mouth and tongue go. Pet-u-lant.

I listen to my mum again and she's mad as hell. After the yelling and screaming—which is so distorted that it's hard to tell exactly what she's saying—there's this pause until she says, 'Right Madam, you've really fucking wound me up. You get your arse back here or we're coming for you.' There's a long pause and I can hear her breath coming all shallow like she's been running. 'Mistyann, I'm serious. Get back here.' There's a sigh. 'Right. Right. Harry's still in hospital so I've got to spend all bleeding day there which I need like a hole in the fucking head. And no one will have William because you know what a toe-rag he is. Yes you are, you little shit, going on about your fucking mobile all the time like I give a flying fuck'

And I can picture William clinging onto her while she makes the call. He's got no sense that boy.

'Anyway you better come back today or don't bother to come back at all. You can go to your father's and see how he puts up with all your crap. I don't need this. I really don't need this. And what the bloody hell do you want now? Can't you fucking stop whinging for one second…?'

And the call ends just like that with her ranting at William, who I almost feel sorry for. Just then the phone leaps in my hand. A text. U WAIT and I'm thinking yeah Mum, I get it. You're proper jarred with me.

There's a banging on the door. Charlotte.

'Come on, Mistyann, I'm dying for a wee-wee.'

A wee-wee? For fuck's sake. How old is she? I can feel the tension building up like it does sometimes. I can feel my shoulders getting tight. I'm getting to the stage where I'm going to give someone a slap. I try to think about what Michaela in Anger Management said. I start to count to ten and breathe really slowly. And I look at myself in the mirror and tune Charlotte out by trying to decide exactly what colour my eyes are. Jade. In the end I go for jade. I was going to be called Jade until my mum read this American novel by someone called Mistyann and so I ended up with her name. I wonder if I would have been a different person if had a different name?

These totally random thoughts manage to make me feel a bit less like a bomb about to go off. It's a funny thing a temper. It's like losing contact with the real world. Like a weird kind of time travel. One second you're in one place doing something normal and the next second time's gone on and you're in a different place and things have happened that you don't even know about, that you have to be told about. Terrible things mostly, but good things too sometimes.

I come out of the bog and Charlotte goes 'at last' and does this big thing of staggering past me, trying to walk with her legs crossed, which is sort of stupid and sort of funny too. She leaves the door open while she has a piss.

'You're down to cook dinner today, Mistyann,' she calls.

'I know!' I call back. 'You don't have to go on.'

To be honest I had forgotten. I'm not worried though cos I cook all the time at home. Charlotte comes out of the toilet still buttoning up her jeans and it's like proper quick so I know she can't have washed her hands. These floss girls can be really scummy, that's one thing I've learnt already on this course.

She says, 'You've got Zak as your cooking buddy, you lucky thing.'

'Yeah, and Amber,' I say.

'True, but Zak. I mean come on Zak. He's like so the best looking boy here. Him and Julius. They're top equal I reckon. And your teacher of course. He's pretty fit for an old guy.' She gives me a sly look. I'm not rising to that.

'You should wash your hands after having a piss,' I say. 'You'll spread germs if you don't. You would have thought that for 15K a term your school would have taught you that much.'

And I'm going through the door and I can hear her going, 'God. What is your problem? You are so uptight.'

Like she is one of those girls on American TV. One of those princesses who need a slap. I can feel my shoulders go tight again but I don't answer and I head off for the kitchen.

I like cooking. And I do it loads. Good stuff too. William and Harry are always moaning about it, so I must be doing something right. I'm well strict. They only get burgers once a week. Twice at most. They have chips a lot but I get the good kind, the chunky kind not the thin and crispy ones that they like. And they always have something green. Broccoli. I give them broccoli loads. Harry likes it. Says that he's like a giant eating trees. And they get fish fingers, but the good kind made with 100% fish with the picture of that creepy old man with the beard on the front of the boxes.

I still like food tech. I used to love it. It's just that it's got a bit boring now that we have to do stuff about food marketing and packaging. All that coursework stuff. I used to like it when we actually did some cooking. We did loads of cooking at Edith Cavell and then when we went up to St Teresa's I thought we'd do more cos we were older, but we actually did less. First term at St Teresa's we spent all our food tech lesson making up new sandwich fillings and then designing posters to advertise them.

Anyway. I like cooking and I'm good at it. But Zak is the cook in our group. The rest of us just get to be his peelers and choppers. I get to the kitchen and he's waiting there with a pinny on, sharpening knives. He looks like a crazy man. He has all his hair under a sort of black bandanna thing and he looks well serious. It's obvious that he's going to be the top chef in our kitchen. We've got Amber and Julie who is one of the girls who hasn't really said anything yet. Julie's there staring at the floor but Amber comes in after me.

'Sorry,' she says, 'just had to call the fuckwit boyfriend, check that everything was okay back at the ranch.'

I guess that Amber is the worst kind of teacher. She's one of those that want to be liked and will talk to you about make-up and boys and getting lushed up and all that.

Pathetic. If you want to be popular don't be a teacher. Simple as. End of.

Susie's there to help tell us where everything is.

She says, 'You've got a treat. You're doing a simple chicken casserole. It's a classic recipe. It's delicious and you can't go wrong.'

Zak sucks his teeth. He's letting us know that he thinks the recipe is kind of beneath him. He's real professional though—proper slick with an electric whisk and brilliant at moaning about the equipment all the time the way all good chefs are meant to. The knives aren't sharp enough, the garlic crusher is pathetic, the surfaces are unhygienic, the casserole dishes are second rate. He says even the fucking napkins are cheap and tacky. Everything's crap basically and not what he's used to. Susie gets fucked off with it and leaves after a quarter of an hour or so.

'It looks like you know what to do,' she says. 'I'll be in the office if you need me.' The rest of us all say bye and cheers and thanks for your help and all that but Zak just flaps his wrist at her like she was a slave or something. Doesn't even look up from his chopping. I notice that he has taken his weird jangly bangly jewellery things off.

He hardly looks at the recipe which Susie has got printed out on a nice laminated card. There's a bit of a row when he goes to chop some chillies.

'Oh God, it's not going to be spicy is it?' whinges Amber.

Zak is well rude. 'You'd miss it if it wasn't in,' he says without even looking at her.

She goes, 'I bet I wouldn't.' Just like a little kid.

Zak just sighs and still doesn't even look at her and gets on with chopping the chillies.

Amber won't let it lie. 'I can't stand foreign food,' she says.

Now Zak does look at her. He gazes at her for a few seconds.

'I'm surprised to hear that there's any food you don't like,' he says and Amber goes really red.

She's not fat. Not really. She's plump. In the olden days she would have probably been a top model or something. Have you seen those old pictures where the girls have got big tits and big arses and it's funny because they all look like they know they're pure fit? They have the exact same expressions that you get on the skinny princesses at school. The ones that think they're it cos the boys go a bit weird when they come into a room.

Amber's got a pretty face under that black bob and she's wearing stylish clothes, this black jumper and a brown skirt with a wide rock chick belt with this massive buckle that says 'Triumph' on it. She's good with make-up too. She's got this pale face with this strange coloured lipstick. It's red but so rich it's almost purple. I think, you've made an effort here girl, haven't you? And I wonder why.

She stays calm.

She says, 'You, Zak, are a male chauvinist pig. And you're not exactly Brad Pitt yourself, are you?'

Zak just laughs and turns back to the chillies. I can't be doing with rows and all that so I distract Zak. I ask him about being taught at home.

'Not being funny or anything, but aren't you a bit of a loner. What about friends?'

He says, 'I have friends. And they're real friends. They're not just the random people whose names happen to be close to me in the register.' And he talks about his band and his drama group and his book club.

'Yeah, it's really tofftastic,' he says, 'Fine wine, fine food and talking arse about literature in a fine Georgian house. Got to be better than being in a classroom having to wait while the chavs try to keep up with *Of Mice and Men.*'

I ask him what a typical day is like and he says that he gets out of bed about ten, plays guitar for a couple of hours, goes to the gym for a couple of hours, gets back home and watches a documentary or something and then in the evenings he might have drama or band practice or go to the movies or something. When I ask about GCSE's and the syllabus and everything, he just shrugs.

'I watch a lot of Open University programmes and I do a lot of past papers. They haven't been terribly taxing so far.' Turns out that he already has four GCSEs. I ask him about grades and he gives me this strange look.

'What grades do you think I got, Mistyann?' Which I guess is his way of saying that he got A stars in all of them.

Amber comes back into the kitchen, bringing the smell of fags with her. 'Hark at the genius,' she says.

He turns to face her and looks straight at her as he says, 'We're all geniuses Amber. That's why we're here.'

'Yeah, but not everyone is quite so big-headed.'

Zak sighs but doesn't answer and just asks me to pass the garlic.

'Oh Christ, not garlic and chilli.' Amber puts on this proper whiny voice.

Zak goes, 'I'm sure we can rustle you up some fish fingers and smiley potato faces.'

Amber huffs off and Zak keeps unwrapping garlic bulbs until he's got about twelve. Then he slices up another couple of chillies.

'Just for luck,' he says and smiles.

The next thing that happens is that Amber slices the top of her thumb off. She's chopping something and the knife slips. Yeah, right. As if. I've seen this before. The kid who isn't centre of attention does something fucked up just to make sure we all have to look their way.

She holds up her thumb like she's holding up the world cup or something. She looks like she just won something major. God knows why, she's made a right mess of her thumb with the skin flapping off at the top like some kind of mad hat. The blood—which I notice is the same colour as her lip-stick—runs down her thumb and over her other hand which she has squeezing it tight. Her eyes glitter.

Zak goes over to her. He doesn't rush though. He's easy. Calm. And then he says something weird.

'Oh, what a thrill. My thumb instead of an onion.'

And I'm thinking what frigging onion?

Amber laughs even though the blood is pure sprinting down her hand and dripping onto the tiled floor of the kitchen.

She says, 'The top quite gone except for a sort of hinge of skin.'

Then she stops and frowns. Zak fills the sudden quiet space with, 'A flap like a hat. Dead white. Sylvia Plath.'

I butt in now, excited. 'That's what I was thinking. That the skin looks like a hat.'

But they aren't listening to me.

'Well done,' says Amber looking straight at Zak.

He wriggles a bit and says, 'I love Sylvia Plath.'

Amber looks at him for a slow second.

'I used to. But I find her work very adolescent now. I think Plath is a phase you go through. Something you grow out of.'

Zak says, 'Poppycock.' And he moves back over to the oven. Julie comes across with a big plaster and fixes it around Amber's thumb. Amber's still smiling and it's obvious that she's thinks she's scored a few points somehow.

And I think that I'll have to tell JD about this little incident. Find out what it means. But I don't have to cos as we serve up the dinner Julie goes to me. 'Why do people always like to flirt while they cook?'

And I pause cos I think it's a joke and I'm waiting for the punch-line and then I get it. Amber and Zak. They were flirting. Jesus. I never flirt. Who can be bothered with that? Who's got the time?

TWENTY-THREE

That night, when Susie asked everyone to toast the cooks we did it with real enthusiasm. Hard to believe that you, Zak, Amber and one of the anonymous girls had rustled it up. I wouldn't have been able to do it. These days I try to be a bit imaginative. Every time I think I'll just have a Fray Bentos pie I think that it might mean I'm sliding into depression and force myself to scramble some eggs. Then I have the pie as well.

I also force myself to have a shower every day and to resist day-time TV. I read somewhere that people who survive death camps are the ones who keep washing, who keep up some sense of routine. I deny myself telly until *The Weakest Link* comes on. *Countdown* at the very earliest.

There was only one person who didn't seem to appreciate the meal. Charlotte just sat there toying with the smallest of portions. Ariel asked her if she was alright.

'Yeah. I just don't do food,' Charlotte said.

Ariel laughed which caused Charlotte's face to curdle still further. Charlotte aside, it was a convivial party that Saturday night. The room had a festive giddiness about it. Snow brings that, doesn't it?

Ray and Susie told us about some of the pitfalls of running a place like Cefn Coch. The fights, the affairs and high jinks that go on during adult courses; the troubles with school groups who get their hands on the liquor cabinet; the poets who go midnight skinny dipping in the stream. Amber took the piss out of The Fuckwit Boyfriend, while Ariel showed us that she was a good sport by mocking her fellow Americans for their ignorance of the world around them. Even Kendra smiled a bit and I could see how, if someone could persuade her to be properly Prozaced, she might be a reasonable person to hang out with.

Most of the students seemed happy too. You sat between the two anonymous girls at the opposite end of the table and I wondered how you'd cope, but you seemed to be doing fine. There was lots of smiling and nodding and enthusiastic whispering going on. It was another of those moments where I took notice of your gift for friendship. Looking at you then you could have been mistaken for a normal, happy go lucky, middle class teenager.

I was on washing up duty with the athletic looking black kid Julius, the rangy laconic Indian lad Dalwinder, and the edgy Chinese boy, Stephen. That was one of the things that Ariel said most impressed her about the UK—the way that we genuinely seemed happy mixing with different races. At dinner she told us that if there had been a group like this in the States then some racial incident would kick off within the first couple of days. I talked to her about Burnley and Bradford and the BNP and the racial segregation that you find even in Bedford. She didn't really take it on board.

'I appreciate all that, Jon, but generally racism doesn't seem as deep here. I mean look at this group: doesn't it make you feel that there's hope?'

And I felt some of my default cynicism drain away. So what if this trip was part of some social engineering project? What if some of these Diversity Officers and all the other sundry Equal Ops flunkies were actually doing some good?

This mood carried me through the clean up routine as Ray showed us how the cupboards were all numbered, with lists of what went into each cupboard pinned up in the four corners of the kitchen. We worked skilfully and quickly with Julius and Dalwinder washing what couldn't go in the dishwasher, Stephen and myself drying.

When you popped in to make some squash or something I was able to say, 'Hey look, Mistyann, we're like a well oiled machine in here. Bodes well for the cooking tomorrow.'

'We did most of the cleaning up for you,' you said.

'Augurs,' said Stephen.

You and I both said 'what?' simultaneously and Stephen elaborated.

'It's "augurs well". Bodes is what you say if something bad is predicted. It bodes ill and augurs well. It is English you teach, isn't it, Jon?'

He was smiling, but I caught an edge in his voice. Stephen was the boy that always wanted to do some proper work. Do you remember? He was always asking when we were going to start writing.

We'd just put away the last glass when Ariel came in with the plan to walk to the top of the lane to the ruined chapel.

'Ray is going to bring his storm tent,' she said, 'It'll be exciting up there in the dark and the snow, surrounded by ancient spirits.'

To be honest I didn't fancy it. I was attracted by the idea of stretching out in one of the battered armchairs in the sitting room and talking or reading till lights out, but she was the guru. The boys must have felt the same because they raised half-hearted objections. Ariel met them easily, swatting them away like so many feeble returns to a demon serve. What about the dark? Ray's providing head-torches. What about the cold? Wear a warm jacket. What about the heavy snow? We asked you to bring stout walking shoes.

To Stephen's slightly more forceful, 'Why? What is the purpose of this night-walk?'

She said, 'It'll be fun.'

Then she paused and said, 'And it's preparation for a written task.' Which was the perfect answer because he immediately left the kitchen to prepare himself.

I found Ray and asked him if he had any spare walking boots or wellies in a size six. 'I would have thought you were a bit bigger than that,' he said, ever the comedian.

'Not for me. I'm just sure that Mistyann won't have brought any boots. Or a proper coat either.'

He went and found me some of Susie's old gear and I took them to your room. When I got there I felt suddenly

130

shy and hovered outside for a minute. I had just raised my hand to knock when I heard a voice behind me.

'Boo!' it said. It was Charlotte. I jumped. 'Scaredy-cat,' she said. 'Are you here to see my oh-so-classy roomie?'

'Watch it,' I said.

'Oh come on,' Charlotte said. 'You must admit she's a bit, you know, a bit plebby. Of course you're her teacher, aren't you? You are probably a bit biased.'

She was as tall as me and looked me straight in the eyes and I have to say that her celluloid looks and aristocratic manner unnerved me slightly. I couldn't think of anything to say. Nothing. After a moment Charlotte laughed, twinkled past me and pushed open the door.

'You can come in, she's decent.'

I followed her in. You were sitting on the bed glowering beneath knitted eyebrows.

'What do you want?'

And the thing is, I didn't know because you were lacing up what looked like pretty expensive hiking boots. You had thick socks into which you'd tucked a pair of water-proof trousers. You had on a chunky knit jumper and on the bed was a fleece-lined jacket. You looked like you'd been kitted out at some special top of the range hiking store and I was standing there with Susie's battered cast offs and a coat Ray had liberated from the depths of some musty cupboard.

'I didn't know if you'd have any boots,' I said in a breathless rush. 'I managed to get a spare pair and a coat.'

Your frown grew darker. 'Why? It said in that letter you gave us about all the stuff we needed to bring.'

'Yeah. Course it did. I just thought…' And what had I thought? That you wouldn't read it? That you wouldn't be able to get some hiking kit together? That you were too poor? I'd leapt to lots of conclusions and I couldn't tell you what they were. Not in front of your sniffy room-mate. 'I just thought that you might have forgotten that's all.'

'Have I ever forgotten stuff before?'

And it was true, you didn't forget stuff. You always had your books with you at school. Your problem, in fact, was that you remembered too much. You squirrelled away insults, real or imagined, more or less for ever or until you decided to visit a whirlwind on the perpetrator. My best tactic was to make the most dignified withdrawal I could.

'Sorry, Mistyann, my mistake. See you downstairs.' And I shuffled out. You said nothing as I left, though I heard a clear stage-whispered 'prat' from Charlotte.

The walk itself was pleasant enough. Hard work though. The hill was a steep half mile and, what with the snow and the borrowed wellies, I would have found it hard going had it not have been for Ariel keeping my spirits up with more stories from her time trying to reassure parents that their broken kids could be fixed or that there's some way to create a genius from the most unpromising materials.

'A thing that I used to like about England was the way people just got on with things without making a fuss. Now it seems that every second kid I meet has ADHD or Dyslexia or Aspergers and wants the world bent to his or her own special needs. The truth about these conditions is that you just have to work harder,' I said.

'Ritalin can help a bit,' she said.

'Ah, The Chemical Cosh,' I said. 'Who wants that? Surely it's better to try proper food, proper exercise and good parental example and if the kids still don't achieve, well, someone's got to stack the shelves.'

She didn't really answer my point.

'There's a lot of pain in the world and people need to be able to express it, Jon. They need to be heard.'

But once you've been heard and nothing changes, what then? Don't you have to carry the embarrassment of having confessed to weakness as well as the original problems? Haven't you outed yourself? I said some of this.

'It's like Pete. It doesn't matter how much we hear his pain about his illness, he still can't come up here. Some burdens you just have to shoulder alone.'

It fact there had been a short but lively debate about whether or not we could take Pete. Kendra was spirited in advocating that if we couldn't take him we shouldn't go.

'That's the law,' she had said with nervy emphasis. 'If you can't offer Pete the same as everyone else, then you are in breach of the Disability Discrimination Act. If you go he has to go too. That's all there is to it.'

In the end, Ray had offered his sledge and we had fixed up a plan where the lads would take it in turns to haul Pete up the hill.

'We'll be his huskies,' cried Zak. 'Hey, Pete man, we're going to be your husky bitches!'

It was Pete himself who had demurred. 'I think I'll stay here and read. I'm happy not to go on any stupid walks in the ice and snow. Go if you want. I'm not going to be offended by staying in the warm with a mug of Cadbury's drinking chocolate while you lot freeze your nuts off.'

Kendra still wasn't happy. Just before we set off she grabbed Ariel's arm. 'He's just being noble,' she hissed in that fierce whisper that she specialised in. 'He's gutted that he can't go really.'

Me, I wasn't so sure about Pete's nobility and Ariel was pretty brisk too.

'Honey, it was his call. These kids have to be in charge of their own lives.'

And she couldn't say anything else because at that moment the boy himself wheeled himself in from the kitchen.

'Hey Kendra, what about this hot chocolate then? It won't make itself. Chop chop.'

Kendra flashed us a look of sort of despairing contempt before bustling off to make her boss his drink.

After ten minutes it became obvious that we could never have pulled him. After fifteen minutes no-one was talking. All we could hear was our ragged, emphysemic breathing. It was beautiful out there at night though, wasn't it? The moon and the stars and their light reflecting off the snow. And the silvery vapour trails we were all leaving. The most eerie thing was the way the head-torches gave the impression that we were some kind of strange war party.

From the top of the lane it was a matter of a couple of hundred yards to the ruined chapel. I'm an atheist. I'm even what you could call an evangelical atheist but still there's a special kind of trespass involved in setting up camp on gravestones. All that was left of this church were the two end walls that rose sharp against the sky. The snow had drifted against the furthest of these and against the low stone walls that surrounded the graveyard which meant that gaps appeared in the already sepulchral carpet. All around were dozens of jumbled memorials; some lying on their sides, many flat on the ground, others broken.

The drifting snow meant that the floor of the ruined church was covered in just an inch of fine powder and Ray produced a spade and quickly cleared it from a space roughly ten square feet. He then put a modest rucksack on the floor, touched some kind of trigger or wire and jumped back as a lime green rubber house pinged out fully formed. It reminded me of the kind of bouncy castles you find at village fetes. If anything could call forth outraged spirits then this blasphemous temple of man-made fibres would do it. Ray was, of course, very proud of himself.

'All-weather, high-vis, hurricane-resistant and self-erecting. And less than two hundred quid.'

It was cramped inside the tent but once Ray had placed his retro hurricane lamp in the centre— 'An exact replica of the kind Amundsen would have used in the Antarctic'— then an infectious kind of Boy Scout euphoria spread through the group.

I had been in this kind of situation only once before. Cadet Force camp 1982. The Modern school ran a well drilled compulsory army unit. The school had been set up in the 1840s with the specific intention of producing soldier-administrators for a growing Empire. Friday afternoons would see Mr Page with his swagger stick and epaulettes taking drill by the fives courts, followed by rifle practice on the range by the cricket nets. Mannequins representing Johnny Foreigner were peppered with .22 pellets on a weekly basis, the idea being that when the time came the Modern boys would not be found wanting. The dining hall was decorated with the sombre record of the names of the fallen from the school, not just in the two World Wars, but those who had taken hits fighting the Pathans, the Boers, and the Zulu; as well as those who had bought it in more contemporary—and more futile—rearguard actions in pointless colonies such as Aden and Northern Ireland. One ex-Head Boy has recently managed to get himself wasted by a roadside bomb in Afghanistan so some traditions have clearly lingered.

Anyway, in 1982 the Cadet Force was a big deal. We had green berets, combat trousers and our hands on live guns once a week. And we had a yearly camp.

My main memory of that camp was playing The Biscuit Game. Five boys in a flapping and noisy ex-army tent wanking onto a ginger nut. Last one to cum had to eat it. I told this story to Army Dave once. He assured me that it was mild compared to what the real Army gets up to.

He said, 'There's a point to it, hazing I mean. It might sound disgusting but when you're taken prisoner by the Mujahidin, there's not much they can do to you that's worse than what your mates have already done.'

Have you heard of hazing? It's an American word. Means violent initiation. Apparently sororities and female soccer teams are big on it. There are some very graphic hazing sites on the web.

And I think Army Dave is right about the uses of bullying and terror. I think a big reason women are so nervous of men is that they see what we routinely do to our friends. Okay, so it is only in the forces that open brutality is encouraged, but even in supposedly civilized offices you find blokes ripping the piss out of each other in ways intended to leave the victim weeping real blood on the carpet.

In the hi-vis, bargain-priced, self-erecting storm tent, no-one suggested the Biscuit Game but that didn't mean that the tent wasn't filling up with pheromones. It was quite a squeeze and I was sandwiched between Ariel and Charlotte. It got pretty warm, pretty quickly. Very soon there was an intoxicating scent of evaporating snow, boot leather, teenage sweat and the fruity notes of feminine hair products.

I have to say that the task Ariel had set for us was pretty lame. She must have known it too. It was a simple story exercise. We had to go around the room saying one word each to construct a story. I think the first go went something like this:

TheBigRabbitSatOnAPorcupineOwSheExclaimedAsThe RocketPlayedTableTennisWithHimself.

And the second and third efforts were worse. These may have been gifted kids but spontaneous surrealism clearly wasn't their bag. After the third feeble story a silence fell. I could feel Ariel stiffen slightly next to me. That's when Zak spoke up.

'Did anyone really look at the gravestones out there? Amazing aren't they?'

Charlotte piped, 'Yah, I'm going to write about them. Imagine how weird it must be under the earth with all the bones and coffins all mixed up and everything.'

And Stephen spoke softly and said, 'It's been done.' And he recited that Thomas Hardy poem.

I've just looked it up now and it was so perfect for the moment. The voices of the dead conjured up in that desolate bone yard. Do you remember it? It's the one that begins 'It is not death that harrows us...' And he did all seven verses. Word-perfect. He gave it just the right delivery too. Not too actorly or rehearsed. Just called it up as though the words were just occurring to him for the first time.

And the silence stretched afterwards.

Someone said, 'Good work, Stevie-boy.'

And Charlotte said: 'Yah, kudos, but I think my writing group are going to expect something with a bit more of a sperm count if you know what I mean? I'll have the dead arguing about who has got the right bones and trying to put themselves together properly. Like all the dead geezers are playing a massive game of Twister, yah?'

On the way back I caught up with Stephen and asked him why he had learned that particular poem. I had to blink and shield my eyes from the beam of his head torch as he turned towards me so that it shone full in my face. When he spoke he sounded snappy, cross.

'In Singapore, where I was living until this September, we often learn the classics by rote. I think it is an essential skill for a civilized person, don't you?'

He turned his head and continued his steady tramp down the hill towards the gothic shadow of the house, which stood etched against the clear sky with its needle-pricks of star-light.

'This country,' he continued wearily, 'This country, Mr Diamond, is very careless of its history and its culture. It seems strange to me that in Singapore we should have more respect for your heritage than you do. It's depressing. No offence or anything.'

And I thought back to the night before when he had been the only one to laugh at Ray's harmless milky gags. He'd clearly been thrilled that he had been chosen as part of a special gifted group and we'd managed to let him down within twenty-four hours.

'No offence taken,' I said. 'Stephen, the poem was perfect. Exactly the right thing at exactly the right time. If people don't have the patience for it, fuck 'em.'

I could feel him wince beside me at the f-word. He lengthened his stride slightly. If I had wanted to keep up I would have been almost jogging so I let the gap between us grow. Then you were at my elbow.

'Weird kid isn't he, JD?' I remember starting at the way that you used my initials. It was the first time you called me that. 'I reckon he's a serial killer. If this was a movie, he'd be the murderer deffo.'

'Deffo?' I said, smiling. 'What a quaint speaking style you have, Mistyann.'

And then there was the hour we sat—me, you and Ariel —in front of the fire with a cup of something herbal— chamomile? Rosehip? Some kind of poofs tea anyway—I was reading an old copy of the *London Review of Books*. She had a *TLS*. And you were finishing *Dark Sister*.

Later, in my beautiful tiny room, showered and damp, the air full of the generalized tingle of pine fresh gel, I reflected on how easily my life was flowing. Jon Diamond was more or less the same age Elvis was when his colon had imploded. He hadn't shaken up the world of rock 'n' roll, but he was alive, clean and sober. And able to take a dump without fear of pegging out under the strain of it. Jonathan Diamond was a success.

I wondered idly for a minute about how England was doing in the Test. In other words, I was a fool. A blind, smug, time-wasting fool. For complacency alone I deserved everything that came after.

TWENTY-FOUR

So I get to my room proper smecked out. I haven't done PE for ages now. I don't like the skanky school showers and girls PE is crap anyway. Netball, what kind of a game is that? A shit one. A game where you're not allowed to move more than half the time. How dry is that? Anyway I reckon I'm proper unfit cos the walk to that spooky church and back has left me with all shaky legs.

But of course I can't take it easy when I get to my room cos Charlotte is there spliffing up with Julius. She's got a little stash tin out and some skins. Giant rizlas. I'm jarred cos I want to go to sleep and I don't want Julius to see me all sweaty and I don't want to have a shower with him just the other side of the door. And I'm not a big fan of the idea of Charlotte rolling around on her bed with my Jules. And if they're doing draw they'll be awake for hours talking shite. Then they'll be sneaking down to the kitchen in the middle of the night to make a sarnie or raid the cookie jar or something and I'll feel like crap in the morning. I'm sure Charlotte can see all this on my face but she's such a princess that she doesn't give a shit.

'The alarms will go off,' I say.

It's well lame but I can't think of anything else at the minute.

'Oh don't be such a party-pooper. Just chillax, girl. Anyway I can't believe that you just say no to drugs.' I can feel my shoulders go tight. 'Or is it still glue and lighter fuel where you live?'

She is begging for a slap now. My shoulders go mega-tight. I give her a look. I hate it when people say chillax. The person who first made it up was kind of clever. Everyone else who says it is just an asshole.

Charlotte is stretched out on her bed wearing her three hundred quid jeans and a little camisole thing that shows the top of her tits and her belly button. I'm bloody sure that she wasn't wearing gear like this when we went for that walk.

I wonder how long Julius and her have been up here. I try to think when I last saw them. I've been sitting in the lounge for the last hour or so listening to Ariel talk about America. I've been thinking I'd love to go there. Not just New York but some of the other places Ariel knows. She tells us about the deserts and the plains and the strange small towns and the Indian reservations and the places you don't see on films or TV. Yeah I'd love to go there. After I've lived in London, I'll go travelling around America.

Now Julius is sitting on my bed facing Charlotte with his hands on his knees. They don't look like they've been getting jiggy or anything. Julius looks like he's her counsellor or something. In fact when I go to Anger Management, Michaela, the girl who tries to get me to breathe, she sits the way that Julius sits, all stiff and awkward and twisting her fingers and that.

Fuck it.

'I'm going to have a shower,' I say. And I go over to my bed and reach round Julius to get my pyjamas from under my pillow. He doesn't look at me. He looks at the floor. I'm close enough to smell his deodorant which is one of those special boy ones. The ones that make you think of the dentist.

The shower is amazing. Freaked me the first time, but I'm getting used to it now. It's like a million jabs of light trampolining on your skin. I let the room fill up with steam and use Charlotte's mega expensive body-wash so that when I step out of the shower I feel totally worth-it. My shoulders are back to normal. Who gives a fuck about Charlotte and Julius? Plenty of lads to go round.

I come out in my jimjams. I'm not exactly sex-on-legs but I don't care. I feel good now. Warm and sort of drowsy and I think I'll just kick Julius off my bed. He can sit next to

Charlotte and they can fool around or whatever and I reckon that I'm tired enough to just sleep through.

The surprising thing is that they haven't started smoking yet. Charlotte still has the tin of grass and the rizlas next to her. Julius is still sat twisting his fingers. They look like they haven't moved or spoken for the last twenty minutes. I think maybe they're worried about the smoke alarm after all. But it turns out that neither of them can actually roll a joint.

'Mistyann,' Charlotte whinges, making my name sound as if it's got about ten more a's in it than it has. 'Mistyaaaaaaaaaanne, can you skin up for us? Julius has never done it and I always get someone else to do it.'

Now as it happens I can roll a mean joint. Ty taught me so he could show me off to his mates when they came around for poker sessions or to watch WWF. I was about seven and producing these A star doobs. Ty used to say that I had the perfect thumbs for it. They're kind of a bit deformed I guess. Sort of flat on top. Anyway it's probably bollocks but Ty was convinced that gave me the edge in rolling draw.

I whiz up a couple of joints for them and Charlotte's so jarred at having to ask me that she can hardly breathe. And then I climb on a chair and use a pair of Charlotte's nail scissors to unscrew the alarm. And then, finally, I can kick Julius off my bed and crawl in under the cover.

I think I'm going to have to listen to slurping and squelching and heavy breathing and all the crap that goes on when kids start making out, but instead I just hear coughing. Coughing that goes on and on and on and on. It gets so bad that I sit up in the end. Julius looks like he's having a heart attack. His eyes are watering and panicky and wide and there's a thin stream of snot dangling from his nose. He's not my lovely J any more, he's just another kid who can't handle his drugs.

As it happens I hate dope. Dope makes you pure thick. What I love are eggs. Tamazapan. What I like—what I used to like—is getting some proper fine car, like a Subaru Impreza or something and just racing around the countryside. You feel the speed and the danger and that but you also feel above it all. It's like watching a movie and being in it at the same time. Music helps too. It's funny, but old style classical music works best. Anything else makes the movie seem like a comedy and when you're racing around the countryside in a nicked motor, what you want is action or horror.

I discover this by accident. We nick this motor once—top of the range Audi—and the guy who owns doesn't have any CDs. So we're flicking through the radio pre-sets and this mad piano music comes on and for some unknown reason, we leave it on. Well freaky, speeding round all the lanes with this crazy music. It keeps breaking over us like cold waves at the beach. It's impossible to listen to that kind of shit at home. But in a top car going ninety. Well ace.

So Tamazapan is okay and you don't have to fiddle around with baccy and rizlas and it won't give you cancer, but I don't feel like talking about drugs with Charlotte and Julius. They're so not worth it. You see that a lot up town. Floss kids giving it the big one about drugs.

There are four floss schools in Bedford and it makes me laugh. They all live in the villages so you see kids like these a lot. Hundreds of Charlottes clogging up the bus station and all trying to talk like they're on Eastenders. They all smoke and get lairy—all the girls swearing and talking about cocks and booze and who might be pregnant. And all the boys tossing their floppy hair and talking about guitars and bands. They all need to fucking get real.

Anyway, I sit up. I think I'll have to have a piss or something. Charlotte springs up like she's been waiting for me to make this kind of move.

'Hey Mistyann, sweetie, can I have a private word?'

She bounces herself up off the bed and comes over to me, grabs my hand and pulls me up. She flashes a smile and fires off 'Girlie chat time' at Julius who looks like his fucking dog has just died. Sick and miserable. If I wasn't so tired I could feel sorry for him. I can't believe I ever fancied him. In the bathroom Charlotte turns on both taps.

'So he can't hear us,' she says. Then she says. 'Miz, you've got to get rid of him for me. He's such a drip.'

I can't decide whether I am prepared to put up with her saying 'Miz' like this. It's so fake. But then again, no-one has ever shortened my name like this before and I quite like that. The newness of it.

'Why can't you do it?'

'Oh. Just because.'

'You could just say "Julius I'm knackered. I need some kip".'

'Oh, you can't say that sort of thing to boys. Especially when you've invited them up here. You can do it. He won't mind if you're rude.'

'Why not?'

'Oh, you know what I'm saying. Cos you're rude to everyone. He won't take it personally. Please, Mistyann. I'll owe you one.'

I can't believe it. She's got a lad back to her room to get high and fool around and then she's worried about not being a polite hostess. I just pull open the bathroom door. At that moment I'm just going to go back to bed and leave Charlotte to sort out her own mess.

But what I actually do is say to Julius, 'Come on mate, time to split.'

He looks pure grateful. Like I've rescued him from a fire or something.

'Yeah, I need to hit the sack. They're working us pretty hard aren't they?'

And I'm thinking, are they fuck. So far we've played a couple of kids' party games, had a snow ball fight, a walk around the gardens and then made up some crap stories while sitting on some dead people.

'Night then.'

'Night.'

'Night.'

And he hovers about for a while like a mook, like he needs to say something else. But he doesn't and finally ducks out of the door with a funny gay flick of his hand.

Charlotte lies back on her bed and takes a drag.

'Jesus,' she says, 'You really can't tell who is going to turn out to be an utter geek can you? I mean, he looks so good, but is actually so bloody sad. What a loser.'

I don't answer. Everything she says annoys me. But she can't take the hint and just carries on. I lay on my side looking at her, using my mind to tell her to get undressed and go to sleep.

'I reckon Zak is the best bet out of this lot, don't you?' she says. I think about Zak in the kitchen and the way he took charge. Yeah, he probably is the best bet. He looks like someone who'll probably end up running some mega company. Zakspace. Zaktube. Something with his name in it anyway.

'He's a twat,' I say.

There's a moment of silence while Charlotte smokes and thinks.

'No,' she says, 'He's a dude.' And she sits up and pulls her top off. I don't know anyone who would do that, just get their tits out in front of someone they hardly know. I've been in the same room as people shagging and I've never seen any breasts or nothing. Just heard the noises. I feel myself blushing and it pisses me off. I close my eyes. But somehow Charlotte's perfect tits are still there sort of printed on the inside of my eye-lids. It's upsetting.

Just then there is a knock on the door. Charlotte slides under the covers. Neither of us says anything. The knock comes again. It's a shy knock. I know who it is.

'For fuck's sake,' I say and get over to the door and pull it open. It's Julius. Had to be. I smile but I make sure that he knows it's a false one. 'What is it, Julius?'

He doesn't look me in the eye.

'I can't find the way to my room. It's all a bit confusing.' He looks so fucking beaten up. For a minute he looks like Carboot did when I saw him shitting it outside school. He looks about five years old.

'Come on,' I say, 'We'll go down to the kitchen and work it out from there.'

'Oh yeah, thanks. Yeah I should be able to find my way from there.'

I'm not so sure. I don't look back at Charlotte because she'll probably wink or something crap like that. Or she'll say, 'Have fun' or something and laugh in that totally jarring Tinkerbell fairy voice she puts on.

When we're outside and walking along I can feel Julius begin to relax a bit.

'Well. What a player you are,' I say.

Julius laughs and says, 'Yeah. I screwed up big time. The thing is I thought we were going to talk about Oxford. You know, which colleges to apply to. And then she got out the grass and I'm like…' His voice fades away.

'Yeah, I know. You were like crap,' I say. But I say it nicely and he laughs again.

'I don't know why I even tried it. I don't drink and I've never even had a cigarette. I'm sort of straight edge really.'

Straight Edge are these hard core Christians. You see them in town asking you if you want to live forever. Who the fuck would want to do that? I don't think Julius is Straight Edge. I think he just means that he goes to church on Sundays with his mum. He's just a nice boy.

I say, 'I think you're just a nice boy, Julius.' He jerks away like I've slapped him. 'I'm sorry, but you've just got to face up to the truth, mate. And there are worse things to be than nice.'

He doesn't look like he believes me. He looks like being nice is the worst possible thing to be.

We get to the kitchen and the stone floor bites at my feet. I skip over it and Julius follows. He looks like that old dog of Mr Negus. That was a dog that always looked like it had just had her ass kicked. We go out of the other side and I'm aware of the way the house seems to watch over us. I mean it's like all the people in it are asleep but the house is awake, holding its breath to see what we're up to next. I have the thought that all the people through history have just been some kind of soap for the house. Just entertainment. Everything that any of us do, it's just to fill time for the house.

We come to a corridor and Julius says, 'Hold up. I think this is the one.' And he moves past the first two doors. He's doing it in slow motion, stretching those bendy arms and legs pretending to be a spy. I think it's meant to be funny. I think it's meant to be cute. God, he's such a geek.

When he reaches the third door he puts his finger to his lips and crouches down with his head pressed flat against it like he's listening. He's keeping up the whole 'I'm a spy' thing. I'm thinking that he found his room a bit bloody easily and I'm wondering how lost he really was. He pulls the handle down and pushes the door open a crack.

'Fuck's sake, Julius. In or out.' It's Dalwinder's voice. Julius straightens up immediately.

'Sorry, mate.' He does that weird gay flapping thing with his hand, which this time means 'I best get off then'.

'Night.' I say. I say it loud. Louder even than I meant to. For some reason I don't feel like playing these let's be quiet games. 'See you tomorrow, Julius.' I make my voice a bit quieter but not much and I smile at him. He looks shocked. Obviously I have broken some rule. Boys have tons of rules for girls. Don't make jokes, don't run, don't answer back, know a bit about football but not too much, look mint at all times but don't spend ages in the bathroom. There are some 'do's'—Do love me. Do love my mates. Do love my music. Do love my clothes. Do laugh at my jokes—but mostly it's don'ts. Don't be funny. Don't shout. Don't be loud. Don't be quiet. Don't be clever. Don't be thick. Don't nag. Don't make a show. Millions more. Don't don't don't. There's like a basic law which all lads agree with and then each lad has tons of other don'ts which are like unique to him. If you want to have lads as mates there would be millions of rules to learn. I have two don'ts of my own. Don't give a fuck. Don't waste your time.

Julius whispers, 'Night.' And disappears into his room like a robber going over a garden fence. Sneaky and quick.

I stand in the corridor for a second, feeling the house wondering what will happen next. And I think that this is the first time all day that I have been on my own. And I think that if I ever win the lottery this is what I'll buy: time on my own. This is what I'll have when I live in London and then New York. Time by myself. If I get married I'll have a pre-nup that will lay it all down. A minimum amount of time my guy will have to give me on my own.

It's then that one of the other doors opens.

'Hey, Mistyann, come in here.'

And I follow Zak into his room. I don't know why. Yes I do. He asks me. He has that thing about him. Like he expects you to do what he says. He's looking fine too. I don't know if that has anything to do with it because I swear that at that moment I don't really see what he looks like. It's only when we're actually in his room that I notice that he looks fit as fuck.

His hair's not so floppy now, it's sort of standing up. He's not wearing a shirt and he has a TV body. A swimmer's body. You know, tight and tanned and toned and all that. He's got a pair of grey sweats on and there's just a golden flicker of hair leading down from his neat and tidy belly button. I think—this is a proper man. Except I know that he's not. He just has a man's body. The only boyish thing about him is that indie necklace which I notice he's still wearing. He stretches his arms above his head which shows his body off even more. I think maybe he knows this. Or guesses. He's a kid that is used to being fancied anyway.

I need to do something to stop staring at his pecs and his six-pack and his little trail of hair and so I look around the room. It's huge. Miles bigger than Charlotte's and mine and I had thought that ours was pretty big. The other thing I notice straight away is that it only has one bed in it.

'You're not sharing,' I say.

'I don't believe in sharing anything,' he says. 'My mum told them about my medical condition, said that I had to have a room to myself.'

'What's wrong with you?'

He shrugs. 'I don't know. She just made something up. I said I wouldn't go on the trip if I had to share a room. And she was desperate to have a bit of a break from me to be honest.'

Zak has pure made himself at home. There are scarves over the lamps which gives the room a strange spaceship glow. There's a guitar standing in one corner. The floor has piles of books on it, looking like those giant jenga games you get in pub gardens. The floor also has today's clothes on it. There's a desk which is covered in papers and some of the papers are covered in scribble and some of the rest are bank notes. Twenties as well as tens. And there is a dressing table that has lots of bottles of potions and stuff. Aftershave and shit like that.

'I get a bit freaked out if other people are in my space that's all.'

'Me too,' I say.

'Hell is other people.' He smiles. He has a heart-breaking, breath-taking smile. Better than Julius. There's a silence and it goes on and on and I can feel myself getting panicky. I'm finding it a bit hard to breathe.

'What's that smell?' I say.

He looks embarrassed.

'Incense. Joss sticks. A bit hippy-dippy I know, but it relaxes me. And makes the place my own somehow. Don't you like it?'

'It's okay.'

The truth is I don't know whether I like it or not. On the one hand it's better than that socks and trainers boy-smell. On the other hand it's not helping with the not being able to breathe properly thing. It's making me feel unreal somehow. It's a bit like that wobbly eggy feeling. Like when they're just kicking in and mixing with the cider or the voddy or whatever you've been drinking. I feel a bit like how I feel on a dark country lane with the piano music on and the leather of a pure rocking car underneath me. I can't think of anything to say. Normally my brain is full of things to say. All the words I could ever need are just there waiting for me. And I'm not used to not finding the right ones whenever I want. The only time I've felt like this is in French. I'm good at French but I have to scrabble around for the words. They aren't just there. That's why I don't like it.

Zak doesn't seem to mind the silence. He's just smiling. He goes over to the chair by his desk and sits down. There's nowhere else to sit except the bed so I sit on that. I see the guitar making faces at me. I think maybe the house has that kind of magic, that because it's alive it can make other things come alive too. Anyway. That guitar seems like it's gurning away. I nod at it. Zak follows my look.

'Can you play that?' I say. I don't care if he can or not, it's something to say.

Zak gets up and sort of glides over to the guitar, which gives me the chance to look at his back which has the proper v shape. He grabs the guitar by the neck, like it's a naughty kid or something.

So then he's back on the chair and he can proper play. And he sings. No boy I know sings. Not after about Year 9. They can rap, yeah, or freestyle but Zak is proper singing. He sings quiet. It's a whisper really so he doesn't wake anyone. I don't know what he sings. I know hardly any songs. I listen but it's hard to hear the words. In any case they don't make much sense but it's a beautiful song and he sounds so blue as he sings it. Like you can hear the tears in his voice. I think that is when I decide to shag him. Course there is a part of me that thinks that he's learnt the guitar and singing thing just to get off with girls. But then, so what? At least he's learnt something.

Shagging's easy. Getting started is hard. But Zak is smooth. He puts the guitar down and stands and stretches again.

'Fancy a drink?' he says. I don't say anything. All my words have gone again. He moves over to this little wooden cabinet thing by the bed. He comes so close to me now that I could put my hand out just a few centimetres and touch that soft pathway of hair if I wanted. I don't though.

He bends down to open the door to the cabinet saying, 'Excuse me,' as he does it. He's leaning right over and now I can see the bush of hair in his pits. I sort of feel my insides go melting and warm. Funny the things that can set that off. I mean, it's just pubes isn't it? Zak's pubes making me go funny. Making me wet. It's mad.

He gets out this bottle. Whisky from the shape of it.

'You had this before? Jim Beam?' I shake my head. I can't remember. I've had loads of different drinks. I might have had this Jim Beam but best to say no. One of the don't/do rules with boys is: don't know too much. Do let them show you stuff, teach you stuff.

He takes a big swig from the bottle. And doesn't make a face or anything. He makes it look like he's just swigging

OJ. Now I feel like laughing because this is all ordinary lad stuff. The guitar and the singing and the being in control thing, even the being properly grown up thing—that is a bit freaky. You know, a bit gifted and talented. Pretending to be hard, well that's just normal.

I take the drink and swallow. It's Jack Daniels basically. No big deal. JD. We call it that. Same as what I call Mr Diamond. I think about him for a moment. All that worrying about if I had the right gear for a walk in the snow. He can be too much like a dad sometimes. A granddad even. And it's a bit funny cos all that walking gear is from the school. You can get anything in lost property. It's like a free shop.

I reckon if you went to see Mrs Thornton in the office and said 'has anyone handed in an elephant?' she'd say 'wait a minute, dear' and then she'd be back with a dirty fuck off elephant on a piece of string going 'we were wondering when someone would claim this'. Dozy old mook. And how can people forget where they've left their stuff? Pisses me right off.

And then I hand the bottle back to Zak who is standing right in front of me and our hands touch. It's the first time we've touched and he jerks back just a little bit. And I feel it too, the little shock, the little spark and I look at his sweats right where his cock is. I don't mean to. I just do. And he's hard. Half hard at least. I put my hand on him. Feel how strong his cock is and I feel my stomach start jumping up and down. I stroke him and keep my eyes on his face. He looks surprised. Getting started is hard but you can make it easier. Making all the first moves makes things easier.

I pull the sweats down and now I look at him properly and take a breath. I put him in my mouth. They say that all cocks taste different, but they don't really. Just depends how clean they are. They all taste of salt and they all taste of shower gel. Nearly all anyway, thank God.

He sighs and time passes. I'm good at this. I'm pure A star at this. My hand is stroking him softly moving up and down the whole length and around his tight balls and the fuzz of his pubes. More time passes and I feel Zak's hands in my hair. Then I move over on his bed and his sweats are off and my jimjams are off and it's all hands and tongues and slapping, slippery skin and noises. All the stuff you expect but that still catches you out.

Things get ruder. We kiss hot and the alcohol stings inside our mouths and the room just melts into lights and shadows and then I know that he has to be inside me. It has to be now. He feels it. I feel it. Right now. Right now. And I say this to him or something like it and I'm full of him and my head is full of his noise and his breath and I'm pulling at him and we're both saying stuff and I don't know what any of it means. I'm pulling him into me and from far off I can hear this banging which later I realize is the headboard knocking against the wall. And then I'm back in the room and time is passing again and I can feel the weight of him and then the wet heat right inside the centre of me.

And the room rebuilds itself out of the light and shadow and everything comes into focus again and you can tell how noisy we've been by the hard shape of the silence now. Zak guesses what I'm thinking—another thing he's gifted in.

'Don't worry,' he says. 'These are proper walls. About a metre thick. Proper rooms for bonking in.' And the word bonking makes me feel a bit shit. 'Anyway,' he says, 'we weren't that noisy.'

And maybe we weren't. Maybe most of the noise was in my head.

I sit up and feel spunk cool on the top of my leg. I don't want to stay and I don't want to go. Zak is up on one elbow looking at me. Trying to see inside my head. But he doesn't ask me if I've come or if I enjoyed it or anything stupid. He keeps quiet. A bright boy. A talented boy. A boy with a gift.

We sit for a bit and he fiddles with his guitar for a bit and then I feel a bit of an idiot just sitting all quiet in the dark on this posh kid's bed. He watches in silence as I search for my jimjams.

'You are fucking beautiful,' he says. 'Fucking beautiful. Don't ever forget that, Mistyann.'

And I'm like yeah right. As if.

'See you at breakfast,' I say, like we've just been chatting or chilling or something.

And then I'm back in my room. I sneak in but of course Charlotte is awake and sits straight up and puts her light on.

'You've been hours,' she says. I shrug. 'Did you snog him?' she says.

'Who?' I ask.

'What do you mean, who? Julius of course. The boy you like so totally fancy. The boy you took back to his room. You know. Tall? Black? Fit but can't roll a joint?'

'No,' I say, but she won't let it lie.

'What did you do then?'

'We chillaxed,' I say, 'just chillaxed.'

TWENTY-FIVE

I was avoiding the kitchen with its dreary crush of adolescence. I was taking my breakfast al fresco. By breakfast, I mean of course, instant coffee and a Silk Cut.

There was a fresh snowfall and the day felt sharp with new hope. I felt unusually cheery as I stomped around to the secret garden. My intention was to look at the amazing snow heads and see if the new fall had disfigured them. It might have done but the artist herself was at work changing and developing, revising and redrafting her creations.

'Hey Susie,' I called. 'So these are your work?'

She smiled and raised the garden hoe that she was using to carve a new shape from the white silo in front of her.

'Hey Jon. Yes. All mine. I love snow, don't you?'

Surely everyone loves snow? Everyone loves the illusion of starting over that it gives; the way it offers the prospect of new shapes and, of course, fun and games. I trekked the ten feet or so towards her.

'Snow's great,' I puffed, 'but wouldn't a simple snowman have done? An ordinary rotund fellow with stick arms and a carrot nose?'

She laughed.

'Ray and I, we went to Osaka in our back-packing days. They have this amazing snow festival there. You can see the maddest things. Some of the sculptures there were awesome. Huge. I mean some people take it too seriously and use grid patterns drawn over their initial sketches. And then use chainsaws to do the rough carving. Or they get their snow into blocks which they can use like ordinary house bricks. But who has the time?'

Susie herself was simply using a gardening trowel, the hoe and a shovel to work her figures. She had beaten the snow with a shovel to form a taut hillock. After that she just cleared a space around the site of the statue and then it was just a matter of working carefully with her trowel and hoe. She had used kitchen items like spoons and knives for the detailed work like eyes and lips. And there they were: alive and shining with mystic power. She'd turned dead water into magic.

'Each figure took me about two hours,' she said. 'But it's creative and burns off a few calories.'

Six hours in the cold making snowmen. On her own. Did she not feel just the slightest bit eccentric?

'Snow is so rare in Malaysia. I still get excited by it and I suppose... I was an artist when Ray met me and this feels like I'm keeping in touch with that part of myself. With the added benefit of not cluttering up our house with my installations. These will just melt away and next year... with any luck... I can do some more.'

'But most artists want an audience don't they?' I said. 'You didn't even tell people that they were here. We had to stumble into them.'

'But Jon, I love that idea. I love the fact that people will come across them and not know what to make of them. These figure-heads will be beautiful mysteries. Like snow itself. A beautiful inexplicable mystery. And also...' She paused slyly. 'Owen the Gardener will be especially freaked out. He already thinks I'm some kind of whore witch who sold herself.'

And so I got a glimpse of Susie's discontent. I stared into my mug, empty save for a sludgy residue.

'I better head back,' I said. 'I'm running low on fuel. I need some more FC.'

Susie raised an enquiring eyebrow.

'Fresh Coffee,' I said.

Of course FC doesn't mean Fresh Coffee. It's St Teresa's staff room slang for fucking coffee. In other words the highest octane rocket fuel we can find. The stuff that gives us the strength to survive those tricky lower sets.

You'll find a lot of recovering alkies take their coffee very strong and in large amounts. Addictions find you out, are assiduous at spotting gaps in the market. Meet a guy who is genuinely obsessed with something—car boot sales, chess, running marathons, traction engine rallies—and the chances are that there is another more pernicious addiction in the not so distant past. The need to mainline caffeine is a pretty minor one, compared to pot-holing or work.

Susie looked suddenly shy.

'The best coffee is in the cottage. We only get the rubbish catering stuff for the main house. Or do you need to be back for the first workshop?'

I probably should have been at that workshop, but it was a Sunday morning and strictly speaking I wasn't there as a teacher. I was there in *loco parentis*. And what could be more parent-like than spending Sunday morning having coffee with the neighbour?

So I was soon thawing in Ray and Susie's kitchen, a room maybe twelve foot square and as cosy as a digestive dunked in warm milk. There was a heavyweight iron Much Wenlock stove squatting like a little Sumo wrestler in the fireplace. Through the latticed grill I could see flames doing a frenzied dance; flames reflected in the flag-stoned floor that shone where the boots and clogs of generations of farm hands had worn channels and grooves. A Welsh dresser of dark wood stood brooding in one corner, while in the centre of the room a table of similar wood was saved from slanting too dramatically by the distinctive tangerine addition of a penguin classic under one weathered leg. Some free standing units of utilitarian design and a butler sink at the far end completed the furniture. It was about as un-Ikea a kitchen as you could find.

There was also a large painting propped against the wall. An original nude in oils that reminded me of a Lucien Freud; paint thickly applied, the colours streaked and the face's features blurred. Nevertheless it was possible to see that the woman was dark, lithe and Oriental. I obviously stared at it a little too long because when I looked round Susie was blushing.

'One of Ray's,' she murmured, 'From when we first met.'

'He's an artist too then?' I said breezily, though it was clear from the ham-fisted execution that he wasn't.

'No, no. That was just for fun. Ray doesn't have the stamina to be an artist really. Or the concentration. He gets bored easily.'

And again I caught it, the scent of unwanted seclusion. She turned back to the little rituals of clattering cups and milk and the cafetière.

I let a suitable pause elapse before I said, 'And where's Ray now?'

'He's in Merthyr Tydfil. He's at a Conference of Literature Education Activists.'

There was another pause while Susie allowed me to digest the absurdity of this idea. The way she stressed the capital letters told me exactly what she thought about the concept of being an activist for literature education.

'In this weather?' I said. 'He's a brave man.'

'Yes. He was up at five clearing snow from the lane. Luckily we get a Landrover with the job so we can get out.'

She brought over the cups and coffee things on a tray. I got the feeling we had talked enough about Ray. I told her about my short inglorious career taking my clothes off for money. It's a funny story and considering that there was a picture of a naked Susie in the room, not inappropriate.

Skint during my first year at uni, the weary slob at the job centre offered me the choice of flipping burgers in the Wimpy or being the life model for the Art Foundation class at the tech. I'd turned up, slightly buzzing from a couple of nerve-settling Red Stripes, without any of the basics. No-one had told me that I would need a robe. The instructor, a man who looked so much like a painter that he had to be a fraud, gave me an insolent once-over. There he was in his black but oil-streaked polo-neck, with his close-cropped grey goatee and film-star cheek-bones, gesturing for me to change in a store cupboard. I heard the students arrive, the fizz of teenage girls. I was naked in a store-room surrounded by broken easels and bottles of squeezy paint.

I heard this low rent Lautrec say, 'We've got a bloke today.'

The fizz turned itself up a notch.

'Oooh, about time,' someone said. 'What's he like?'

'Let me put it this way,' I could hear the smirk in Lautrec's voice, 'he's not exactly Arnold Schwarzenegger.'

And he swung open the store-room door forcing me to emerge into the laughter of a roomful of girls, which is probably the cruellest sound there is, wouldn't you say?

I told Susie this story. And then, spurred on by her giggle, I told her the story of being stranded in that first PE lesson at the Modern school wearing nothing but my Union Jack knickers.

The stories added a little sexual heat to the room. We were both thinking of the other naked. She was no beauty Susie, her face had too many odd folds and shadows for that, but she was sparky and intelligent and had the most amazing eyes; so dark they were almost black. Eyes you could hurl yourself into. She was also easy to talk to, quick to laugh and had enough of an accent to lend her exoticism. She was good at spinning stories herself too. She moved the conversation on from nude modelling to shit jobs in general and from there to teaching jobs and her jet eyes grew wider as the room grew warmer.

I spoke about you and about the staff room at St Theresa's. I gave her my line about it being like Hitler's bunker with 'none of the *joie de vivre* that implies'. It always goes down well. And Susie talked about the Malaysian education system where you don't apply for jobs at individual schools; the government simply posts you to where you are needed. And where the national curriculum is fixed so that the whole country turns the page of the text books at more or less the same time. And where one teacher armed with a bamboo cane can teach a class of sixty in silence.

We were getting on great.

I've had a lot less sex since becoming sober. The drunk's smile can be a beguiling thing; particularly for other drunks. Two drunks together aren't so much fucking as mixing a cocktail. One drunk nearly always has the ingredients that other drunks need. And let's not forget that even people who aren't drunks by vocation or training tend to get wasted before embarking on any kind of love affair. Other cultures may have careful and protracted negotiations before any kind of union can be contemplated, but the British have getting arse-holed and tumbling sloppily onto a stranger's mattress.

Of course even drunks can't stay drunk for twenty-four hours so there are a lot of terrible surprises for the drunken lover. There are girls who wake in the night and start beating you up. Girls who weep disconsolate for hours. Girls who are sick in the head or in the bed. Girls who aren't girls, but women far older than you thought. There are the scarred and the scared. But the worst is the girl who thinks she can change you. Pour yourself into the warm and hopeful bed of the woman who thinks she can help and you are turning the self-loathing meter from merely high to unbearable. And these nice girls are so high maintenance. You have to stay trashed just to give them a purpose. They don't really want you to change. It's about the journey for these girls.

And since I've been sober? Well, there was Beth the primary school teacher. Carol-Anne the travel agent. And Angela the librarian. That's it. All of the liaisons starting with shy glances, building up to frenzied sex on a carpet somewhere, settling down to coupling four or five nights a week after a film or a play, before finally fading away amid a low level guerrilla war of bickering about chores, of which sex was soon just another. Beth, Carol-Anne and Angela. They came within the first two or three years of sobriety and since then I have found it easier not to bother.

Every so often I scan the soul mates sections of the *Guardian,* but it's invariably depressing. A directory of opinionated professional women every one of whom is into 'the usual *Guardian* interests'. By which I think they mean a large glass of half-decent Shiraz at around six o' clock. Perhaps I should have pursued the racier alternatives in the Singles Out section of the local rag: Buxom, broad-minded single mum, 26, size 16 seeks older man to spoil her.

Seems both more honest and more enticing.

The year leading up to Cefn Coch had been entirely and happily fallow. I liked to think that the quiet phone and unexciting credit card bills were signs of long delayed maturity.

We fell silent for a while.

'What are you thinking?' she asked.

I was thinking what if I reached across the table and took her hand and kissed it? Or what if I stood up, walked around the table and kissed her on the neck? What if I slid my hand down between her shirt and that butternut skin and cupped her small tight breast? I was thinking what if I asked her to go upstairs and we spent what was left of Sunday morning as all Sunday mornings should be spent?

I was thinking that the Undead would approve. In my head I heard the papery rustle of ancient men applauding. 'Go for it, my son,' they would say. 'Get in there. You won't regret it. Not in the end.'

What I said was, 'Nothing. You know I really had better get back. Thanks for the FC. I really needed it.'

And I heard the anguished howling of the Undead all the way back to the sullen black slab of the main house.

Back in the house the kids were having a break. The kitchen was crowded and I couldn't see you anywhere. I asked Charlotte if she'd seen you and got an unhelpful shrug as a reply. I was on my way to look for you when Ariel stopped me by the stairs.

'Hey Jon,' Ariel said and I was struck again by the terrifying perfection of her American smile. It wasn't just ideal in terms of the physical orthodontic facts of it, but also in the perfectly judged emotional weight, modulation and heft of it. It stopped me in my tracks. 'We missed you this morning.'

'Oh sorry,' I began, 'I was…'

'It doesn't matter. Kids were all fine. There are more than enough adults here to cope. And look Jon, I hope you don't mind, but it's Sunday and I've given all the kids five quid to buy lunch and said that they can go off into the village today. We aren't going to do any more lessons, though they do have a task.'

I thought this sounded risky. I was worried about the snow. I was worried about the lack of street savvy of some of these kids and, ridiculously, I was worried about paedophiles. What Mum would have called, with grim emphasis, Strange Men.

Every Saturday Dad would drop me at the pictures, the old Empire by the river, and I would watch the flickering black and white of *Flash Gordon* episodes that were ancient even then, and wait for the Strange Men to come and put their hands on my knee. This never happened, but every week I was convinced that it would.

Now, like my mum thirty years ago, I feared Strange Men and I had nine kids to worry about. I mentioned some of these concerns to Ariel.

'Oh Jon, I think these scare stories are horribly exaggerated, don't you? I've told the kids to stay in twos or threes, not to get into conversations with strangers, not to get into cars and we've given them back their cell-phones so they can call the centre if they get lost. The village is tiny, Jon. A street of shops, two pubs, two cafés, two churches, a children's' playground and a 7/11. I really don't think there's too much that can happen to them.'

'Well I guess if you've told them already then I can't really stop them going now in any case. What's the task?'

The dazzle and gleam of her smile seemed to develop a watt or two of extra radiance.

'They've got to each find a person in Llangow and follow them for at least fifteen minutes making notes about their clothes, speech, behaviour—whatever strikes them. And they should do this without being observed.'

It sounded like a recipe for chaos, violence and possible law suits. Imagine if she were followed around Smallville, Iowa by notebook-toting foreigners. But I didn't say this. I said that it was a cool idea and maybe I would do it too.

TWENTY-SIX

Would I fancy Charlotte if I was boy? Course I would. She has the fuckable ass, the swollen lips, the over-sized tits that bounce like basketballs as she walks. She has all of that going on. And she looks clean and dirty at the same time, which is the look boys like. Like she could be taking it up the ass one minute and making a Sunday dinner for their mum the next. She's proper bendy too. Some of the yoga poses are pure freaky. The last thing she does is stand on her head. That can't be good for you, can it? She does it for more than five minutes and I laugh because it makes her head go purple. I can tell Charlotte is dying to say something to me but she can't cos she has Made A Decision to ignore me. Fine, I think. Fuck her.

I go into the bathroom, taking my phone with me. There is another message, loads of missed calls and a text. I can't bear to hear mum ranting on so I look at the text first. It says: SAY YOUR TEACHER WE KNOW WHERE YOU ARE COMING TO GET YOU which gives me a real fucking shock until I think that she's bulling. She can't drive and she's got the brats. She can't even handle predictive text. Say your teacher. Jesus.

But I don't like her knowing where I am. She can make trouble. The good thing is it's Sunday today and the school is closed next week so she can't cause trouble there. Of course she'll go ape when I get back and she'll probably come down the school and try and give JD a smack in the middle of assembly or something but that's all in the future.

I can't face listening to her voice screeching at me so I grab the phone and come out of the bathroom. Charlotte's pissed off to breakfast. I don't need to go down because I've got coco-pops which I eat dry from the packet.

We do proper work for a bit this morning which makes the Chinese kid happy anyway. First we have to write about our own funeral. We have to imagine who will be there and what people might say about us and then we read out the speeches. That takes quite a long time and is actually pretty interesting. Everyone is pure honest. Zak's is the longest. He puts in all the music that is going to be played, where everyone is going to sit, everything; like he's been thinking about it for years. It's funny too because he has all these world leaders coming and pop stars and actors and he has people who can't be there in person sending in video clips like it's an award ceremony or something.

I don't look at Zak in the workshop. I still think he is as fit as fuck and when I think about him and me on the bed in his room I feel hot and achy between my legs. Proper achy. I don't think I've felt that before.

I'm thinking about me and Zak doing it so much that I don't listen very carefully to everyone else's writing. But the other person that I do listen to is Pete. He doesn't want to read it out at first. Ariel has to make him.

Kendra starts to say, 'Oh Pete, you don't have to if you don't want to...'

But Ariel talks over her. She says, 'I'd really like to hear it, Pete.' And you sort of know that it's an order. Kendra looks like she's been slapped.

Anyway. Pete tells us about the little church on his estate which will be full of people from school and his drama group and youth club and Boys Brigade. And you can see that everyone is a shocked because they've just realised that Pete's funeral won't be years away. And we realise that it will happen exactly like he says.

And he tells us about being buried in his Tottenham kit with the football that was signed by last year's first team squad. And about how he'll have his DS and PSP and Wii and all his games with him, in case he needs them in heaven. And he says his little cousin won't know what's going on and will keep asking when he's coming back. And he tells us that everyone will look sad but actually some people will be relieved because it's already hard work looking after him and it's going to get harder.

And he smiles when he looks at Kendra and he says, 'You'll be there won't you? You won't be in the front row with Mum and Dad and Gramps and Nan. But you'll have grabbed a place in the second row and you'll probably be crying and sniffing the most out of everyone.'

And we're all looking at Kendra and we can see that she's nearly crying. And Pete puts his hand on her hand and he's quite gentle and I can see dying is not for wimps.

And he tells us about the small white coffin which he has already chosen from the internet.

'Not EBay,' he says and smiles, but no-one else does because it's not fucking funny is it?

And then he says about his mum and dad and how they will look small and broken and how they will say that they will never forget him. And then they will. His brother and sister first and then everyone else. Friends, relatives, close family, he'll fade away from all of them. And he says that somebody at the funeral, maybe his uncle Ken, will say, 'Just goes to show, doesn't it? Just goes to show that you've got to seize the day. *Carpe Diem.*'

And the last thing Pete says is that it's a bit hard to *carpe* fucking *diem* when you can only move from the chest up. And there's this silence after. It's not a perfect silence because you can hear Kendra sniffling, but it's pretty quiet.

And then Ariel just says, 'Thank you, Pete. That was charming.'

Which was the last thing it was.

And it's funny because after Pete has finished talking I'm sitting in the silence and I think about how I want to go back to Zak's room and get him to fuck me and I feel myself getting wet and I have to move around in my seat because it's not comfortable. And then I sort of get embarrassed because I wonder if people can tell.

We do some other writing stuff which is alright but not really that different from a normal English lesson. I'm thinking how fucking weird it is doing English on a Sunday.

When we finish Ariel tells us that cos it's Sunday we have the rest of the day off to explore. They are going to give each of us a fiver to buy lunch and we have to be back by four, which is when it starts to get dark. She also says we have to keep in twos and this is a pure result cos it means that I can spend the day with Zak. She tells us to wrap up warm and to take a watch and that Ray and Susie will let us have our phones back so that we can call the house if there's an emergency.

Stephen asks if we have to go to town, can't we stay and read instead? And Ariel says that yes she would like us all to go and she explains about the task. She says we have to follow someone and make notes on what they do or say and then write it up for Monday's workshop. It sounds like a laugh and everyone starts buzzing about the idea.

I go to the nearest bog and finally listen to the message my mum left and it's fucking bad news. She's not screeching now. In fact she sounds proper up. Three glasses of white wine up, I reckon.

'Mistyann? Mistyann? Fucking hell. It's your mum. I've sent a text. We saw that Mrs English and she told us about your little trip to Wales. So we're coming to get you. Yeah, Ty came over last night.' She giggles now, which almost makes me vom if I'm honest. She sounds like a kid. Not a teenager, I mean an actual snot-nosed kid.

'And anyway, he said that he wouldn't mind a trip to Wales.' There's a muffled sound in the background which I reckon is Ty fucking sticking his beak in. 'He says it'll give him a chance to run in his new motor. It's an Audi Quattro. And test out the Tom Tom. Anyway, we're leaving about eleven so we'll be there about four Ty reckons and we're going to bring you back home. No arguing.' There's more mumbling that I can't hear. 'We're bringing William and

Harry. This car's got DVDs in the back and everything so they'll be happy. Anyway, you just be ready when we get there. And you can tell that Mr Diamond that he's in the shit as well.'

This is proper bad fucking news. And my shoulders are well tight straight away. It feels like there's a metal bar right across the top of my back. The first thing I decide is that I'm not letting Ty and my mum drag me back home. No fucking way. Especially if Ty is back on the scene. What are they doing back together anyway? And then I think that maybe it was me nicking William's mobie that brought them together. So it's my own fault in a way.

Anyway. I think about the other options and there's only one. And for the first time I'm glad I nicked those twenties off Zak's desk cos I'm going to need cash. I didn't take them all. I mean he might not even notice for ages, but it still means I've only got £80 plus the fiver we are going to get for lunch. £85 doesn't get you anywhere.

I go to look for Zak but he's already gone which puts me in a right mood. In fact most people have gone. The only ones left are the girls who don't hardly speak and Pete who takes ages to get ready. Only one option again.

Pete and Kendra are in the kitchen arguing about how many layers he should wear.

'For fuck's sake, Kendra. I'll be sweating like a pig.'

She says, 'Well you won't be burning off as many calories as everyone else.'

And he says, 'And thanks for reminding me that I'm a cripple. Again.' And Kendra goes pink. You could feel proper sorry for her sometimes.

'Hey Pete,' I say. 'Do you want to come up the village with me?'

Now it's his turn to go pink and I think fucking hell, he fancies me. And Kendra sees and a big old black cloud zooms right across her face. She's got problems that girl.

Pete recovers well. 'Yeah, It'll be a laugh. And it means that you can have a rest, Kendra. Have some time to yourself.'

There's some more pointless chat about whether she has to come with us. Health and Safety. Qualified staff—yada yada yada—but in the end Pete settles it.

'Kendra, for God's sake let me have a little bit of a life, okay? I mean what part of 'only a few weeks left to live' is so bloody difficult to understand?'

We don't talk as we go up the huge hill. The fact is, I can't. Pushing him up that hill is pure murder. I have to stop for a rest every five times. The snow isn't as bad now. It's starting to turn to muddy brown slush and in any case someone has been clearing the lane and put salt and grit and stuff down otherwise we would never make it. Even so I'm well smecked by the time we finally make the top and I'm sweating all over. I take my jumper and sweatshirt off so I'm just down to the Pink Ladies T-shirt which I got from my mum's drawer. I've always liked it. *Grease* is one of my favourite films. I've seen it about twelve times. They're always putting it on at school on the last day of term and stuff. And I've seen it about five times at sleepovers. Everyone loves *Grease*.

There's three kinds of girls in the world: Sandies, Frenchies and Rizzos. Every girl can divide their friends into these groups.

When we finally get to the top of the hill there's a vicious wind blowing and I have to stop to put all my clothes back on. My sweat is cooling down and I feel itchy. I'm wondering if I've done such a smart thing going to the village with Pete.

But it's miles easier at the top and by the time we've gone past the ruined church, I start to enjoy it. Me and my mates, we never walk anywhere. We get the bus if we're desperate, but there's usually some lad with a car who will take you where you need to go. Now though, I start to feel fresh and good. Our PE teachers are always going on and on about exercise providing feel-good endorphins and I reckon I can feel them buzzing around my blood. And maybe it's the endorphins that don't make it such of a downer when I ask Pete about when he found out about his illness.

He says, 'I just started banging into things. I was about four and I'd be bumping into people in the playground or tripping over the furniture at home. They thought it was my eyes, then my hearing and then I had tests and now here I am.'

He says about how every time he went to hospital it was the worst possible news. And I wonder how you deal with that. I mean, there you are thinking to yourself that it's going to be all right, that it's probably nothing, probably something they can sort out with an operation or pills and then you find out that it's not alright, it's something complicated and it doesn't matter how many pills you take or how many operations you have, eventually you'll be trapped in a chair, talking by blinking once for yes, twice for no. And then you can't even swallow or breathe on your own and your mum and dad have to decide when to turn off the machines that keep you alive. And you never even get proper started with life. It sucks.

It should make me feel better about my own problems, like my mum and Ty coming to fetch me. But it doesn't. It does make me feel more certain about not letting them fuck things up for me.

Then Pete asks me about my worst day. And I think about it. There have been tons of days when proper bad things have happened, but sometimes they haven't made me feel bad. And then sometimes there have been times when something small happens and it makes me feel pure shit for ages. And I say this to Pete and he agrees.

He says, 'Yeah. When my guinea pig, Blackie, died I was miles more upset than when they told me about the muscular dystrophy.'

And I think, yeah, I was more jarred off when Roy Keane left Man U than I was when Mum kicked Dad out.

And then I think about all the times when bad stuff happens and you can hardly remember later. And sometimes you do remember, but it's just funny. And I think about telling Pete about the time I smacked that old German teacher, but it's a long story and we're in the village now and I want to get out of the wind and have a bit of a sit down.

'Let's find a caff or something,' I say.

It's a bit stuck-up this village. I mean it's pretty and everything. It looks a bit like that village in Emmerdale. Stone houses. There are quite a few people about and most of them are dressed up like they're going for a posh meal or something. When I mention this to Pete he laughs.

'They're on their way back from Chapel, I think.'

And I'm amazed. Hardly anyone goes to church in Manton Heights. There's a Baptist church on Brickhill Drive but you only ever see old ladies going in and out.

There's nothing to do here. I think anyone young would go mad. It's not just that there's no Maccy D, but there's nothing at all. Actually we don't see anyone under forty so maybe it doesn't matter. The people we do see stare straight at us, like they've never seen a guy in a wheel-chair before, which is plain rude. And anywhere else doing that would be dangerous. You don't stare people in the face unless you're prepared to back it up.

The only café we can find that's open is in this museum. We have to pay £1.50 to go in even though we're just going into the café bit, but I'm feeling floss so I don't bother arguing. We are the only customers and it's got to be obvious that we aren't local. Still the waitress comes over and asks what we want in Welsh. I'm about to tell her to stop mucking about when Pete does something proper smart. Smart and surprising. He answers her in Welsh. And then she says something back to him and he says something back to that and they both smile and the waitress goes off again. I watch her for a moment. I watch the back of her as she moves around the tables. She's a big woman and she reminds me of when you're in a car in the country and you get stuck behind a tractor. She looks like she does everything pure slow.

'What was that all about?' I say. 'You're not Welsh.'

'No, but I thought I'd make the effort to learn a bit of the lingo.'

And I like that. Who says 'lingo'? It sounds cute.

He says, 'I get ignored enough as it is. You know when you're in a wheel-chair people either completely ignore you or they make a huge effort to give you all their attention. You know, like they're waving a sign 'look everyone, I'm not ignoring the cripple. I'm a good person'. I thought if I spoke the language a bit then they might treat me a bit more normal. It's bloody hard though. Some words are all vowels and other words are all consonants.'

'So what did you actually say?'

'I said, 'Hello. Good morning. Could we have two cups of tea and two scones please?' I hope you like scones. And then she said, 'Jam on your scones?' I think and I said 'yes please.' I hope that's okay.'

Well I don't really drink tea or eat scones and if I did I wouldn't have jam on them but I don't want to piss on Pete's chips.

'Yeah, fine. Whatever.' I say. And his face sort of falls.

When the waitress comes back her big red apple face is smiling and the scones are huge. They're like footballs. So it was probably a good call, the whole speaking Welsh bit. The tea's not the best. It's dark like soup but I put four teaspoons of sugar in it and it's drinkable after that.

Me and Pete talk about the course and we talk about football and then we talk about Zak. He comes up because Pete is talking about all the waste he sees. He says, 'I see blokes like him and I get really mad. You know he can do anything and he just fucks around.' And I think about Zak playing guitar and singing and I think that he doesn't waste time, not really, but Pete's got a thing about it.

'When I was younger it was sort of easy to make the best of things. Getting a new wheel-chair or going for physiotherapy or going to Disneyland. You just accept stuff as a kid, don't you?'

'You've been to Disneyland?' I say. 'What's it like?'

He shrugs. 'Okay. Gets a bit boring after the third time.'

'You've been three times?'

'Four. If you're a spastic you're always being offered trips to Disneyland. Especially if you're a spastic who's going to die young. I reckon if it wasn't for the spazzes Disney would go bust.'

He's quite funny, Pete. Sitting in that café, I look at him properly for the first time. I know that we had to do that getting to know you exercise together but I hadn't really looked at him. He's looking down at his tea and his scone and he has this proper thin face. His cheek bones stand out like cliff-tops. He has this very pale skin with black hair that is gelled so that some of it falls forward and some of it stands straight up. It's kind of carefully messy. It looks like Zak's hair in fact. He has very bony shoulders and I realise that he only really uses one arm, so it isn't just his legs that are affected. He has crazy full-on lips. In fact he has a proper pretty face. It's almost like a girls face. An anorexic girl's face.

'Actually, I'm not a spastic.'

'No?' I say

'No, I'm a Scopie. That's what they call us since the Spastic Society changed its name to Scope. Kids like me, we're Scopies.'

172

I don't know what to say to this but I guess he doesn't care if I don't say anything.

'I'm not scared of dying you know,' he says suddenly. 'I mean that might be a real adventure. Disneyland—that's just a big kid's playground really but it taught me some things about life. It taught me that everyone, even people who are normal, spend their lives in queues waiting for twenty seconds of adventure. They have that and move off to join another queue.'

I don't really get what he means and I make him try and explain it a bit more.

He says, 'My dad goes to work in an office and that's a kind of queue so that he can have a nice house. But the house has got a mortgage so that's twenty-five years more queuing before he can enjoy it properly. We go on a family holiday once a year. We always go to La Rochelle in France. We rent this specially adapted bungalow. It's okay there but my dad and mum save all year to pay for it. That's fifty weeks queuing for two week's fun. And Christmas. Everyone loves Christmas and everyone goes mad with the credit cards and then spends the rest of the year paying it off. More queuing. Do you see?'

He looks up and his eyes look just amazing. A proper clear blue like you get on the best winter days and the whites round them are pure like snow when it's just fallen and he stares right at me.

'Yeah,' I say, 'I get it. I totally get it.'

And I do get it. And I think I'm not going to be doing any queuing. Ever.

And then he says, 'At least as a spaz you don't do much queuing. We're front of the queue every time.'

And I can see that he might not be frightened of dying, but he is fucking angry about it.

We buy more tea and sit quiet for a while. And then I tell him about my plan. This means that I have to tell him about Mum and Ty and William and Harry and everything so it takes quite a long time and I'm not used to talking about it. I try and make it funny and interesting and I can do that. I always get A-stars in my Speaking and Listening coursework.

Pete doesn't laugh much but he doesn't look bored either. He sits there staring at me and his eyes sort of shine.

When I finish he says, 'Mistyann, why don't you have my debit card?' And I think that he's sorry for me. There he is in his wheel-chair knowing that someday soon he's going to die and everyone else will go on and get jobs and have kids and forget all about him and he's sorry for me.

He carries on, 'Go on. I'm loaded. Got a trust fund. Got lottery grants. Got shit-loads of money from relatives. Everyone round where I live is out doing sponsored walks and shit for me all the time.'

And he scrabbles around in this bum-bag thing that he holds in his lap and pulls out a wallet. It's leather and black. It's a proper quality wallet. And then he takes out a card. It's also black so you know it's worth a lot. It's funny—all the cheap crap cards are gold. Even the cards they give school-kids are gold. The good ones are black.

'Here you go,' he says. 'The pin number is 1.9.6.1.'

'The year Spurs won the double,' I say.

'That's right,' he says, pleased. 'See, I knew I was right to give it to you. There's over four grand in that account. Plus my signature is really easy to forge. Look.' And he shows me. It's like a little kid's scribble. It's just a P and an M all muddled together like the letters have been stirred together with a stick. Harry could do better.

'Poor muscle control,' he says, almost like he's boasting.

I take the card. It will pure help and he pure wants to give it to me.

'Pete,' I say, 'I'll never be able to give you any of this money back. You know that, don't you?'

'You can't take it with you,' he says and he smiles. He really has got a pure dutzi smile and I can see the other

Pete, the Pete there would have been without the muscular dystrophy. He might have been it.

'I owe you. Big time,' I say.

'Oh forget about it. Just give me a hand job or something next time you see me.'

And it's a crap thing to say and it jars me off for a minute and I look at him and I see that he just said it because he is shy about how grateful I am. He's just kind of trying to flirt and it's no surprise he's shit at it, he's had no practice. And lots of lads are shit at it even when they've had loads of practice.

I stand up and go out towards the museum proper. I'm following the sign that says toilets and find what I'm looking for pretty quickly. So I go and have a quick word with the waitress who gives me what I want with a sad little smile. Then I walk back to our table and go behind Pete's wheel-chair. I put my hands on it.

'You should get an electric one,' I say.

'I've got one. Top of the range. German. But they said it wouldn't cope with these hills. Anyway, Kendra could use the exercise. Where are we going?'

'Ssh,' I say and begin to push him.

The museum has three toilets. Men, women and disabled. I knew it would have, being a public building and everything. I put the key in the lock of the disabled one. Pete blushes. It's quite cute. I decide that I quite like taking charge. I have a sudden memory of the warmth of Zak's cock through his sweat-pants last night. It feels like a million years ago.

'What are you doing?' He whispers it.

'I told the waitress that I was your carer and that you needed to go to the bog.'

He doesn't say anything.

The toilet is the cleanest one I've ever seen. It smells a bit chemical but it's all white tiles; floor, walls and ceiling

175

and everything is really shiny. I feel a bit like a nurse as I wash my hands proper thorough.

Pete still doesn't say anything even when I tug at his trousers, but he does sort of raise his bum off the seat of the wheel-chair to make things a bit easier. I ask him if he can still feel things and he says that yes, his problem is with his muscles not with his nerves.

My hands are all soapy when I first touch him. I want to make sure that he is proper clean so I soap him all over. He's really big, or maybe it just looks that way because the top of his legs are so skinny and shrunken.

'You're circumcised,' I say and then I feel a bit stupid.

Pete just smiles and says, 'Well spotted, Sherlock.'

And the mood changes. It doesn't seem so heavy or serious, so I'm glad I said it.

I had thought that he would cum proper quick but it seems to take ages. I don't really want to suck him off, but I'm getting worried about the waitress knocking on the door and asking if we're alright, so I'm just about to go down on him when I feel his cock jump and there's spunk on my T shirt, dots of it like when you spill bleach, and then hot all over my hand.

We're quiet for a moment and I can hear his breathing.

'Can't get that kind of care from the NHS,' he says.

'Would you want it from Kendra?' I say and then I feel bad because Kendra does all the worst jobs and Pete is proper mean to her.

'Oh, Kendra's alright,' he says, 'She just fusses.'

And suddenly we're having a normal conversation again and it's easy to pull up his trousers and it feels just like we've been doing something really ordinary.

William's stupid phone bleeps. It's a message from Mum. STAYING OVERNIGHT IN SHREWSBURY STILL COMING 4 U 2 MORROW DON'T WORY And this is fantastic news. It means I have loads more time than I thought and, with Pete's card, I'm proper candied.

I bet the car's broken down. Knowing Ty he will have gone for the flashiest, shiniest motor at the auction and bought some heap of crap.

On the way out of the café the waitress gives us that sad little smile again which jars me right off and I feel a sudden tightness in my shoulders. I make a special effort to breathe like Michaela always tells me.

We spend the next hour or so wandering around the village playing the zap game. This is something I used to do with my dad when I was little. Basically you go out for a walk and are allowed five zaps. If you see a thing you want real bad like a particular car or a house or something then you say 'I zap that house/car/tree' or whatever but you've got to be careful because it's proper sickening when you've used up your zaps and then the perfect thing appears round the corner and someone else sees it and gets it.

I play at home with William and Harry sometimes but they always zap the same things. William ends up with five 4x4s and Harry zaps dogs.

Pete loves the zap game. He makes me stop every few metres so he can decide whether something is zapable or not. Once it's an old fashioned Herbie car. Once it's a strange black wooden house that stands in the main street on its own. It looks old from a distance but close up you can see it's pure modern. It still has the builders sign outside. An exclusive, individually designed eco-house.

He spends ages outside that. It looks proper sweet to me. The thing I like most about it is that there are all ordinary houses around it. Houses like the Lego ones that William builds. Square with four windows and a door facing out at you. Boring. This black house is really thin and really tall with these small windows. It's like a house in a fairy story, but it's proper new. I decide I like that in a house. To be new and old at the same time.

Pete takes such a long time looking at it that in the end I zap it. He moans but I just tell him to make his mind up faster. As we walk on Pete doesn't look like he's going to zap anything. I tell him that when we're back at Cefn Coch he'll lose all his zaps

He just says, 'There's clearly nothing I want badly enough.'

But on the way back he zaps the museum and the café and we argue about whether that counts as one zap or two.

'Why do you want it anyway?' I say, but he doesn't answer. And then I think I know why and I feel my face go hot, so I don't say anything for a while either.

In the quiet I think about what I wrote about my funeral. I remember writing all about the flowers and my mum making a scene—probably by yelling at my dad. And I make everyone laugh when I write about how William will be trying to play some game on his PSP while the vicar goes on about my lively personality and unique outlook on life. But I think now that it was all crap. Because at my real funeral no-one will know about me as I am now. There'll be no-one who remembers me as that mad girl from Bedford.

Who I am now isn't the real me.

I'm not sure who I am but I'm going to do like Ariel said. I'm going to find out who I am. Then I'm going to become that person. And when I've done that, then I might not mind dying.

TWENTY-SEVEN

So there I was, an hour or so later, sweating slightly as I struggled out of Ray's duffle coat and feeling the blood fight its way inch by agonizing inch back into my feet. I hadn't fancied waddling to and fro and around the village in a pair of over-sized gumboots, so I was wearing brown Chelsea boots which, in Bedford High Street, are the height of footwear elegance for the GQ reading male. In Bedford they make you feel slightly like Bryan Ferry. In Llangow, however, they looked what they were: impractical and suspiciously effeminate. In Llangow they made you feel a lot like John Inman. You won't know about John Inman. He was a gay icon of 70s British TV. One of the many panto dames the BBC entertained us with back then.

I was in a pub. I was in the Telyn a Chan—The Harp and Song. I started going back to pubs when they grew up enough to serve coffee and food that was more than two slices of bread, a slice of rubber cheese and a small plastic tub of pickle. This pub, however, had yet to partake in the gastronomic, family friendly revolution. The way to the bar was across a minefield of strange sticky patches and also involved groping your way through a cinematic haze of cigarette smoke. Perhaps they were still using a different calendar round those parts because it was as if April 1 2007 had never happened. There was nothing passive about wading through that fag fug.

I'm a fan of smoking. If I ran a bar, a cinema, a theatre or a night-club it would be compulsory to smoke. Smoking is big and it is clever. It's like dry ice at a rock gig, it's an essential part of the atmosphere of any social space. I was thrilled to find a nicotine-friendly space that the Health and Safety Nazis hadn't been able to jackboot out of existence but I admit that this was something a bit too max strength even for me. I could feel the tar attaching itself to the fertile plains of my lungs before I even reached ogling distance of the absurdly generous décolletage of the landlady.

I have always found the noise of wide screen tellies, fruit machines and adult orientated rock far more polluting than nicotine. One of the fieriest levels of Hell will surely be a 'family friendly' fun pub where a cinema sized wall-mounted plasma screen babbles hysterically about football, while Bon Jovi's 'Living On A Prayer' plays on repeat.

Naturally they didn't serve coffee or tea in the Telyn a Chan—'Too much faff, sorry'—so I ordered a ginger beer.

The pub was a traditional Welsh boozer in every respect. It felt like drinking in a museum. Four old boys in trilbies and battered suit jackets supped pints of mahogany brown Brains bitter. They looked like they hadn't moved since 1944. The Elvish hum of their desultory Welsh provided most of the background noise; with the irregular clack of pool balls from a room I couldn't see providing the rest.

I'd been in a reverie for ten minutes, watching smoke waltz in the sunlight that was not so much weak as exhausted by the struggle to get through the grimy crust of the windows. Then I saw her, her broad black back at the bar. Boudicca. It was only the day before yesterday that we met and already it felt like another life. Was my ghost with her in the back room losing at pool? He wouldn't be winning. I was sure that Boudicca would take losing very badly indeed.

Boudicca ordered Stella with an agile laughing Welsh and was answered with a quick fire retort that had both her and the landlady quivering with mirth. No dilettante, stumbling incomer traveller crustie Welsh this. This was the real deal. The language of Arthur and Owen Glyndwr, refashioned in bible-black by the chapel. The language that the Victorian English couldn't quite birch out of the population a hundred odd years ago, which is now protected in its reservation by EU statute.

Boudicca and the landlady continued a sprightly kind of conversational table tennis across the bar. Every now and again the Tolkeinesque polysyllables were cracked open by ordinary English words crashing their way into sentences like stones through a window. Noticeable among the Celtic music were the words 'Parcelforce', 'EBay', 'Google', 'bubble-wrap' and 'sellotape'. All of which vandalised the prehistoric poetry of the Druidic tongue more than once and which lead me to deduce that among the subjects being covered was the joy of buying stuff over the interweb rather than having to go into an actual shop.

I smiled to myself. Somewhere, I was sure, the founding fathers of Plaid Cymru were restless in their graves. Is this what they had been fighting for? The freedom to buy and sell old tat in the language of the bardic heroes?

When Boudicca turned, pint in hand, she clocked me straight away. She stopped and gave me a frank stare. From the subtle sway of her, like she was dancing to distant music only she could hear, I guessed that this was maybe the third or fourth pint that day. She came to a decision and strode over, calling over her shoulder to the landlady as she did so.

Seconds later I was drenched by toxic Belgian fizz. Too stunned to do more than gulp like a landed guppy through the fringe that was now plastered to my forehead, I just sat there while Boudicca delivered a verdict upon me more damning, more lucid and more eloquent than any magistrate or pontificating local journalist has so far managed.

The gist of her speech was that I was an ungallant cad. Not only this but I was a smug hypocrite who had the effrontery to look down my nose at her and her young lover while clearly entertaining thoughts of an indecent nature about the youthful female that I had been escorting on the train. She expressed plainly her doubts concerning my virility and ability to maintain erectile function. She maintained that if I were ever able to achieve sexual congress with anyone, no doubt the process would be Hobbsian for my unfortunate partner. In other words, nasty, brutish and short, much like my member itself. She reminded me that I was English and should endeavour to return to my country at the earliest possible opportunity. In fact her parting shot was, 'Fuck off back to fucking England you fucking patronizing English fucking cunt.'

So Boudicca was bilingual. Equally at home in Welsh or Anglo-Saxon. Her biggest complaint seemed to be that I had, in her hearing, referred to Wales as a 'cartoon country'.

She returned briefly to the bar where she picked up the new pint her friend had poured. The significance of the shouted sentence before her assault becoming clear. Forward planning. Having taken possession of a brimming glass of premium lager, she made the landlady laugh with a quip in her native tongue before passing me, head in the air, on her way to do further battle in the pool room.

Even through my dampness and humiliation I could see that she looked magnificent. She looked like that new double-decker jumbo jet that's been all over the news recently. She looked like she could fill the sky.

I headed for the gents. We've all of us, have we not, spent moments of quiet repentance in the toilet? Sitting on the lav or lying clutching the bowl amongst the piss and filth, we've all made vows to change some aspect of our behaviour; to work on some personality flaw. And so it was that I was looking in the dark, truthful mirror wondering if I *was* a smug hypocrite. Maybe I had allowed my surface to harden. Maybe Boudicca was right. Maybe, in fact, I deserved a lot worse than a baptism of Stella.

I emerged from the bogs invigorated, purged even. A new, less complacent, less detached Jonathan Diamond had been born. Boudicca had, in the finest traditions of rural Wales, become my Baptist lay preacher. I should thank her. Buy her a drink, if she'd accept one.

I re-entered the bar to a ripple of applause. Clearly I had made the day of the pickled Trilbies. I gave an ironic bow, which went down very well. The new Diamond was already beginning to connect. I made my way to the pool room. Boudicca was bent over the pool table stretching for her shot; one leg straight, supporting her while the other was bent up on the table. For a big woman she was clearly very flexible. Everything about her that I could see, her buttocks, back, shoulders neck was taut and clenched. She had the pure stillness of distilled concentration.

At the side of the room, leaning on his pool cue, was a short, butternut coloured man who was entirely circular. He looked like Benny the Ball from *The Top Cat* series. And you say it's not a cartoon country, I thought. Benny smiled at me revealing a mouth completely *sans* teeth. Just another small black circle within the beige circle of his face.

Boudicca's shot rifled towards the pocket and I noticed that her opponent had all seven of his balls still on the table. He grinned and gurgled something at Boudicca who laughed easily back.

'Fancy a game?' I said.

Boudicca turned, frowned and gave me a stern look; not dissimilar to the one I see on the face of Maggie the Magistrate.

The heat of the place had led me to take off my jumper as well as my coat so it was only my head, neck and T-shirt that had taken the lager deluge. My head and neck I had dried, albeit inefficiently, in the gents using a combination of crunchy green paper towels and a wall mounted hand dryer that blew a ferocious cyclone of scalding air. My T-shirt I had wrung out over the single tiny cracked sink.

Despite my efforts I was aware that I was still sticky and clammy and carrying with me that pungent industrial perfume of Belgium's gift to world culture.

'Okay,' she said at last. 'Rack them up then but don't drip on the pool table mind.'

TWENTY-EIGHT

I'm not on cooking duty, but Charlotte is so I know I'll get some peace in my room. It's weird how we never saw anyone from our group in town but then we went to a museum and one thing I know is: if you want to stay hidden go to a library or a museum. In Bedford I go to the library a lot. Not the central one. I go to the one that looks like a Lego castle past the station and near the river. There's never anyone I know there. It's full of people just reading and thinking. Nothing bad ever happens there.

I need to think.

I've got money so I've got options. I phone the National Rail Enquiries help line which makes my shoulders go all tight again. Where do they find the people who work in call centres? Do they go round every school asking for the names of the special needs kids for a massive data base to offer them a job the minute they are kicked out of school?

Anyway. Eventually the mong on the other end discovers that there are fuck all trains from here. And what are the chances of hitching on a rainy Sunday night?

It's very fucked up.

I've got a card worth 4K and I'm still stuck. The plan looks shit. I don't know what to do. It would be good to talk to someone but JD is not back from the village and can I trust him? End of the day, he's still a teacher and all that.

In the end I go to the desk in our room. There's a stupid notebook on it with a big picture of a daisy on the cover. I open it and flick through. I already know what it is. It's so obvious. Charlotte's diary, isn't it? And it's as pathetic as you'd expect. Me and Angus; Me and Kerry; Me and Jessica. It's boring. Charlotte's life: she goes shopping with her mates and sends texts to lads. There's bits which she has written in a kind of code. She uses sort of foreign words— Spanish or Italian or something—I guess these are the bits where she has sex or something. I reckon it would take me a minute to find out exactly what those bits say. But I can't be arsed. She's so obviously left her diary out on purpose. She wants me to be impressed or something. So after about ten minutes flicking through it I put it on her bed. I tear a page out of the back and write a note which I leave with it.

I write: 'Charlie darling, you left this out. I haven't read it. Don't worry.' And I sign it M with a big X. And I know that will jar her big style because it's pure fucking obvious that she's desperate for me to read it.

The only thing that's interesting about Charlotte's diary is that at the bottom of each page she writes a little list. It goes Monday April 8 and then a page of crap about shopping and stuff and at the bottom this list which goes half a Weetabix, two cups of chamomile tea, one and a half digestives. Cup-a-soup, crispbread and marmite, no butter. That makes me feel sorry for her. I tried to be anorexic once, but it's proper hard work. Who can be bothered? Respect is due. So in the end I rip up my mean note.

After that I get out my note-pad and I write about the waitress in the museum restaurant. That was the task we were given and something makes me want to do it. I proper get into it and end up doing a drawing of her as well. I don't just describe her. I try and imagine what her house is like and her fat, lazy husband and kids who are nearly grown up but don't want to leave home, but moan all the time about living in a village where's there's nothing to do.

And then the gong goes and I go down to dinner. I still haven't thought about how to sort out my plan but I feel a bit better now and think that something will turn up.

I'm not looking forward to dinner. I don't want to see Zak. I don't want to see Pete. I don't want to see Julius. And I don't want to see Charlotte. I can't be bothered with them. JD's not around. I ask Amber about him. She says she's no idea and it's pure obvious that she doesn't give a shit. And then she turns back to Zak who looks at me for a proper long time before pretending to listen to whatever crap she's going on about.

I've got Ariel on the other side of me and when I turn away from Amber I find she's staring at me too. I feel my face getting hot. Ariel's pure like some kind of white witch. It's like she can see inside your head. She's like a scientist. You can imagine her picking up each of your most secret thoughts and turning it over in her hands, which will be in those plastic gloves that they have in hospitals, and she'll be saying 'Hmm interesting'. She's like an alien. Scary.

I start to chat to Ariel about going into town with Pete and about the waitress and everything, but I'm talking too fast so I just stop. I'm sitting there thinking that she's going to think that I'm well weird.

There's a bit of a silence and Ray suddenly says, 'A toast to the cooks! Another fine repast!'

And we all drink blackcurrant squash and clap. I haven't noticed the food. It's some kind of sausage stew thing with mashed potatoes and broccoli. It's alright. Nothing special. And Ariel looks down at her plate, then turns to me, smiling.

'I was a vegan once upon a time. For seven years. Can you believe that?'

And I ask why, and she goes, 'Oh, the usual reason, I guess. My boyfriend was.'

And I ask if she has a boyfriend now and she laughs.

'Hell no, honey, I don't have the time for that.'

And I ask why she broke up with the vegan and she says, 'Well I guess that one day I woke up and I wanted a steak real bad. And he couldn't deal with it. That's the kind of guy he was. You weren't allowed to fail.'

'You really split up over a steak?'

'Well. I guess it was about me not wanting to be controlled by him. I said I fancied a steak. He got mad. So I got mad too. I thought 'screw you, buster' I'm having a 10oz steak with fries, the works, you know? And so I did. I

186

went to this real sleazy diner downtown and got myself one. Except that once I'd bought it I didn't want it anymore. I took one little bite and pushed my plate away. But it showed me that Leonard wasn't the one. He was cute though.'

'It's funny isn't it?' I say.

'What?'

'That your first boyfriend was a vegan. And then you married a guy called Hamburger.' Ariel laughs then and I feel like laughing too.

'Bless you, Mistyann, I've never thought of that before. I guess I must really have hated Lennie, huh?' And she laughs again. It looks like I've made her day and I feel warm ripples start in my tummy. I love it when I make people laugh. Love it.

Amber says, 'Don't you want a partner though?'

And Ariel says, 'Well, I'm thirty-three years old so I guess the old biological clock will kick in some time soon, but it hasn't so far, touch wood.' And she taps the table at the side of her plate. 'Besides there's too much to do and too much to see first.'

Thirty-three. That means that Ariel is the same age as Mum. I try to imagine them sat side by side at school. I imagine what my mum and her mates would have said about her. Or maybe Ariel would have been different. Maybe if she'd been at Pilgrim Upper when my mum was there, then she'd have had a kid my age by now. She's not thick my mum. You don't want to get in a row with her. She can destroy you in a row. She's vicious. She doesn't care what she says.

Some nights she gets together with a couple of her old school mates and I sit upstairs and I can hear them screaming and hooting and going ape about stuff that happened about a million years ago when they were at school. It's all blokes and fights and stuff. And they say 'it was all different then' and it seems like it was pretty much the same, only without computers. And computers are crap anyway. Mum and her mates do internet dating sometimes. It's always a fucking disaster. The bloke is always married, which is normal I suppose, but what's worse is that he's usually some speccy geek who has been trying to pretend that he's like a billionaire with a Porsche and stuff.

The other thing my mum and her mates do sometimes is dress up in their old school uniforms, tits and bellies bursting out all over, and they go to this club night at Esquires called Last Night of Term where they dance to cheesy nineties music. But it's crap isn't it? I mean no-one ever wears their school clothes to a disco, do they? I say this to my mum when her and her mates are getting ready and she stands up really shaky and puts on this floss voice and says, 'Goodness, Mistyann, don't be so literal minded.' Like she's a teacher or something. And then she falls over and everyone's laughing. They nearly piss themselves. They've all had about five WKDs but even so it's not that bloody funny.

Some mornings after Last Night of Term I come down in the morning and my mum is lying on the sofa wearing her white shirt and her mini skirt and her stockings and she still has her old blue and yellow Pilgrim Upper School tie wrapped round her neck and she's snoring and stinks of fags and alcohol and farts and I think that she could be my sister. But your mum should be a mum, not a frigging sister. When I have kids I'm not going to be their sister or their friend.

After dinner I have to wash up, which I think I'm going to hate, but which is a laugh really. Ray tries to get everyone organized but we ignore him and it's funny to watch him try not to show that he's annoyed. Zak's funny because he was so good at cooking and cutting up chickens and that, but he's pure scared of putting his hands into dirty water. He makes this joke about wanting to keep his beautiful hands soft but I can see that he hates putting his hands in the water for real. He makes a big fuss about having to have a pair of marigolds on. Marigolds turn out to be these big rubber gloves that are bright yellow.

Amber says to him, 'Hey, that's well sexy. I do like to see a man with his hands in the sink. Turns me on.' And she puts this funny, deep, husky voice on.

She can't see Zak sort of roll his eyes and make this face like he's going to puke. But I do and it makes me laugh.

She does nothing to help either. I bet her boyfriend does all the washing up and all the cooking and all the cleaning in her house. I feel sorry for him. I hope that he's gone out and got lushed up and got off with someone while she's been away. It would serve her right.

When we've done the dishes all the others start talking about playing some dumb ass game so I go outside into the secret garden to look at the snow heads.

It's been raining quite a lot today so they've kind of shrunk. They're not just smaller, they're all sort of twisted too. They looked crippled. Monged. And they're dirty. Not white like they were yesterday, more a kind of skanky grey. It makes me feel sad about how quick everything gets fucked up and dies. But it also makes me think that nothing ever really matters, does it?

There's a swishing sound behind me. Kendra. Looking like her gran's just died. As ever.

'Hiya,' I say, trying to be friendly.

'Did you have a nice time with Pete today?'

'Yeah, it was easy thanks.'

'Because he can be a bit difficult.'

'He was a laugh. We went to the museum.'

Kendra sort of grunts. She's letting me know that the Pete she knows wouldn't be seen dead in a museum. Just for a second I feel like telling her that I jerked him off in the disabled bogs. But I don't.

We stand looking at the snow heads for a bit.

'I better go in,' she says, 'See if he needs me.' And I think: just leave him alone you mook.

When I get back to the house I find that there's a bit of a party atmosphere. Amber, Charlotte, Dalwinder, Julius, Stephen and Julie are at the big kitchen table playing Trivial Pursuit. I don't do board games, no-one I know does, but I watch for a while. I didn't realize how loud you could be, playing games like this. They all look happy. They look like one of those families you see on adverts. Everyone is pure good at it. The only person who gets any questions wrong is Amber, which is quite funny seeing as she's the teacher. She giggles every time she messes up.

In the end Stephen says, 'You know, I think professional people who are happy to remain ignorant should be sent to Guantanamo.'

And Dalwinder says, 'Yeah, Amber, which university was it you went to again?'

But Amber just laughs. She's got a big old glass of red wine and her eyes are sort of sparkly. She looks like she's having a pure easy time. Or that she's about to cry. It's hard to tell the difference.

JD's still not around so I think I'd like to talk to Zak. I'd like to talk to him about my plan, see if has any ideas. And to just see what he says, but I can't because he is in the sitting room with Pete. Pete is on the big green sofa and it looks well weird to see him out of his wheelchair. In his tight black jeans his legs are all twigletty. His top half looks much too big for him. He looks like he's going to topple over. In his chair he looked sort of normal in a way. Out of it, he looks like a freak.

Sitting in Pete's wheelchair and using it like it was a BMX bike or a skateboard or something, is Zak. He's doing wheelies and spins and racing around the room like it's a rally course. Pete's just laughing.

He says, 'Go for it, mate.'

And I can't decide which of them is the bigger twat; Zak for messing around with a wheelchair or Pete for letting him. But that's what lads are like. Anna's in there too and she's doing the oddest thing of all: she's knitting. It's the truth. I've never seen anyone knit before in real life. Even my gran doesn't knit. Anna says she's doing a jumper for her little nephew. He's eighteen months, just starting to walk and talk, she says. Mum says that I started to walk at nine months. Walked from the ironing board to the TV and turned it off.

'And I was watching it. It was *Blind Date*.' Mum loves to tell that story. But I don't tell Anna that her nephew might be a bit slow. A bit special needs.

After a while I go up to Zak's room and just wait outside. It's nearly ten o clock now so he's going to be here soon. I've only been there five minutes when I hear footsteps. But it isn't Zak. It's Ray. He looks proper nervous and confused. He is a complete hole. He's losing his hair at the front but he still tries to spike it up in a punky style. He looks like a Muppet. Really. Like one of the Muppets. Beaker or someone.

He says, 'We don't really encourage the girls to go to the boys rooms.'

I have an idea. I don't answer him but I say, 'When's your birthday, Ray?' He looks confused. I say, 'I'm really into astrology. Star signs and that. I'm trying to work out everyone's horoscope for the week.'

He says, 'Er, I'm a Pisces.'

I'm not sure which that one is, but it doesn't matter.

I say, 'No. I need your actual date of birth. To do it properly.'

I can see him hesitate. He doesn't want me to know how old he is. But he goes with it in the end. 'Er twenty-seventh of February nineteen sixty-nine.'

'Thank you,' I say, proper cheerful. And he dithers for a little while like he is going to say something else, but he doesn't. He just nods and walks on past.

It's another twenty minutes before Zak comes to his room. I spend them thinking about my plan. Working out the details. Of course I might not even get started. There's only a small chance of the first bit working and if that doesn't work, then the rest is fucked. But I can't worry about that.

Zak's gone off me. You don't need to be gifted to work that one out. As soon as he sees me sat outside his door it's like he switches off. He lets me into his room, but he doesn't look at me properly. I try to ask him about what he saw in the village.

He just says, 'We went to the old church again and then went the other way, away from the village.' I ask him what he saw there. 'Fuck all,' he says. 'Sheep, a farm, a guy on a tractor.' I want to ask him who he went with but I can't. I know anyway.

'Charlotte's a snobby bitch isn't she?' I say. He laughs then, which is a good sign. 'Yeah, she is,' he says, 'And a bit thick too.'

'Nice tits though,' I say. Which makes him laugh again.

'You noticed that?'

'Hard to miss seeing as she's shoving them in my face all the time in our room.'

'Really?' he says. He sounds interested now. Lads are so fucking obvious.

'What did you talk about?' I say.

'Not much. Her school. Her family. Her life generally. She's a bit messed up.'

And I think: everyone's messed up. If you're not messed up, you're not human. You're not even alive. There's a silence after that. I think about talking about my plan but I can tell that he wants me to go. He's embarrassed about us having sex. He's decided that I'm not his type or something.

192

Decided that he could do better. Well, fuck him then. I just wish I'd taken more of his cash. I'm sitting on his bed, he's sitting on the chair next to it. I can see that all the cash is still out, all muddled up with the books and papers and shit. He's so fucking floss he hasn't even bothered to pick it up. He's like William. Just a spoilt brat. But I don't want to be jarred with him. Don't want to remember him as just another wanky boy.

I say, 'Play that song again.'

'What?' he says. He looks amazed. Scared even.

'That song. You know the one with the strange words.'

'Solid air?'

'Yeah, that one.'

And he goes over to the corner of the room and picks up his guitar and takes it back to the chair. He fiddles about with it a bit and then he plays. I close my eyes and remember him playing last night. I remember him playing that other song naked. I remember the feel of him as he went inside me. It makes me warm in my tummy.

I open my eyes to look at him and he's totally into it. He's got his eyes shut too and his hair flops down over his face. He'll never be lonely, I think.

I clap when he finishes, but it sounds pathetic. Stupid. One person clapping. It sounds sarcastic somehow.

So I say, 'That was brilliant. Fan-fucking-tastic.' But he just looks uncomfortable, so I say, 'Better go. Don't want Charlotte Super-tits to worry.'

Zak tries to kiss my cheek on the way out, but I'm not having that bollocks, so I just sort of duck under him and say, 'Bye then.'

He says, 'See you in the morning, Mistyann.'

My eyes are all filled with tears as I walk down that stupid corridor, which kills me. What the fuck am I crying for? I never cry.

TWENTY-NINE

There was a good buzz about the house when I got back, which wasn't till nearly ten. Yes, I felt guilty that I had deserted my post for so long but Amber, Ariel, Ray and Susie were all around. Like the guru herself had said, more than enough adults for nine fifteen-year-olds, however gifted. And it was half term for God's sake. And if Amber wanted to go off to Zorro's—Llangow's very own club—the following night, then I'd cover for her.

I was ridiculously cheerful, though my teeth ached a bit from the ginger beer. I must have had seven glasses of the stuff. It had been a fine night. Surreal, but I thought then that most of us didn't get enough strangeness in our lives.

I played Boudicca—who was christened Caitlin—five times at pool. She won the series 3-2 but I eased off in the final game. In my experience of playing women it's best to let them win if you can do it without looking patronizing. Boudicca was an okay player, but I was better and sober and it was easy to make it look like she'd squeaked it on the final black. It put her in a very good mood.

That last ball had just gone down when in walked my alter-ego, making me shiver. A confusion that lasted a good minute or so. With him was a plump, short, bald man about my age whose black NHS specs contrasted starkly with his pale complexion. He eyed me warily.

'Jon,' Boudicca boomed, after kissing both the newcomers, 'Let me introduce you to the two loves of my life. My lovely Welshman Derec and my English rose, Justin, the father of my child.' My ghost nodded but Derec scowled and headed off to the bar. I raised an eyebrow at Boudicca who met my gaze placidly.

'It's a lot less interesting than it looks,' she said at last.

It turned out that Derec and Boudicca had been a couple for years. He was a tattooist by trade whose passion was for the mandolin. They also ran a Welsh language poetry press and edited a fanzine devoted to Welsh punk. They organized music festivals and poetry events and got involved in various campaigns mostly to do with the Welsh language, but also the environment and animal rights. When money was especially tight Derec would tour the small towns and villages with his tattooing kit.

'And then I met Justin at an animal rights thing in Cardiff and fell in love all over again.'

'And Derec?' I was intrigued.

'I managed to fall in love with Justin without falling out of love with Derec. He's been brilliant. He did Justin's tattoos. And he's so good with Carmel. He's like an extra Dad. And what's really good about it is that he only ever speaks Welsh to her. That's really good for Carmel.'

'And you all live together?'

'We've got a big house on the edge of the village. Derec has the top floor. He has all his instruments and equipment, see.'

'And...?' I was aching to ask the obvious question.

'Your sex life is none of my business, Jon, and ours is private too. But it's just ordinary. Pretty suburban in fact.'

'But really, Derec doesn't mind?'

'He has more freedom now. He's always had the odd fling to be honest and now he doesn't have to feel guilty about it. And, yeah, I go up to the top floor every now and again.' She smiled. She had big strong square white teeth. If she was a horse there would be no shortage of buyers.

'I want to play some pool.' This was Justin who had clearly had enough of this discussion. I gave him a game. Thrashed him. Twice. Derec and Boudicca watched. I noticed that they hardly spoke, though whether their silence was companionable or hostile was hard to say.

My last frame of the evening was against Derec, who played a fiendishly defensive game full of safety shots and percentage plays. He was pretty much silent through the match too. Softly banging his cue on the ground in appreciation of a good shot. Or murmuring to himself before making one of his own cautious efforts.

He won and we shook hands and I spent another pleasant hour listening to the trio's plans for a weekly Welsh language comedy club in Llangow before walking back through the steady rain to Cefn Coch.

I made myself some FC—it would keep me awake but at least it would drive away the sugary residue of ginger beer.

You were waiting outside my door.

'Where have you been?' Your tone was hard, accusing. I was instantly annoyed. That would have been the guilt, I guess. I spilt some of the hot coffee over my hands.

'Fuck. Jesus. Look what you've made me do. I just went for a walk, Mistyann. Why? Did you miss me?'

'No. Yeah. Maybe.'

There was a pause during which Amber appeared on her way to her own room. You were silent, looking at the floor.

I said to Amber, 'Look, sorry about today. Can we have a chat tomorrow?'

Amber said, 'You, Jonathan Diamond, have fucked me right off and I'm never going to forgive you for going off enjoying yourself, leaving me in charge when you're meant to be the senior teacher. You're lucky that I don't make a formal complaint and get you sacked.'

Of course she didn't really.

What she actually said was, 'Don't worry about it. We managed.'

And she said it in a fake Northern accent which is the kind of thing women do when they are really pissed off but can't bring themselves to say so. She went into her room after looking you up and down in a way that was outrageously rude and, I guess, would have been very risky if you'd seen it.

You said, 'Can we go into your room? I need to talk to you. It's important.'

So then it all came out. The fact that you hadn't got permission for the course, that your family was coming up with the intention of taking you back to Bedford so that you could spend the rest of the week being the unpaid baby-sitter for your brothers and what was I going to do about it?

I said, 'I know exactly what I'm going to do, Mistyann.'

'What?'

'I'm going to have a cigarette.'

'Fucking top, thanks. That's helpful.'

'What I mean is that we need to think things through calmly and carefully without making any rash decisions. And having an unhurried fag will help with that process.'

'Well give us one then.'

So I checked that the shower cap was still secure over the smoke alarm and then we sat smoking in silence, thinking.

You wouldn't believe how much time I've spent thinking about your mum since then, Mistyann. Hers is the face I see in my worst dreams. Pinched and pale and scowling and looking like she wants a kitten to strangle. Though she is a master at dealing with the press. She's found her vocation now. Anyone wants a PR guru they could do a lot worse than use your mum.

It seems amazing now, when her face is as well known to me as my own mother's, that at Cefn Coch I actually had to struggle to conjure her up.

I had met her of course. Parents' evenings in Year 7 and 8. I remember a stick-thin blonde with restless eyes that flickered over my shoulder like she was expecting trouble from that direction. Nervy. Looked like she needed a fag and, sure enough, I saw her outside smoking as I finished my appointments and left. I remember smiling to myself because your mum looked like she needed a fag even when she had a fag. Younger than me—maybe ten years younger than me—she looked brittle and pointed. Everything about her was sharp. Except her walk. As she walked to my desk in the sports hall she moved with a careful, viscous sway that I recognized. The walk was liquid and spoke of more liquids that it would have to contend with later. It was the walk of a drunk.

I remember recounting a few of your choicer moments in that first year in high school.

'And what's Mistyann like at home?' I said

Your mum snapped back, 'She's a fucking nightmare.'

And suddenly there had not seemed much point talking about home-school contracts and Individual Education Plans and the rest of the apparatus we use to contain those who refuse to fit to the shapes we want.

The following year she was accompanied by a heavyweight black man who looked like a grid-iron footballer and whose laugh, which was employed easily and often, was the deepest rumble from the heart of his belly. She seemed softer and her walk less liquid. They made an attractive couple. The retiring sports star and his trophy wife. And they stood out amid the grey faces of the council accountants and various other middle management types that make up most of the parental intake at St Theresa's.

'I've noticed a marked improvement in Mistyann's application and, consequently, in her results this year. How is she at home now?'

Your mum held my eye. 'Oh, still a fucking nightmare.'

But she laughed, which was something. It was another short interview. What more was there to say?

She might be outside now. Smoking and staring. I've started getting terrible headaches. In the skull-crushing vice of a migraine it's easy to imagine your mum beaming voodoo from her spot in the Audi all the way into my brain. She feels like Nemesis now (another one to Google—the goddess who destroys the smug, basically), but back then she was just another problem to be solved. That used to be my mantra to students who whinged about coursework or exams. Do you remember?

'Life isn't meant to be easy,' I would say, 'Human beings are a problem solving species. We crave challenges.'

And it's true. When life is too easy people start making plans to sail across the Atlantic in a bath. We need life to be difficult otherwise we'd be sheep. Alcoholics, in particular, are in revolt against the ovine life. The self-destruction that goes with the alcoholic path makes for a challenging existence. Half the people you see in AA have been led there by boredom.

In the quiet of that study bedroom I had no idea what I was going to do about your mum. I suppose I was thinking that we might try to persuade her and the family into a B&B at the state's expense. My expense if it came to it. I was also counting on there being some residual authority in being a teacher and therefore 'knowing best'. If I could add to that some judicious flattery about how bright you were—with its implications about where these genes had come from—then perhaps I had the vague beginnings of a strategy.

And if she wasn't willing to be bought off in this way and insisted on taking you back, was that really so bad? You'd miss the rest of the course and that was a shame, but hardly devastating. It was clear that we needed back-up. We needed Ariel on side.

THIRTY

I'm waiting for Charlotte to go to sleep. The trouble is she's talking about lads and it's like her specialist subject. She can go on about them for hours and I don't have hours. She especially wants to give me some chat about Zak, which totally jars and makes my shoulders go tight.

'We got on really well today, you know. Don't you think he's really sensitive for a boy? And he is so goddamn hot!' which she says in a crap American accent and she generally talks shit like this for ages and doesn't seem to notice that I'm not talking. Not for the longest time anyway.

When she finally gets the message, she goes, 'Well, you're Miss Happy tonight aren't you? What happened? Julius not fancy you anymore?'

Which makes me want to tell her that I've sucked Zak's cock. I want to tell her that I've pulled him into me. That I've felt his spunk on my leg. That I made him need me even if was just for a little while. But I don't.

I just say, 'Charlotte, anyone ever tell you that you talk too much?'

She goes mad. She starts screeching, 'Everyone tells me that! I'm not having it. I'm not having you say it too. You can't say that! You can't!'

And she switches the light on next to her bed and she's sitting up and those perfect tits are heaving up and down under her T-shirt and her face is bright red. It's vivid red. That's the right word. She's vivid and livid like a lizard and I almost laugh out loud.

'Alright,' I say, 'I take it back. Don't sweat it. Take a chill pill.'

And she gives me the hairy eyeball for a second before she turns the light back off. And pretty soon I think she's asleep but she isn't because after a while she says, 'I do want us to be friends you know, Mistyann.'

And I say, 'Yeah,' and I'm going to say 'whatever' but I don't. Suddenly I don't feeling like being mean to Charlotte. So I say, 'Me too.'

Then she does go to sleep. And I know what I've got to do but I lie there and toss and turn and kind of put it off. In the end I get up and go into our en-suite and sit on the bog seat and read my book and I do actually get into it and time goes past and some time in the early morning I know I can't put it off any longer. I stumble back to my bed and pick up my bag and stop for a second to look at Charlotte. She looks sweet when she's asleep. She looks like a little girl. It's too dark to be sure but I think that she might be sucking her thumb and that makes me smile. I take a deep breath and I'm thinking about that song they sing at Man U. *'Que Sera Sera…'* I remember years ago I asked my dad what it meant and he put on his pub quiz face.

He said, 'It's Latin for "fuck it, let's get pissed".'

I go down the stairs and through the kitchen and into the hall. I find the cupboard with the key pad where Ray put all the mobile phones on the first night. I tap in 27021969. It doesn't open. Course I knew that there was a risk that even a tosser like Ray would be a bit more sensible than to use his birthday as the code, but even so I am surprised. I'm normally right about these things. I can feel my shoulders getting tight and I realise that I'm not really ready to give up on the plan. Anyway, it's all I've got left. I take a deep breath. I count to ten and I try again cos I've just thought of something. This time I tap in 27021968. It still doesn't open. I take another breath. I try again. Last time. 27021967. Bingo. Stupid fucker. He's lied about his age by two stupid years. Like that's going to make any difference. Like I'd fancy him because he's 39 instead of 41. Blokes are so weird.

There's this funny clicking sound and I pull the cupboard open. And there they are. The crown fucking jewels. A bunch of car keys tied to a fuck off big wooden triangle. I bet Ray's the kind of person who loses his keys all the time. I bet the huge triangle is meant to make it easy for him to see them when he puts them down. Well, you've lost them now, you mook.

I look at the time on my mobile: 02.30. It's really quiet. I'm probably safe but I feel a bit scared all of a sudden. I need a dump proper bad. So I find the bog in the hall near Pete's room. I see there's still a light under his door. I bet he's listening out for me.

My poo is pure runny, like I've eaten something a bit dodgy, so I go back to the kitchen and get a big pint glass of water. I take my time drinking it and I'm not quiet. I clink the glass and clonk about, but no-one comes. I sort of feel the house watching me, but it's just a house. It can't move. It can't stop me.

I look at my mobile again: 02:37. I decide to count to sixty real slow and listen proper careful. There's no sound at all for a whole minute. Only my breathing, so I go for it.

I'm out in the courtyard. I see the car. I yank open the door, climb up the step and I'm into the driving seat. Pull the seat-belt on. Key in the slot. Head-lights on. Turn the key, put it into gear and off. Only it's not as smooth as that because this is a heavy old fucker of a car, so we sort of stagger and leap and jerk up the cobbled driveway to the lane and then I can get it into second gear and it's proper tarmac and it's all much easier.

It's pure noisy though, this car, and any moment I expect the lights of the house to come on and Ray to come running out. But then Ray's in his own little house and maybe everyone else assumes that I'm him, because they can't have slept through all that row. I know that Pete's still awake and he must have heard me. I wonder what he's thinking?

202

At the top of the lane I have to decide to turn left towards the ruined church and the village or right, the way that Zak and the snob-bitch went this afternoon. I've never been right and at first I think I'll go that way, but then I think that in the village there might be sign-posts towards a big town. This is what I'm thinking: eventually I'll find a sign to a town that's big enough to have signs to London, and it'll be easy then. It would be a lot easier if this car had sat-nav but of course it doesn't. But I can sleep in here if I need to. I'm not in a hurry now.

The car's a right state. There are sweet papers everywhere. I notice that Ray has a big thing for Maltesers and Minstrels. Kid's sweets. And there is a pile of old newspapers on the passenger seat underneath a box of Kleenex. What a loser. I look in the back and there's a manky old coat and a couple of quilts with all mud and oil and that on them. When I get a car that's properly mine I'm going to keep it nice. People judge you on your car. It should be like your front room, a place you can take people. A place you can be proud of.

It's hard work just keeping the Defender straight and by the time I reach the village my arms are pure aching. I drive down the main street looking for sign-posts. I'm nervous when the first houses appear but I don't need to be because there's no-one about. It's proper dead and I think again how shit it must be to grow up here.

I don't concentrate much cos there's no-one around so I don't need to, but also I'm thinking about the shit meeting that Diamond and me and Susie and Ariel and Ray had up in the LRC.

They're all sat there talking about me like I'm not in the room and about my mum like she's some kind of psycho bitch from Hell. Thing is my mum is like some kind of psycho bitch from Hell. Sometimes. But that doesn't mean that other people can talk about her that way. She's still my mum. They should have more respect.

JD doesn't diss Mum but he doesn't really stick up for her either. He doesn't say much at all. Ray's all for just letting me go home with her when she turns up.

He says, 'You signed a contract, Jon. It clearly states that all pupils must have signed permission from their parent or guardian. I don't see we've got any choice.'

And he's pure whiny like William when Harry's broken up his Lego Viking ship. It gets on everyone's tits and at first I think that's quite good cos it means that no-one will admit that Ray is right and they'll do anything to find a different way of doing things. Human nature that is.

No one asks me anything. No one even looks at me.

'And you definitely want to complete this programme, Mistyann?' Ariel says this out of nowhere.

It shocks me when she uses my name because I've been thinking about Roy Keane. What if Keano's mum had tried to keep him away from a special Man U soccer camp when he was fifteen? I bet she'd have fucking regretted it. But the answer is yes, I do want to stay here. For one thing I hate not finishing stuff and for another I've never met people like Zak and Pete or even Charlotte. They're kind of freaks but kind of interesting and in any case I'd only be looking after Harry and William if I went home. And I'd have to put up with Ty's big fat arse plonked on our sofa every fucking night going 'make us a cup of tea, love' in that stupid voice he has. Fact is, if I go home then I'm going to be looking after three kids instead of two. I tell them all this and Ray sighs.

'But you signed a contract,' he says again. And I see Susie move away from him just a bit. He's jarring everyone off big time.

Ariel says that it seems to her that the way forward is to 'stop her mouth with gold'. And this is where JD leaps in and goes yes that would probably work. And Ariel says about the Foundation having a contingency fund and that this seems to be the kind of thing they ought to spend the money on. So basically they are going to bribe my mum into letting me stay.

And they're all agreed when Ray says, 'Look, I want a solution too but this is er public money, let's not forget. And we have to account to the Arts Council for every penny. I don't think we can assume that Mrs Rutherford's hotel bills will be just waived through as necessary expenditure.'

'Her name's Mrs Eve now,' I say, 'Claire Eve.' But no one's listening to me.

Ariel says, 'I'm sure that I can square it with the Arts Council, Ray. Just give me the name of someone to talk to.'

But Ray just says, 'If it was down to me then I wouldn't mind but the fact is that Mistyann came here without proper authority and now we're proposing spending money that's meant to be for educating, er, gifted children on keeping an angry parent quiet. What if that comes out? We'll all be in the soup, frankly.'

Susie looks at me and says that perhaps we should discuss it in private and I look at JD and he nods and I go out of the LRC. I make a big deal about not slamming the door. What I really want to do is smash Ray in his stupid face. And on the way back to my room I think that if he's worried about bad publicity then I could do something that will make him shit himself. And that's when I decide to nick his car and drive to London.

But now that I'm actually doing it I can't find a sign in this poxy village that makes sense and the buzz of nicking the car has gone and the thought of driving for hours and hours is exhausting and I feel more smecked out than I've ever felt and then the warning light comes on that says I'm running out of gas. That's Ray, again. Shit for brains. Can't even keep his car filled up. But it means I have to stop, so when I come to a bumpy lane on the edge of the village I turn up it and switch the engine off.

The silence pure freaks me out. And I just sit there and listen to it. It's proper weird to hear nothing. Nothing at all. But after a while I can hear some noises. Little rustlings and twigs cracking and all that and I think thank fuck for that and I get the coat and blankets from the back. I'm nearly asleep anyway so it I can curl across the back seats of the Defender and kip down pretty easy. I think that in the morning I'll find a way to get to the train. Travel in style.

THIRTY-ONE

Ariel woke me by rapping fiercely on my door like some kind of absurdly beautiful bailiff.

'Jon,' she called, 'We have a situation.'

I sat up as she let herself in. She brought her sun-ripened mid-west good looks into the room and I become aware of a flabby British mustiness that had built up overnight. It was like I had been pumping out school canteen smells in my dreams; the air cabbagy with stale hopes.

'The police are here,' she said. And then, natural actor that she is, she paused. 'And so are Mistyann's mother and step-father.' She paused again and I felt trapped in the narrow student bed, disadvantaged to say the least. Under the thin cover I was wearing nothing but boxers and socks. Not a great look even if maybe I shouldn't have been worried about appearances at such a time. Ariel smiled slightly as she picked up on my discomfort.

'Hey, Jon,—it's okay. I'm not easily shocked. And I thought you'd want to know straightaway. The police are here, the parents are here and Mistyann's gone.'

As I dressed she fleshed out her take on events.

'We need a strategy, Jon. I'm not prepared to lose Mistyann just because of some dumb escapade with a car. She needs this course and she's just about the most interesting person here. I'm not going to let her fuck up. It's obvious isn't it? The reason for this kind of self-destruction? Mistyann's on the brink of changing her life and that's scary. She's moving out of her comfort zone, out of the familiar into a place where she can really fly. That's terrifying for her. How much safer to just run away from everything. Well, I'm not letting her go, Jon. Mistyann's a special person. She just needs to be forced to be free.'

When I speak—when I make a speech as long as this—people tell me that I use my arms and hands as semaphore, like I'll be more convincing if I can turn my words into pictures at the same time. It has been pointed out to me that it doesn't look good in court. It looks like I'm trying too hard. But Ariel hardly moved her hands at all. I noticed how still her body was as she spoke; ballet dancer straight almost the whole time. This calm must serve her well in those TV debates American politicians have to indulge in. At that moment it annoyed me.

I said, 'Yeah, well, I think we need to find her first.'

'I tell you one thing: I'm not doing no fucking televised appeal.'

This was your mum five minutes later in the library. She had definite views on how this crisis should be tackled.

'I don't think we're quite at that stage yet, Mrs Eve.' murmured the woman PC.

There were two plods in the room. A chubby red-faced bloke of about thirty who kept smoothing his hair down nervously and pulling at his collar like it was too tight for him, and a woman, also plump, who looked about sixth form age and kept her eyes on the carpet. They looked like they would last about a minute in the inner city. They carried no authority. In fact they looked like they would struggle to enforce a parking ticket. Compared to them, milky Ray was a model of resolute management.

Together we reviewed the known situation: You'd gone off with Ray's car sometime in the early hours. After that it was speculation, but we were agreed that you were probably holed up somewhere fairly nearby; that you were capable of looking after yourself; that there was no need for panic yet and that you would probably come back when you got hungry or thirsty enough. We didn't know that you had Pete's bank card or we might have been more worried. The police representatives mumbled and muttered that 'all units' had been notified of the make, model and registration number of Ray's car. In the interests of maintaining a united front I didn't voice my opinion that 'all units' probably meant three middle-aged fatties on push-bikes.

Ariel determined to take workshops as planned—'I think we need to keep the excitement to a minimum, don't you?'

Susie would oversee things behind the scenes and your mum, Ty, Ray and I would wander around the village and its environs looking for you and/or the car. In other words, business as usual as far as possible. Blitz spirit. Keep on keeping on. That kind of thing. It was a reasonable plan and your mum wasn't having any of it.

'Bollocks to that. I've got two kids in the car. I've had to take sick leave because of that little madam and you want me to trail all over the flippin countryside looking for her. We're going back to our B&B to try and keep the little'uns amused. You phone me as soon as she makes contact.'

I held open the door as she passed though it and she stumbled as she did so, grasping my arm for a second to steady herself. And I caught it. The unmistakeable sweetness of an early morning voddy and tonic. She looked right at me. She knew that I knew and her eyes were full of fire and challenge. She brought her face close to mine.

'And after she gets back here then you, Mister Diamond, better start looking for a new job.'

She released my arm and strode on, heels clicking fast on the cold, chequered tiles of the hall-way. Ty shrugged at me sheepishly as he followed her out.

Your mum stopped half-way towards the doors at the other end, turned. She was almost smiling. A thin, tight smile, but inappropriate.

'And remember what I said. No bleeding TV appeals. I'm not letting her humiliate me like that.'

And in that defiant moment she reminded me of you.

The male plod was just behind me as I moved out into the hall. 'Phew-ee,' he breathed, 'Wouldn't want to get on the wrong side of her.'

What an idiot. We were all already on the wrong side of her. The whole world was. That's what kept her going. It was what forced her to get up in the morning, that sense that someone somewhere had stolen her real life and was hiding it from her. And she was going to bloody well track them down and force them to hand it over.

Ray and I did several silent and morose circuits of the village as snow became sleet and then full-blown rain. After a couple of hours we had exhausted all the possible places where you might have gone and Ray determined to go back. To his credit he hadn't mentioned the theft of his car once and when I brought it up, he shrugged.

'Just a piece of metal, Jon.'

Despite our signal failure to find any trace of you or the car and despite our absolute conviction that you would come back unharmed in your own good time, I couldn't bring myself to go back to Cefn Coch with him. And, to be honest, our inability to find anything to say to each other was growing oppressive.

As I watched him go, his high-vis nylon cape shimmering like a shadow glimpsed through a shower curtain—the rain was that heavy—I was splashed by the wheels of a car pulling up next to me. It was the chubby PC from the meeting earlier in the day.

'Get in the dry, man. You look like a drowned rat. Here, have a sandwich. Wife made them. Hope you like peanut butter and marmite. Not to everyone's taste I know, but my Liz see, she knows the way to my heart.'

And I realized that I was starving and that actually peanut butter and marmite was just what I fancied. And so we drove through and around the little settlement again and again and again till it got dark. And in the course of our searching I learned a lot about PC Leo Minhinnick.

He was fundamentally a Heartbeat kind of bobby; warm-hearted and out of time with the target-led demands of the modern force. He was thirty-two, two small children; three and a half and thirteen months. Big rugby fan 'used to play a bit, you know—before the kids'. Singer in the police choir — 'Well, I am Welsh you know. But I do enjoy it'. Studying for a degree in History of Art with the Open University. Nice bloke. You'd have torn him to shreds. Me, I quite liked his chuntering. It was like having local radio on in the background. A nice person talking about nice things. Every day things. His favourite band? Public Enemy.

I know: shook me up too. But he wasn't faking it. PC Minhinnick knows more about the life and work of Dr Dre than any other man in Wales. It could be his *Mastermind* subject. Goes to show, you never can tell.

It had been dark for a good while when he dropped me off in the centre of the village with an apology.

'That's it I'm afraid, Jon, end of my shift. Got to get home. See the kids, you know how it is.' His face flicked through a few trial expressions before settling on 'concerned'.

'I'm sure you'll see her tonight. She's not going to be able to tough it out for long and if she's as bright as everyone says she'll come to her senses. You sure you don't want a lift to the centre?'

I shook my head. I said I'd do just one last circuit of Llangow on foot and then walk back. I was stiff from sitting in the squad car for so long and the walk in the cold night air would do me good especially since the rain had stopped.

'Mind how you go then.' And he was off, gunning that plod-Focus like it was a pimped up Gary-boy motor. Mind how you go. Straight out of *Dixon of Dock Green*. I stared after his fading tail-lights for a while and then found my way to the Telyn a Chan, sorely in need of a song.

THIRTY-TWO

I'm watching *Toy Story* with Carmel. We're both pure smecked. We're cuddled up on the sofa under a duvet. The duvet smells of weed and Carmel smells of bubble bath and bacon. We're munching on bacon sarnies for our tea. I reckon *Toy Story 2* is better than *Toy Story* but they don't have it here. Anyway the original is still a good film. I've watched it about a zillion times with William and Harry.

Caitlin asks me not to let her watch too much telly or DVDs but I reckon this is okay because we have a well busy day. In the morning we make snow men in the back garden. I have a go at making a snow head like up at the centre but it comes out all wrong and keeps collapsing, so we just make normal ones. Then it starts to rain so we come in and watch a bit of telly before we do some cutting out of pictures from magazines and sticking them onto paper. Then we play hide and seek about a million times. There's loads of places to get lost in this big old house even though we don't go to the top floor. Carmel says that's Derec's and we can only go there when we're asked.

I say, 'Who's Derec?'

But she just says that he's her friend and looks at me like I don't know anything. Obviously everyone else in the world knows who Derec is and only an idiot would have to ask, so I let it drop.

Then we have lunch and go kicking slush and splashing in puddles down the lane. There are loads of holes in the road so plenty of puddles for us to jump into. It's a proper laugh actually. Carmel has got this super sick giggly laugh and it just makes me want to laugh too. And every time she makes a splash—well, she thinks it's pure hilarious.

We don't go near the end of the lane where it joins the road cos someone could see us. When we've had enough of splashing we go back up to the house.

In the afternoon we do reading books and drawing and then we make a house by pulling the cushions off the sofa and using the chairs as walls and we play a game where we're going to Goblinland and Carmel keeps wanting to shoot goblins and kill them while I'm trying to say that no, these are nice goblins, friendly ones. But you can't stop little kids shooting things, so in the end I give up and I become the chief goblin and I reckon I must get killed hundreds of times and I make my death proper noisy each time and Carmel does her dutzi giggling laugh.

And then we do a game where she sits in the duvet and holds on while I swirl it around. It's knackering but she wants me to do it more and more and faster and faster. In the end we're both cream-crackered so it's time for bacon sarnies and *Toy Story* and it's dark outside and I wonder if Caitlin will be back soon. Her and Justin have gone to some meeting somewhere.

It's pure luck that I'm doing this baby-sitting. A bit of a head-fuck too. This is how it happens. I'm in the car and awake even though it's still more or less dark cos it's cold and stinky in Ray's Defender and I'm pure frozen right deep in my bones, when I see this face staring at me. And I tell myself not to freak out, that I'm dreaming or it's a squirrel or something cos it usually does turn out to be something boring and normal when you get freaked out.

But the face doesn't go away and in the end I get out of the car and it's this little kid, the one we saw on the train coming up here. Carmel. The one with the old mosher mum and the young mosher dad. The ones who were making a big show of snogging.

We just look at each other, the girl and me, and then we hear this shouting from the house, 'Car-mel! Car-mel!' like that, with her name all split in two. Then the kid just takes my hand and pulls me towards this gate that leads to this house and for some unknown reason I go with her. I've parked just next to this big old red brick house which I never even saw in the dark.

Anyway. Me and Caitlin get talking and she's a bit freaked out to see me holding hands with her daughter but I tell her that we've got a day off from studying. It's obvious that she doesn't believe me, but it's also obvious that she doesn't give a flying fuck and she looks at me for a bit and then asks if I fancy baby-sitting and I ask how much and she says four pounds an hour—which is okay. She asks if there's anyone I should call and I say I'll do it later and she says okay and then Justin appears and she explains to him that they don't have to take Carmel to the meeting anymore and Carmel is jumping up and down going 'hooray!' and she punches the air and goes 'yes!' like a footballer scoring a goal and we all laugh. Justin and Caitlin start to go for the door and Carmel goes, 'Daddy! Daddy!—a kiss and a cuddle!' and we all go 'aah' and Caitlin takes my mobile number—she hasn't got one herself—and then they're off. Which is how come I'm sitting in the dark watching *Toy Story* when Derec comes home.

Derec is small and bald. He brings the smell of fags in with him and I realise why all the walls are pale brown. He doesn't say anything either. You can tell Carmel loves him though, she leaps up and hangs from his neck and talks at him at about ninety miles an hour, but in Welsh, and I guess that she's telling him all the stuff we've been doing cos he looks over at me and nods and gets Carmel off from round his neck and comes over and shakes my hand. He keeps his eyes on the floor though. I tell him I'm baby-sitting for Caitlin and Justin and he nods again.

Carmel says, 'Derec doesn't speak English. Well, he can, but he chooses not to. That's what my mum says.' And Derec smiles and I notice that he has really small teeth and they're a bit yellowy too. 'He's a tattooist, look.' And right there and then she takes off her jumper and T-shirt and vest and on her skinny chest is this huge green and red dragon. I

214

don't know what to say but then I feel relieved cos Carmel says, 'It isn't real. It's just a drawing. I've got to wait till I'm big to have a real one.'

And I laugh because for a second I did think that Carmel had a huge fuck off tattoo on her chest.

Derec laughs and says something.

Carmel says, 'Derec says have you got any tattoos?' And I say no, I believe in being a bit more individual, I like to stand out. Everyone I know has tats. And Derec laughs at that. He laughs like he's choking. Like he's got a disease. Then he disappears upstairs and when comes down again *Toy Story* is nearly over and he's all washed and clean and smells of cheap aftershave as well as fags. And he says something to Carmel.

'Derec says can he have a bacon sarnie?'

Which is pure cheeky but I do more for everyone and I set the smoke alarm off. Derec gets a chair and takes it off the ceiling and I notice that the smoke alarm is stained all browny-yellow and that makes me laugh—a nicotine stained smoke alarm. How crap is that?

After we've eaten Derec says something to Carmel.

'Derec says is it alright if he goes to the pub? Mum and Dad should be home soon.'

I can tell she's proper enjoying being the translator so I look seriously at her when I answer. Don't even glance at Derec. 'Tell Derec that will be perfectly fine,' I say.

She turns to Derec and even though the words are Welsh it still sounds just like me speaking. She's got my way of talking down perfect. She's a right little actress.

Derec struggles into some kind of anorak and Carmel hugs and kisses him goodbye like she did with Justin.

As he leaves she says to me, 'It's croaky night tonight.'

I say, 'Do you mean karaoke?' And she says yes, that's what she said. Croaky night.

THIRTY-THREE

Eleven hours straight, the dim light of the endless afternoon, the Elms Nursing Home: All around the man with the trolley old ladies stare venomously. As the ladle crashes through the brown gloop of Wednesday's lamb stew with dumplings, the ancient metal pan seems to flinch at the gristly specks that mark its sides, as if it grows alive to the horror of the brevity and indignity of human life. He feels suddenly as if the air itself has dementia, as if the brutal loneliness in the room has infected it. Once this was all gloss and brittle laughter. His mind can easily conjure cocktail parties and the spinning brightness of Christmas charades. Now the atmosphere is a soup of putrefaction. The gristle of rotting memories. The morning bustle and loud good cheer of the staff can sometimes challenge the stale breath of the room, force it into a semblance of lightness and coax the weary furniture into giving the space an appearance no more depressing than the average hospital ward, but the afternoons are heartless. The afternoons yield and give and he feels that he could disappear into them like a sailor swallowed by the thoughtless yawn of a whale.

The man with the trolley and the ladle and the gloop is me by the way.

And will prison, if it comes to that, be much different? Maybe all lives end somewhere similar. And prison might at least mean a reprieve from the glowering kids at the end of Gladstone Street. Even the littlest kids are at it now. Whipped up by older siblings or by their mums and dads. Three year olds—less than knee high—shrilling 'perv!' as I struggle back from Mr Joshi's's temple of tinned produce once a week. It should be laughable. It is laughable.

I've given up going further afield. I'd rather run the gauntlet of baby vigilantes in my own neighbourhood than face old friends staring through me in Waitrose.

And the Telyn a Chan on that wet winter's evening. That felt like the Elm's too; like a nursing home that dispensed real ale rather than cholinesterase inhibitors. At least in a rural pub on a late Monday afternoon you don't get the lightweights. No amateurs. When I was drinking, my least favourite night of the year was New Year's Eve. Pubs full of people who only drink once a year and can't handle it. We called them Sunday drivers because of the chaos and the hold-ups they caused in our favourite bars. A seething mass of flushed humanity intent on being offensively jolly. Grim. Hogmanay was the one night when I definitely stayed in. I'd far rather watch some middle aged professional Scotsman on telly try to gee-up the nation with jokes about what's beneath his kilt.

I had thought that the Telyn would be empty but no, over on the far left hand wall, a skinny, acned youth was setting up some decks and speakers. The landlady was as chipper as the day before, already pouring me a ginger beer as I made my way to the bar.

'Brought a spare set of clothes?' she quipped and giggled girlishly at her own gag.

I smiled weakly and accepted the drink. I knew that you hadn't come back yet. I had the school mobile in my hand so that I could feel it vibrate just in case I missed it ringing. Even so I checked it every ten minutes for a text or to make sure it was still working.

I was at a loss to be honest. Exhausted too. Hours scouring roads and hedge-rows with PC Minhinnick had left me stiff and headachy. I drifted. Killing time by eating crisps and mulling over the only English language paper in the room. A two day old copy of the *Daily Mail*. Asylum seekers were driving down house prices, teaching assistants wearing the veil were giving our kids leukaemia, Inheritance Tax was causing widows to starve in the streets. All the usual stuff, so I was more than amenable when a sharp prod on the arm caused me to look up.

It was Derec, jerking his head towards the pool table. Derec's aversion to speaking English made him the perfect pub companion. No dull anecdotes, no opinions. We just played steady, careful pool and took it in turn to keep one another's glasses full.

He was a better player than me but the amount of Brains bitter he was taking on board meant that he was bound to make mistakes in the end, so we grew more evenly matched as the afternoon passed into evening.

Emerging from the bogs into the main bar after our fourth game, I found that there was suddenly a bit of a crowd in the pub. Clearly Monday evening Karaoke was a big deal in Llangow. I was intrigued. I'd never heard Welsh karaoke before. I glanced at my watch. Just gone seven. Still no word from anyone up at the house.

It occurred to me just then that maybe the pub was the best place to find out where you'd gone. Maybe I was rationalising my presence there. Justifying my inability to go back to the house where the adults would be worrying and pacing and biting their lips and jumping at every noise.

I racked up the balls again. No one else had yet tried to get on the table but there were a few young lads gathered round the bar so I guessed that it wouldn't be long before someone's 50p went down. That was fine by me. A last game. A last ginger beer. A chance to hear a few classics desecrated by the locals. A walk back through that hyper-oxygenated air that would leave me ready to deal with all that hysteria and emotion up at Cefn Coch. I was thinking that by now all the other kids would know about your exploits and the mood up at the big house was bound to be too melodramatic to bear.

I won the final game and Derec nodded as we shook hands. He still hadn't spoken. We moved over to a table in the main bar. The booklets for the karaoke had been distributed around the pub and people were gathered

218

around them pointing at the various tracks on offer and laughing. A flip chart next to the DJ's equipment showed who was down to do what song. So far only two people had their names down. Derec startled me by suddenly speaking a sentence in English. It was a short one, mind.

'Do you sing?' he said.

'Used to,' I said, surprised. And I told him all about Be Nice and our short and inglorious career. He didn't interrupt.

'I'm going to do Mustang Sally,' he said at last.

'Good choice,' I said. 'Hey, I thought you didn't speak English?'

'Everyone has to speak English sometimes.' And then with a kind of leer, 'Caitlin talks some right crap you know.'

He rolled off toward the young guy running the karaoke and I could see that Derec was really quite slaughtered. I watched as he spoke to the kid at the machine, pointing out the relevant track in the book and I watched as his name was written on the flip chart. He wrote two tracks down, but I couldn't see what they were.

Derec circulated around the bar, joining groups and, from the nods and smiles, I could see that he was popular and well known. The four Trilbies from last night were in and Derec had a laugh and a joke with them too. At one point someone thrust another pint in his hand and he came rolling back to our table. If my estimate that he was on his fourth pint when I came in was correct, then the one he was now holding was his eighth.

'I put you down to do London Calling,' he said.

'Bollocks.'

'You said you used to sing. You like The Clash. Make a change from all the fucking Tom Jones we normally get.'

'I've got to get back.'

'You'll be on in half an hour. If you don't do it people will think you're a typical English wuss. This is for the honour of your tribe, mate.'

'No pressure then,' I said.

Derec smiled. I wasn't sure I liked this new voluble, sociable incarnation. On the whole I think I preferred him when he was cautious, careful and silent.

I looked at my watch again. 7.10. I could do my song at 7.40. It would be over by 7.45 and I'd be back at Cefn Coch by 8.15pm at the latest. Did I want to do it? Yes and no. Fear and vanity were at war, but curiosity was the final motivating factor. When I'd been in bands I had jumped about, rolled around the floor—really flung myself into it like a combination of Iggy Pop and John Lydon. And of course I was always pissed. Could I now, twenty years later and sober, do anything like the same? And London Calling was pretty much one my favourite songs, I knew all the words so I wouldn't have to look at them scrolling across the screen waiting for the bouncing ball to hit the one I was meant to be singing. I knew every breath Strummer took, every beat of Topper Headon's drums, every guitar chord, every note. If PC Minhinnick could do *Mastermind* on Dr Dre, I could do it on the rhythm and structure of London Calling. And there was the whole surreal thing about performing in a remote Welsh pub where I knew no-one. So, curiosity came down on vanity's side. I'd do it. What a story for Cog and for the staff-room. What a story for you, Mistyann, come to that.

You can still see the resulting fiasco on YouTube. 40,614 hits as of last week. Nothing like a court case to generate publicity. Derec was a star. His performance is on YouTube too. Only 6,711 viewings. Lacking in the notoriety department you see.

He went up on stage like a seedy Philip Larkin or, more accurately, like Penfold from the *DangerMouse* series. He left it like Jim Morrison. He rocked the house. He had a voice as rich as Scott Walker and he had that authentic soul mix of swagger and desperation. Which, actually, Scott Walker never had. He became leaner, almost sinuous under the

220

lights. He was the real thing. The transformation from meek and bespectacled to pouting rock god was staggering. He went down a storm.

I couldn't follow that. And there were so many reasons why I shouldn't have attempted it. But the chopping chords of London Calling began and I took a deep breath, closed my eyes and hurled myself in, only to find that I'd landed many miles from the tune. I could glimpse it—but it was as though it was on the distant far side of an eight line highway filled with speeding vehicles—and I spent the rest of the song trying unsuccessfully to crawl towards it. I'd gone in girlishly high and it's a song that needs Strummer's deepest, desperately raw range to pull it off.

There had been genuine goodwill and good humour extended towards me as I had taken the tiny stage, but staring through the pub's smog at the mix of incomprehension, faint distaste and disinterest of the audience, I felt a hollow rage. I had let vanity seduce me again, after all these fucking years.

Derec was smiling and that was the one thing that kept me going. The sight of his smug little face, twinkling away, awoke a peculiar and stubborn sense of irritation in me. I was determined to finish the song whatever happened. So I gave it everything. Flailing arms, contorted face, spastic dancing: the works. I re-visited my whole long buried repertoire of front-man moves. I looked—I know it now—an utter turd.

It all kicked off during the bridge before the final choruses. There was a sudden commotion near the bar. Two lads in their early twenties pushing and shoving. One skinny and rather beautiful with glossy hair flopping over his eyes, the other prematurely paunchy, flabby-faced. Obviously I couldn't hear what was being said but arms as well as voices were being raised. A crowd gathered as though an impromptu bare-knuckle boxing ring was being thrown up. A proper band would have stopped but the machine and I ploughed on providing a ludicrous sound-track to what had become the main event.

The lads stood nose to nose. Paunchy was clearly incandescent about something while Skinny was silent, immobile. Slowly, deliberately, he tapped his glass on his table. It shattered and then, with equal casualness, he raised the base with its new shards gleaming as jagged as an alpine mountain ridge and flicked his wrist towards Paunchy's face. There was a scream that cut through the music and the fat kid lurched back clutching his eyes. Skinny sprung forward and his arm moved back and forth two or three times before his victim fell towards the floor and a little scrum of customers grabbed the other kid by the shoulders.

Someone finally had the presence of mind to turn the music off. There was a hush in the room. You can see it in grainy videoblog on your PC if you've got one. The fat kid still on the floor, hands to his face, flip-flopping like a landed fish. His assailant shaking his shoulders; the hands clutching him and falling away. It looks vicious enough all smudged and blurred on my ancient desk-top. Live, it was extraordinary. The blood and the speed of it all. So sudden and vivid.

Skinny looked around, pushed his way through the crowd and left. No one tried to stop him. I walked over to the fat lad who was subsiding into a foetal question mark on the ground. And the YouTube version ends there, with my useless intervention. I've seen it dozens of times and I still can't get over how much of a teacher I look.

'Is he okay?' I said fatuously.

The girl kneeling over him didn't look up. 'He's just been fucking glassed. Do you really think he's okay?' she spat. She prised his hands away from his face. It was a pulpy, spongy mess, scored with wet, scarlet trenches that glittered horribly where tiny bits of glass were lodged.

'Come on,' the girl said tenderly, 'let's get you to hospital.'

She turned to the onlookers and let fly a torrent of Welsh as bitter and forceful as her words to Paunchy had been quiet and gentle. Someone turned and walked away, presumably to get a car.

Physically, the kid was a mess, but the worst thing was the way his face was crumpled up like it was his feelings that had been hurt the most. He was crying, sobbing with damaged pride. He raised himself to a sitting position, hands still to his face.

'There was no need. No fucking need. He owes me twenty quid that's all… has done for months… won't fucking pay me…'

'Sssh,' whispered the girl, 'It's going to be alright.'

Then he was on his feet and the girl—who I recognized now as one of the waitresses from our first night here, the one who had been teaching you Welsh swear words—was leading him out gently. Then the barmaid was there scrubbing at a sticky red stain on the floor with a grubby cloth. And somehow I was at the bar.

I looked down as the barmaid's mottled wrestler's hand pushed across a pint and then a chaser.

'On the house, love. I reckon you've had a bit of a shocker.' Her English was being used carefully. Like it was a dangerous tool, a hedge-trimmer that she didn't use much and needed to take extra care with.

I had a clear flash of myself taking two fierce swigs of Dad's Laphroaig moments after seeing the ambulance take its leisurely leave from Curlew Crescent. It had arrived, TV drama style, in an ecstasy of nightclub lights and apocalyptic sirens. I arrived more or less as the ambulance did. There I was, hurling my bike into the front garden and lurching up the gravel of the drive through the special lung-bursting agony known only to the chronic pub-dweller forced to undertake sudden exercise. Inside, the body-bag was zipped and the ambulance men were moving unhurriedly through the drill of packing up bits of shiny kit. Kit that had been useless and unnecessary, despite its expensive gleam.

'There's nothing anyone could have done.' A tall spindly paramedic was speaking to Mum. Despite his neon yellow vest he had so much the look and manner of a cartoon undertaker that I guessed he was the one who always performed the task of dispensing platitudes to the newly bereaved. He shook his head sorrowfully, nodded respectfully and took himself and his colleagues off at hearse speed to the mortuary. It was then that I made my move straight for the bottles kept in the G-plan dresser in the lounge. The purchase of this dresser had been the subject of what had felt, to a ten year old trapped in the wasteland of the Northampton Furniture Emporium, like many hours of debate. Now I was older I could appreciate its charms more fully. Chief among these was the fact that it contained the household supply of liquor.

It took a matter of seconds to find the forbidden bottle and seconds more to take those final swigs and turn and face the abject face of my mother. She looked like all the bones of her face were melting. Her voice, when she found it was steely enough however.

'Aren't you going to give me one of those? In a glass, dear, if it's not too much trouble.'

I didn't say anything. I poured two fingers of the pale caramel into one of the best glasses, the ones that were reserved for dinner parties and special occasions. I added lemonade and handed it to her. Then I up-ended the bottle for another long chug of my own. Wiping my chin and feeling the drink do its usual fiery thing in my stomach, I felt suddenly foolish.

I walked over to the sink in the kitchen, keeping my eyes away from the bowl of Alpen on the table and poured the remainder of the bottle away. And Mum watched while the rest of the family booze supply went the same way. Everything. Even the little bottles of piss-weak Co-op own brand lager kept for summer Sundays in the garden; even the Calvados, forgotten souvenir of a coach trip to Normandy. And the next day, in the morgue, I had my last ever drink.

Twelve years had passed since then. Twelve years of a proper job and evenings spent marking; of five a side football and badminton and jogging; of Friday night curries and girlfriends and building a decent credit rating in order to buy my little house in Gladstone Street. Ten years of solid, decent, unspectacular effort. Fuck it. Fuck it all.

And it was, despite everything, a great session. After that first pint and chaser I bought a round for the entire pub. Medieval the Telyn a Chan may have been, but it took debit cards. The gesture felt good. I sat with Derec and the Trilbies and explained about you going missing but no-one knew anything.

After the next pint Dave the taxi driver walked in and he didn't know anything either. We retired to my table to talk bollocks. Sport bollocks, political bollocks, teaching bollocks, car bollocks, aren't the Welsh all barking bollocks; all kinds of entertaining bollocks that I can't remember a word of now. He got the next round.

The pint after that Boudicca and Justin walked in and Derec intercepted them and had a conversation that involved a lot of emphatic hand gestures and I thought that he was telling them about the fight, but when they came over I started to tell them about you going missing.

Boudicca said, 'Yeah, Derec told us about that but I'm sure she's going to be okay. Certain of it and I'm never wrong about these things. Got a bit of a gift I have, see.'

And Justin confirmed it. 'Yeah, she's never wrong when she gets one of her feelings. Never.'

And they looked at each other and smiled and Boudicca reached over and squeezed her lover's hand. And she radiated certainty. I turned my phone off.

And Dave, Derec, Boudicca, Justin and I sat at a table with the four Trilbies singing along with the karaoke. New York, New York; Dancing Queen. A buxom, red-faced matron belted out 'Mama's got a Squeezebox…', some Welsh stuff of the fiddly-dee-fiddly-fucking-dee, finger in the ear kind that I normally abhor but somehow sounded just right and there was an impromptu language lesson for the two tin-eared English guys and lots of laughter. And the Trilbies were great fellas, insisting on getting their rounds in and, some time later, there was a row with Dave about something. The budget before last? Inheritance tax? Something meaningless and financial anyway. Then agreeing to disagree. And whiskies to celebrate our renewed friendship. And then there was the strong-arm of the land-lady on my neck and I was suddenly alone at midnight in a silent main street. Everyone had vanished into the night and I was leaning against the pub wall vomiting carelessly over my Chelsea boots and beginning, though I didn't know it yet, my journey to becoming one of the Strange Men. And I had simply forgotten about you, Mistyann. Forgotten all about you, your mum, the course, everything. Forgotten myself. Call it a moment of madness. Call it pushing the big red self-destruct button. Call it Nemesis, destiny, or just being a twat.

Then I wasn't alone in the street any longer: I was with Justin and Derec and Boudicca and we were stumbling back to their place for a night-cap and they were laughing and gabbling in that shared pixie language of theirs and we were falling through the door of some brooding manse and there you were, hands on hips, looking like everyone's mother. I half expected you to say 'And what time do you call this?' and tell us that we were all grounded.

THIRTY-FOUR

It's Justin that catches me. Everyone else is too old and too shit-faced. Soon as I see them coming through the door I'm off. They try and hold on to me but I mental them out by screaming and whirling my arms and stuff cos I can't fucking believe that they'd grass me up like that. I should always remember. No one can be trusted. No one is ever your friend.

I'm slipping and sliding down the path cos it's all iced up but I get to the gate and I know that they're still fucking about near the door. I think I can hear a kid crying too. The stupid fuckers have woken Carmel up.

My mistake is to go for the Defender. Well, my first mistake is to leave the keys in there cos some wanker has taken them. Derec probably. I go ape when I find this out and that wastes more time and by the time I'm out of the car, Justin is there and he grabs me. I'm belting him and screaming and going pure heavy mental on him but he clings on and then we fall over on the ground and he's got me wrapped up so tight I can hardly breathe but I'm still thrashing about and I catch sight of JD just standing there like a dumb ass so I yell, 'You're killing me! You're killing me!' or something like that and Diamond says, 'That's enough. Leave her alone.' Which is what I want and Justin let's go just a tiny bit and then I'm up again but I run straight into Derec who just goes bang against the side of my head and I fall back down in the lane. It proper fucking hurts. And then JD tries to smack Derec.

I see him like he's in slow motion. He pulls his arm back like someone in one of William's stupid comics. Like someone acting being in a fight and Derec just twats him one and I see JD spinning round and falling down like he's a statue. As he hits the ground I swear he says 'Gosh'. I hear Derec say, 'Dickhead,' clear as a fucking bell.

So I say, 'I thought you didn't speak English, you fucking egg.'

I call him that cos it's what he looks like—an egg. But it's not the best thing to say because it just makes the others laugh.

And Caitlin says, 'I'll make some coffee.' And we all stay in place for a while, sort of frozen, and it's JD who makes the first move. He stands up and wipes his nose with the back of his hand and tries to brush the ice and shit from his clothes and he doesn't look too steady but I don't know if it's the punch or the drink.

He says, 'Well, I'll clearly have to work on my in-fighting technique.'

And him and Derec shake hands. And then I stand up and I look straight at Derec.

'You're fucking dead, you are,' I say. And I work hard on making sure that I say it proper quiet so he knows I mean it.

I'm most jarred at Caitlin. When her and Justin came back there was a note from Derec which must have said where he was.

Caitlin goes, 'Fancy a drink, Jus? Karaoke night. Derec's there.' Justin shrugs and I think he doesn't give a shit about going but Caitlin says, 'That's alright isn't it, Mistyann? Means more dosh.'

I don't like being taken for granted but Carmel is begging me to stay so I think it'll be okay. And now she's dropped me right in the shit.

We're in the house and I keep looking for chances to run but I feel sort of tired and they're watching me all the time. They all have coffees with whisky in them, even JD.

Derec says, 'A nice drop of Welsh, Jon?'

And JD says, 'Welsh whisky. No wonder you have it with coffee.' And it's like they're all fucking friends again.

And when JD says, 'Come on, Mistyann, time to face the music.' Everyone stands up and kisses each other on the cheek like we've been at some floss party or something. Freaks me out. Caitlin asks if JD is alright to walk back and he goes, 'Yeah. Nothing like finding a runaway student to sober you up. Not to mention a punch up the bracket.' And everyone smiles and laughs and it's all so nice and polite that it makes me want to puke.

I say, 'You owe me sixty-four quid.' Everyone looks a bit shocked. 'Baby-sitting,' I say.

So then they have to scramble around to find the money. Stupid fucks. But they do in the end. What did they think? That I would just say 'Okay—don't worry about it.' Carmel's a nice kid but no kid is that fucking nice.

It's proper cold on the walk back and JD and me both keep slipping and sliding and skidding. In the end we have to hold on to each other just to keep from falling over but it's still hard work and slow. It's like when you run the three-legged race in primary school. For a start JD is much taller and heavier than me and for another thing the drink has messed him up. It takes us about twenty minutes just to get to the end of the lane and by then our teeth are chattering and my muscles feel tight and JD is having to stop for a rest every five seconds. The last time we stop JD has his hands on his knees and his head hanging down. He looks like he could collapse and die any minute.

I say, 'This is messed up. You know that, don't you?' But he can't even speak. Just looks at me.

In the end he goes, 'Yeah, but what can we do? We can't go back to the house of the Free Wales Army.'

I have no idea what he's on about but I guess it's a teacher-joke. I have an idea then. I put my hand in his pocket and there they are. The keys to Ray's Defender. Derec must have given them to him in the house.

JD says, 'I can't drive, Mistyann. I'm way over the limit.'

And I say, 'I know that dum-dum. I'm going to.'

JD says, 'Bollocks.'

But I can see him thinking about trying to walk back in the dark and cold and ice. And then he doesn't say anything but turns around and starts heading up the lane so I know he agrees. I go after him and link arms again.

It's quicker going back. Pretty soon we're at the car and we get in. JD straps himself in and I switch the lights on and we can see snow all around on the fields and trees and hedges even though it was raining quite a bit today.

He says, 'The land of ice and snow. That's the Ancient Mariner, Mistyann.'

And I say, 'I know, you taught us it in Year 8.'

'For Christ's sake don't crash, Mistyann.'

I say, 'Thank God you reminded me otherwise I'd have like proper mashed us up big style.'

And I turn the engine on and the heater and the little petrol warning light comes on but I can't worry about that now and I bump down the lane. And I can feel JD all tense next to me but he relaxes as he sees that I can drive. And I can handle this old beast of a car now no worries. By the time we've left the village it's well warm in the car and JD's fallen asleep and I'm thinking fuck it all. Fuck everything.

Fucking car runs out of petrol about half an hour later. I've just been driving, haven't looked at the signs, just kept on going wherever, so I have no fucking clue where we are but it's still the middle of nowhere. After the car coughs and dies I sit there listening to JD's breathing and the odd sheep that's got insomnia and wants to tell the world.

I feel proper lonely and want to wake JD up even if he just has a go at me and starts shouting. And I think again how decent he is and how he always wants to do the right thing. Then I realise that I can't hear JD breathing and I panic a bit but when I go to shake him I see his eyes are open and he's just watching me and I get a tiny whiff of sick so I move back away from him.

He says, 'Where the fuck are we, Mistyann?'

And it feels good to just have him say my name even if I'm shocked at him swearing and know that he is pure total mad at me. I know he's proper cross cos his voice is so quiet I can hardly hear him even though he's in the seat next to me. I don't say anything.

He says, 'Christ.'

And I say, 'Just ran out of petrol. Not my fault, is it?'

'Yes, Mistyann, but we're not actually anywhere near the centre are we?'

And I can't think of anything to say so I keep quiet. He says, 'Christ.' Again.

I say, 'I need a piss.' And I get out and go a little way from the car.

It feels well weird to have a cold wind moving on my bare legs and pubes and everything and I can hear JD having a piss the other side of the car and I think about how much easier it is to be a bloke. It's just zip down, knob out, do the business, knob in. Zip up. But we've got to fiddle about all crouched over and running the risk of getting piss on our jeans. Fucking inconvenient.

When we're back in the car I try and say this to JD, just to try and have a normal chat but he's still all mardy and won't talk so we just sit in the car in silence getting colder. I think we're going to freeze to death. I've got my mobile but I'd rather die than call anyone. I watch my breath make shapes in the air in front of my face for a while

Then I say, 'There's some covers in the back. And some stinky old quilts.'

And JD still won't say anything, so I crawl over and get everything and try and make a little nest for myself along the back seat.

It still feels freezing so I say, 'Come on, Sir, we have to snuggle up otherwise we'll be like those geezers who went to the North Pole and froze to death on the way back. You know, Captain Scott and that.'

He says, 'Don't call me Sir.'

And we laugh and then he tells me it was the South Pole and I tell him that it's all the same isn't it and he laughs and crawls into the back with me and he lies one way and I lie the other and our legs are all tangled up in the middle and we share the duvets and it's not exactly comfortable but it does feel warmer and I decide that yeah I actually like the smell of booze on his breath. He asks if I want a fag and I say yeah and he has one too and I see all the shadows in his face as he lights them with this match and I think that it's like we're in some mad film.

He hands me the cig and I think about reaching out and touching the stubble on his cheek. But I don't. We just smoke for a while and then I notice that my feet are like totally numb and I ask JD about what happens when you get frost-bite and he tells me about gangrene and having to have limbs amputated. Even noses sometimes. And he must know that I'm panicking so he tells me to take my boots off. And it's a hassle but in the end I do and my socks and feet are soaked and he takes hold of them and rubs them really gently and it hurts as the blood starts moving in them and then they feel warm and dry and nice. JD carries on stroking and rubbing them for a while and then he stops and tells me about soldiers getting something called trench-foot in the First World War and I don't really care but it's sort of like getting a bed-time story when you're a kid. It's just good to hear his voice droning on and my leg is trapped right between his and the bottom of my foot is resting on that bit you get on blokes jeans where it all bunches up over the zip. And I push my foot forward just a bit. Just to see what will happen. And he puts his hand on my leg and says, 'Don't, Mistyann.'

And I go, 'What?' But I don't make a big deal about it. And then somehow we go to sleep cos the next thing that happens is it's day-light and I'm on my own and proper stiff and achey. I look out of the car window and I don't see JD at first but I do see where the car stopped.

We're at the side of this fuck off lake. Miles and miles of water all surrounded by mountains and there's this mist hanging over the water. It looks like magic. It looks like Lord of the fucking Rings. It's like a dragon could rise out of the water at any moment and start breathing fire over everything. I'm gobsmacked.

And then I see JD standing next to the water with his hands in his pocket. Smoking. I open the car door and the cold slaps me in the face. It's unbelievable and there's a wind too. I can feel the tears coming into my eyes.

'Hey!' I shout, 'You better have saved me a fag.'

And I put my bare feet in my big old lost property boots and stumble across the mud and grass and snow to where he stands. He doesn't look at me but does give me a cig.

'Breakfast,' he says, still without looking at me.

I say, 'Aren't you going to light it for me then?'

But he doesn't answer. He just says 'It looks so easy doesn't it? Like you could just dive in and you'd feel so clean and you could keep swimming and every part of you would be alive and new and everything would be sorted out. It would be like diving right through the world and leaving all the mess behind. You'd take nothing with you except what mattered.'

'You dive in,' I say, 'And I'll go straight in after you and we'll both die of hypothermia and that won't look good will it? Teacher and star pupil drown together. It'll look like Romeo and Juliet or something.'

He turns and looks at me then. 'What makes you think you're my star pupil, Mistyann?'

And that's when we hear a car and turn around to see the fat copper shouting.

THIRTY-FIVE

I was in the cross-country team at the Modern school. It wasn't intentional. We'd never done cross-country at my old school. Let the kids run around the estate in school time? That would be madness. It was hard enough to get most of them into school in the first place. So the first time the games master at the Modern sent us off like a pack of hounds across the fields that surrounded the Victorian turrets and towers of the school I had no idea of pacing myself. I treated it as a three mile sprint and was amazed that I could keep going through miles of that special Autumn ooze of leaves and mud and cow-pats. I didn't come home first—some boarder fuelled by the freedom of being outside on his own for the first time in months managed that—but I was up there on the leader board.

I didn't stick at it. I was already finding the shock of Saturday morning school an assault verging on actual abuse and spending the afternoons chasing the long-limbed children of colonels around nondescript Midlands woodland rapidly lost its novelty. And as I moved up the school the discovery of music further sapped my motivation, while the drink began to undermine my speed. But I discovered it again a few years ago as a way of sweating out all the many kinds of nonsense that go on in a modern comprehensive. Something loud and fast on the Walkman; breath forced from your body by trying to sprint up past the cemetery and through the allotments and the world of league tables, reports and percentages of children gaining five A-C grades at GCSE all seemed slightly silly.

I've even done the London Marathon. And I did the Great North Run the year half the race seemed to suffer heart failure at the ten mile mark. I've worn the T-shirts of the Meningitis Trust, the Alzheimer's Society, MIND, the British Heart Foundation, all sorts. I've even run for PETA, in fear the whole time that I'd be booted off the team when they discovered that my trainers had leather uppers. I must have raised thousands for good causes. I don't do it now obviously. But all that training seemed to come in handy when we saw PC Minhinnick on the brow of the hill that Tuesday morning.

You took off like a frightened hare, unlaced boots clearly impeding your progress, but you managed to somehow keep going while getting them off and tossing them aside in a way that any Ethiopian Marathon virtuoso would applaud. Then you were clambering across that extraordinary furred and speckled landscape, that mixture of ice and slush and mud and grass, in your bare feet. I went after you with no thought in my head beyond catching you but as I got close you breathed, 'Fat fuck's got no chance.' And it was as easy as that, the line was crossed. I was no longer your teacher, I was your accomplice. I could have pulled you down or back, held onto you till that amiable plod came puffing up to us. But I didn't. As you stumbled, I pulled you up and became, instead, your coach, exhorting you to keep your knees up, giving you the encouragement to keep going.

We lost him soon enough, darting away from the reservoir and into a scrubby patch of woodland; scratching our way through nettles and thistles, until you were unable to keep your curses at a muttered volume.

You called out, 'My feet are getting all fucked up here!' Which is how I came to be giving you a piggy back down a narrow and ancient footpath, a girl nearly as tall as myself, but giggling like a child at the nonsense of it all.

We came to a stile and climbed over it and you were okay to walk again on the other side, though you clutched my arm as we skirted the bored cows who occupied it.

'Cows won't hurt you, Mistyann,' I said and you gave me one of those dark and penetrating looks.

On the other side of the field we could see a village. Or a row of cottages anyway. It turned out to be four houses, a shop and a pub.

'Top,' you said, 'I need a shit. Badly.' I must have winced or showed some sign of distaste because you followed up hotly with, 'Well, even girls shit you know. And I've got a real tortoise head coming. It's poking between the hills. Know what I'm saying?'

'Yes, I think I get the general picture. The thing is, the pub is unlikely to be open at this time.'

'Well I've got to go. Have you got any tissues?' And I did. I had a crumpled pack of handies because a teacher in charge of a school trip should always be prepared.

So there you were squatting by the dry stone wall at the edge of the field.

'Turn around then, Sir. Don't be a perv,' you chirruped. And I turned my back on you and stared at the cows who stared back unperturbed. I heard you sing out from behind me, 'Sorry. Didn't mean to call you Sir.'

I didn't answer. I thought about the Army Cadet Force back at the Modern. We didn't mind playing the biscuit game, all of us tossing ourselves off onto a ginger nut but there's no way any of us would have taken a dump next to one another. Not even the ones who later ended up in the proper army.

We stumbled into the hamlet, no sign of life anywhere, to find that the shop was not the predictable post office cum general store. It was instead a shop that announced itself as Tom Price: Bicycles and Footwear. The footwear wasn't even bike related. It wasn't even sport related. Do you remember? The window display was a random mix of bike helmets and old ladies bingo-creepers in various shades of cream, beige and brown.

I wouldn't let you come in with me. You gave me your size and shivered outside. I didn't want a row about shoes in the shop but your feet were butchered by this point and you needed something even if it was going to be a pair of mules of a style you wouldn't touch again until pension day sometime in 2055. If they still have pensions then. But I had sorely misjudged Tom Price.

'Trainers? Of course we've got trainers. Kids won't wear anything else round here. Don't put them in the window in case they get pinched, see?' And so a pair of size five turbo-charged Air Jordan gti max or whatever were produced at a price that would not have disgraced Bond Street. £180. For a pair of pumps. £10 for a pair of hiking socks. I declined the patent cleaning fluid that came in a three inch tube, a snip at another tenner.

'I only wear Nikes,' you said straight-faced. But you put them on.

Bikes and shoes. What was all that about? I didn't really question it at the time, did you? When I was at the University of Clearing there was a shop in the town called Bacon TV, and we used to joke about picking up a few rashers and a VHS recorder. And Salmon builders who work out of Stanley Street always made me laugh. The idea of freshwater fish leaping high to fix roof slates, but Tom Price was doing it for real, making a living from selling two completely unrelated items in the same tiny space.

The pub was even stranger. It was old, walls bulging oddly and sloping noticeably to the left, leaning against the short terrace of cottages like a drunken great-grandmother at Christmas, relying on her younger, slightly sturdier relatives to keep her upright. Apart from that little family of labouring cottages there was nothing around for miles except fields, emaciated woodland and a reservoir. And yet the Forester's Arms—written in English—proved to be a gastro-pub that was aiming high.

We studied the menu. Who out here, I wondered, would really appreciate a stir-fried salad of king prawns and baby courgettes? Where was the market for Gressingham duck with pink grapefruit and passion fruit sauce? You told me off for being a snob and pointed out the obvious.

'It's open for breakfast, look.'

The interior of the pub was all flag-stones, exposed brick, big fireplaces and cast-iron stoves. There was one customer, a slate-faced old man breakfasting on real ale the colour of oxtail soup. He raised his glass to us as we made our way towards the thirty-something blonde at the bar. In looks and manner she was more city lawyer than rural Welsh bar-keeper and sure enough her accent told a story of Surrey gymkhanas and Young Farmers' balls. She made a heroic effort not to give us questioning looks. We must have looked a sight. Hungover, unwashed, clothes in disorder, me unshaved and the two of us oddly matched. Perhaps we passed for a father and daughter on an ill-advised bonding holiday, but it seems unlikely.

We both had a full Welsh fry up which seemed, to my undiscerning palette, the same as the traditional English kind.

And it was only then that we began to talk about our situation and its implications. I began in the role of chief investigator and prosecutor: What were you thinking? Where were you going to go? What was your plan? Did you even have a plan? And then you put it to me, gently really, that actually I was the one that was really fucked here.

You said, 'God, JD you're such a teacher. Look, nothing bad will happen to me. Either I get to London or I go back to school. Mum's going to go mental, but then that's nothing new. You, though, what are you going to do? Out on the lash then found next day with one of your students, sprinting away from the pigs when they turn up—looks shit doesn't it? I'm sorry by the way.'

'It's not your fault.'

'I know. But I'm still sorry, because you're going to have to look for a new job. A whole new career.'

'Your mum said something similar actually.'

'Yeah well, she might be a psycho but she's not thick.'

And you sat shovelling bacon and fried egg and tomatoes into your mouth, egg dribbling down your chin and making you look about six.

'You've got egg on your chin.'

You laughed. 'Our problem isn't what to do about me. It's what to do about you, man. You're going to get crucified when we get back. Maybe you can work with school refusers or special needs or something. Maybe they'll still let you do that.'

I doubted it. You shrugged.

'You need some kind of plan, JD. See I can go to London, get a job, get a flat. I can disappear. It's less than a year till I'm sixteen anyway and I can sort myself out. You're proper shafted though. Maybe you can open a shop. They don't do checks and that on people selling stuff do they. Maybe you can do stuff on EBay.'

'Selling what, pray?'

'I don't know, do I? Rare books and shit. Just saying, you've got to have a plan.'

My head was aching. I asked if you were still going to run away.

'Probably. Not sure.'

I told you to at least wait until after your GCSEs. You howled, 'I don't believe it. You can't stop, can you?'

'I know, Mistyann. It's just... well, you can take the bloke out of the staff-room but you can't take the staff-room out of the bloke, I guess.'

You looked at me carefully. 'It's a fucking shame that is.'

We didn't talk about the night before in Ray's freezing Defender. We didn't talk about your wet and frozen foot coming back to life under my hand. We didn't talk about the way that same foot had pushed between my legs. We didn't talk of my dreams where you had lowered yourself onto me saying, 'Ssh, it'll be alright' silencing my protests with a kiss. And then a breast. We didn't talk of the fear I felt on starting awake or the relief when I realised it was just a dream and that you were sleeping soundly and fully clothed at your end of the bench-seat. Three times I must have had a variation on that dream and each time had to rip myself from sleep, sure that I'd wake to find myself heaving and writhing on top of you.

We sat in silence. An ancient Labrador padded over and lay down at your feet. You scratched her behind the ears. Satisfied, she put her head on her paws and went to sleep.

I said, 'Where do you see yourself in five years time, Mistyann?'

And so I heard about your creative business dreams. The money you were going to make and then the way you'd use it to travel. How you were going to put many frequent flyer miles between Bedford and your future self.

You said, 'I wonder what everyone else is doing now?'

I said, 'We should call them. Tell them about the car at the very least.'

'They'll know by now. Police radios. In fact we should get out of here. Before it's too late.'

'Yes, but we do need to make a few decisions first.'

And that's how come I used the pay-phone in the Forester's to call a taxi. You were going to the nearest railway station and then I was going to face the music and dance. The taxi company said they'd be fifteen minutes and they were true to their word, arriving exactly quarter of an hour later and at exactly the same time as four—four! —police squad cars appeared, all lights blazing. The mid-Wales police establishment couldn't have got more excited if they'd received reports that Osama Bin Laden had been caught in flagrante with Lord Lucan in the pub toilet. It was the most absurd overkill and you know what was the worst thing about the arrest? They sent me a bill for the cost of the taxi.

It's true. When all the legal paper-work arrived at the offices of poor old Wayne's superiors it included an invoice from the police for £17.25 because they'd had to pay off an irritable cabbie who turned up to find his fare being bundled into the back of a police Astra.

I didn't make a dignified exit, being first spread-eagled across a pub table and then cuffed and man-handled out into the clean, crisp blue of a fine clear morning. A clean crisp blue which I only experienced for a few seconds before being shoved into the back of the car the way the remains of a Friday night takeaway gets forced into an over-flowing pedal-bin. Those impassive coppers couldn't bear the sight or smell of me. I made them physically ill.

You, they had the good sense to leave to walk to a separate car under your own steam. Something in your look kept them polite and at arms' length. It's a good trick, Mistyann, being able to keep the authorities in check with a glance. You should keep that. Practice it. Don't lose it

THIRTY-SIX

I'm pure fucking bored. The graffiti is mostly in Welsh so I can't pass the time reading that. I know that they are going to leave me in here for hours so I should just get my head down but there's this crap strip lighting which is one thing that makes it hard. Another thing is the cold. I've only got this wooden bench thing to lie and one itchy blanket that pure reeks. The worst thing is the smell. Old men's piss is what this place stinks of. I keep waiting to get used to it. But I don't. There should be a law against keeping people in conditions like this. If you kept a dog like this in Bedford, someone would grass you up to the RSPCA. Or shove shit through your letter box. One or the other. They pure love dogs in Manton Heights.

I shout and scream for a bit. I tell them I'm only fifteen and they can't keep me like this, it's against the Children's Act. I don't know if it is but it's got to worry them, but no-one comes. I'm not even sure if any police are in.

In my head I sort of make this movie where I go to the bogs in that pub just before the police arrive and see that they're coming and get out of the window and zoom across the fields. I think about loads of fat coppers trying to get me but not being able to and me waving to them as I disappear out of sight and they have to call up helicopters to try and catch me but I've used Pete's card to check into some fancy hotel and I just stay in there watching TV and using the internet and ordering from room service until there's some other big crime and they can't be bothered to look for me anymore.

No-one talks to me till I'm in the car. There are two of them. It's the fat one who speaks first, probably trying to suck up to the boss one.

He says, 'You alright, love?'

And I say, 'Fuck you.'

And he says, 'Oh, so it's going to be like that is it?'

And I say, 'Yeah it is.'

And he can't think of anything else to say. So that's him stubbed out. I stare at the back of his neck. He's got these folds of fat that hang over the collar of his shirt and there's thick grey curly hair on it and you just know that he'll have a hairy grey back. I ask him if he's married and he says that he is, not that it's any of my business. And I ask him if he's got any kids and he says yes he has, two and then he remembers that he's meant to be arresting me and treating me like shit, so he tells me to shut up.

And I say, 'Charming. Politeness costs nothing.'

And I start smiling to myself. I can see him checking me out in his mirror. I see his little piggy eyes flicker and slide across me like he's reading me like a book he finds a bit difficult. He can't tell me to stop smiling can he? But I can see that it's winding him up.

They give me a cup of tea at the police station. It's not a proper station. It looks like someone's house. The police station is all white and the lights are really bright and I can see that the boss one is well younger than I thought at first. He's maybe around twenty-eight or something, but he has a chubby red face and it makes him look older. He probably drinks too much. Probably needs to eat some more vegetables. I tell him this and he tells me to shut it. Which isn't very original. He's getting jarred with me. And it's worse for him because the fat one is smiling and that's going to jar him off even more. Which is good.

There's another policeman behind a counter and he is older and just seems tired. He looks like a granddad, the kind of granddad you see in adverts that surf and go hang-gliding and skiing and all that shit. The kind of granddad that doesn't really exist. This granddad sends the blokes who arrested me off to do something or other. All of us know that it's just to get them out of the way.

The granddad-guy says that his name is Alun-with-a-u and it's him that makes the tea and puts four sugars in it when I ask him to without looking surprised or making any sarcastic remarks or anything. He fills in some forms and when I tell him where I'm staying he says, 'Oh, Willy Wonka's' And I ask him why he says that and he says it's because everyone thinks of the Cefn Coch centre as being like Willy Wonka's chocolate factory.

'You never see anyone come in or go out see, and no one is very sure what goes on in there.'

And I say, 'Oh, it's just school stuff. Writing and shit for gifted children.'

And he says, 'Oh, so you're gifted are you?'

And I say, 'Well, some people think I am.'

And for some unknown reason I end up telling him the story about Mr Negus calling me a genius and what my mum said and then I find that I'm crying. Proper does me in. I never cry. And that's twice now in two days.

And when he says, 'There, there, love.' And goes to fetch me a tissue. It just makes me cry more. And I almost tell him everything else. I nearly tell him about the joyriding and Mum being a bit of an alkie psycho and Ty and William and Harry and JD and coming from Bedford and all of that, but I don't. And in the end I'm glad that I don't. I'm not sure that he would have been able to handle it and he'd probably have to report it all to someone and then there'd be more shit to deal with. And it would go on and on and there'd be meetings and social workers and just more and more crap. Anyway, after a while I don't feel like talking so I just sort of sit there.

So I get another cup of sugary tea, two chocolate hob-nobs, this scratchy blanket that smells a bit like the covers in Ray's car and the kind, granddad policeman tells me that they'll phone the centre and tell them where I am and that someone will be down to pick me up in the morning.

I sit in that crappy cell trying to get used to the stink with a billion thoughts running through my head and pacing about. And that's when I start shouting and all that, but nothing happens so I sit still and just try and hypnotise myself by staring at a crack in the grey wall for hours.

I'm not bothered. Really, I'm not. I'm thinking how this will make it easier to get to London. In a way, everyone will be expecting me to run off now. I won't be letting anyone down. I've already done that. It's too bad about Pete's credit card. I guess they'll give that back to him and he'll die with 4K in the bank and I'll be scrounging for a fiver, but it did feel sort of too easy.

I try to imagine my life in London. I think that it'll be shitty at first. I'll have to work crappy cash in hand jobs. I see myself as a waitress or something, but not for long. Soon as I'm eighteen I'll get bar work and then go abroad to somewhere sunny. Learn a language, manage a pub, meet a decent bloke.

I see myself on a beach, two kids, my own bar, SUV, watching footie on satellite, maybe even serving drinks to players and their girl-friends. I'd have the kind of place where you can chill big-style. Big sofas, a bloke in a posh suit playing the piano. And I'd be with someone who works in an office, but who keeps himself fit with five-a-side and running and the gym three nights a week. A funny guy, a brainy guy, so our kids would be clever. And after a while I'd earn enough so I'd only work behind the bar when I wanted to. We'd serve the sickest food too. Healthy but proper tasty. People would talk about our place. We'd be in magazines. And then we'd build our own house. Something wild and spectacular. I imagine it all. The colour of the walls, the material the sofas are made out of, names of my kids—Freda and Katie—everything. Keeps me going for hours.

THIRTY-SEVEN

In contrast to the common-or-garden roughness of the police who arrested me, they were pretty decent in the cop-shop. I imagine that they were worried that unless they treated me with courtesy then I might get off on a technicality. Despite the breakfast and the adrenalin rush of the arrest and the unnecessarily high speed journey to the nearest town, I was now feeling the delayed effects of the drink and lack of sleep.

My mouth tasted like someone had painted all my teeth with thick, oily glue. My brain had shrunk inside my head. I could picture it—a desiccated walnut rattling around the inky emptiness of my bruised skull. I felt like shit. But it was a whole lot better than I deserved. What was a headache in the grand scheme of things? A headache—even an apocalyptic, biblical one like this—was nothing.

I made a humble request to take a shower and not only did they allow it, they even provided a clean and ridiculously fluffy pink bath towel. They even gave me shower gel. Ginger and eucalyptus.

I was escorted to a large bathroom and left alone. I looked in the mirror. I had grown old overnight. In the shower I was able to examine honestly whether falling off the wagon had sent me tumbling straight back into addiction. I know that's what they tell you in rehab or AA. They say 'a hundred drinks are not enough and one is too many'. But I was gratified to find that the thought of drink was repellent to me. I felt more or less fully prepared to accept whatever bad things were coming my way. One of the other tropes they have in AA is 'Even this will pass'. Which you are meant to be able to cling to while all the rest of your life sinks around you. It's meant to keep you alive, afloat and sane until you float within swimming distance of dry land and a new start. It's bollocks. Nothing passes. It just adds a layer to the weight we carry.

I used a lot of shower gel. And I spent a lot of time and attention on my bloodied feet. They didn't look like my feet at all. They were the tortured soles of an Arabic political dissident. They were raw and crusted across the toes with the ruddy brown of dried blood. I soaped and rinsed them back into some kind of normality. I wondered what condition you were in. All that running with no shoes.

And then I scoured my mouth with a great deal of turbo-mint toothpaste. I was equally liberal with the sandalwood shaving gel which the police service had provided along with a Gillette mach 3 razor. The best a man can get. I'm sure suspects aren't usually given the wherewithal to kill themselves in police custody. It occurred to me that perhaps I was meant to do the decent thing. Perhaps this was the Welsh police equivalent of handing a disgraced officer a loaded revolver and a glass of whisky. And I was reminded of that great Evelyn Waugh novel where an officer responsible for some regimental fiasco is handed the drink and the gun and left alone for a discreet minute. In Waugh's story he drinks up and flees through a back door unable to save his honour.

Was I meant to freshen up and then slice my wrists as a way of avoiding the shame I had brought on myself, my family, my employer and my profession?

There was a dinky bottle of some sort of après lave, something some young PC was using to mask the smell of fear and loathing out there on the mean cart-tracks of Wales. I splashed some on my stinging cheeks and neck. Whatever my doom was going to be I was going to face up to it. And I was going to face up to it smelling pretty.

And it was only then—when I was scrubbed, rubbed, scented and scraped—that I really thought about you. I realised that the police—being in my experience creatures of limited imagination—were going to assume that we'd been 'carrying on'. I also realised that this kind of mud sticks fast and hard and that my teaching career was, as both you and your mum had been quick to point out, over. There were going to be choppy waters ahead but I had no wife, no kids. No-one other than myself to be hurt by the implication that I was a scum-bag nonce. Only my mum.

Just think, if they hadn't had London Calling on the karaoke machine in the Telyn a Chan; if I hadn't called Wales a 'cartoon country' in Boudicca's hearing; if I had announced that I was an alcoholic when offered a pint by the landlady; if I hadn't let you drive back to the centre; if I hadn't fallen asleep in Ray's Defender... If any one of those things... perhaps, instead of sitting here watching day-time telly behind drawn curtains, I might be introducing Year 9 to the dirty magic of *Macbeth*. I could be producing a newspaper front page with Year 8 or queuing at the photo-copier behind Mrs English counting how many times she sniffs. You know, sometimes it almost seems worth all this humiliation just to have escaped the whole dreary business of mass-producing young workers with the vocational skills necessary for today's fast moving globalised economy. And all that bollocks.

And what if I had accepted the invitation of your naked foot against my groin in the dark of that car? What if we had made love and then eloped to London in the romantic Welsh dawn? Where would we be now? Would we be eating hot buttered toast in our rented mews apartment in dock-side London? Or would I be in another jail while you gave hell to some unlucky foster family?

PC Watt was a soft-faced thirty-something who may well have been the most depressed man I've ever seen. Did you see him? He had a ruddy complexion and his uniform was crumpled and shiny. There was a stain on one shoulder. He looked like he'd been sleeping rough.

He began with some small-talk, presumably to put me at my ease. It must be a difficult job being a teacher, what with the behaviour of young people today, no respect etc. His heart wasn't really in it and I didn't encourage him.

'Perhaps you should give me your side of things, Jon?' he said.

And I looked at him and he looked at me. He seemed genuinely puzzled. It didn't look like he wanted to make an arrest, more that he wanted to set his accounts in order; solve the riddle. He looked like one of the dim but hard-working kids in Set 3, Year 9. The kind who can somehow concentrate on the painstaking labour of writing the diary entry of one of Macbeth's soldiers before the battle of Dunsinane, and then illustrate it nicely with a picture, despite the noise from the disruptive elements. Maybe this made me want to help him out. I told him everything.

Then I waited around in a squalid cell while they fetched a special detective from Aberystwyth, a brisk efficient woman called Detective Sergeant Linda Edwards and I told her the whole thing too. And they told me that I'd be staying in the cells overnight while they thought about what to charge me with.

And yes, as I'd known from the moment I was bent double over that pub table, what they were interested in of course was whether there was anything 'between' you and me. The air in that stuffy little office was thick with innuendo and speculation. It made me tired. I know getting off with the students is an occupational hazard for male teachers, but you? The trouble is an affair, a 'thing' as Linda put it, between teacher and pupil is much more understandable than a platonic moon-light joy-ride. As far as Linda was concerned the story went: unhappy pupil looks for a father figure, predatory teacher takes advantage. Predatory teacher organizes a trip away the better to indulge his sick desires. This despite the obvious point that if I had actually had those kind of sick desires to indulge, then I would have been far better off having my half term at home. If I hadn't put you up for the course we could have been at it 24/7 in the comfort of my terraced kinky sex den, or whatever the tabloids call it.

I wonder how they told Ariel and Susie? What did they tell the kids? I wonder how Amber reacted? Did she fire off an immediate text to the long-suffering fuckwit boyfriend?

I know that by three o' clock they had decided to cancel the course rather than try to find another suitably qualified adult to act as guardian for the week. Linda told me this as soon as she arrived. I was left in no doubt that ruining the life chances of gifted students was merely the least of my heinous crimes.

I was up in a Welsh court the next morning charged with abduction. In addition to the expected, the drink-driving. Abduction. Despite the fact that if anyone had been kidnapped it was me. I had been bringing you back to the centre, not eloping with you. They dropped it eventually. Did you know that? Did you follow anything to do with the court case?

Well, in case you didn't—they couldn't make it stick. After months of suspicion and finger-pointing and hints and innuendo, all of which still goes on, they couldn't pin that one on me.

While I was helping police with their enquiries, back in Gladstone Road a forensic swat team clad in sterile combats was filmed going into my house and removing my computer. Another team went in to take away my sheets for a thorough sniffing. What filthy minds the people who do these jobs must have. And once someone shines their prurient light into all the rooms of your life, you can't avoid looking evil or, worse, ridiculous.

Imagine how it looked for me. I lived on my own. I was, therefore officially a 'sad loner'. I became 'Sad loner,

Diamond, 41' who was 'revealed today as a pathetic alcoholic who once nursed dreams of being a rock star'. And there was a string of ex-colleagues and current neighbours eager to ink in the painting-by-numbers portrait of a sinister loser who, it turns out, they had always had doubts about. After a while nothing you read or hear about yourself surprises you. Nothing catches you off guard because you expect it all. The cat-calling in the street; the mates who blank you; the spitting; the punch in the face from an ex-student when you answer the door-bell; the breathy calls in the early hours where the number of the caller has been withheld; the misspelt graffiti on the wall of the house—'Peedo', I mean, come on, who teaches these kids? And then there's your mum. It's like life during war-time. You get used to the bombing and dig around for some Blitz spirit.

Where the fuck are you, Mistyann?

THIRTY-EIGHT

There's Mum. She's skinny and bony and looks even more like a witch than normal and she's smiling which makes my shoulders go tight. It's the fat cop who brings me out of the cell. He seems a bit shy now. Like he's nervous of me.

'Come on,' he says, like he's trying to be hard, 'People to see you. You're a lucky girl. You might get away with this.'

I like the way Welsh people speak, like they are singing even when they are just gassing about the weather or something, but I don't like the way this guy talks. There's something about the way his voice goes up and down that makes my shoulders tense. I take a deep breath.

So there's my mum by the counter in that stupid toytown police station, smiling. And there's Ty looking huge like a super-size elephant and smiling too. My mum's smile says 'I knew you'd fuck up'. And Ty's smile says 'I'm genuinely pleased to see you and I think that you are pleased to see me'. Ty's smile pisses me off the most.

I say, 'What the fuck are you doing here?' My mum's smile doesn't change or shrink, that's how false it is. Ty looks proper upset. He looks like a little boy that's had his bum slapped. That annoys me even more. 'What are you looking at me like that for?' I say. 'Fucking perv.' And my mum's fake smile disappears now. She crosses over to me proper fast. She's wearing heels and they click-click-click across the stone tiles of this office place proper loud. The policeman guy stops her.

'We've got some paperwork to do, love,' he says. So she can only give me the hairy eyeball for a second or two. Then she looks at the copper and gives him this big grin. I can see him turn away from it. It really is an ugly smile. She looks like some kind of shark. Like the proper evil ones you see in cartoons.

'Where are William and Harry?' I ask.

'In the car outside,' Ty says quietly. He's still acting all hurt. Wanker.

'That's illegal that is,' I say to the cop, 'They're only little kids. They can't leave them on their own. You should arrest them.'

The cop just sighs but Ty says, 'I'll go and check on them,' and mooches out of the door. He's so tall that his head brushes the door frame, even though he ducks down. Mum looks jarred off, but she doesn't say anything.

Me and the copper have to go into this small back room. He has to give me my stuff back and I have to sign a form. He tells me that he is releasing me on police bail and that I'll have to come back in a month or so.

'All this way?' I say, 'To fucking Wales?'

'That's right, love. To fucking Wales. I said you were a lucky girl.'

I decide to tell him about my mum being a psycho witch and I add some stuff about Ty looking at me funny and making me nervous. You hear about families where they take the kids away just because their parents took a photo of them in the nud. When my mum first started fighting with Ty—when she first found out about him fucking other women—we were going to click on to some kiddie porn site using his credit card. Then Mum was going to phone the police all in tears and say she'd discovered these disgusting images on his computer. It was my plan. Me and Mum were getting on pure easy then and she was well impressed. She should have done it. Ty would be in prison now. Out of our lives anyway. They always remove the perpetrator from the family environment. Any TV show will tell you that. The cop listens to me for a bit and makes loads of notes in this note-pad like the ones I use to do my GCSE coursework. I nick them from the English Department stock cupboard. After a while he interrupts me, which is just plain fucking rude.

He says, 'The thing that I don't get, love, is why your teacher was with you?'

This 'love' business is getting on my tits but I decide not to worry about that for now. I don't say anything. I'm waiting for a chance to tell him more about my freakish family. But he keeps on about Diamond. I don't answer him and in the end he has to change the subject. He asks me about Cefn Coch.

He says, 'I know they have some pretty weird kids up there.'

I say, 'They're all totally normal except that Dalwinder is a Paki, Julius is proper black, Charlotte is a stupid spoilt rich bitch, Zak's never been to school and Pete's a spastic. Oh and there's two other girls who are always too scared to speak and look like they are about to cry all the time.'

He asks me about stealing the car.

'Not much of a policeman are you?' I say. 'It's not stealing—it's Taking Without the Owner's Consent. TWOC. There's a difference you know.'

'Is there?' he says.

'Yeah, and actually there was someone else in the car with Diamond and me. It was Pete the Spastic. He heard you coming and he got up and ran. His legs began to work all of a sudden and he went pure fast and got away from you. It was a fucking miracle.'

And I get this sudden picture in my head of that day when I had the school baby and it started to cry after I had whacked it. I remember JD shouting 'It's a miracle!' and all the kids laughing and I remember that I felt angry because it was like he was taking the piss. And here I was protecting him from getting accused of doing under-age sex with me. Makes me smile. And that makes the cop mad.

'You think this is funny?' he says, and his red face is getting redder. It's almost purple.

'Yeah, I do actually,' I say. 'Your face is funny anyway. It looks like a tomato.'

And of course he goes redder. I can tell he wants to twat me. You can always tell when people have run out of words and don't know what else to do. He swallows and takes a deep breath.

'You want to do anger management,' I say, 'It works for me. Most of the time anyway.' And I smile at him. He looks away.

'You're a nutter, you are,' he says.

I ask him what he's going to do about all the things I've told him about my mum being an evil witch and Ty being a weirdo and he says, 'I tell you what I'm going to do, love.' And he takes the pages of notes that he has been writing and he tears them up in front of me and throws all the pieces into the bin by the door. And I suddenly think of Ariel and her amazing smile.

'You're a timewaster,' the copper says, 'You know that's a crime, don't you? Wasting police time? Now I suggest that you go back home. Get some GCSE's, get a job in Tesco, try and stay out of trouble and have a decent ordinary life.'

'A decent ordinary life,' I say. And I laugh. And then I have to go and deal with Mum and Ty.

As I get into Ty's stupid new car, William and Harry are scrapping. I give William his mobie back.

'You did have it!' he cries.

And I say, 'Well done, Sherlock.'

And he makes a mong-face and I'm thinking of Pete's cock hot in my hand and how weird it must be to have all normal feelings, when everyone else sees you as a freak.

As we drive away from the police station we pass Susie and Ariel and JD in the old white Landrover. I wave and wind down the window and shout but they don't see me.

And Mum says, 'Just sit down and be quiet for fuck's sake.'

And Harry goes, 'Yeah, Mistyann, for fuck's sake.'

And Mum goes, 'And you can shut up, you little shit.'

And Ty puts the radio on. It's a rap and hip-hop station but the presenters are all speaking in Welsh so you get all the weird talk and then you just hear them say 'Snoop' or whatever every once in a while and then they play some tune that's all about slicing hoes in LA. And the car is so cheap that the radio's already bust and Ty can't change the channel. And Mum starts banging on about how she's going to sue the school and JD so I just tune her out. I think I'll put up with it all till the end of the holidays and then hitch to London, meet up with Pete, see if he'll give me his debit card again and just disappear. I reckon they won't even look very hard. Maybe I'll get an apartment with some other girls like me. It'll be like *Friends*. Only I won't share with anyone like that hippy one, Phoebe, or the one that is manic about cleaning. Or anyone who's like Jennifer Aniston. Like *Friends* without anyone annoying.

Imagining this apartment cheers me up and I don't mind playing this game with William and Harry where we get points for spotting different kinds of lorries. It's a game Dad taught me. I see a Norbert Dentressangle almost straight away which is ten points and I take this to be a good sign. The kids get bored quickly and plug themselves back into their DVD players. William is watching something called *Sacrilege* about a football playing Buddhist monk who is also a Kung Fu expert. Harry is watching some CGI animation thing about a farting cat. I look out of the window at the rain and think some more about London. After a while I notice that they are speaking in English on the radio. Some crap about how many million new houses have to be built in England in the next twenty years and I want to go to sleep. I hear Harry going, 'Mistyann's leaning on me.' Like I'm torturing him and it's then that I lean forward and yank on the hand-brake.

THIRTY-NINE

The plods did a thorough job of ransacking my house. The search for evidence left my place looking like it had been burgled. They'd taken my computer, my DVDs, my old videos, random paperwork, address books, novels. My first edition of *Lolita* went too I noticed—a present from an old girlfriend (Angela? Beth?). Anything which might somehow be waved in court as proof of my ingrained depravity had been swept up and taken.

They'd also used up all my coffee and tea-bags, the bastards. What a finely calculated piece of police brutality that was. Especially as it was so cold. The house felt violated and dead, as though the assault of police boots and throatily coarse police laughter had killed it. As though it had collapsed, exhausted, under questioning, and they had let it die.

I shivered and began to close the cupboards the plods left open. That was all the tidying I felt up to. I checked for phone messages. I had several. There was one from the head, one an hour later from the director of the education authority—a great honour I can assure you. There was a squeaky, teenage voice from the *Bedfordshire on Sunday* asking if I would like to put my side of the story and a cheery one from Army Dave asking if I'd like to meet for breakfast at Asda on Saturday morning as usual. Dave's voice felt like a message from a better world.

And so it turned out that he was the first person I saw. I spent most of the intervening time in bed, getting up only to piss, eat bowls of crunchy nut cornflakes or drink boiled water. I wasn't up to nipping to Mr Joshi's to restock.

We went to the big new Asda. Army Dave is a big non-drinker like me. But unlike me, he did the whole AA, twelve step therapy. He's got the drinking sorted, but he's still in recovery from therapy. I met him when he came to talk to the sixth form about the perils of binge-drinking. They thought he was an idiot but me and him, we just clicked. He's an alcohol counsellor, who does shifts for the Samaritans in his spare time. His new addiction is good works but it doesn't stop him being cynical and outrageously self-absorbed. He makes me laugh and one thing I've learned is that you hang on to people that can do that. And he never wants to talk about me. In fact he hardly ever wants me to talk at all. My job is to listen and nod. Listen and nod. Whenever we get together it's always the Army Dave show. He's probably a really shit counsellor. But it suits me fine.

That Saturday morning Army Dave and I met at eight for the Asda big breakfast. £1.99p—can't argue with that. Army Dave works as a warden at a half way house for people coming off drink and drugs. He still hasn't kicked the desire to help. It'll kill him if he keeps it up, I tell him. He doesn't listen. I do like his stories from the front-line however. I follow them the way other people follow soaps.

He began, 'Abi and Carl are homeless again.'

'You're joking. Why? They were doing so well.'

'Yeah, they were.' Dave started to sing softly, but loudly enough for other diners to pause over their full Englishes and stare in our direction.

He sang The Jackson Five 'Blame it on the Boogie', ending, 'Blame it on the bingo…' He broke off in a wheezing chuckle, the hard won product of a warped sense of humour and sixty fags a day.

'What do you mean?'

'I mean that in an effort to replace the destructive joys of drugs and alcohol with something less damaging, Abi and Carl go to the bingo on Wednesday.' He paused.

'And?'

'And they win. One hundred and fifty notes.'

'And?'

'And they celebrate in the only way Abi and Carl know how to celebrate.'

'With a drink.'

'With a drink, followed by another drink, followed by a couple of bags of whiz, followed by a pipe or two of finest oak aged crack. They get back to the Haven at eight this morning to find that Himmler has changed the locks. They're out man.'

Himmler is Dave's boss at the hostel.

'After a year of staying clean. Jesus'

'It's a fine line we walk my friend. A fine line.' Army Dave took a sip of Colombian style mild blend cappuccino. The nearest he comes to hard-core vice these days. He stirred thoughtfully with his little plastic agitator.

On the table next to us was a copy of the *Sun* screaming about the porno shame of a bit part politician caught shagging an under-age Latvian hooker. Actually he was caught 'romping with' the teenage stunner. People only romp in papers. Everyone else fucks.

Army Dave followed my gaze. He said, 'In the future everyone will be a paedophile for fifteen minutes.'

That's all. So I knew that already my case was common currency on the streets around town. We didn't discuss it further. It's still all he's ever said about the whole affair. I guess he meant to show that he was on my side, that he knew that we were living in mad times. I felt my eyes fill up. Pathetic. Army Dave grabbed my hand and squeezed and put on his most earnest therapist voice.

'This too will pass.'

My how we laughed.

FORTY

The car is upside down. We're all upside down hanging by our seat belts. There's a moment of quiet. No engine noise. Nobody says anything. There's just the radio jabbering. Then Ty is saying, 'What the fuck did you do that for?'

And he doesn't even sound angry. He just sounds whingy. And then everyone is screaming. William, Harry and my mum are all screaming and it blots everything out and I notice the blood. There's blood everywhere. It's like someone has taken a bottle of fizzy cherryade, shaken it up and sprayed it around the inside of the car. Only it's thicker than that. Like someone has sloshed thick red oil around.

I hear my mum go, 'Oh my God. Harry's lost his tongue. He's lost his fucking tongue.'

And it's true.

The blood has come from Harry's mouth. There's tons of it and it's gushing. Not spraying, but like there's a tap in his mouth.

I can smell petrol and I suddenly think the car is going to explode like they do in films. I scramble out of my seat belt and under Mum cos I can see her window is smashed and I can squeeze through. A piece of glass scrapes my neck as I wriggle through, but it doesn't really hurt. It does later. Later they put three stitches in it but just then it doesn't hurt at all. As I get clear of the car a proper scary thing happens. Harry stops screaming.

I start kicking at the upside down car with my feet and screaming and yelling. There are other people around now and some men start rocking the car.

I hear a woman shout, 'Leave them, you might make their injuries worse.'

And someone else says, 'They might fucking roast alive.'

And the first woman says, 'I'm a nurse. I'm a nurse.' And then she starts crying.

The men have stopped rocking the car. They think the nurse-lady might be right. And I feel desperate. Harry's stopped screaming. I can only hear Mum and William.

Then Ty goes mad. Proper yelling, 'Turn this fucking car over!'

And the men start again, rocking it and it's suddenly the right way up looking like one of the wrecks they use in banger racing with the top all bashed in and everything. I can hear sirens and above that I can hear Harry. Thank fuck. Thank fuck, I think and now we're all pulling at the doors and someone has a crow-bar thing and there's a tearing sound as the door comes away. Mum sort of falls out onto the ground and she's got blood running from her nose into her mouth, but she doesn't care.

'My baby!' She's yelling, 'My baby!'

And then Ty's out of the car and him and some other guys get the door open near William and he leaps out into Ty's arms, but Ty just sort of shoves him to one side and reaches in for Harry.

Harry has both hands to his mouth and there's blood all over them and down his arms and all over his T-shirt. Suddenly there's an ambulance nearby and Ty gets into it with Harry in his arms and blood is still flooding from Harry's mouth and going all over Ty. And Mum dives back into the passenger seat of the car. She kneels on it looking into the back. And I wonder what she's doing. And then we see it. Harry's tongue. It looks like a little pink fish on the back seat. I half expect it to twitch.

I reach for it first, going through the back door. I pick it up. It's small. It's not his whole tongue. Maybe not even half. I stare at it for what seems like ages but is probably only a few seconds and a paramedic lady says, 'Oh, you've got the rest of the tongue. Good girl.' And she sounds just like this is a normal thing. She doesn't sound stressed or anything. And she takes Harry's tongue off me and puts it into a little bag like a freezer bag and seals the edge like I do when I make sandwiches for William and Harry if they're going on a school trip. I just stare at her and she smiles at me and ruffles my hair.

'Don't worry,' she says, 'It'll be alright.'

And I remember the last person who said that to me. It was JD when we were standing outside Derec and Caitlin's house in the snow.

They're all in the ambulance now. Mum, Ty, William and Harry. And the crowd of people who helped turn the car over start to move away and the ambulance speeds away with its siren on and I think that's good because Harry will love that. And then I feel a bit faint and I put my hand on my head and there's definitely a bump there and I have to sit down suddenly at the side of the road and the nurse-lady comes up with a cup of tea with loads of sugar in it the way I like it and someone else says, 'She should be in hospital.' And a young guy says, 'I'll take her.' And I sort of fall asleep in his car but it can't be for long and then he says, 'Here you are.' And I say thank you to him and notice then that he's quite fine. He has big oily hands. He sees me looking at them. 'I'm a mechanic,' he says. I don't know if I'm expected to say anything else or not. He says, 'Look after yourself.' And he drives off. It's a VW Fox, I notice, though it's bit pimped up with a spoiler and that.

FORTY-ONE

I had to do a sad thing yesterday, Mistyann. I had to see a patient's mother. Mrs Delderfield came to look around The Elms. She came with her son. Mrs Delderfield is 92 but she wasn't looking for herself, she was looking for the son. Mrs Delderfield is as bright as a button. She's lived in Rothsay Gardens all her adult life, brought all her kids up there. Her husband was a Council architect, designed the Eagle Street car park, may have God have mercy on his Philistine soul. No, it was her youngest who needed care. Jack Delderfield is 66 but well on the way to joining the Undead.

Mrs Delderfield said, 'It's his temper, you see. He gets frustrated when he can't remember things and starts lashing out. He's always been a big lad and I can't control him.'

She's probably not even five feet and there was Jack, a six footer who still carried with him the sense of having once been a powerful rugby prop forward. He stood there drooling slightly and smiling vacantly as his mother described how he'd been living at hers for the last three years but had become much worse recently and now she was at her wit's end and her doctor had told her that she absolutely must find Jack a good home or he would be the death of her.

And I thought that of all the duties of being a parent one of the most unexpected and painful must be that of checking out your child's senile dementia care plan. People say that out-living your children is a crime against the natural order of things and yet it happens all the time. Car crashes, war, illness, pub fights, domestic anger, lunatic drunken impulses of all kinds. There are a million ways in which the lives of your kids can be snatched away, but to see them lurching ahead of you into the darkest reaches of old age must be one of the hardest.

Mrs Delderfield looked around our communal room where fourteen zombies sat in slack-jawed worship of the forty-two inch HD plasma screen on which, at deafening volume, two acned lads fought for the right to be called the father of a beautiful scrap of a baby that belonged to a girl not old enough to shave her legs. Jeremy Kyle. It's riveting stuff, you must admit.

She wrinkled her nose at our bathrooms. And she sat openly weeping as the dinner trolley with its piles of steaming mush made the rounds. The Elms wasn't good enough for her son. But it would have to do and that broke her heart. Jack smiled throughout.

I'm only forty-one. I could yet have children, plenty of men my age are only just getting around to it, but I don't feel ready and Mrs Delderfield at 92 isn't ready. She squeezed my hand as she left the home.

'You're a good boy,' She said, 'I can tell. You're kind.'

And then she was crying again and I cried with her.

I came home to find a carefully parcelled human turd in my hall-way. Someone had crapped into a copy of the *Bedfordshire on Sunday*, wrapped it neatly and shoved it through my letter box.

You know they're making me sign the sex offenders register? Well, they aren't making me. You can volunteer apparently. It was poor old Wayne's idea. You can add your name to the list even if you haven't been convicted of a sexual crime. It's meant to make everyone involved in supervising criminals think that you're a model crook who is managing his own offending behaviour and beginning to show some insight into his own deviancy. Then they go easy on you. That's the theory.

I wouldn't have agreed to it but I'll admit I was I was taken aback by those court statements. I shouldn't have been, but I was. And if I was taken aback, poor old Wayne was wrecked. He gave me the paperwork and then disappeared to get himself a happy meal or something, so I 'could read the prosecution case undisturbed'. 'Undisturbed' was entirely the wrong word.

Mrs English well yes, of course, she was first to cast a stone, being so pure in thought, word and deed herself. Her testimony was entirely predictable. She had often been concerned about my closeness to pupils. I didn't seem able to keep an appropriate distance and so on and so forth.

Old Hoy, the Head of St Teresa's gave a statement that was as bland and meaningless as the man himself. Mr Diamond always appeared to carry out his duties in a conscientious manner. I feel very let down but fully accept my share of responsibility for this regrettable situation. There followed several pages of weaselling justifications intended to make it clear that his share of 'this regrettable situation' was actually nothing at all.

But there were other, more wounding statements. Susie for example, provided the prosecution with an essay on the damage child prostitution and sex tourism has wreaked on generations of Malaysian children. At a stroke I was right there with your Gary Glitters and all the other vermin who pay to be jerked off by five year olds in gym knickers.

And then there was Amber who claimed to be 'worried sick' when she realized that she would be in sole charge of these vulnerable young adults while I was off on a drunken spree. She needed three weeks off when she got back. Got a doctor to sign her off sick on the grounds of the stress she'd suffered being placed in that position of authority while still a Newly Qualified Teacher.

And what about Kendra who said that she was 'disgusted' by my callous and indifferent attitude towards disability? She described my remarks about Pete being the 'token cripple' on the course as being unbelievable coming from a teacher, which only shows that she hasn't ever been in a staff room. The thing about Kendra's statement was that she was right in a way. I did think that, in a selection designed to show how wonderfully inclusive this gifted and talented programme was, Pete was the token crip. But I'm sure I never said it out loud. Kendra is one of those twisted mystics who can divine an evil thought in someone a mile away. You can imagine her at the head of some Social Work SS Thought-Crime unit, hauling screaming children away from parents deemed unfit because they once considered smacking a kid going ape in a supermarket. Pete clearly hates her. His dying breath may well be used telling her to go and stick her PC sensibility where the sun don't shine.

And where did they get Dave the taxi driver from? And what induced him to repeat what I said about the virginity game? All the teachers used to play this game during invigilation of summer exams. It wasn't just me.

The thing about invigilation is that it's very boring. You can't talk, can't read. The only thing that breaks the monotony is racing to be the first to give the swots new pieces of paper when they run out of space in the answer booklet. That and trying to spot the virgins. It's a harmless enough game. You let your eye run over the kids and simply decide if they've done it yet. It passes the time. I can't remember how it came up in conversation at the Telyn. But there it was, a sheet of A4 signed by Dave, detailing his outrage that people like me could be eyeing up girls like his daughter while she was taking her GCSEs.

The most damning statements were from the kids. Dalwinder said that I was 'weird', Julius that I 'seemed very aloof'. Hardly the kind of stuff which would normally convict anyone of anything. Zak tried a bit harder, saying that I had 'become very aggressive during a harmless snowball fight' and that he had thought then that I was 'unstable and not a fit and proper person to be in charge of school-age children'. Nice work, Zak. Go to the top of the class. The Anonymous Girls each seized their moment. They really unleashed their creative selves. Ariel would have been proud of them. Each of them detailed, in exquisitely honed prose, how I had made them feel uncomfortable by brazenly giving them the eye. The truth is, I hardly noticed them at the time and can recall almost nothing about them now. Did one have a pony tail? Were they carrying a few pounds more than they needed? What should have undermined them was that their exquisitely honed prose was almost identical. There was clear evidence of collusion. Poor Wayne missed it of course.

How come we have this kind of system anyway? How can it be justice for the prosecution to write to more or less anyone who has ever come into contact with the defendant saying, in effect, we have this terrible villain who has been kiddy-fiddling, is there anything at all you can add to the imposing stack of evidence against him? Is there anything you can give which will help rid our streets of this monster?

I wasn't expecting sympathy. After all in Iowa, under the rule of someone like Ariel La Rock, I would be facing chemical castration or the real thing. So I was actually a lucky boy. And so I was grateful. Really, I was.

FORTY-TWO

I'm at Nan's in Manchester. Everyone knows I can't go home after what I've done. Mum wants to pure batter me. The police and social services have to sort out a foster home for me. They want to charge me with loads of stuff. Mum's up for being a witness but Ty says he won't testify. They have a row about it in hospital in front of everyone while Harry has this operation. No one knows whether he's going to able to talk properly. The worst thing is that William hides from me. He runs away if I go near him.

I'm in the first foster home ten minutes and I'm hiding in the bathroom. Well, not exactly hiding because everyone knows where I am and they keep banging on the door to get me to come out. I ignore them. I've got mates who would cut themselves in this situation. I think about it. I look in the bathroom cupboard but the only thing that I could use is the razor Mrs Pynchon—the foster mum—uses on her legs and it's pure manky. I'd probably get hep B or something. There's also a big box of condoms which makes me shiver. It's the first time I think about being pregnant. I normally make blokes use johnnies and if they moan I tell them to forget it and they usually see sense.

But I didn't with Zak. It feels like years ago that I was with him. Him singing—the line of hair leading into those jeans—everything. All gone. I wonder if the whole of my life will be like this. Just moments that burst like bubbles and then disappear so you can hardly remember them. At least a baby is a moment that stays with you. A moment that gets better and bigger than the original moment.

I sit on the edge of the bog and think about a life where I don't run away to London but stay here with Zak's baby. Perhaps I get a council flat in Goldington or somewhere and go to the park and mother and toddler groups and that.

It's an okay idea, but London's better. I wonder how long before you can have a pregnancy test? Mrs Midgley tells us that they have these really good kits that can tell if you are pregnant like a minute after you've had sex. She's not a proper teacher. She comes into child development classes to do support or something, but she acts like a teacher and she's got about eight kids at home so she should know.

The next few days are crap. I still don't know if Harry's going to be alright and everyone keeps asking me why I pulled the hand-brake but I don't know. I really don't know but they keep asking. And I'm having these fights with the foster mum every day, mainly because she keeps trying to get me to eat and I don't feel like it. In the end everyone says that I can go and stay with my nan in Manchester, which is okay even though she keeps going around with this sad face that she puts on because I'm there. She says I'm breaking her heart which I think is pure total bullcrap.

There's a bad day when I have to go back to the police station in Wales and it takes all day to get there and when I get there they tell me about JD being charged with abduction and try to make out that him and me had sex.

I go mental when they say that. I go for the fat woman copper with my nails and she gets this really long scratch under her eye. My nan and the man copper and my solicitor are all trying to pull me off but they can't. In the end it takes all of them plus three other police to get me off her and I've got a fist full of her stupid blonde hair. And she's crying and shouting and she goes to run out of the room, but she turns and comes over to me and spits in my face and screams, 'You fucking stupid English chav bitch.'

And then Nan goes for her and there's a big ruck all over again. And Nan catches her right on the chin with her fist and that fat bitch copper goes down in a big heap and we all see her huge pink thighs. They look like something you see in the meat section at Asda. And when it's all calmed down they realise that they've left the tape running.

The man copper has to say, 'Erm, interview terminated at 11.03am. PC Corrigan has left the room.'

And everyone laughs because it just sounds proper stupid after all the crap that went on before.

My solicitor says, 'I look forward to hearing that tape in court.'

We have to sit around for another couple of hours. They keep offering us tea. What is it with the police and fucking tea? And then we go back into the interview room and there's two different coppers and one of them asks about my relationship with Mr Diamond. I tell them that I don't have a relationship with him. He's my fucking teacher. And they ask why I was in the car with him.

I say, 'We had to drive. We were too pissed to walk.'

Which isn't true cos I wasn't pissed. And then they ask why I took the car and I say because I was going to London. And they ask me why I was going to London.

I say, 'Because my mum is a fucking stupid chav bitch.'

And it's sort of a joke but Nan looks like I've smacked her and runs out of the room. I wonder what's the matter with her till I remember that Mum is Nan's daughter. It's weird but I've never really thought about that.

Mr Unsworth sighs and the copper who is doing all the talking gives me a bit of hairy eyeball and they can't ask me any more questions because there's not a parent or guardian present. But I tell them that JD might be a bit of a twat but he isn't a perv. And that is kind of how I feel now. I feel a bit embarrassed by how much I used to like him. He seems a bit of a loser when I think about him now. I keep seeing him in my head. I see him getting up off the floor in that hippy house in Wales going, 'I've got to brush up on my in-fighting technique.' And I see him looking out over that lake looking proper sorry for himself.

Ariel turns up on the day I get it together to go to London and see Pete. Ariel in Nan's flat in Manchester. It's mad. I'm meeting Pete so he can give me the credit card. Then I'm going to get myself a flat share, pretend I'm eighteen or a student and get that first job as a waitress. I can do that. I'm talented and gifted. I was part of the TAG crew. I'll need to arrange an abortion too, but how hard can that be?

I haven't actually done the pregnancy test because I'm too scared but I know I must be having a baby. I feel different. I feel all weird and bloated and I've been proper tired and I haven't been eating or sleeping much. I'm late too. At least I think I am. I must be. But I never check the dates when I have my periods. Who can be arsed?

It's not been the best at Nan's. Nan has got a new boyfriend for a start. He's from Guyana and they're either rowing or shagging and I can't decide which is worse. Nan's got this real pattern when she comes. Starts like one of those steam trains on *Thomas the Tank Engine* and ends like something from a horror movie. If I ever go into her room just after one of her orgasms I think there's a chance I'll see her head spinning round.

It wouldn't be so bad if they kept to her room and to the night, but they are always groping each other. When she's not throwing things at him, that is. Cos Nathaniel doesn't stay every night and she wants to know where he is the rest of the time. Well, she wants him to lie to her, because actually she knows where is: he's fucking someone else, isn't he? It's obvious. He's forty-five and Nan is sixty and she's not stupid. She can work it out.

I say this to him one time, when Nan's at work. I can see it's true. He doesn't deny it, just winks, which makes him look like the elephant man and reminds me of Pete.

That's the day that we hear that Harry is going to be alright that he'll be able to speak properly and everything.

Anyway. The day comes and I'm all packed. I've checked the train times. I've spoken to Pete. It's weird to hear his voice because it's only been a few weeks but he sounds different. I think it's because it's always strange hearing someone on the phone. Especially a phone as shit as mine, which makes everyone sound a bit like a robot.

Nan's at work. I'm bunking off. I've got a new school but it's shit and I don't like anyone and they don't like me but I don't go very often. Nan doesn't care. I'm missing English, Maths, Science and Business Studies. All shit subjects with shit teachers. The only good thing about any of these lessons is that we get to do Business in the new room with decent chairs and it's always kept clean. In this school they go fucking mad if anyone messes up the business room. You can get expelled just for putting your feet on the desks, while all the other classrooms are proper shitty with holes in the walls and fuck off big pictures of knobs along the back row of chairs and gum under the desks. If you turn any of the tables over in any of the rooms, except business, there's so much dried gum there that it looks like one of those 3D maps they have in geography that show you all the mountain ranges.

Then Ariel is on the door-step wearing jeans and trainers, looking like a model even though she's thirty-three. She looks proper out of place. I don't know what to say.

Ariel says, 'Hello, Mistyann. How are you?'

And I say, 'I'm fine, how are you?'

And she says, 'I'm fine.' And then she says, 'Mistyann, can we go inside?'

And I think about her sitting in Nan's flat with all her stupid nick-nacks and ornaments and shit around.

'I was just going out actually.'

And Ariel says, 'Oh, anywhere special? Are you in a hurry? Maybe I could give you a ride?' And then I notice her car which is this huge black SUV with tinted windows. It's like a president's car. It makes me laugh.

'You won't be able to park in town in that,' I say. 'And I wouldn't leave it here too long or the kids will have all the wheels off. It'll get trashed.'

'Really?' She says and her forehead crinkles up, but only a bit. And then she smiles and says, 'Well, hey, it's only a rented car. Mistyann, we need to talk. And I need to talk to your grandmom.'

And I don't know why, but this makes me laugh too. Or maybe it's just that Ariel makes me happy, because she never says anything that's exactly funny.

So we go inside and I sort of run around tidying up and throwing stuff into cupboards while Ariel just sits. She sits on the edge of Nan's brown leather sofa with her back proper straight like she's the queen on a horse. She doesn't want tea and just has a glass of water. She asks for mineral water and that makes me laugh too. Like my nan would have that. I give her tap water but if she notices then she doesn't say. And then she tells me about Pete.

'He can't fucking die,' I say. I can feel my shoulders go tight. 'I only spoke to him yesterday.'

'You spoke to him? When?'

'Yesterday about three o' clock. He was fine.'

She looks well stern.

'He wasn't fine, Mistyann. He has a serious respiratory infection brought on by his condition. The muscles that control his lungs are giving up and he was moved to hospital three days ago. It's very serious.'

And I think about how faint and smecked his voice had sounded. 'But he's expecting me. We were going to meet tonight. He gave me his address.' I show the bit of paper to Ariel and yeah of course St Andrews House, Warwick Street, London SW1.

'It's a hospital isn't it?' I say.

'It's a hospice.'

'Same difference.'

'No, not really. A hospice is where people go when they are preparing for...'

'For what?'

'For whatever comes after this, Mistyann. The after-life, heaven, whatever.'

'You don't believe in heaven.'

'Yes I do, Mistyann. I believe that the soul lives on, though what form that life takes is, of course, unknowable.'

'Bollocks,' I say.

Ariel laughs. 'Mistyann, you are a hard person to debate with.' And then she tells me her plan and it's probably a better plan than mine. Scary and huge, but better.

Basically her plan is to buy me. She doesn't say that but that's kind of what it is. I get to go to some fancy school in America. I have some important questions about this.

'What's the uniform like?'

'Mistyann, schools in America generally don't have a uniform.'

'Where will I live?'

'Well, you'll live in my house. But I'm not there most of the time. You know I travel a lot, so your full time guardian would be Esperanza De La Hoya, who is my house-keeper in Iowa.'

'How far away from New York is that?'

'A long way, Mistyann. A long way in miles and culturally even further.' This is like a joke. Ariel is one of those people who shouldn't make jokes.

'Will there be any other kids there?'

She looks at me for a minute but I can't tell what she's thinking, which worries me a bit because normally I can tell that sort of thing easily. It's not reading people's minds exactly but a bit like that.

In the end she says, 'I have four girls on this programme at any one time. And when each girl finishes High School, that leaves a vacancy. So you would be expected to live with me for nearly three years and then you could come back and go to school.' She sees I'm a bit confused. 'I mean University or whatever you wanted to do.'

'What are the other girls like?'

'You'll like them. I think you'll like them. I hope so.'

I've saved my biggest question till last. 'Why?' I say, 'Why me?'

And Ariel smiles and says, 'Why not you, Mistyann?'

So I say yes. I think that it doesn't matter about me saying yes because Nan will come back and she'll say no and that will be that and I'll have to work out some other plan, but when Nan comes back it's not like that. Her and Ariel go into the kitchen and come out half an hour later and Ariel's smiling and my nan is smiling and she gives me a hug and says, 'America. Fucking America. Imagine that?' And Nan wears masses of perfume but I can still smell her sweat underneath it. Then Nan signs some papers and that's that. I'm an American kid. I've been sold. It's taken about twenty minutes.

Later that night we're watching a crime thing on the telly that Nan likes. She comes to the sofa and sits next to me.

'You can stay if you want,' she says, 'You don't have to go to America. You know that, don't you?'

'Yeah, right Nan,' I say.

'I just thought that with all the stuff with that scum-bag and everything...'

She means JD. Normally I would have lost it then and started ranting and all that, but I think I'm starting to get used to all the people calling him a perv and a paedo and a nonce. Maybe he should have taken his chance in Ray's car cos I would have done it with him.

Anyway. I don't start ranting to Nan.

I say, 'What about Harry and William. And Mum?'

And she looks a bit surprised. She says, 'Don't worry about them. I talked about them with Ariel and her charity is going to give them enough money to have a live-in au pair. Like a nanny. She's going to have your room. Ariel's going to help us arrange it.'

And I think. Top, when I wanted to go to Wales with JD I had to fill in the form myself and sneak off and now I'm going off to America for years they can't wait to move someone else into my room.

'You can't blame her. Not after… and it's a good opportunity, Mistyann, really. The best thing probably.'

'I know, Nan, except I can't go.'

And I tell her about being pregnant. And she goes pure fucking heavy mental. We're still shouting at each other when Nathaniel gets home.

He yells, 'Can't a man have a moment's peace when he gets home from work!' After a while he just runs off. Slams the door too, the tosser.

Nan's main thing is that she wants to know who it is and I can tell that she thinks it might be JD which is just disgusting but anyway I'm not telling her. About twenty minutes later Nathaniel comes back with this packet he's got from the chemists. He shoves it at me.

'What's this?' I say.

'It's a fucking pregnancy test,' he says.

'Don't fucking swear at me,' I say.

'Don't talk to Nathaniel like that. Give him some respect,' says Nan.

'Damn right,' says Nathaniel. And he looks like he's done something pure top. Looks like he deserves a prize. Nan sees it too.

'Oh shut up you big oaf,' says Nan. And Nathaniel fucks off. Doesn't say anything just grabs his coat and is gone.

'That's the last time you'll see him,' I say.

'Good,' she says.

Anyway. I have to admit that I haven't even done a test yet. I just know I'm pregnant. I go off to the bathroom and piss onto the little stick and wait. And while I'm doing it I can hear Nan phone Mum. And then she phones my dad.

FORTY-THREE

Shortly after I got home from all the final indignities of the court I had a visitor, Mistyann. Charlotte. She'd used 192.com—the stalker's friend—to track me down to Gladstone Street. It was about 3.20 in the afternoon, a difficult part of the day for me because it's when the school-kids come out; reminding me of everything I've lost. I'd almost given up on answering the door. It's never good news, the unsolicited ring at the door.

Oddly, since I became a pariah, my door-bell has worked a lot harder. Given a choice between the boot-faced troop of Probation Officers and Danny, the retarded Betterware guy, I'd go for Danny every time.

As you know Charlotte is quite an insistent sort and she leant on that bell until eventually I hauled myself from the arm chair and waddled to the hall-way. I've put on about two stone since the court proceedings got started. I can't really do any exercise. Generally, getting fit involves going to places where you can be seen. I suppose I could do some kind of DVD work out at home, but I don't have the moral fibre to be bouncing about to the instructions of some Z-level reality TV celeb in legwarmers.

So I dragged my fat and ever-spreading arse to the door. There she was, Charlotte, with her back to me, giving the finger to some wolf-whistling tosser on a scooter.

Hair as black and shiny as seal-skin, dark purple sweatshirt, pink knitted scarf, denim mini-skirt, just slighter wider than the chunky belt that was loosely draped around her skinny waist. Black leggings and chunky Goth boots. She looked not unlike girls used to look back in the 1980s on demos and at gigs. These days, however, an attractive teenager on my door-step is the worst possible news.

'Charlotte?' I said. Or stammered I don't suppose I carried any authority in my voice. It's amazing how quickly you lose that. She spun round with grace that was all the more impressive for being executed in heavy duty S&M footwear.

'Mr Diamond.'

There was a long moment between us.

'Best come in,' I said.

I made her tea. Charlotte was very precise about how she had it. She liked, she said, a pot of tea made with strong tea-bags but with just half a spoon of Earl Grey mixed in. I was, unbelievably, able to meet her requirements. She stood silently behind me while I did all the to-ing and fro-ing.

We sat at my breakfast table and made conversation about the vicissitudes of her journey to Bedford. She told me that she had got a bus from the station to Manton Heights.

'Why?' I asked.

'I wanted to see where Mistyann lives. Lived.'

'At the risk of seeming like an annoying child, can I ask again, why?'

'Well I thought it would be a scummy estate. A shit-hole. But it's alright. I mean suburban and aspirational and grim as fuck, but not,' she searched for the word and lit up as she located it, 'Squalid. That's right, it's not squalid.'

'Why did you think it would be?'

'Well, you know how Mistyann is. Gobby. I thought she was from a real tough background, but it's just ordinary.'

I thought about Manton Heights. Charlotte was right. It's hardly the Chicago projects. It isn't a ghetto. There is no street-corner crack for sale. In fact there isn't even all that much litter, just ugly sixties semis climbing up the hill above equally ugly nineteenth century terraces.

'Yeah, Manton Heights. Nothing special.'

'She is though, Jon, isn't she?'

'What?'

'Mistyann. She's special. I mean she's beautiful and clever and she's got all this fantastic energy. Too good for a place like this.'

'What are you getting at Charlotte? I agree, by the way.' I could see where this was going. The sly innuendo. Charlotte was playing good cop but the thrust of her questioning, was I thought, quite clear. It made me tired. 'Did you talk to anyone? See her family at all?' I said. She shook her head.

'I stood outside her house for a while. But I was too shy to knock. Maybe I will after I've left here. Tea's nice.'

She took a thoughtful swallow.

'Thanks,' I said, 'It's nice to be appreciated.'

We sat in this damp patch of silence that spooled out around us gradually. I thought that Charlotte was the only school age person who had ever sat at this table. I had never had any of my students call round and what was gratifying about this encounter was that there was no sexual heat in the room at all. Charlotte, chocolate and cream limbs and all, stirred nothing inside me. I thought about the ache over tea when I sat in Ray and Susie's cottage. There was no echo of that here. It was a relief to feel nothing for this kid with her wanton lips and hair.

I sighed. 'I never slept with Mistyann. We weren't planning a romantic escape or anything. She's just a kid.'

'I know,' she said, 'I know.' And Charlotte walked around my kitchen table and she put her arms around me. I allowed myself to be held there for a moment. She smelt of some ripe fruit that I couldn't quite place. Mango? And then I pushed her away—gently I hope—and stood up to get some kitchen roll with which to wipe my eyes.

She said, 'You know Zak and Amber were shagging in the bathroom the night Mistyann went missing. Amazing, huh? He blogged about it.' She paused. 'He shagged Mistyann as well. All the gory details are in his blog.'

Army Dave once suggested that I start blogging.

'You'd be brilliant at it,' he said, 'And you've got a good story.'

But it seems like showing off to me. I do follow quite a lot of blogs. Homeless women living in cars. Lesbian call-girls. Taliban insurgents in Afghanistan. Plods blogging about how much paper-work they have to do, poor dears. But I don't feel the urge to add to this incoherent pile. Would Pepys have blogged? I don't think so.

I asked Charlotte to leave. I did it nicely. Just said that I was tired, it was a stressful time, found it hard to deal with visitors and with the court case it probably wasn't such a good idea for her to be around. The sort of thing you would expect. She didn't look too shocked at being evicted.

I said, 'You should go down to the embankment. It's nice there. You'll see Bedford at its best.'

She nodded like I had just said something incredibly profound. Like I had sorted everything out for her. She asked if I ever had any contact with Ariel.

'She said she'd stay in touch,' she said, a whiny note creeping into that cut-glass RP. 'But I haven't heard from her at all.'

I said, 'I doubt very much that either of us will be hearing from Ariel La Rock any time soon. I suspect, Charlotte, that we've all been air-brushed from her resume.'

She looked up and smiled thinly. I have to say that Ariel's made an enemy there.

Ten minutes later, Charlotte was out and marching down Gladstone Street like it was a Milan cat-walk. It was a strange experience seeing her, Mistyann. Like someone walking out of a dream and into your life. She's possibly the unhappiest kid I've known. I wonder if she's aware of just how miserable she is? Probably. She's not thick is she? She's gifted too, remember?

I sat for ages in my kitchen smoking and thinking and then I went upstairs and got all those old GCSE revision books out, spread them all over the spare bed. And then I got all my notes out. All my lesson plans. Every hand out I'd ever fed to the kids. All my disks with their PowerPoint presentations, all the literacy strategies and school improvement policies—every piece of paper or plastic related to my profession and filled three of the big black plastic containers the council put out for us to save the planet with.

I hauled them out into the garden and burnt their contents. Despite the damp afternoon my whole professional life was quickly reduced to sooty and glowing specks that rose up and spread over the gardens of my neighbours like exotic and sinister beetles. A small plague of educational locusts humming over the district.

I came back in and ran a bath. I had added smoke and ashes to the clinging sourness that is the smell of the court-house. Max-pax coffee, sweat broiled under the strip lights and shame, of course; these are the ingredients that create the distinctive sticky odour of the habitué of the court system. The smoke and the clear out made me feel a bit cleaner but still I needed a good soak.

I took my clothes off in my spare bedroom, the bedroom where the full-length mirror ended up and took a look at myself. I'd like to complete the cliché and say that it was an unflinching look, but that would be a lie. No-one after forty looks at themselves without flinching. I tried to look at my reflected image through Charlotte's eyes. What had she seen? How would she describe me in her blog?

I really have put on a lot of weight. My belly swells like someone in the second trimester of pregnancy and I've got little paps growing: Man-boobs. Moobs, the young people call them. And my legs have shrunk as my torso has swelled. As though all the muscle and flesh of my thighs and calves has been sucked up to feed the newly voracious appetite of my chest and stomach.

The result of the court case was never in any doubt but nevertheless we were obliged to hang about to hear it. And in truth nothing very bad happened. I was banned from schools. Not just from working in them. I am not allowed within a hundred metres of them. And, to use the current teenage vernacular, am I bothered? Only failures work in schools. Everyone knows it. Any man with a favourite chair in a staff room after the age of thirty has failed. I'm tagged too. I've got to wear a plastic ankle bracelet so the plods can keep tabs on me. They are quite sought after now amongst young people; confer a kind of credibility.

They also banned me from going to Manton Heights because of the distress I might cause to the Rutherford family. What about the distress the Rutherford family causes me, hanging about near my house in such a threatening manner? In any case I hardly ever went to Manton Heights. Why would anyone go there?

And they banned me from having any contact with you. I almost laughed. I would, I must admit, love to hear that you're okay. If only so I could pop outside my house one night and tell your mum.

When I've finished up here; when I've put the invoice from poor old Wayne, my ASBO and the certificate that shows that I'm sex registered in a safe place—perhaps in the drawer where I put my Advanced Skills Teacher diploma—I'm off to meet Cog and talk about our new band.

And tomorrow I'm going to spend the day in London. Cog thinks it's a really bad idea. He told me that there are still pictures of you in the ticket office. Badly photocopied missing posters that he says will be bad for my mental health. He's very concerned about my mental health these days. It's his big thing. He says, and I know he's right, that I won't find you and that even if I do it'll make things worse. I'm doing it anyway. I should never have let you go.

I had hoped that there might be a ritual for adding my name to the sex offenders register. I thought they might hand me a special quill like you might use to sign a wedding register and I'd sign with a flourish before handing the pen on for Cog or poor old Wayne to be my witness. Surely for something this momentous I wouldn't have to use a common or garden bic. There wasn't anything like that of course. Just a bored clerkette asking if I could check that she'd spelt my name right and could I confirm my address please. Civilised but matter of fact.

Our band. We're going to call ourselves the Rattle Bags and the idea is to cover old psychedelic songs that have disappeared from the pop cultural radar. We have rules: no hits, nothing by a group that had hits, nothing earlier than 1965 or later than 1969 and only tunes that we both love.

We'll never play of course. Army Dave suggested that we form a Gary Glitter tribute band and that's the kind of tasteless joke that I treasure him for, the same way that I treasure Cog for trying to keep up my spirits with his sweet, pointless talk of rehearsals, sets lists and tours.

Wayne wanted to appeal. He said that he thought we'd have a good chance. You've got to admire his guts. Willing to go for a rematch after being comprehensively mugged in the first round.

I was ludicrously cheered by the absence of an affidavit from Ariel. I had, I must confess, feared the worst. In court they said that attempts to contact her had been unsuccessful due to the international nature of her work and the pressure of the campaign for the state senate. They adjourned the case three times to try and get her co-operation. So well done her for avoiding PC Plod and his mid-west associates.

I may lose the house. I had life cover and critical illness cover, but I foolishly neglected to take out 'getting summarily dismissed and barred from practicing your profession' cover. It's something I'd urge newly qualified teachers to consider, if any were ever allowed to talk to me.

And most other jobs are a bit too visible. I can't even work on a till at Asda. For a teacher branded a wannabe paedo the risk of meeting a vigilante in the eight items or less queue is just too great. I don't want some beer-bellied former pupil venting his anger on me. It will be nothing to do with me of course. Nor will it be about my alleged crime. No, what will be fuelling the blows will be his anger at a life that has brought him to Asda on a Friday evening looking for sugar puffs and chicken nuggets. It wasn't what he was hoping for when he laboured over that first poem about Spring when he was six and full of joy and hope.

No, it's homelessness or keeping on with the Undead. The Undead don't care what you've done. In any case, those Undead that still function at all approve of any efforts at sexual gratification. There's no perversion that the Undead don't wish that they had sampled for themselves. Caligula has nothing on the inventiveness of the late stage Alzheimer's patient in that agonizing moment of lucidity. The Undead understand.

FORTY-FOUR

Because Nan is proper jarred off with me now, I'm meant to stay in Burntisland and my dad has arranged for me to have 'a termination' in Scotland. You know the weird thing about being pregnant? You suddenly see babies all the time. They're everywhere. I'd never noticed before. They say in England you're never more than twenty metres from a rat. Well, you're never more than five metres away from a baby.

I'm in Leeds station waiting for the train to Edinburgh and it's like Baby Central. White ones, black ones, chinky ones, crying ones, smiling ones, twins. I even see a specially made buggy with three little identical faces sleeping under three identical woolly hats. They look like three little piglets. And I mean that in a good way. There's this one baby that looks kind of mongy until she (or he) gives me this dutzi big no teeth smile and it just makes me feel good.

And that's when I think, fuck it, and change my mind. Why should I have an abortion? Babies are the sickest. Babies are it. And lots of people have babies and manage to have good lives. Rich people have babies. There's this woman I was reading about. She runs like the world's biggest bank or something and she has eight kids. So a baby is not the plague. Everyone likes babies, so why should I have to get rid of one? Doesn't make sense.

Leeds to Bedford is well slow but that gives me the chance to come up with a plan. I come up with lots of ideas. But the simplest one is the best.

'Alright, Sir?' I say when he opens the door. I nip inside before he can close it. He tries to stop me but I'm too quick. His mouth is opening and closing but no sound is coming out. 'You look like a fish,' I say. 'Got any food? I'm proper starving.'

I go down his hall-way to where the kitchen is. I'm being all up and everything and trying to sound buzzy but I'm thinking that I might have made a mistake. JD's house is a fucking pig-stay and it pure reeks. And he looks a mess. He's let himself go big time. It's only been a couple of weeks but he looks years older. Sort of pathetic. Maybe I should have gone up to my dad's after all.

'Mistyann,' he says and then he starts shouting.

He tells me to get out of his house and that he can't be seen with me and what the fuck am I doing there and do I really want to see him in fucking jail and he goes on and on and there are little bits of spit on the corners of his mouth. He looks ugly and he pure fucking scares me but I don't show it. I just wait till he's finished.

By the time he stops going mental he looks smecked. He's all out of breath and his shoulders are going up and down and he's breathing well loud. I wait till I'm sure that he's finished yelling.

'You should get an inhaler,' I say, 'You sound like you've got asthma.'

'Fucking hell, Mistyann,' he says, 'You are fucking amazing, do you know that?'

'Yeah,' I say, 'Course. Have you got any tucker?'

We have a proper Tesco's finest meal. Chicken Kiev and wild rice. It's like a restaurant meal and only takes five minutes to cook. We eat this, then I tell him my plan.

'You can't live here, Mistyann.'

'Why not?'

'Oh for fuck's sake…'

'You swear a lot now, Sir. You didn't use to.' I don't think he's going to say it at first. But then he does.

He says, 'Don't call me Sir.'

And everything stops for a minute. It's like someone has taken a photo. It's like there's a flash in the air. After a second he smiles and I feel happy. Proper happy for the first time in ages.

And then we talk. We sit in his front room and proper talk. I tell him about Harry and my nan and the crappy Manchester school and everything. But I don't tell him about the baby. I don't think he's ready for that.

And he tells little stories about all the interviews he's had with social workers and probation officers and policemen. And he tells me that he's going to have to go to court and he makes it all sound boring but kind of funny too. And we talk about Wales and laugh about Ray and his stupid little jokes and about Ariel. And I tell him about how I'm meant to be going to America and he gets serious for a minute and says maybe I should go and I don't want to spoil the mood so I say maybe and he asks me when I'm meant to be going and I say in a couple of months. And he looks thoughtful. And it goes quiet again.

I say, 'Your house is a tip, man. I know you're poor and everything now that you don't have a job but even so…'

And he tells me that he does have a job. At least he's still getting paid. They haven't sacked him yet. It sounds mad to me.

'They're paying you while you sit on your arse in this shit?' I try and say it nice but I'm shocked to be honest.

'They'll sack me soon, Mistyann, don't worry about that.'

'Anyway, it's a proper mess. You should have more respect for yourself.'

And I see him look around at his house like it's the first time he's seen it. So we clean it up together and it's quite a laugh because when it comes to cleaning it's like I'm the teacher and he's special needs. He's useless. It takes him about half a year to wash up a plate or he'll start clearing crap off his living room table and I'll come in and he's standing reading some year old paper and I have to tell him to shift his arse. Every now and then he comes in and asks me to check if this room or that room is okay and I ask him if he's done under the furniture and he goes, 'Oh shit, forgot about that. Sorry.' And goes off and clears up properly like a good little boy.

When we've done it all he tells me again that I can't stay with him and that it's mad and so I drop my bomb. I tell him that if he doesn't let me stay then I'll run off to London —which is actually the truth—and work for an escort agency or do massages. And that stubs him out. He can't say anything after that.

So I end up in his spare room, which is like an office really. It's where he keeps his computer—which is one of those well flash Macs—and it's a room full of books and papers and I don't sleep much, just listen to the night outside and feel like a spy. And I think about why I've come to JD's—it's a bit because I'm worried about him but mainly because I'm sick of being on my own. At Mum's I was on my own. At Nan's I was on my own and at my dad's I would be especially on my own. Unless I went up to the pub quiz with him. It's funny—when I'm with my family then I'm on my own but I'm never left alone, but here with JD well, it'll be the opposite: I'll be with someone but I'll get left alone when I want. And it'll be cosy here. Now that we've cleared all the shit, we'll have a nice little place. And I can keep an eye on Harry; make sure he's getting on properly and all that. Makes total sense.

Takes me the whole night to work this out though cos the truth is I wasn't sure why I'd come at first. When I first walk in—when JD pure starts shouting—I think I've messed up. But it'll be okay, I think. I can rest up here for a while. Chill, get sorted and all that. And JD will be good at dealing with all the housing and benefits people and everything. He'll know all about that. It'll be good here. A place where I can decide on a name for the baby.

FORTY-FIVE

What should I have done that first night, once you were upstairs asleep? What would a decent citizen have done? What would Ariel or Amber or Kendra have done? A phone call to social services? To your mum? I thought about it. My hand hovered over the phone, but it seemed easier to do nothing. The night leaked away and with it the opportunity for action. I sat in my lemon fresh house—the house that had come back from the dead—and smoked and played slow country records so quietly that the songs surrounded me in the same way the fag smoke did, just hanging in the air, a blue gauze through which I saw the living room shiver as I grew more tired. I stayed downstairs all night and was roused next morning when you brought me a cup of FC and a shopping list.

'You've got fuck all in, Sir. You need to stock up.'

'Don't...'

'Yeah, I know. Sorry, slip of the tongue or whatever.'

When I look back now I see those days as a sort of charmed time. The days were surreally domestic, a kind of parody of marriage. Every day I'd make one trip out for groceries and the rest of the time we would talk, play scrabble, or watch entire series of comedy programmes. I taught you the rules of chess and you got into that for a few days. You were a fierce competitor; merciless, which is how I knew that you, unlike me, had the proper chess-playing gene. Chess is not a sport for the civilized. It's all about teeth and blood and leaving your opponent with his entrails hanging out.

Sometimes we watched the racing on Channel Four. I'd get the tabloids and a couple of bags of change on my morning trip and we'd study form in a kind of library quiet before staking small sums. We used proper odds and had ourselves a little competition going, tallying up each other's winnings at the end of the afternoon. When we got bored of this we watched old films and you showed a surprising taste for Technicolor musicals. For a while we passed the time in this ludicrously companionable way. It was like some kind of nuclear horror had destroyed the outside world and we were under orders to lock all doors, seal the windows and wait for orders. Orders which wouldn't come.

I did try to get you to take some exercise but instead you curled up on the sofa eating Green and Blacks chocolate, taking the mick while I strained with the rope and pulleys of the rowing machine, hauling myself up some choppy, imaginary Thames. I suppose it was laughable. After all, there you were with those ludicrously long, athletic limbs; radiating energy and speed despite doing nothing more strenuous than hoovering or looking for the TV remote.

Of course it couldn't last. Daily I expected a visit from the plods or the social work swat team to come abseiling through the windows or else Ty and your mum and their tooled up friends. I felt no fear though. My old orderly life of teaching, marking and lesson-planning felt like some kind of peculiar dream. And so did this new time of parlour games and banter. Though you'd thought things through a bit and did your best to reassure me.

'I've told my dad that my mum's changed her mind and is letting me back home. And I phone Mum sometimes and tell her what a wanker Dad is and how miserable I am in Burntisland, so she's happy. They're both happy. They never talk so they'll never find out where I really am.'

Getting sacked these days is like a job in itself. After a while the letters started arriving suggesting dates for hearings and meetings and discussions. Everything polite, everything formal. The hearings were the same but with added human awkwardness; conducted entirely without eye contact. Bottoms shuffled on plastic chairs, throats were cleared, papers rustled. After a few of these I was no longer a teacher. I didn't defend myself and my union rep was hard to distinguish from the prosecution, so desperate was he to show that the modern trade unionist is more committed to professionalism in the ranks than any mere manager. I worried that you'd be bored while I was out going through these motions but you waved my concerns away.

'Maybe I'll use the rowing machine.' You smirked.

On the day I stopped finally being employed by the Local Authority, I bought a bottle of champagne on the way home. It seemed important to mark the occasion in some appropriate way, alcoholism or no alcoholism.

I let myself in and called, ironically, 'Hi honey, I'm home!' And listened to the silence as it rolled back at me.

It struck me then that it wasn't our joint cleaning that had brought the house back to life. It was your presence in it. It was clean enough now but felt lifeless again. You weren't in. I toured every room to check and then searched again, more thoroughly, in case you'd left some kind of note. The thought that you might have just taken off made me simultaneously numb and panicky. And though I knew that our time together had been an impossible dream, this sudden consciousness made me feel wretched and lost. I popped the cork on the champagne, letting it ricochet off the kitchen ceiling while the foam fizzed over my hands in that pantomime of the male orgasm which I'm sure is the essence of champagne's appeal. So it was that when you returned I was half-pissed but also maddened with grief and shame. You knew of course. Without a word passing between us. You nodded at the champagne bottle.

'You going to give me some of that, or what?'

Ludicrously I told you that you were under-age and at that second I would have fought you for the bottle if you'd made a move towards it. You shrugged. Champagne made you feel sick anyway. You walked past me into the living room, turned the TV on, left the remote on the arm of the chair, the same arm over which you draped your legs. You looked at home and it really irritated me. I followed you, picked up the remote and zapped the telly off. You didn't even look at me, though you allowed yourself a sigh.

I took in your profile. You were—are still I hope—a beautiful girl. It was a kind of secret power that would destroy you when you realised what you had. When you got wise to the full extent of your gifts you would be unstoppable. An unstoppable monster. And right at that second I don't know what annoyed me more; the scope of your talents or the fact that they were still hidden to you.

'Where have you been?' I said, making an effort to sound reasonable, neutral.

'You're not my dad.'

'Who did you see?'

'No-one. Look, do we have to do this now?'

'Yes, Mistyann, I think we do.'

You turned to face me. Your eyes flickered like light through stained glass. You had the look of some kind of holy warrior. The kind of look Joan of Arc might have had before pitching into the English. You were ready to fight and I was suddenly aware of my own unsteadiness, how unprepared I was. Naturally, I turned the heat up, hoping that sound and fury would do the job. You saw through me in a second. Your movie star lips twisted in regal disdain.

'Are you saying that you want me to leave?'

'Yes, I think that is what I'm saying.'

'I'm no help?'

'No.'

A stretch of silence cooled between us. I felt rising panic and into that came the sound of the door-bell followed by a bailiff's knock and a voice calling through the letter box.

'Oi, Diamond, get your arse in gear and open the frigging door. It's freezing out here.'

Cog.

You unfolded yourself, rose as tall and elegant as any finishing school product, and headed for the stairs.

'Come on, mate. I know you're in.'

I sighed and opened up. Cog came in rubbing his hands. 'So I enter the lair of the infamous Jonathan Diamond, child-snatcher.'

'You shouldn't believe all you read.'

'Tell me what I should believe then, mate.'

I gave Cog the edited highlights. We went to Wales. You ran away. I got pissed and fell asleep in the car which you drove away with me comatose beside you.

'So you're the victim?'

'I didn't say that.'

'Do you fancy her?' I didn't answer straight away.

'That's a yes.'

'No—it's me thinking about it.'

'Of course you fancy her. I saw the photo in the *Beds on Sunday*. It's an occupational hazard, isn't it? Must happen to everyone in a career. How many kids have you taught over the years? A thousand? Five thousand? You wouldn't be normal if you didn't have a little spark with one of them.'

'Really, Cog. It's not like that.'

'Okay. I believe you. Thousands wouldn't. You know what we should do?'

'No. What should we do?'

'We should go out and get insanely drunk.' His eyes flickered to the champagne bottle. 'We haven't done that for years.'

I thought about it but I wasn't quite ready for that emphatic surrender to the fates.

'No, I'm just going to watch some telly and go to bed.'

That's when he suggested the band. He got all fired up, stalked the kitchen monologuing about possible set lists and venues and other band members and names. It was exhausting to listen to. After three cups of tea he was still going, refusing to take no for an answer. Even as I threw him out into the drizzle, ideas were still fizzing from him.

'What do you think about 'Psychotic Reaction'? You know, The Count Five song?'

'How about you just go home, Cog?'

You came back into the room smiling. I smiled too.

'You going to form a band then?'

'No, I don't think so.'

I wondered what we would have done if Cog had discovered you in my house.

'He wouldn't have. I was under your bed. It's quite roomy under there actually.'

It's true. It's a big black reproduction Victorian wrought iron number that stands high off the ground. Beth, Amy, and Angela had all commented favourably on the bed. You had lain up there reading and eavesdropping on Cog's delusional schemes for middle aged creative fulfilment.

You made dinner. Bacon, onion and pasta in cheese sauce. We watched *Carry On Cleo* on DVD. You laughed a lot.

'This is classic, this is.' And then you told me where you'd been. 'I went to see Harry. He's still in hospital you know. I went just after visiting hours. Saw Mum and Ty leave, then I nipped in and they let me see him for a little while. He was asleep when I got there though. I love him. Even though he can be a whinging little sod. But he opened his eyes and he saw me and he started crying. The nurses asked me to leave.'

'Shit. I'm sorry.'

'No, it was okay because just as I was going he made this sound and I turned round and he had his arms open and he wanted me to cuddle him. It's going to be alright. Have you finished the champers? I could murder a drink.'

You went upstairs for a bath. I nipped up the road to Mr Joshi's for more booze.

FORTY-SIX

We're snogging. JD and me. I come out of the bath wrapped in one of his super-size fluffy towels and he's just standing on the landing holding two mugs.

'Only cava,' he says. 'Old Joshi doesn't run to the good stuff.'

So I know we're proper friends again. And I lean forward to kiss him on the cheek but he sort of twists his face and our noses bump and then our mouths are locked together and his tongue is in my mouth and searching around in there like a hungry snake. And I'm shocked for a second but then I start kissing him back and it feels fierce. Almost like fighting. He's gripping my neck with one hand and the other is on my back where the towel meets my skin. It's awkward because we're still holding the mugs. And it's exciting and I feel my insides go hot and liquidy. And then he pulls away and he's breathing heavy and he's sort of squinting and I can see the little bristles just under his nose where he hasn't shaved properly.

'I bet you thought you were in there,' I say. And I'm suddenly worried that my towel will fall down so I move away from JD and into my room. I turn and give him a smile before I go in. I don't want him thinking I'm disgusted or anything. I'm not. I just don't fancy it.

He breathes out this heavy sigh. 'I'm more than twice your age,' he says.

'So what?' I say. 'I've been with blokes older than you.'

This isn't actually true as it goes. The oldest guy I've been with was twenty-seven, though he acted older. Kept banging on about what good value a Toyota Yaris was.

I go into my room and close the door and take the towel off so I can feel the air on my skin. I feel sexy, sort of extra alive and tingly but I don't want to shag JD. I want to shag Zak. It's funny, I know he's a wanker but every time I think about him I think about my legs gripping him and pulling him into me. How hard and how hot he felt inside me.

Obviously I've thought about shagging JD. Of course I have. Thought about it when he was still my teacher to be honest. He's fine and funny and fit and handsome. Or he was then. He's got pure X factor cheek-bones and soulful eyes and thick dark hair. Best looking geezer on the staff easy. And he smells nice. Some kind of lotion but also smoke and booze and soap. It's a good mixture. Me and my friends are always saying how older guys are better than young blokes. They've got more wedge. They've got their own houses. They can talk about stuff. And they own stuff. And if I fucked him he would be the first man I've gone with who I liked. I mean I've liked them all at the time but then got jarred with them pretty soon afterwards. I think I might still like JD afterwards and that's one of the things that stops me going any further. I get under the covers and JD knocks at my door. It's a soft knock. An 'I'm-sorry' knock. Who can be bothered with that?

'I'm asleep,' I say, but he comes in anyway. He sits on the bed. There's no light in here except from the street light outside shining through the curtains. JD looks like a proper super-size bear. All shaggy and shadowy.

'Are we okay?' he says.

'Yeah. Course,' I say.

He sits there for a while not saying anything.

Then he says, 'It was kind of an accident.'

'Thanks,' I say, 'That makes me feel top girl, doesn't it?'

He does this sort of grunt which I think is a laugh. I hope it is anyway.

'We only snogged,' I say, 'It's no biggie.' And then I say, 'We can't have sex anyway. It might hurt the baby.'

What a fucking stupid thing to say. The second it's out of my big mouth I want to scream. I can't believe I've said it. There's this humungous silence. It's like this pure heavy big hole has opened up and swallows every sound into it.

Then—after a while—I hear JD's breathing. He starts to breathe like he's in hospital on a machine. Like he's nearly dead. For fuck's sake, people have been having babies for about a hundred billion years and it's treated like some kind of mega-disaster. And everyone knows that young mums make the best mums. Obviously all the dried-up old bags who work in telly don't want us to think that, but it's true.

JD doesn't say anything for ages. I guess he's trying to work out if I'm fucking with his head and I almost tell him that I'm just messing, but I don't and then it's too late cos I start getting a lecture. And I don't listen to it. I work hard at not listening to it. I'm concentrating on breathing, counting backwards from a hundred and all the other things Michaela talked about in anger management. My shoulders are so tight I think they might snap. JD moans on and it's all the usual teacher crap. Mustn't waste my life. Think of the child. Where am I going to live? How am I going to manage for money? And I'm thinking that we were just having a chilled out time. Why does he have to go and spoil things? I should have shagged him but it's too late now. I just have to blot him out and wait for him to go.

He gets proper worked up and it reminds of that time in English when he was going on about something or other, getting all excited about I don't know—commas or something—and Denny Hanzlik puts his hand up. JD stops, sort of shocked at being asked a question but pleased too cos Denny doesn't usually take much interest.

JD goes, 'Yes, Denny, do you have a question?'

And Denny goes, 'Sir, do all teachers have bad breath?'

And suddenly the whole class is proper excited cos it's the kind of thing people like to talk about. And some people are going 'It's all the coffee they drink'. And other people are saying which teachers stink the most and the whole lesson is fucked up and JD looks totally stubbed out. He's pure forgotten what he was saying. I want to do something like that now. I want to stub him out with something but I can't think of anything, so I just lie there under the covers concentrating on the little green light of his computer and trying to pretend that JD's voice is just the TV or something. And it works because when he stops and leaves the room I don't hardly notice.

After he's gone I get up and get Pete's letter out of my bag. The one he sent to my nan's after Ariel came round. The one that had his bank card in it. I pretty much know it off by heart. It just tells me where he's going to be buried and how much Kendra is fucking him right off. When I'm sorted I'll go and put flowers on his grave.

Anyway. In my bag I've got £3,740. There wasn't as much in Pete's account as he said there'd be, but I was expecting that. Everybody bullshits and bigs themselves up. I know that. But it's enough. Too much even. Took me over a week to get it out. Pete's card only let him take out £500 a day.

The day he sends me the cards I send him a card to say thank you. A proper good one. I found it at a boot sale. It's of the Spurs team that won the double centuries ago. They don't look like footballers. They look fucked. They look like smokers. They must be young in the photo but they all look like granddads.

Now it's time to write to Ariel. I've got a normal card for her. A crappy Purple Ronnie thank you card.

I write, 'Sorry I can't come. Too complicated.'

I feel a bit grey inside for a second when I do it. But only for a second. It costs three quid to send a card that size to America which is a right rip off.

America is not ready for me yet. One day it will be, but not yet.

FORTY-SEVEN

I woke late after a difficult night. That Serbian plonk Joshi had sold me had sat in my stomach fizzing, the way a detergent tablet does in a washing machine. I felt it scour and bleach me most of the night. My brain had been fizzing too. It was going to be a difficult day, a demanding day, but at least it was going to be an important day, full of movement and change. Then a treacherous kind of sleep had mugged me in the darkest hours and left me behind schedule and groggy. I felt befogged and numb. All the fizz and pop had gone leaving numerous aches which fought a dense lassitude for control of my limbs. I struggled out of bed like a man who finds himself waist deep in manure.

You'd gone of course. No note, nothing. You'd made your bed and only a handful of treacle-dark hairs on the pillow told the story of your visit. What was the point of phoning your mum now? What would be achieved by doing the decent thing?

I went back to bed and surfaced again amid the wastes of the afternoon in time to watch the racing on *Channel Four*. I sat picking winners as they paraded around the enclosure and thought idly about killing myself.

I had made the effort once before at the end of my first term at the Modern school. It had been an impulse thing, unable to face double maths with Mr Hendry on a Saturday morning when normal kids would be watching *Tiswas*. I grabbed the bottle of paracetamol and tipped the tablets down my neck and went back to my room to die.

I think nearly every boy thinks seriously about killing himself somewhere between the ages of twelve and fifteen. Adolescence is a life-threatening disease. There's a well documented slide in self-esteem for kids between these ages and while girls are forming social networks of like-minded bulimics and self-harmers, boys are just hanging themselves, or jumping under trains or choosing the less dramatic route of swallowing everyday poisons. Usually on a whim or in a sudden rush of passion. And the thing about a boy's lack of self-worth at these ages is that it is entirely justified. The girls he knew from primary school are daily turning into unattainable goddesses fixated on tattooed fairground operators twice his age, while he's left with the Lego set which somehow doesn't do it for him the way it once did. And despite the chemical warfare that he wages on his breath, arm-pits and face, he knows he smells and looks like a refugee from some burns unit with his flaking, reddened and pustule-ridden skin.

Obviously my attempt at suicide didn't work. It didn't even work as a cry for help. Maybe my parents were ripped off by their dealer. Maybe the chemist was cutting his paracetamol with low cost placebos, but I didn't suffer any effects at all. When the poet Sylvia Plath first attempted suicide she lay in a coma in a shed or somewhere for three days and nights. All I got was a mild headache. These pain-killers actually gave me a head-ache. And the drug didn't even cause drowsiness. If we had had any heavy machinery I could have operated it without any trouble. Maybe the adrenalin released by the fear of dying had neutralized the toxins, ambushing and coshing them on their way to my liver. Whatever, I passed a restless night and went off to school to be bollocked for not doing my homework. I've been reluctant to use paracetamol ever since.

The big thing that suicide has to commend it is that it is the coward's way out. If you're in trouble rely on a coward to find the speediest, most pain-free exit. In a plane-crash follow the coward. They'll be at the front heading for the emergency exits having memorised them on entry.

But to kill myself just then I would have had to get dressed and go outside into the drizzle and walk up to Sanjay Joshi's. I'd have had to talk about cricket as I purchased the vodka and pills. And I'd have had to write notes for family and friends. It was too much effort frankly.

I did some marking instead. Pointless really. I'd had the books of 8X since before we'd gone to Wales. I had been intending to mark their attempts at writing ballads in the style of *The Highwayman* on the weekend after we'd returned. But I never went back to work and no-one had called for the exercise books. They must have issued new ones at a cost of at least 45p per book to the tax-payer. I sat and marked books for kids I would never teach again. I marked them thoroughly. Pointlessly. But it was calming, the way that some housewives tell you that doing the ironing is relaxing. Then I looked up www.bedfordjobsearch.com and rang the Elms. And later that day I got the word that even scum are allowed to hang with the Undead. I think that they might even have been pleased to see me again after all those years.

FORTY-EIGHT

I'm sipping champagne—proper champagne from France—on my yacht while the kids play with remote controlled cars on deck. Sometimes I get calls and emails on my Blackberry. Mostly I ignore them. My PA does all that. I only deal with stuff that's proper urgent. Tom—that's my partner—gets pure jarred if I work too hard. He wants to get married but I'm not going to, not without a pre-nup. I'm not letting him get his paws on my candy, no way.

I'm on the phone to Roy Keane. Can he manage Man U? I'll pay whatever he wants, plus decent money to strengthen the squad. I want success, Roy, I tell him. I want Champions' League. He doesn't need to worry about the board; they'll do what I say. I own all the fucking shares.

I'm cutting the ribbon at the opening day of my school. My academy. It's my bit for charity. They wanted to call it after me. I said, 'Mistyann Rutherford High School?' Schools should be named after the streets they're on. Brickhill Drive High School. I've bought Pilgrim Upper. They closed it after my mum left. Turned it into social work offices. Now it's a school again. It's like a private school only no-one has to pay or have a stupid uniform.

I'm one of the top women in business. Girls write to me all the time asking for advice or wanting to do work experience. I have a secretary who spends all day writing back to them and two others who deal with begging letters.

I have houses in Spain, Bulgaria and Florida. I have a Bentley convertible. My company sponsors an F1 team.

And still no-one is sure what I look like. I can go anywhere and do anything. I never get mobbed. I only need one bodyguard but no-one messes with him. I look ordinary but I do amazing things and that's what freaks people out when they first meet me. But they always say how down-to-earth I am. On my holidays I go into space and take some of my best mates with me. We have girlie trips away to the new space station and bitch about our boyfriends who we leave behind on earth and who shit themselves about what we get up to.

I've made it up with my family. William and Harry both work for me now and I can proper trust them and Mum lives near the sea in a house I bought for her. I go and see her sometimes and we have a right laugh.

Or maybe I'm a teacher. I do all the special needs kids and everyone says that I work miracles. I get in a bit early and stay a bit late and give them all time and attention and they love me so they start to do things no-one else thought they could. Sometimes they get exams and stuff and go to uni and send me cards and presents to say thank you for I've done. They have Facebook groups about me. And my classroom is always tidy and no-one gives me any lip.

Or maybe I'm just married to some candied-up bloke and live in a floss house in Hampstead and meet my lover in the afternoons before the kids get home from school.

But right now I'm on the train to London.

Getting away is easy. I keep thinking something will happen, that some copper or Ty or JD will be there at the station. But that's movie world and in the real world you just buy a ticket and a magazine and a burger. And your train is announced and you get on and nothing happens. You go where you want to go and do what you like.

I think I might see the kid who checked the tickets when we went to Wales. But I don't and I'm pleased. I don't want to see anyone who knows me. I'm out of here. I sit on the train pretending I'm invisible and it's no prob cos everyone else has their own thing going on. There's a couple of tired geezers in suits. An old lady sleeping with her mouth open. An Asian girl who thinks she's it. You can tell by the way she nods her head in time with the sounds on her phone.

There's a pensioner bloke with dyed black hair. He looks like he's going to cry.

I've got enough cash till I'm sixteen and then I can do whatever. I've already got the little card with my national insurance number on it. I've been trying out baby names. Robyn. Bryony. Menna. Elsie. Hannah. None of them are right. The baby doesn't like them. Baby talks to me now. I don't hear a voice. I'm not schizo or anything, but she tells me stuff. I know she's a she. And I know she's happy and excited about London. And she proper trusts me. Sometimes she gets worried and upset, but I can calm her down. I tell her everything will be alright and she believes me and goes to sleep. This baby is going to be special. I'm telling you—this baby is going to shake the world.

Maybe I'll go round a graveyard when I get to London, nick a name for her from there.

I go into the bog and think about doing my make up but the train is rocking too much. I'd just smear it everywhere. I'd look like a clown. I check the cash in my bag. £3,694 now. I'm well floss. Mum, she would divide that into shots. 1800 shots of vodka. I make a note of every penny I spend in a little notebook. I look at my face in the mirror. Proper examine it. I can see the beginnings of lines under my eyes and along my forehead. No-one else would notice, but I do. I run my fingers along them. I can't feel them. I get in closer. The light is harsh and the lines are clear.

I'm fifteen. I'm Gifted. I'm Mistyann fucking Rutherford. I'll be fine. No-one needs to worry about me.

And then I'm back in my seat and smiling and that's when I start writing my name on my new bag. Putting little faces in all the o's. Doing it careful. Doing it well. And when I've done it I'm going to write JD a post-card. Going to start it, 'Dear Sir…'